SURTR'S FURY

SHATTERED WORLD
BOOK ONE

AMANDA S. GREEN

E-book ISBN: 978-0-692-47008-4

Print ISBN: 978-1-949901-58-0

Cover design by Amanda S. Green.

WELCOME TO THE SHATTERED WORLD

The last few years have been challenging for many of us. For some, the world changed in ways we never would have expected before Covid and other factors. It was from this sense of change that *The Shattered World* series was born.

I've had a lot of fun writing *Surtr's Fury*, the first book in the series. Two more books are planned, and I've already laid the groundwork for them. Of course, my muse being such as she is, I've learned to never say a series will only be so many books. Myrtle—yes, my muse has a name—will rise up and prove me wrong, cackling almost insanely as she does. So don't be surprised if the trilogy turns into something else, something bigger.

To keep up-to-date about the series as well as other books coming out, sign up for my Substack or follow my fan page.

Thank you,
ASG

For my Family, whether by blood or by choice.

The boundaries which divide Life from Death are at best shadowy and vague. Who shall say where the one ends, and where the other begins?

— EDGAR ALLAN POE

LIVING UP TO MY NAME, HEAVEN HELP ME

"You're late."

I closed the door and leaned against it, blowing out a long breath. I didn't need to look up to know the gruff voice matched the gruff expression on my foster father's face. Of course, it was nearly impossible for him not to look that way. Part troll, part dwarf, and part who knew what, Redmond Oakley no longer bothered with personal glamours to hide his true appearance.

And why should he?

The world now knew elves and fairies, witches and ghosts, even vampires and other things once thought to exist only in ancient myths and bad Hollywood movies were real. The Upheaval changed the world forever. No matter how badly anyone wished otherwise, that was one proverbial genie that wouldn't be returning to the bottle.

Even now, more than two decades after the Upheaval released wild magics across the globe, there were those who resented paranormals, who feared us, and who wanted us locked in cages or zoos. Others wouldn't mind if we found ourselves strapped to examination tables in some black site, dissected and worse all so they could find out what made us who and what we are.

Fortunately, they're in the minority.

Even so, any para with a sense of self-preservation made sure to watch their back and not call attention to themselves. That was something Red excelled at. He was short, barely five feet six inches tall, with a barrel chest and thick arms and legs. His skin was a deep russet. He sported thick greying hair, except for the sides of his head where he shaved it close to his scalp. But it was his almost black eyes and the way they seemed to see everything that one remembered.

The mistake came when someone judged him only on his appearance. That sort of mistake could prove to be fatal—either financially or in a more permanent way. Being smart, Red always managed to do it within the letter of the law, even if only barely at times. But he never took such extreme action for his own benefit. It was always to protect those he took in, his "family" so to speak.

People like me.

My name's Ellen Ripley Walker, Ripley or Rip to my friends. Yes, my parents were big science fiction fans. For some reason I'll never understand, they thought it would be a good thing to name me after one of the most kick-ass heroines in the genre. The fact I was born the same year the world turned upside down and inside out only confirmed—to them, at least—that they made the right decision.

For me, well, that's a different story. The family legacy weighs heavily enough on my shoulders. Add in the name and, well, there are times I want to disappear and become Mary Sue Jones, worried about nothing more dangerous than watering my plants and feeding my cat.

But that's all a dream and a far cry from my reality.

Welcome to my world. A world where, when I'm not tending bar, I work for the North American Conclave of Paranormals. You might say I'm following in my parents' footsteps. For generations, since long before the Upheaval, we've served the Conclave to help keep our kind in check. The memory of all witch hunts, the religious persecutions over the ages, the fear that caused otherwise rational people to become a mob reminded us of the danger of exposure. Fortunately, there were those who understood the danger.

And that's where my boss, Red, comes into the picture.

Red runs what he euphemistically calls a reclamation agency. Most of his employees focus on finding paras who have gone missing.

Sometimes they disappeared of their own accord. Sometimes it's because they crossed the wrong person. On very rare occasions—fortunately—it's because someone abducted them, wanting to find out what made them "special" and didn't care what they had to do to find out. Those were the tough assignments because they rarely had good endings.

But that's not the only work we did. Just as Red's bar, The Red Dragon Brew Company, served as a front for some of his other just barely legal interests, the offices here had another less well-known purpose. Here, Red and "the team" did research and trained. It's where clients come to discuss their cases. It is also where Red ran interference with—and sometimes for—the Conclave. Not only did that let him protect our town and "family", but Red was nothing if not mercenary. The Conclave paid well for information and even better to make sure our kind did nothing to stir up trouble with the "normal" humans. The bar allowed us to gather information and monitor those paras who love their drink and drugs and couldn't hold their tongues if their lives depended on it.

Yes, we. Because I spent most evenings and all too many weekends slinging drinks behind the bar at The Red Dragon Brew Company. It might not be the sort of job most parents want for their kids, but it fit my needs and, well, my folks weren't around any longer to object. I owed Red for taking me in, and this was one way of repaying him.

"Well? Anything to say for yourself, girl?"

I glanced at my watch and rolled my eyes.

"Late, Red? Really?" I crossed the office and dropped onto one of the two chairs in front of his battered desk. As I did, I considered reaching out with one booted foot and nudging the corner of the desk to see if any of the stacks of files and loose paper would topple over. In the five years I'd worked for him, the stacks had grown and multiplied until there wasn't a bit of the desktop visible. "It's barely noon and I'm not scheduled to go on shift at the bar until six."

"Then why're you here, Walker? I'm not gonna pay you overtime." His black eyes glittered, and one corner of his mouth lifted in what someone might generously say was a smile.

I barked out a laugh and crossed my legs. "When have you ever paid overtime, Red? You're a stingy bastard, but we love you anyway."

I grinned as he growled. But the sparkle in his eyes gave him away. I might frustrate the hell out of him at the best of times, but he liked me. More than that, he liked the bounties I brought in when he managed to get me to agree to take the job. Besides, I always got my paperwork in on time and did my best to make sure the other marshals did as well. That meant money in my pocket and his, something he appreciated more than just about anything else.

"You say that to every guy who signs your paychecks." His voice rumbled deep in his barrel chest.

"You haven't signed a check in years, Red. Everything's digital now."

"You're such a bitch, Walker."

"No argument there, Red."

Survival in this post-Upheaval world meant being able to take care of yourself. Doing what I did, you'd better be a ball-buster who wasn't afraid to draw blood if you wanted to live to see the next day. That was the first lesson my mama taught me when she sat me down at the ripe old age of ten and told me this was my legacy. She'd been a marshal until she disappeared on a job for the Conclave. My dad had been one until a feral wyvern killed him protecting its nest.

I'd been nine when Dad died and almost thirteen when Mom didn't come home. Red took me in, and it didn't take long for him to put me to work. First, I helped around the office, sweeping the floors, running errands, that sort of thing. Oh, he made sure I finished school, but he also saw to it that I got the training I needed to carry on the family legacy. When I asked him about it a couple of years ago, all he said was he promised my parents and he always kept his promises.

"As long as you remember you're my bitch." He grinned and cracked his large, hairy knuckles.

I arched one brow. Nothing else. I didn't need to do or say anything, not when he paled and swallowed hard, realizing how badly he stepped in it.

He licked his lips once. "You know what I mean, Ripley."

I waited, watching as sweat pricked out on his forehead. Then I grinned. I didn't mind letting him sweat, but I knew what he meant.

"No worries, Red. Just don't say something like that in front of anyone else." That was all the warning he'd get. "Now that that's out of the way, why did I need to drag my tired ass out of bed before my alarm went off? I assume this warm greeting is your way of saying a job's come across your desk and it's not something you want one of the others to deal with."

He nodded and reached for one of the files. Then he stopped and dropped that hand back onto the desktop. A flicker of concern tickled my spine and I waited, wondering what was going on.

"Red?"

"Something's going on, Ripley. I don't know what or I'd tell you." He lifted a hand to stop me before I could say anything. "Gemma called before I rang you up. She's worried about something." Another pause, and this time he frowned. "She didn't come out and say it. You know what she's like. She'd not one to get right to the point. But I could tell she's scared. I heard it in her voice. When I asked what's wrong, she said she Saw something. It's bad, and it's coming this way. She asked—*asked*, Ripley—if I'd send you out to see her."

My mouth fell open and I did a credible imitation of a fish out of water. At the same time, my blood ran cold. As far as most people were concerned, Gemma Blackrock is a Native American witch with a touch of foresight. I knew better, as did Red. Gemma's a Seer, one of the most reliable I'd ever known. If she said trouble was coming, I believed her.

"She asked for me specifically?"

That simple request scared the shit out of me. Gemma might look like someone's sweet old grandma, but I knew better. Behind that innocent-looking exterior lay one of the most powerful witches and Seers around. The only other time she asked Red to have me deal with something, I'd come damned close to losing my life and I still bore the scars to remind me.

I was in no hurry for a repeat performance.

"She did. Said for you to come ASAP."

He didn't look any happier about it than I felt. This was so not good.

I closed my eyes and gnawed my lower lip. Then I blew out the breath I hadn't realized I was holding.

"All right. But I want double my usual rates and hazard pay as well as full access to the armory and anything else I might need. That includes any wards I want from Razor." I thought for a moment. "And, Red, that's just to go see her and it is all on your dime." We'd argue about additional contract terms later, after I found out why she wanted to see me and decided just how involved I wanted to be.

"Agreed." He levered his bulk out of his chair and moved around the desk. "Sign and add your thumbprint."

I probably should have thought twice, maybe even three times, before reaching for the tablet he held out. Not only because he didn't argue with my terms, but because he already had a contract with those terms included prepared. The fact he didn't want to spend a few minutes negotiating terms—something he loved dearly—only confirmed how bad things appeared to be.

Frowning, I scanned the contract. I trusted him, but I also knew he was a shrewd businessman. That meant making sure I knew what I was signing. This time, at least, I saw nothing I needed to clarify or change. The terms were simple. He'd pay what I asked, and, in return, I would meet with Gemma as she requested. I was not obligated to do anything else, and he would contact her once I signed to let her know when to expect me. He would also make sure she understood I was under no obligation to do anything more than hear her out and then report back in.

Simple enough. Then why did I have this sick feeling in the pit of my stomach that it would come back to bite me—hard—on the ass?

With my luck, it would not only bite me there but take out a big chunk and I really liked my ass, especially the way my jeans hugged it this morning.

I signed and added my thumbprint before handing the tablet back to him. He took it with a single nod.

"I might not be a Seer like Gemma, but I have a bad feeling about this, Ripley. Gear up, weapons and coms, before you head out. Take one of the SUVs instead of your car. And keep your head on a swivel. If Gemma's worried, I'm worried."

"Understood." I thought for a moment. "I am going to stop by Razor's first. If I'm heading out to Gemma's and if it's as bad as we both suspect, I want all the mundane and arcane protections I can get."

Red and his arsenal could handle the mundane. Razor would take care of the arcane for me.

"Good. Once you get there, tag me and tell me how long you'll be. I'll let Gemma know your ETA then."

"Thanks." Seeing the worry lurking in his dark eyes, I smiled in reassurance. "Don't worry, Red. I won't take any unnecessary chances."

With that, I turned on my heel and left his office. If I stayed any longer, I'd start second-guessing my decision to go see Gemma. Tempting as it was to suddenly come down with a case of the "I don' wannas", I couldn't do that. Not to Red, and not to Gemma.

Hell, I couldn't do it to the rest of us.

After all, I was a Conclave marshal. That meant it was my job to deal with problems like the one it seemed might be about to land in my lap.

Welcome to my world and when can I get off?

2

THE SHAMAN WILL SEE YOU NOW

The heady strains of heavy metal music and the exotic aroma of incense greeted me as I pushed open the glass door. As I stepped inside, six heads turned in my direction: four human (or as human as anyone living in this part of town happened to be) and two canine. One of those canines looked at me with surprisingly bright golden eyes. That told me all I needed to know. Not lycan but certainly not a dog. A shapeshifter of some flavor. Well, I'd leave him alone so long as he left me alone.

Not that I wouldn't ask Razor about him. I knew almost everyone in town, but not this one, at least not in this shifted form, and that worried me. Especially in light of Gemma's call.

One of the "humans" sat on a stool behind the glass display case. An ancient cash register sat on top of the case. Inside merchandise celebrating *Razor's Tats and Mods* was almost carelessly displayed. At other similar shops, the meaning of the shop name would be clear: tattoos and body modifications. Here, however, it took on a different meaning. Razor was a master at crafting spells into amulets, drawings, and so many other things. While some of his spells were offensive, it was his defensive expertise I needed just then.

"He's expecting you, Ripley." The young man behind the counter pushed a lock of dark hair behind one pointed ear before nodding to the back of the shop.

I nodded at the elf, trying not to frown. The fact Red let Razor know I was coming only confirmed how worried my foster father happened to be. That, in turn, worried me.

"Ripley, come, tell me what I can do for you."

Roberto "Razor" Pantoja excused himself from the others and motioned me forward. As he did, I dipped my chin but stayed where I was. I knew him. Too well, some might say. I also knew Aras Silverthorn, the elf manning the register. I did not know the two men sitting at the rear of the shop with Razor. That, coupled with the unknown shifter, set off all my mental alarms. First Gemma's call. Now this. Something was up and I needed to find out what.

Razor's eyes narrowed before widening in sudden understanding. Almost instantly, he drew himself up to his full height of almost five feet seven inches. He reached up and smoothed a hand over his dark brown hair. As he did, I winced inwardly, making a mental note not to shake that hand until he wiped all the hair product off of it. Then, to my surprise, he motioned for the two men to stand.

"Welcome to my shop, Marshal. Allow me to introduce you to my cousins, Carlos and Antony Pantoja. They have come from their home in São Paulo on family business and to pass along information you may be interested in.

"Cousins, this is Conclave Marshal E. Ripley Walker. You will treat her with respect. She is a friend, and she is always welcome in my shop."

The threat that he would deal with them for any perceived insult or threat remained unspoken. Interesting. So was the way he introduced me, especially since Razor knew I preferred not to advertise my role as marshal. Suddenly, the feeling that the day just became even worse—and that was saying something considering everything so far—filled me.

"Gentlemen."

I nodded to each of them. We didn't shake hands. That might be an insult in human society but in para society, it was normal. Too much could be revealed about a person through a touch. Too much could be stolen through the transfer of DNA. The dangers outweighed what normals would view as common courtesy.

"Come, Marshal. We can discuss what brings you here this fine day in my office. Aras will keep my cousins company."

The elf smiled, making no attempt to hide his very sharp and pointy teeth. It was a warning he wasn't one of the gentle elves who would do no harm. Far from it. Aras most closely resembled the Dökkálfar, the dark elves of Norse mythology. More interesting was the fact the warning was aimed at Razor's cousins. For whatever reason, he didn't trust them and that had my mental alarms screeching even louder than before.

I made a quick decision, one I hoped didn't backfire on me.

"Gentlemen, you are welcome in the North Texas Zone as long as you obey the rules. I assure you, it wouldn't be wise to go afoul of your cousin." I nodded respectfully in Razor's direction. "And trust me, you do not want to cross me."

The two paled, not easy when one's complexion is as dark as theirs, before assuring me they understood. Good. I had neither the time nor the inclination to deal with two idiots foolish enough to push me. Not this morning.

"Come, Ripley, and you can tell me what brings you to my shop." Razor motioned me inside his office and then closed the door behind us.

"I didn't mean to interrupt."

I watched as his fingers drew a series of sigils in the air. A moment later, I sensed more than felt the slight change in the air I'd learned to recognize. He'd just ensured whatever we said could not be heard beyond the office walls.

"You didn't interrupt, Ripley." He waved me to a seat and moved to pour out coffee from a carafe resting on his desk. Before handing me one of the heavy earthenware mugs, he waved a hand over it, a look of concentration crossing his expression. Then steam wafted from the mug, the coffee heated to the proper temperature. "I was going to contact you later today, after I made a few calls about why my cousins showed up unexpectedly on my doorstep last night."

"Trouble?" Nothing else explained his expression or worry darkening his aura.

"Perhaps. If what they said when they arrived is true, most definitely. But I know my cousins." He gave an almost bitter laugh. "And I know my family. There is a reason I left Sao Paulo so long ago."

"So you've said." He never told me exactly why he left home and came north while still a teen. All I knew was that he felt he had no other choice. That was enough for me. At least until the reasons impacted our people here. "I take it that concern is why you introduced me as you did."

He nodded. Then he grinned and spread his hands in front of him. "It was also to warn them not to try to get in your pants. My cousins are, shall we say, rather full of themselves."

"Unlike you." I grinned, reminding him of our first meeting when I threatened to cut off his dick if he didn't keep it there.

"Most definitely, my friend. But I knew you would cut off my dick and probably try to feed it to me. They are foolish enough to ignore your warning and my dear aunt and uncle would be most upset to learn they would never be grandparents. Not that Tio Benício hasn't threatened to do exactly that more than once after bailing them out of trouble of their own making." His hazel eyes sparkled with humor before he sobered. "Now, tell me why you've come. Red only said you were on your way."

"I've got a job, hopefully a quick and uneventful one. But there's a chance it can go south very quickly. So, I'd appreciate some general protections."

He sat back, studying me over the rim of his mug. "Will you be remaining in the Zone or heading into the city?"

I shrugged. "Starting here, but I'll be going closer to the rift. I don't know where I'll head from there."

If anywhere.

"If you are going toward the rift, don't take your car. Use one of Red's trucks or SUVs. You can leave your car here. I'll even ward both vehicles for you. I will add personal wards as well."

I narrowed my eyes, worry once again spiking as he echoed Red's request.

"Why don't you want me taking the car?"

I leaned back and studied him. We knew one another well enough for him to know I much preferred my ancient Camaro to any other vehicle. It was fast. It could still outrun almost anything else on the road. I couldn't remember him ever telling me to leave it behind.

What did he know that I didn't?

"Ripley, I am hearing concerning things about the area closer to the rift. The rift storms are increasing, not only in frequency but intensity."

I hissed out a breath. Growing up near the rift, I knew the dangers of being caught in a rift storm. Imagine torrential rain, winds as strong as a tornado, all coupled with wild magics shooting through the air and that was a rift storm. They often resulted in a change in the landscape, and anyone caught out in one risked more than just death. If there was even a small chance of getting caught outside during one, I'd take one of the SUVs. Especially if Razor warded it for me.

"All right. I'll take one of the SUVs."

"Good." He blew out a breath, obviously relieved I agreed so easily. Then he set his mug to the side and leaned forward, reaching for my left arm and pushing up the sleeve of my leather jacket. His fingers lightly traced the markings on my forearm before he frowned. "As I suspected. These wards have faded. You should really let me do a permanent tat. It is quicker and easier to recharge the wards tied to my inks."

I shook my head. We had this discussion whenever I came to him. Each time, I declined. I can face down many things that most folks balk at, but when it comes to needles, I turn into a puddle of cowardly goo.

"Maybe later, but I'm in a time crunch right now."

"All right." He stood and pulled a padded table away from the far wall. "Strip and let's get this started."

An hour later, I finished dressing, my skin tingling as the personal wards he'd put in place settled around me. This time, instead of drawing the protective sigils on my arms as he usually did, he turned my back into what I assumed was a piece of art to anyone with the ability to see the wards. But, by being on my back, no one would see them unless I wanted them to. Not that it would fool Gemma. She knew me well enough to understand I'd come to her warded to my teeth. She'd also sense the wards as soon as I stepped foot onto her land.

But then, the wards weren't there to protect me from the old woman. There were bigger, meaner things in the world than her. Not that I ever wanted to get on her bad side.

"Take this." He handed me an intricately woven leather wristband about two inches wide. "It has additional protections attached to it as well as a little extra that should boost your own talents if you need to call on them without preparation."

"Thanks." I quickly fastened it around my left wrist. Once I had, he touched a forefinger to it, and I felt the *zing* as the protections activated. "Charge everything to Red?"

He nodded. Then he looked at me, his head cocked to one side. "What else can I do to help you, Ripley?"

"Your cousins?"

"I will find out why they're really here and will let you know."

"Thanks." I started out, but paused before reaching the door. "Razor, who's the new shifter?"

"Stefan Janusch. I vouch for him, Ripley. He's a client and friend from Tulsa."

That was good enough for me—for now.

"All right and thanks. I'll touch base later."

"You watch that very attractive ass of yours, Rip. I'd still like to show you how much fun you've missed out by turning me down."

He gave me a sly smile and I couldn't help grinning in return. It would never happen, and we both knew it. He wasn't my type. I also liked my head attached to my shoulders, so I wasn't going to risk his wife's anger. After all, running afoul of a naga was anything but smart, especially one very much in love with her husband and who possessed a wicked temper when riled. But there was no harm in teasing since we both knew where we stood.

And so did she.

"Talk to you soon, Razor, and thanks again."

With that, I left him to deal with his cousins. I had other concerns just then, and I pulled out my phone, sending a text to have one of Red's SUVs prepped. I wanted to leave as soon as Razor's protections were in place. Hopefully, the garage understood. Otherwise, there would be hell to pay.

3

THE WITCH IN THE WOODS

F ive miles outside of town, the SUV slowed to a stop and idled at the crossroads. I held the steering wheel in a death grip and leaned back, considering my options. This was it. If I drove on, there would be no turning back. Gemma would "feel" me the moment I crossed into her lands. The fact her house lay several miles away didn't matter. She'd know, just as she'd know if I chickened out and ran back to town.

Not long before she disappeared, Mom and I made the drive to see Gemma. Mom stopped the car right here that day. She sat as rigid and looked as uncertain as I now felt. When I asked her about it, she explained what she called Gemma's arcane security system. The Seer's wards would warn her of anyone approaching. Spells would turn them aside unless she approved of their presence on her lands. If that failed, well, Mom said not to risk the "what happens now" factor where Gemma's concerned.

That was one of Mom's many lessons I took to heart and now it resonated through me almost as strongly as the magics from the Rift.

I hissed out a breath, cursing softly for letting memories distract me. Then I inhaled sharply. Ten yards in front of the SUV, a large, tawny-colored feline slowly crossed the road. Mouth suddenly dry, pulse beating a loud rhythm in my ears, the fingers of my right hand slowly pried themselves from the steering wheel. Even more slowly, I reached for the 1911 resting on the passenger seat. Not that it would do much beyond pissing the cat off if I had to use it.

As if reading my thoughts, the cat swung its large head in my direction. Green eyes blazed above a scarred snout and fangs that left no doubt about the damage it could inflict if it wanted. The fact it also outweighed me didn't reassure me any.

I waited, holding the gun in my lap, hoping the cat would move along. I didn't want to kill her—assuming I could—not when her teats told me she probably had a litter somewhere nearby.

I didn't dare close my eyes, but I could roll them. This was just what we didn't need: a litter of monster cats that bore more than a passing resemblance to the long extinct smilodon. Assuming I got out of this alive, I needed to warn Gemma. I also needed to let the local authorities and then the Conclave know.

The cat gave me one last look and padded off, disappearing between two of the abandoned houses down the road. Relief washed over me, and I let out a shaky breath I hadn't realized I'd been holding. Then I swallowed hard. The cat's appearance was a reminder monsters bigger, badder, and meaner than me lived in the area and I was the trespasser. If I continued down this road, I risked everything and for what?

What the hell did Gemma want with me?

One primitive part of my brain wanted to turn and run back to town just as fast as I could. Another part wanted to embrace the danger and release the darker part of me from the bonds of this mortal form. But the rational part knew better. I could not become one of the monsters, not if I wanted to stay true to myself and to all my family stood for over the years. But it was tempting, especially as the wild magic of the rift called to me.

Like it or not, I had only one choice: I had to find out what the Seer wanted from me.

I slid the transmission into gear and slowly drove on. As I did, I moved from one world to another. The road, well-maintained until now, turned rough. Potholes created by time, weather, and other things best not thought about, put the SUV's suspension to the test. Overhead, the once clear sky turned dark. Clouds swirled as the wind picked up. Lightning streaked across the horizon. I didn't need the faded red and yellow signs warning the unwary of the danger presented by nearing the rift. I felt the wild magics in the air even through my personal wards and the wards Razor placed on the SUV.

This wasn't good. Not good at all.

What the hell was going on?

I slowed again, taking careful note of my surroundings, looking for any indication of a change since my last visit with Gemma. Nothing. At least nothing easily noticed. I didn't know whether or not to be relieved.

Before the rifts appeared, this area had been part of the suburbs north of Dallas. Farm and ranch land to the north turned into housing developments and business parks the closer you got to the Metroplex. Then the Upheaval happened. One of the first North American rifts appeared less than twenty miles north of my current location. Like anywhere a rift opened, wild magics escaped and things changed, not always for the better. Hell, rarely for the better. The normals living here fled to the safety of the Dallas or Fort Worth. Some moved further north to Oklahoma City or Tulsa. Others fled south to Austin and San Antonio. They abandoned their homes and offices. Most left with what they wore and the few things they could quickly throw into a car. No one wanted to take the time to pack up properly.

Who could blame them when the world suddenly went mad?

They saw family and friends turn into things they didn't understand, things they thought only existed in books and movies. Now those family members and friends were the things of nightmares, and no one understood why.

No one knew why the rifts opened. All anyone knew for certain was that the authorities told them to leave and report to processing centers well away from the rifts where they would be checked out and given any assistance needed.

Of course, in the immediate aftermath, that help often amounted to heavy sedation or jail to "protect" those not changed by the rifts.

In the years since, some braved the dangers long enough to collect their belongings. Most simply walked away without looking back. Scavengers took what they could. Now nature was reclaiming the area. But it was a twisted nature that made the area look like a scene from a dystopian story. Houses and office buildings stood abandoned, windows broken and roofs sagging. With overgrown yards, peeling paint, and cracked concrete sidewalks, it was hard to believe this had been an upper middle-class neighborhood before the Upheaval.

In another mile or two, the scenery would change again. Buildings would give way to fields and then to trees. The latter had been encouraged to grow by Gemma, creating a buffer of sorts between the town, her lands, and the rift beyond.

I'd been a child, probably no more than five or six, when she first moved out here. No one understood why she left the relative safety of town, but no one wanted to be the one to tell her they thought the move foolish. Not that it mattered all that much to my parents, who brought me out here to learn from her and to understand there are predators out there bigger and meaner than me.

Mom taught me it was my job to learn how to be deadlier.

I cursed softly as unshed tears burned my eyes. I needed to stop thinking about what was and what might have been. I needed to find out what Gemma wanted and letting my memories overtake me wouldn't get that done.

Less than fifteen minutes later, I pulled off the road and headed down a narrow dirt drive through trees that once upon a time might have been oak trees. A shiver ran through me as the shadows seemed to close in all around me. Unless Gemma lifted the wards, my cellphone wouldn't work out here. There was no way to send for help if I needed it. Fortunately, I trusted the old woman, at least up to a point. Besides, Red knew where I was. At the very least, he'd send someone out to check on me if I didn't report back within a reasonable time. Of course, Red being Red, he might contact the Conclave and leave it to them to follow up. Not that I blamed him. No one from the local Zone wanted to cross Gemma.

At least no one with an ounce of common sense and a reasonable sense of self-preservation.

A few minutes later, I parked in front of the small house, little more than a cottage. As I did, the front door opened. Gemma Blackrock stood framed in the doorway. Her iron-grey hair hung in a single braid down her back. She wore a pair of black slacks with a white cotton shirt tucked beneath a wide black leather belt. Her blue eyes scanned the front yard, as if making sure I brought no one with me. Then she smiled and lifted a hand in greeting, the morning sun glinting off her rings and the silver cuff on that wrist.

"Thank you for coming so quickly, Ripley." She stepped aside so I could enter the house.

It never ceased to amaze me how normal the house seemed. At least so long as you didn't look beyond the obvious. If you did, you couldn't miss the power resonating through it or the various magical implements that would send those unfamiliar with Gemma and those like her running in fear.

"Red said it was important." I sat on the well-worn sofa and leaned forward, elbows on my knees. "How may I help you, ma'am, and is this something that might be best suited for your student, Rip, or for the Conclave marshal, Ripley?" It felt strange to phrase it that way, but her answer would tell me a great deal about why she sent for me.

"That is a question I don't have an answer for, Ripley." Her usually serene expression looked troubled. "At least not yet."

"Perhaps if you explained why you sent for me?"

"Of course, but please bear with this old woman for a few minutes."

She rested a light hand on my shoulder before moving into the kitchen. Part of me wanted to get up and follow. But I knew what she expected. We'd danced this particular dance before. She would leave me to think about what she said—and hadn't said—while she brewed tea and produced some treat I wouldn't be able to resist. She did it the first time I came to visit with my parents, and she continued to do so now that I was an adult.

"Now is the time for talk." Gemma sat across from me, teacup and saucer balanced on one knee. A plate of brownies fresh out of the oven sat on the coffee table in front of the sofa. "I assume Redmond explained my call."

"He said you sounded worried." I wasn't about to say terrified, not until I knew more. "He also said you told him you'd Seen something. He said it's bad, and it's coming this way."

She nodded before sipping her tea. "What do you know about the Upheaval?"

I blinked, surprised by the sudden change in topics.

"I know what we're taught in schools and as well as what my parents taught me. When I became a marshal, I studied the data the Conclave possesses on what happened. I guess I know as much as some and more than most. Why?"

"I've talked with you about my life before the Upheaval some, Ripley, but not a great deal. But you know I've always had my abilities."

I nodded.

"I knew something was wrong before the rifts opened. I Saw something. At the time, I didn't understand what it meant. I saw a world like ours but different, one where our kind walked openly but where the humans feared us. I thought it was a warning. I passed it on to the Conclave and others, telling them we had to take a firm hand over our people to keep the peace. The changes that came with the rifts would terrify most of the humans. They would react with panic if any of our kind acted against them."

I thought for a moment, remembering my lessons. The Conclave existed even before the Upheaval, created to help our kind hide in plain sight. That was something that became increasingly difficult as technology advanced.

"It helped that the Conclave was already working with the federal government before the Upheaval. Safeguards had quietly been put into place over the years to protect us and give us the same fundamental rights normals enjoyed."

Gemma smiled at me like a proud teacher. "Part of our promise to the government, done to reassure not only the politicians but the public as well, included expanding the office of the marshals. Before the Upheaval, there had never been more than one or two of them at a time in the United States. Their main role was to make sure none of our people went rogue and inadvertently revealed our existence to the humans. Afterwards, the marshals became our police, enforcing not only human law but Conclave law as well. It helped reassure the humans we aren't really monsters."

I'd heard the same thing from my folks growing up, so I nodded.

"My dream last night felt much the same as that one so long ago."

I inhaled sharply. I didn't know what life had been like before the Upheaval beyond what I'd been told and what I'd read in various history books. But I sure as hell didn't want to live through a repeat because my gut told me it would be a nightmare of epic proportions and would see the death of many, human and para alike.

Gemma smiled almost gently and leaned over to lightly rest a hand on my knee. "I have learned much in the years since that first dream, Ripley. I do not believe we are facing another Upheaval, at least not to the degree of that first one. However, something is coming, and it bodes ill. Unfortunately, the signs have not shown me more than that. I was hoping you might have seen or heard something that could help me bring the dream into focus."

I started to shake my head. Then I remembered Razor's cousins and their sudden arrival from São Paulo. Could that be related to Gemma's dream?

"Ripley?"

"There are visitors in the Zone, specifically in town. They arrived unexpectedly last night. I think it might be time to learn why they're here."

"Will you let me know what you find out?"

"I will if you tell me more about your dream and why you wanted to see me instead of telling Red about it all."

"When I told the Conclave about my dreams from before the Upheaval, they made me promise to inform them if I ever experienced anything similar. This wasn't the same." She shook her head before I could interrupt. "It wasn't. But it was close. Yes, I will speak with someone from the Conclave when it's time. But I wanted to discuss it with someone here first, someone I trust to learn the truth without being swayed by the politics of the situation." Now she smiled almost sadly. "And, yes, someone with ties to the Conclave should further action be needed."

"Putting the responsibility on me." I didn't like it but part of me understood. "All right. I'll go see what the visitors have to say." I chewed my lower lip for a moment as I thought.

"Have you spoken with Starke about all this?"

The very mention of Griffin Starke had her narrowing her eyes and shaking her head, her expression turning stubborn. Not that I blamed her. Starke could be as frustrating as he was stubborn. For most of my life, I blamed it on the fact he seemed to epitomize everything most folks thought about lycans. Stubborn, proud, quick to anger, loves to fight, and always so damned cock sure he was right, no matter what. Add to that he was now the town's police chief, and it made him a colossal pain in my ass.

"I have not, nor will I until the Conclave or its representative says I must."

The look she gave me spoke volumes. Whether I formally agreed to look into her vision or not, she had decided I was that representative. Great. Just fucking great.

"All right." I tried to smile, having no doubt she saw through the attempt. "Please let me know if you *See* anything else. I don't care if you think it's related or not. I want to know. Understand?"

She smiled, all the earlier tension gone, and I cocked my head, looking at her in question.

"You are so very much like your mother, Ripley."

A hint of sadness touched her eyes, and I swallowed hard. Even after so long, I still missed Mom.

"Thank you. I'm taking that as a compliment."

"As you should. Melanie was a special woman and a very talented marshal."

She stood and motioned for me to stay where I was, telling me she'd be right back. Instead of going to the kitchen as expected, she moved toward the rear of the house. I waited, wondering what she was up to. This was a change in our usual routine, and it worried me, especially in light of our conversation.

She returned a few minutes later. Instead of taking a seat, she stood in front of me and reached for my hand. "I want you to wear this, Ripley." She fastened a silver cuff, much like the one she wore, around my right wrist. "I worked protections into it during its forging and then again when the sigils were engraved. I promise it will serve you well."

The corners of my mouth lifted. "Thank you, Gemma. I appreciate it." I had a sick feeling in the pit of my stomach that I'd need all the protection I could get before this was over. "Is there anything else you can tell me?"

She shook her head. "Perhaps after I've meditated some more, and you have talked with these strangers you mentioned."

"Then I shall take my leave." I carried my teacup and saucer into her kitchen and quickly rinsed them. When I turned from the sink, she handed me a small bag with my favorite cookies and several brownies inside.

"Watch yourself, Ripley." Her eyes took on the out of focus look I learned long ago to associate with her form of Sight. In that moment, her gift spoke to me, not her consciousness. "The darkness coming will target you not only because of who you are but also because of what you are."

I swallowed hard, not liking what she said one bit. "I'll be careful. Promise."

She shook herself and slid her arm through the crook of my elbow. We paced slowly through the house to the front door. Once standing on the porch, she reached up and cupped my cheek with her right hand. The affection in her eyes surprised me.

"You were wise to visit Razor before coming here. You have nothing to fear from me, but there are dangers on the road."

"There always are when this close to one of the rifts." I went on to tell her about the encounter with the *cat* on my way here.

"You were right to leave her alone, Ripley. I will make sure she and her kits move on." She smiled, but it didn't touch her eyes. "You would be wise to allow Razor to make your protections more permanent. Doing so will help in the troubles ahead."

That surprised me. I doubted the shaman had said anything to her about my hesitance to allow him to ink me.

"When I know more about what we might be facing, I'll consider it."

Although her words were enough to make me consider it now.

"I should have more for you when you return, Ripley."

"And I will hopefully have information for you as well." I dug my keys out of my pocket. "I'll call when I've had a chance to talk to the others and do a bit more digging."

She watched as I climbed in the SUV. Instead of going inside, she stood on the porch as I drove off. As I did, I blew out a breath. I hadn't learned much. Hell, I hadn't learned anything other than the fact Red was right. Gemma was scared and she very carefully put me in the line of fire, at least between her and the Conclave. Worse, she hadn't given me enough information to contact the Conclave yet.

Now all I needed to do was figure out the best course of action. Safe money lay on going straight back to Razor's to talk with his cousins. But that seemed too obvious. I wanted to find out more about them first. Then maybe have a private word with Razor to see what he could tell me.

Perhaps it was time to give in and let him finally ink me. If so, we'd do it on my terms, starting with no one but the two of us being around when he did it. If I agreed to having protections permanently inked, I didn't want folks knowing which ones I opted for or where they were located.

First, however, I needed a word with Red, preferably before I returned to town.

"What did she have to say, Ripley?"

"She couldn't tell me much, Red, but you were right. She's seriously spooked, and she basically backed me into a corner. What she *Saw* is enough like what she reported to the Conclave before the Upheaval that she needs to let them know. But she wants to buy herself some time to figure out what might be going on. So, she asked you to send me. She figures that covers her, not that she said as much."

For a moment, silence stretched out between us. I waited, giving him time to consider what I'd said.

"All right. Are you on your way back?"

"I am."

"Come to the office and we'll figure out what our next step should be." Another pause and I pictured him frowning, running a hand over his jaw as he considered the various options. "We'll hold off telling the Conclave for the moment."

"Understood."

I didn't like it but then I also didn't like the idea of calling in the Conclave. Once that happened, the members would insist I finally accept the role as senior marshal in the region. I'd been putting them off for a year now. In that time, they'd been looking for a way to force my hand. Part of that included sending in another marshal to "assist" me. With Gemma worried, they had all they needed to corner me into making a decision, whether I liked it or not.

Bastards.

"Come straight to the office, Rip. No detours."

"There'd better be coffee when I get there." And maybe a large whiskey as well. I had a feeling this was going to be a very long day. It also meant I needed to find someone to cover for me at the bar tonight.

Damn it, I really hate Mondays.

4

NEVER IGNORE A WITCH'S WARNINGS

The small knot of worry sitting like a lump in the pit of my stomach grew into a boulder the closer to Red's I got. Brake lights flashed ahead of me, and traffic slowed to a stop. Traffic, the sort where cars sat bumper to bumper, horns blaring and tempers flaring, was a rarity here. Anyone with two working brain cells knew better than to piss off a paranormal behind the wheel of a car. Doing so gave a whole new definition to the term road rage. Then there was the simple fact there weren't all that many folks living nearby, not like before the Cataclysm. We could wait a few minutes to get to our destination. So, when a car horn sounded and I caught sight of the line of cars stopped ahead of me, the hair on the back of my neck stood on end. Something was wrong. I felt it in my bones. Maybe I was more than a little paranoid after meeting with Gemma, but every fiber of my being screamed *trouble!*

Frowning, I rolled down the window. Almost instantly, the faint sounds of sirens I'd ignored up until then grew louder. Smoke climbed high in the sky, clearing the tops of the warehouses further down the street. The unmistakable smell of a fire filled the SUV. A sense of dread, stronger than I felt with Gemma, washed over me. Worried, I turned off Main Street, hoping to take the side roads to Red's office.

Five minutes later, after creeping along at a snail's pace, I pulled onto yet another side street. But not before I caught sight of the flashing lights of emergency vehicles reflecting off the sides of the warehouses lining the streets in this part of town. My gut told me whatever happened, it was more than a simple traffic stop or medical emergency. Worried, I considered my options, not that I had many to choose from. I could either park and walk to Red's or I could head home. No way was I going to be able to drive the rest of the way to Red's. Not with traffic backed up even on the side streets.

Looking around, I spotted a parking space barely large enough for the SUV. Ignoring the honking behind me, I carefully maneuvered into it. Hopefully, the bail bondsman whose office I parked in front of didn't mind. Even if he did, I didn't care. The SUV was there until I moved it or someone towed it.

And good luck getting a tow on the best of days—something today most definitely was not.

Sitting behind the steering wheel, I frowned thoughtfully. Then I reached for my phone and checked my messages. Nothing. No text or voice mail from Red after our last conversation. My fingers flew across the screen almost on their own as I typed a quick message and then hit send. Then those same fingers drummed impatiently against the steering wheel as I waited for Red to answer.

Nothing.

Damn it.

This wasn't good, not good at all.

I considered for a moment. Then my fingers once again flew across the screen as I sent several quick messages. The first was to my contact on the Conclave, letting him know there was a situation that might need his attention and I'd touch base once I knew more. The second was to Razor, telling him I'd be by later to speak with him and his cousins. The final was to Gemma, warning her to be careful. If this— whatever this was—happened to be related to her dream, she might be in danger.

Of course, I still had no idea what "this" might be.

Unable to delay any longer, I climbed out of the SUV and slid my phone into my hip pocket. Then I grabbed my bag and dug inside. I hesitated a moment before clipping the badge identifying me as a Conclave marshal to my belt. Then I tucked my ID in my front pocket. Then with a frown, I secured the 1911 in its holster to my belt and pulled on my leather jacket. No sense advertising I was carrying, not until I had a better idea what was going on. With that done, I locked the truck and set the anti-theft wards.

Now to find out what the hell was going on.

Getting to the office was easier said than done. People crowded the sidewalks leading up to the converted warehouse. The police, or maybe the fire department, had barricaded the street, preventing anyone from getting closer than half a block away. If that wasn't bad enough, some of those in the crowd recognized me and stopped me, asking if I knew what was going on, had I heard from Red, asking questions I had no answers for.

Even as I shouldered my way through the crowd, promising to let them know something as soon as I learned anything, I kept my head on a swivel. Had Red known something might happen when he warned me earlier to be careful? Why hadn't he said something? Hell, why didn't he say something when we spoke half an hour ago?

I put a clamp on my growing worry and scanned the faces in the crowd. I recognized most of them. Those I didn't, I'd identify later, after I found out what was going on.

Damn it, if only I had a better idea what was going on.

Think, Rip. You trained for this. You know what to do.

I hissed out a breath. My subconscious was an evil bitch. This time, it sounded exactly like my mother during one of our lessons when she started teaching me what I needed to know to be a marshal. Gods above and below, I'd give anything to have her here right now. She'd have the situation in hand and answers for everyone within hours, if not minutes. Unfortunately, she wasn't here. She hadn't been here in more than a decade. But she had taught me. All I needed to do was remember those lessons and pray I didn't fuck it up too badly.

That meant remembering this part of town had a full complement of mundane and arcane surveillance in place. Red told me about it several years ago when a spate of minor vandalism hit the neighborhood. Those systems might help answer my questions and I sure as hell wouldn't hesitate to use them if necessary.

"Ripley!"

Startled, I looked around. A teen, little more than a girl, pushed her way through the crowd. Her red hair sprang in curls around her head. Her blue eyes swam with tears. Through them I saw the anger and fear. But it was the sight of the bruising along the left side of her face and the blood drying under her nose that sent me hurrying in her direction.

I had a moment to brace before she threw herself in my arms, all but burrowing into me. Staggering back a couple of steps, I held her close and looked around. Instead of seeing the person responsible for hurting her, a scene straight out of my nightmares greeted me. My jaw clenched and my stomach turned at the sight. Now I knew the source of the sirens and flashing lights and it was worse than I feared.

Emergency vehicles lined the street in front of Red's building. Several ambulances, their lights flashing, rear doors standing open, waited along with cop cars and firetrucks. Hoses ran from the trucks and the nearest hydrants, wielded by firefighters in turnout gear. They fought what appeared to be a losing battle against the flames devouring the building.

Red's building.

Red's office.

His home.

Hell, home for more than half of his employees and their families.

Not to mention the armory, records room and more.

Gently, I eased back from Dani and tilted her chin up so I could see her face. As I did, I fought down the flash of anger that surged up from the pit of my stomach. Whatever happened, it scared Dani enough her control slipped. Instead of human ears, buff-colored cat ears with black tuffs peaked out from under her curls. Her blue eyes took on a more feline shape. It wouldn't take much for her to finish the shift and I did not want to have to chase down a scared bobcat in this crowd.

I smiled at her in reassurance and rested one hand on her shoulder as I tipped her face up with the other.

"Are you all right?" Much as I wanted to find out what happened at the warehouse, she came first.

She swallowed hard and nodded. Good. She had control, tentative though it might be. Hopefully, it would be enough.

"Dani, you're safe now. I need you to remember that." I spoke softly, praying she believed me.

She nodded again.

"Can you tell me what happened?"

"D-don't know." She shook her head as her teeth began chattering in reaction. "I got off the bus and was heading home when I heard it."

"Heard what?"

"A bang. It was really loud and sounded really close." She closed her eyes and her forehead scrunched up as she tried to remember. "Then I saw the smoke."

"Okay." I looked around, worried because I didn't see Red or any of the others who should have been there this time of day. "Have you seen any of the others?"

She shook her head, tears once again pooling in her eyes. I hugged her, understanding the fear eating at her. Hell, it ate at me. Then I looked around again, this time hoping to find someone to stay with her while I had a little "chat" with the first responders. Relief filled me to see Razor shoving through the crowd, his expression as worried as I felt, as he made his way in our direction.

"Dani, look at me." I waited until she did. "Razor's going to stay with you while I try to find out what's going on." When I glanced at him, he nodded. "I'll be right back. I promise. Then we'll figure out what to do next. Okay?"

"I want to go with you, Ripley." A single tear tracked down her cheek.

I reached out and gently wiped it away. "Dani, I understand. I really do. But I don't know what's going on. Until I do, I need to know you're safe. I can't be worrying about you—and I will if you're with me—and do my job. I promise I'll come right back and tell you what I find out. Okay?"

She stared at me for a moment before reluctantly nodding.

"Wait here for a minute. I need to talk to Razor."

Dani said nothing. Instead, she watched as we moved a few feet away. As we did, Aras appeared at her side. The elf caught my eye and nodded once, his expression serious, and I nodded in return. I might not fully trust him, but I knew Aras cared for Dani in a way he didn't most everyone else. He'd keep her safe until Razor returned. That was all I could ask for, at least until I knew more.

"What the hell happened, Ripley?" Gone was the easy-going tattoo artist. The man demanding answers was Roberto Pantoja, a very powerful shaman.

"That's what I want to know, Razor. This is what I found when I returned from Gemma's." I waved a hand at the first responders. "Dani ran up before I could get to the firefighters to see what they could tell me. Said she wasn't here when it happened, but there's more to it. Something happened to her. Hell, Razor, from the looks of things, someone hit her. She's got a bruise on her face and her nose has been bleeding."

His lips pulled back, baring his teeth as anger radiated from him. "What can I do?"

That's the thing with Razor. We might have our occasional differences and he might keep teasing me about not letting him in my pants, but he stood up when needed.

And damn if I didn't need him now.

"I need to talk to Dani and find out what happened to her. After I do, will you take her back to your shop? I know you and Aras will keep her safe."

"Of course."

"Thanks." I laid a hand on his arm and nodded once. That was all, but it was enough for him to know I appreciated it.

"What else?"

"When I'm done here, we need to talk."

"Agreed. There are things I must tell you and, judging from your text, you have things to tell me."

My eyes narrowed at his tone. "Things to tell me, Rip, or me, the marshal?"

"To be honest, my friend, I am not sure."

The fact he looked uncertain worried me. Instead of asking any of the questions running through my head, I nodded again. I'd learn what was on his mind soon enough. For now, I had other things to deal with, starting with Dani.

"Hey, kid." I smiled gently as we joined her and Aras under the awning outside Cosmic Sisters Café down the street from the office. "You said you were getting back from school when everything happened."

Dani nodded once.

"What happened? How did you get hurt?" I hissed out a quick breath as another question dawned on me. "And why are you home early?" A glance at the clock on my cellphone confirmed she shouldn't have been back for another hour at least.

She stared at her feet and dug one toe against the concrete.

"Dani?" Aras spoke more gently than I'd ever heard before. "You need to tell Ripley what happened. She can't help if she doesn't know."

When she looked up, I saw something in her eyes I never wanted to see again. I saw desperation. Someone or something had scared the teen. Anger building, I pushed it aside. Since she first showed up on Red's doorstep more than three years ago, Dani had been like a little sister to me. If someone hurt her, they would soon discover just how foolish they'd been.

"It's okay, Dani. You can tell me." I slid an arm around her shoulders and pulled her close. When she stiffened, I waited, wondering what the hell happened and who I needed to kill.

"They sent me home because I got into a fight."

I closed my eyes and counted to ten. This was the third fight in as many months. Red promised me he dealt with the problem the last time this happened. Obviously, he hadn't. Great, just great. This was a headache I didn't need right now.

"Dani, we'll talk about this later. Just tell me one thing. Did you start the fight?"

"No!" She shook her head emphatically.

"Then you're not in any trouble. I'll deal with the school later. Promise." I bent and pressed my lips to the top of her head. "What happened once you got off the bus?"

35

"Like I said, I got off the bus and heard the bang. Then someone pushed me. I stumbled and almost fell and then they hit me. They said something and tried to grab me." She looked up at me. To my surprise, pride shone in her eyes and she grinned. "It scared me, but I remembered everything you taught me, Ripley. I kicked him in the shin, stomped his foot and twisted out of his grip. Then I ran and yelled for help. I knew I needed to find you or Red but then I saw the fire." She bit back a sob and buried her face against my shoulder.

"Did the bastard who hit you say anything, Dani?"

She shook her head and then nodded without looking up.

"Yeah, but I didn't understand him. He didn't speak English."

"Did it sound Elvish, little one?" Aras spoke more gently than I'd ever heard from him.

Another shake of her head and then a shrug. She carefully pulled out of my embrace and scrubbed the heels of her hands over her cheeks, wiping away her tears.

"Don't know. Sounded different from how you talk, Aras."

"That's okay, kiddo. We'll figure it out. What else can you tell us?" I shot a look over her head, letting both Aras and Razor know we'd discuss this later.

"Miss Sele stepped out of the café then. He saw her and that's when he ran off."

I caught my lower lip between my teeth and thought for a moment. Something about him running off didn't feel right. If he'd been trying to take Dani, he needed transport close by. Did he run to keep her from noticing his vehicle or, possibly, his accomplice? Or did he panic seeing one of the three sisters—and three witches—who owned Three Sisters Cosmic Café?

Or had he planned on dragging her into one of the nearby buildings and doing who knows what to her?

I needed to find those answers, but not yet.

"You did good, Dani, real good." I glanced to where Razor and Aras stood, grim-faced and radiating with anger. My own anger matched theirs. "Put out the word. I want to have a *chat* with the bastard who laid his hands on her. I'll pay standard rates for information about his identity and where I can find him. Same goes for anyone who was working with him. There's a bonus to the person who brings the bastard to me. My only requirement is that he be not only alive but able to answer my questions. Make that very clear. He's mine to deal with, no one else's. Make sure they understand that."

"I'll see to it." Aras ran a gentle hand over Dani's head and promised to be back soon. Then he disappeared into the crowd, fading into the shadows like a mist.

"Dani, I want you to go with Razor now. He'll make sure you're safe and that nothing else happens to you. I promise that I'll be there as soon as I've talked with some of the folks here." Including Sele to see what she could tell me about the bastard who hurt Dani.

In response, Dani tightened her arms around my waist, holding so tightly I wasn't sure she'd ever let go.

"It's all right, Dani. I promise I'll be there as soon as I can, but I need to stay here right now. I need to find out what happened to Red and the others."

I carefully pried away her arms and turned her into Razor's waiting embrace. The shaman silently told me to go on. Then he turned Dani and slowly escorted her away from the burning building and the gathered crowd. I watched for a moment until they disappeared in the crowd. As much as I wanted to go with them, it was time to get to work and find out what the hell was going on.

But first things first. I needed to update Gemma, even if I didn't know much.

Hell, who was I kidding? I didn't know anything other than the fact the world had just turned upside down and a building that should have been fireproof looked like it might be fully consumed in flames. No way that should happen. Not between the state-of-the-art fire suppression system Red installed last year, the wards on the building and the fact much of it was built from stone.

Stone, damn it!

"Hello?"

Gemma might be the only one who didn't believe in caller ID.

"It's Ripley."

Damn, what was I supposed to say? Someone might have set Red's building on fire, but I didn't know for sure much less how they would have done it?

"Something's happened." She didn't ask, simply told me.

"Yes, ma'am. All I know for sure is Red's building looks like it might have been firebombed. It happened after I left your place." At least I assumed so. Red would have told me when we spoke, wouldn't he? "From where I'm standing down the block, it looks like it's fully engulfed. If there's any good news, it's that the fire hasn't spread."

"Red and the others?"

I shook my head, dread filling me. Then, realizing she couldn't see me, I answered. "I don't know. I haven't seen any of them yet."

For a long moment, she said nothing. I waited, giving her a chance to process what I told her.

"Ripley, I have always understood why you haven't fully embraced your role as our senior marshal. But you need to now. Red and the others need you. This Zone needs you."

I closed my eyes and gritted my teeth. I'd done my duty as marshal before, but she was right. I'd never fully accepted, much less embraced, it. Dad's death and Mom's disappearance happened because they were marshals. As a kid and then as a teen, I'd resented it. But I was an adult now, and it was time to do what I was trained for, like it or not. I had the family tradition to carry on, after all.

More importantly, I had people I cared for to protect.

"I know, Gemma."

"Good." She sounded relieved. "Tell Griffin Starke to put his people on alert, Ripley. Then contact the Conclave. This is somehow connected to my dreams."

Dreams? As in plural? She hadn't said anything about it being more than one dream.

Damn crazy woman. What else was she hiding from me?

"They're going to want to know more, Gemma."

"Don't we all?" She laughed mirthlessly. "When you finish your business in town, come see me. I hope to have some answers for you by then."

The call ended, and I stared at me cellphone in frustration. What did I expect? Gemma Blackrock lived apart from the rest of us for a reason. The best I could do was find out what I could and then pray she had something to add to it. But that came after I talked with the authorities and then armed myself for what I had a feeling might be war.

Welcome to Monday, the worst day of the week.

5

WHO INVITED THE WEREWOLF?

"You need to stay back, lady."

The uniformed cop stepped in front of me as I ducked under the yellow police tape, placing his body between me and the burning building. I arched one brow and shook my head. I might be many things, but a lady I'm not. Especially not when I wanted answers and didn't care what I had to do to get them.

Still, I knew better than to physically move the cop to the side, no matter how tempting it might be. I didn't recognize him—something that surprised me because I thought I knew all the local cops—and I sure as hell didn't want to risk getting arrested. At least not without good reason. But if he didn't let me talk to someone who might have some answers for me and soon, he would regret it.

The fact I might regret it as well didn't matter.

Before I could say as much, another officer turned and looked in our direction. He quickly took in the situation, his eyes sweeping the younger cop's face before his attention turned to me. I watched as he recognized me a moment before he noticed the badge at my waist. For a moment, he lifted his face skyward and his lips moved, possibly in prayer but more likely cursing imaginatively as he read the situation. Then he hurried in our direction. I crossed my arms and waited, wondering if he was going to help or join in the effort to hinder my efforts to find out what happened.

Since I knew him, my money was on helping.

"Let her pass, Conroy."

"But, Britt."

"I said to let her pass, rookie." The older cop stared him down, his frustration obvious. "Look at her belt, you idiot. You might not recognize her—and you should. I know I'm not the only one to tell you to familiarize yourself with the Conclave's reps in the Zone after you transferred in—but you should recognize her badge." When the rookie stared at him blankly, Britt rolled his eyes. "Jesus, Conroy, you're an idiot. I suggest you apologize and beg her to forget about your idiocy before the Chief finds out. If you're really lucky, he'll deal with you before the Conclave gets hold of you. Otherwise, your ass will be grass, very dry grass in the direct path of a firestorm that makes what's going on here look tame."

The young man, who didn't look much older than Dani, swallowed hard as all the color drained from his face.

"S-sorry, ma'am. Just tryin' to do my job." He stepped aside so quickly, I fought the urge to laugh.

As I followed Britt closer to the building, I heard the rookie asking someone who I was. An amused chuckle escaped my lips before I could stop it to hear one of the firefighters tell him he was lucky I hadn't handed him his head. According to the firefighter, I was more than the Conclave's marshal. I was one of the bartenders at Red Dragon Brewing Company and when I was working, they didn't need a bouncer. I chuckled again. Who knew there were folks more scared of my bartender persona than my part-time marshal role?

"Who's the rookie, Buck?" I looked around, noting faces I recognized as well as a few I did not inside the perimeter. Much as I wanted IDs on those I didn't know, I needed to speak with Griffin Starke, Glenham Grove's chief of police, as well as someone from the fire department first.

"New guy, just transferred in from the OKC Zone. Been here a week or so." The look on Keith "Buck" Britt's face spoke volumes and I didn't like the implications.

I glanced over my shoulder and watched the rookie for a moment. "Check him out, Buck. Deep dive, off the record. My authorization if anyone asks, but make sure they don't ask. If my name comes into it, it becomes official. He might just be overwhelmed being in a new job in a new town. He might be a jackass who didn't think he needed to bother learning who lives and works around here, much less who might represent the Conclave. Or he might be someone or something we need to take a closer look at."

Buck glanced over my shoulder in Conroy's direction and nodded. Interesting that he didn't argue. I'd known him long enough to understand how out of character that happened to be. He was as protective of his fellow cops as I was of Red and the rest of our "family". I'd need to find out why, but later, after I figured out what was going on here.

"Chief, got company!" Buck called out as we neared what looked to be the command post for the emergency responders.

A tall man in jeans and a white golf shirt with an embroidered badge on the left side of his chest turned in our direction. He nodded once before scanning the crowd behind us. As he crossed the distance between us, he motioned for Buck to get back to his post. The uniformed officer caught my eye and silently mouthed we'd talk later. Then he moved off, leaving me in the care of Chief of Police Griffin Starke.

"Rip." Starke made no attempt to hide the way he looked me over, or how he winced slightly at the sight of the badge at my waist. "Where've you been?"

"Working." Something about the way he looked at me put my back up. "What can you tell me?" I jutted my chin toward the burning building.

"I think that's my question." He might have said it lightly, but I knew him well enough to know he expected an answer. "It's too early for the bar to be open. So where have you been?"

I bit down on the quick flare of anger. He wanted me to react, and I was damned if I gave him that satisfaction.

"Just like I said. I was working. Red contacted me a couple of hours ago and said he needed me to take care of something for him, something that couldn't wait. After getting the details, I handled the job and was on my back to report in when I found this." I waved a hand at the scene outside the warehouse.

Besides, unless I missed my bet, he already knew I'd arranged for someone to cover for me tonight at the bar. So, I'd give him the truth, just not all of it, not until I knew more about what was going on.

"Red and the others?"

He shook his head, his dark eyes troubled. "We haven't been able to get inside. The flames are too hot and the fire department's worried about structural damage to the building."

One hand fisted at my side. "No contact with anyone?"

He shook his head again, his expression grim.

I turned and took several steps away. When I turned back, he waited, understanding I'd talk when I was ready.

"Starke, there's a safe room in the lowest basement level. It's possible whoever was inside made it there." Or at least some of them. I hoped. "What can you tell me about what happened? This place never should have caught fire." Not built like it was and certainly not with the level of warding Red put in place. "Hell, there's no way the flames should still be present. The building's fire suppression system is state-of-the-art and well above code. You know Red. He had every magical protection he could think of tied to the building as well."

Then there was the asshat who tried to grab Dani, but we'd get to that soon enough.

"We're still trying to piece it all together, Ripley. The FD has been focused on trying to get the fire under control. Nico Cuellar's the captain in charge. He said something about how the fire patterns and behavior don't make sense. He's sent for a fire elemental, but she's got to come from Fort Worth. In the meantime, he's got water and air elementals coming in from Dallas to help."

Left unsaid was "assuming the building's still standing by the time they get here."

"Run it for me, will you? What happened?"

"You asking as Red's employee or as the Conclave's marshal?"

"How about as both?" When he looked at me sharply, I shrugged, deciding to ease off a little before his back really went up. "Look, Griff, something's going on and I don't know nearly enough yet to know

44

how bad it's going to be. The assignment Red gave me is definitely going to fall under the Conclave's jurisdiction. To say I haven't been able to start gathering information is putting it mildly. It also means I can't tell you much more than that until I brief the Conclave and get their okay.

"What I can say is that I don't like what I've learned so far. This," I waved a hand at the building, "happened after I left the office. I can even tie down when the fire started. I spoke with Red approximately forty minutes ago. He didn't say anything to indicate something might be wrong. That means the fire started after we spoke. The fact the flames are strong enough the FD can't get inside worries me. As does the fact the fire appears to be contained to Red's building. I'm not seeing anything to suggest so much as a spark has spread to the nearby buildings. Something's not right about any of this."

He hissed out a breath and his eyes flashed. "You're sure?"

"Of course, I'm sure." I snapped out the words. Did he think I didn't know when I last spoke to the man who'd effectively been the closest thing I'd had to a parent for a decade? Before Starke could say anything, I pulled out my phone and opened my call history. Without a word, I handed it to him and waited as he checked it.

"Fine. Thanks." He pulled his radio and passed the information along to Nico Cuellar. Then he suggested the fire captain do whatever he could to get the elementals here without delay. "I take it you have questions."

God, he was infuriating. That's only one of the many reasons I hadn't agreed to the Conclave's previous requests I accept my role as the Zone's designated marshal before now. Doing so meant having to deal with Starke on a regular basis and that was a headache I neither wanted nor needed.

"Yeah. What the hell happened?"

He shook his head. "Not a clue, not really. Reports came in of an explosion. By the time Cuellar's people got here, the flames blocked entry into the building. I had some of my cops set up a perimeter to keep the onlookers back. Others are taking witness statements and making sure the surrounding buildings have been evacced."

I glanced at the front of the building, frowning as flames danced behind the windows, all but mocking us. At the same time, one part of me felt the pull of them. The fire called to me, a seductive song that touched my very core, enticing, inviting.

And so very dangerous.

My lips pulled back, and I hissed out a breath. Fire rarely felt like this. The only time it did was when magic was involved. This wasn't good, not good at all.

"Ripley?" Starke reached out and rested a hand on my upper arm. "What's going on?"

"I don't know." My temper flared when he looked at me doubtfully. "It's the damned truth, Griffin. I don't know what's going on."

But I planned on finding out.

He pursed his lips, fighting the urge to snap back. Then he shook himself, reminding me of a dog shaking water from its coat.

"Let's try this. Who was inside?"

"I don't know." I scrubbed my hands over my face, trying to think about who might have been there this time of day. "This time of day, there could be anywhere from three or four to more than a dozen inside and that's just talking about Red's employees. There could also be clients, friends, and family, basically anyone." I gave a shrug. "All I can say for certain is Red and Alyce Hampton were there when I came by earlier to see what the assignment was. Several others were there as well. I didn't see them, but I heard them and saw evidence of their presence. That was over two hours ago."

"Dani?"

Gone was the hard-edged cop of a few moments ago. Interesting. Apparently, Dani somehow managed to win him over like she did most everyone she met.

"She's safe. She'd just gotten off the bus from school when she heard an explosion of some sort." I told him what little I could about Dani, including how I'd sent her off with Razor.

"Damn it, Ripley. You know I need to talk to her."

"No one's stopping you, *Chief*." He bristled at my formal tone. Too bad. I wasn't in the mood to play dominance games with him. "But you'll do it away from here and you'll do it when either Razor or I can be there. You'll also wait until we know more about what happened." I stood there, all but daring him to argue. "I mean it, Starke. Red's the closest thing to a father that girl's had for the last three years. You know how he took her in after her parents died in that damned car crash."

A crash I still didn't believe was an accident. Unfortunately, I didn't have any reason to open the case under my authority as marshal. The accident happened in Arlington and the local police closed the investigation after finding nothing suspicious to explain why the car went off the road. Reopening the case without something solid would be tantamount to accusing them of turning a blind eye to a hate crime against paras. Definitely not the way to build a working relationship with any police department.

"If that's not good enough reason to get her away from here for the moment, there's the little fact someone attacked her after she got off the bus. Worse, they hit her and tried to take her with them. Fortunately, she managed to break away. I don't know about you, but I want to know why they were after her and if it has anything to do with the fire."

And that was something I planned to find out. I didn't care whose toes I stepped on in the process.

"You'll leave it to me, Ripley. This is a police matter."

I simply looked at him, wondering if he really thought I'd sit back and just wait for him to figure out what was going on.

"Ripley," he drawled. "What are you planning?"

"I'm going to find out where Red and the others are." And God help those responsible if any of them were hurt—or worse. If Griffin Starke didn't like it, screw him. They were the closest thing I had to family. "Then I'm going to find out what the hell is going on and put a stop to it before anyone else is hurt."

"I repeat, what are you going to do?"

My mouth twisted into a humorless smile, one that sent chills down the spines of customers too far in their cups to know when to stop.

"Watch and learn, Chief. Watch and learn."

His brow furrowed as I shrugged out of my jacket and handed it to him. After a quick text to Razor, I tossed Starke my cellphone. My wallet, badge and Conclave ID followed. Any other time, I'd find some place private to strip. But there wasn't time now. I did like my boots enough that I toed them off. No sense ruining them with what I had in mind. The rest of my clothes could be easily replaced.

"Ripley!" Starke yelled as I walked toward the building.

I glanced over my shoulder and gave him a cocky grin.

"If I'm not back in ten minutes, fifteen at the most, contact the Conclave. Tell them what's happened and tell them I am officially calling for reinforcements."

I easily shrugged off the firefighters who hurried to intercept me. They staggered back, unprepared for the extra surge of strength coursing through me. I barely spared them a look as I continued toward the front door. It had been a long time since I freed this particular aspect of my being. None of those present had ever seen it and for good reason. It wasn't something I advertised. After all, most people, even paras, look at those with the ability to become giant walking columns of fiery plasma with both fear and suspicion.

"Ripley, goddammit!"

I paused at the door and turned back, grinning. Flames that had nothing to do with the fire behind me danced over my skin. My blood boiled and steam rose from the pooling water at my feet. Very few of those who know me realize my bloodline includes Surtr, a Jötnar from Norse mythology. The bloodline, with the exception of a very distant cousin, no longer stands over eight feet tall. Some of us, however, possessed all the abilities Surtr passed down to his descendants.

Fortunately, I was one of them.

"Ten minutes. Have EMTs standing by."

I turned back to the building and held my arms out from my body. Head thrown back, eyes closed, I called my inner fire. The heat raced through me, intoxicating, powerful. The silver cuff on my wrist heated but, surprisingly, did not melt. Nor did the leather cuff. I snorted a laugh. Leave it to Razor and Gemma to make sure their gifts survived this particular aspect of mine.

"Remember," I called, voice rough and low. Then I stepped through the doors into Hell on Earth.

6

YEA, THOUGH I WALK THROUGH
THE VALLEY OF FLAME

Flames rose around me, their dance beautiful and deadly. I drew them close, until they wrapped around me like a second skin. Fire called to fire and I answered. But I didn't give up control. I never would. I knew the danger, tempting though it might be, of doing so. Giving up control meant giving up my humanity and losing control.

And that meant a firestorm the likes of which most people could only imagine in their worst nightmares.

Knowing I didn't have long, I moved further inside, wondering what I'd find.

How many times had I walked this very path, never thinking about danger befalling me here? This had been one of the very few places I considered a safe haven, especially after Mom disappeared: home, work, even a place to retreat to when I needed to escape the demands of everyday life.

That all changed in a flash of fire and magic. Now danger lay not in the flames but in being trapped by a possible building collapse. The flames normally wouldn't harm me, not so long as I stayed in this form. Not that I'd ever remained in it for more than a few hours and then I had not been under duress. But what choice did I have if I wanted to find out what happened to Red and the others?

God, please let them be alive.

I moved slowly through the main floor, checking each office in turn. This time of day, most everyone would be further inside, taking meetings, training, even relaxing. Most of the doors on either side of the reception area stood open, the rooms beyond engulfed with fire. I studied each one, noting fire patterns and wishing I could take photos. They would help Cuellar and his arson investigators. But no camera could survive my hold when I was in this form. I really needed to talk with one of the artificers about that particular problem.

"Red!" I called as I entered his office suite, my voice deeper and rougher than usual. "Redmond!"

I paused at the door to Red's private office. Magical wards danced across my skin, ignoring the flames and stinging like a million ants going to town on my flesh. Gritting my teeth, I reached out, stopping mere inches from the door knob. Think. I needed to think. These wards felt different from the wards on the rest of the building. They felt different than they had earlier. Then they'd been little more than a faint hum as I entered the office. Now they pushed against me, fighting my flames even as they fought the fire working through the outer office.

Protective then. Great, except I needed to see what lay beyond the door.

Hoping I didn't regret it—and praying I didn't find Red or anyone else—I pushed open the door and stepped inside. Unlike the other offices, the fire had not touched the interior. Interesting. Had Red reinforced the wards before getting out or was there an additional layer of protection woven into them, one that would only be triggered in an emergency?

And where the hell was Red?

Why would he leave the safety of his office when Hell on Earth suddenly hit the building?

I knew the answer and took one last look around. He did it for the same reason I would have: to save the others he looked at as family.

I left the office, unwilling to risk the wards any longer than necessary. The last thing I needed was to have my own flames extinguished, especially before I learned what happened to everyone. Hopefully, they made it to the safe room. I doubted they made it out of the building. If they had, they would have contacted me to let me know they were all right. Hell, they would have contacted the Conclave.

Who was I kidding? They'd be outside, doing whatever they could to help the first responders currently working to put out the fire.

Time to return to the search, Rip.

Worry warred with relief as I returned to flames trying to eat away at the building. I breathed deeply and let the flames once again wrap around me. In this form, the heat did not sear my lungs. My skin didn't blister. Instead, it felt like a warm day on the beach, something I could definitely get used to if I didn't mind setting fires wherever I went.

Pushing aside the temptation the power coursing through me presented, I carefully made my way to the stairs. Then I cursed, frustration filling me. One look inside the stairwell convinced me I didn't need to head to the upper floors. Smoked billowed from above, thick enough to kill anyone trapped there.

Down was my only choice. As I carefully picked my way through the smoke, I prayed I didn't come across any of those who worked for Red, people I considered friends and family. The flames wouldn't be kind to them.

Anger flared and with it my fire as I approached the gym that ran along the east side of the first level of the basement. Any doubts I had about the source of the fire ended the closer I came to the gym. It didn't take an arson investigator to recognize the path the flames went outward from the gym. The fire, at least a fire, started here. Any doubts I might have disappeared when I spotted several easily identifiable flashpoints marring the northern and eastern walls.

Steeling myself for what I'd find, I approached the door, surprised the flames that obviously started here were now little more than smoldering ashes. Bile rose in my throat as what I first assumed to be debris from the ceiling tiles falling to the floor assumed the shape of a body, one burned beyond recognition. Thankfully, my sense of smell changed in this form, so the stench of burning flesh didn't assail me.

Still, I swallowed hard as I knelt near the body. At first glance, I couldn't tell whether it was male or female, only that the person died in agony. His—her?—mouth was forever frozen in a scream, body curled into a grotesque imitation of the fetal position, hands more like talons held out as if to ward off the flames.

Damn it!

I stood and glanced around the room I'd spent so much time in over the years. A fury unlike any I'd ever known before filled me. Two more bodies lay further inside. Like the first, I couldn't identify them. I prayed they'd passed out from the smoke before the flames got to them. Not that it mattered. Dead is dead. But their deaths would be avenged, and I'd see to it the Conclave honored their memories. If they had families, they would be cared for. One thing Red, and my parents before him, taught me was to take care of our own and these three had been mine just as much as they'd been his.

Red.

I swallowed hard. I needed to know. I needed to be sure none of the dead were him. Barely daring to breathe, I moved to stand over first one and then the other. I might not be able to recognize their features and their clothes had been burned away. But I could make out height and general build. None matched Red's stocky frame. Relief made my knees weak. But I didn't have time to waste. I needed to find out what happened to Red and the others.

I don't know how long it took to finally make my way to the lowest level of the basement. It couldn't have been too long, but it felt like hours. More than once, I needed to stop to pull debris out of my way. The building still stood but drywall and framing burned and fell, cluttering the way. Over the crackling of the flames, I heard an ominous groaning as supports weakened and stone cracked under the heat. Time was running out and I couldn't afford to get trapped.

How long before the building finally gave way?

Lights flickered and the fire suppression system sprayed water from the ceiling as I opened the last door separating me from the safe room. Behind me, flames licked along the ceiling and walls, searching out fuel and eating oxygen. I could go back the way I came and tell Starke and Cuellar the safe room looked intact. But I wouldn't be able to tell them if anyone made it there and now waited for rescue. I doubted Cuellar would risk any of his people trying to get to the room without some kind of confirmation there were survivors inside.

If I went any further inside, the suppression system would douse my own flames. Not only would I be walking around barefoot and naked, but I didn't know if I'd be able to call on my fire anytime soon. Certainly not until I dried off. But what choice did I have?

Talk about being between the proverbial rock and a hard place.

Praying I wasn't making a very big—and potentially fatal—mistake, I stepped inside the small room and closed the door behind me. Steam rose as water poured down from overhead, dousing my flames. I inhaled deeply, closed my eyes, and pictured the human form I usually presented to the world. Pain followed by freezing cold washed over me as flames withdrew and skin once again covered muscle and bone. Shivering, I shoved my now wet hair out of my eyes and looked around, praying I hadn't just made the biggest mistake of my life.

Padding carefully across the wet floor, I looked around. After the latest upgrades down here, Red explained the power in this room as well as the safe room ran off their own generators during emergencies. That meant the lighting was dimmer than usual, even more so after I spent the last who knew how long walking through fire. I didn't have time to wait for my eyes to adjust. That meant moving slowly but carefully and praying I didn't step on anything too bad.

I blew out a breath, relieved to find no more bodies. All I needed to do now was check the safe room and then get the hell out of there. Time was running out. Not only because I'd given Starke a deadline before he contacted the Conclave but because the smoke in the air made it increasingly difficult to breathe. I hadn't noticed it while doing my impression of a walking column of fire. But now, wet and shivering with cold, there could be no denying it. My eyes burned. My throat felt swollen. My lungs arched as they fought for fresh oxygen. I didn't have much time left.

I opened my mouth to call for Red and then snapped it closed. If anyone made it into the safe room, they'd never hear me.

Think, Rip, think.

I checked the two desks, the room's only furniture aside from the two desk chairs, looking for anything else one of our people might have left, anything that might tell me what happened or where they were. Nothing. But there was a sweatshirt over the back of one of the chairs. I grabbed it up and slid into it. Judging by the way it hung down to my thighs, it probably belonged to Derron, one of our tech wizards. I'd thank him later for the chance to cover up even if only for a little while.

What next?

Check the controls for the safe room. That would tell me the last time the room was accessed.

I reached out and wiped the control panel with a wet hand. Then I leaned forward, praying the ocular scanner still worked. A soft beep sounded as the scanner activated. I blinked and straightened before quickly inputting my security code. Barely daring to breathe, I waited as the screen came alive, line after line of data scrolling across it.

Relief weakened my knees, and I punched in a second series of commands. "Red?"

The speaker crackled and I strained to hear, praying someone answered.

"Ripley?" The woman's voice revealed her fear and relief, a relief I shared.

I closed my eyes and struggled for calm. "Ellie, are you okay?"

"Been better, Rip."

I chuckled softly. Leave it to Ellie to find even a modicum of humor in this situation. Then I sobered.

"How many are in there with you, Ellie?"

"Six."

"Red?"

Please let him be there.

"He told us to get down here and lock ourselves in. We haven't heard from him since then."

That sounded like him. Damned fool.

"All right, Ellie. I'll try to find him after I figure out the best way to get you guys out of there. Is anyone injured?"

God, I hoped not. It was going to be hard enough getting seven healthy people out of this inferno.

"Nothing serious. A few burns and Book twisted his ankle on the stairs."

I studied the readouts, noting in particular the oxygen and temperature levels inside.

"I need you to listen closely, Ellie. Can you all do that for me?"

There was silence and I pictured the scene beyond the reinforced door. They wanted out but knew the danger. Now I needed them to trust me not to leave them without having some plan in place to rescue them.

"Just tell us what you want us to do, Ripley."

"I need you to hang tight a little while longer. You've got enough oxygen for another seven or eight hours, longer if you don't panic. Stay calm and don't move around. Understand?"

"Yeah, we understand."

She didn't like it and I didn't blame her.

"Can't you let us out?"

"I can't take you out the way I came, Ellie. The fire's still burning out here. But the fire department has fire, air, and water elementals en route. Once I'm back outside, I'll start working on finding the backdoor into the safe room." I knew Red. He would never leave just one way in or out of the safe room's level. It might be the sub-basement, but there would be an escape hatch. I just had to find it. "But we will get you out. I promise." That was one promise I didn't plan on breaking. "I'll be back. I'm not going to leave you here for long. I just want to make sure you all get out safely. So, hang tight a little bit longer."

"We trust you, Ripley. But please be careful."

"Always."

I stepped away from the control panel and looked around the room. Nothing screamed 'I'm a secret exit' and I didn't have time to look on my own. This was something best left to the experts. All I had to do was figure out the best way to get my own wet ass out of there without becoming a crispy critter.

7

FIRE AND ICE

I n the end, I was merely singed around the edges by the time I made my way outside. While it hadn't taken too long to bring my temperature up high enough to withstand the flames trying to eat away at the building, it had meant stepping into the corridor outside the safe room. Those few moments in the corridor as my skin dried and my body temperature rose left me with no eyebrows, hair in desperate need of either spellwork or a major trim and restyling, and more than a few blisters. By the time I burst through the front doors, I was cursing not only the bastard or bastards who set the fire, but also Red and the efficiency of the building's fire suppression system.

"Medic!" Starke took one look at me and hurried in my direction.

A few moments later, I was back to my own skin and wrapped in a blanket. I waved off the EMT doing his best to check me for injuries. Instead, I pushed past him, striding to where Nico Cuellar stood conferring with some of his firefighters and a couple of others I assumed were arson investigators.

"Nico, I need blueprints of the building. We've got survivors in the safe room in the sub-basement. There's no way to bring them out through the building. The flames have gotten too strong of a foothold inside. But, knowing Red, there's going to be an exit leading from the sub-basement, maybe even the safe room itself, to safety, one he didn't tell anyone about."

Even me. Damn the man.

Cursing his paranoia, I looked around, hoping to see Red. Instead, I saw another familiar face in the growing crowd beyond the police line. Without a word, I reached out and dragged my jacket away from Starke, who still held it. He looked on in surprise as I dug into one of the side pockets. A moment later, my keys went flying in Yousef Asghar's direction. He snagged them in mid-air and looked at me in question. When I pointed to the side street where I'd parked, he nodded before pelting off in the direction of the truck.

"Ripley?" Starke grabbed my arm. His expression serious, he all but dared me to move away. "You need to talk to me."

"I don't have time for a pissing contest, Starke. It's a damned inferno inside much of the building and everything about it screams that it's magical in origin."

He opened his mouth and then snapped it shut as my eyes flashed in anger.

"Bad as it is, we got lucky. There are seven of Red's people in the safe room. They've got enough air for eight hours or so before things get dicey for them. The emergency generators for the safe room and the office outside are still working, which is a miracle. The fact the sprinkler system in the outer office is still operational is as well.

"As for the fire, Cuellar's right. It's definitely paranormal in origin. Some rooms are completely undamaged, even by smoke, while others have been totally destroyed. Some areas look like a firestorm hit them, doing its best to bring down the building. One thing is clear, the fire had a target."

And all I had to do was figure out who or what that target was. Maybe that would help me figure out who was responsible.

"I'm no arson investigator, but it's safe to say I understand fire. Unless I read everything wrong, it started in the gym. I located several flash points there. Worse, I found three bodies there as well and, no, I don't know who they were. I couldn't tell from a quick glance, and I didn't dare take longer than that to look around. I didn't see any others, but I didn't go upstairs. It's possible there are others there."

I hoped not because I doubted anyone could survive the smoke and flames.

"Also, Red isn't in the safe room, and I don't think his was one of the bodies I found. The body shapes and sizes didn't match." And I didn't know whether that was a good thing or not. I prayed for the former, but feared it was the latter.

"All right." He rubbed a hand over his face and then led me a few steps away from Cuellar and the others. "Ripley, you need to let the medics take a look at you. You scared a decade or two off my life when you did your human flame imitation—and we will discuss that later— but I can see the burns on your face and hands, and I'll lay odds you're hiding more under that blanket. Let the EMTs take care of them for you. Then we'll figure out what our next move should be."

I sighed and shook my head, not so much to refuse medical treatment but in response to his "we will discuss that later" comment. As police chief, Griffin Starke believed he had the right to know all our talents and, well, I didn't like sharing information when it wasn't needed. One of the first lessons my parents taught me was it was best to let people underestimate what I could do. That would almost always give me an advantage when needed.

Before he could press the issue, Yousef trotted up, my go-bag in hand. Because he was one of the Conclave's marshals, Starke couldn't object to his presence, especially since Yousef also worked for Red. But that didn't mean he liked it, and his expression clearly said he did not. Yousef simply arched a brow before turning in my direction. I fought a smile to hear Starke growl deep in his throat. Yousef ignored him and took hold of the blanket I'd wrapped around me, holding it to shield me from onlookers as I quickly pulled on underwear, a pair of jeans and a tee shirt. Once I had, he tossed the blanket over the hood of one of the police cars parked nearby. Then he handed me my boots. As I pulled them on, balancing on one foot and then the other, I breathed in relief. It's amazing how much better I felt to no longer be parading about in my birthday suit.

"I heard what you told him." Yousef nodded at Starke, who glared in response. "What do you need me to do?"

"Start contacting Red's people. See if you can find out who was supposed to be in the office today and who might have been in the living area upstairs." I scanned the crowd, recognizing several of those who worked for Red either at the office or at the bar. "Have Drea and Jayden help."

He followed my gaze and nodded once again.

"I need you to check the bar as well. Make sure no one's tried anything there." I gnawed on my lower lip. "Have Jayden put a sign up that the bar's closed tonight but tell him not to go inside. Not until one of us has checked it. You and Drea can start contacting everyone while he does."

That covered the bases—I hoped.

"I'll be back as soon as I have anything to report."

I watched as he jogged toward the crowd gathered behind the police line. As he did, our people hurried to him, ready to do whatever they could to help. That was the thing about Red. He was a good boss, gruff but fair. More importantly, he built a family with most of us. He had our backs, and we had his. If anything happened to him, the authorities would be hard-pressed to prevent us from exacting revenge on those responsible.

Hell, I'd be leading the charge for vengeance and heaven help anyone who tried to stop me.

With that done, I turned back. With luck, Cuellar somehow managed to get his hands on a copy of the building's blueprints. Before I could say anything, Starke handed me the rest of my belongings. As if that was the signal, my cellphone came to life, the ringtone warning me this was one call I needed to take on my own. I held up a finger, letting Starke know I'd be back. Then I lifted the phone to my ear and walked off.

"Walker."

"Status?"

No introduction. No "how are you?". Right to business. Not that it surprised me. Nor did it surprise me to realize the caller knew what happened.

"It's not good." That might just be the understatement of the year. "Before you ask, I don't know yet how bad it is or how bad it will get."

"Tell me what you do know."

"Gemma Blackrock called Redmond this morning. He contacted me, asking me to come see him ASAP. He didn't tell me why until I got there. All he knew for sure was that she'd seen something in a dream and it worried her." I shook my head. "No, he said it scared her and she wanted to see me. No one else, me. After taking care of the details involved with me accepting the assignment, I went out to her place. Nothing looked or felt out of place, but she's scared, sir, and she did confirm what Red said.

"Here's the thing, sir. She didn't have any specifics she could tell me, only that she has a feeling trouble is coming. She doesn't think it will be as great of a cataclysm as the Upheaval, but she said it has a similar feel. She promised to try to clarify her feelings and let me know."

Too bad she hadn't been able to do so before someone turned Red's building into a raging inferno.

"When I got back to town, the cops and fire department were surrounding Red's office. The building was engulfed in flames. Nothing the FD has done has put a dent in the fire. They've requested a fire elemental as well as air and water elementals, but it will take time to get them here."

"Paranormal attack?" Roderick Drake asked.

"Paranormal in its source, at the very least. Whether a normal bribed one of our kind to weave the spells needed for this or one of our own attacked the office, I don't know." Yet. "But the fire is definitely of paranormal origins."

"You're sure about that?" The head of the North American Conclave of Paranormals sounded more thoughtful than worried.

Could he know something I didn't?

"I am." I described how the flames remained contained to the building, as well as how some rooms were decimated while others were left totally untouched.

"Casualties?"

"We have at least three fatalities so far. I don't have IDs on them yet. Seven others got to the safe room in the sub-basement and we're trying to determine the best way to rescue them before their air runs out. They can't come through the flames and, so far, we can't knock the flames down. As for the rest of our people, Yousef is trying to get a headcount on those he can locate."

"And Redmond?"

Red might not be a marshal or member of the Conclave, but he was an important ally and useful tool. He knew it and so did I, and so did Drake. Losing him would be a personal and professional loss.

"Unknown. He wasn't one of the dead and he's not in the safe room."

Silence followed and I waited, knowing Drake would put together all the implications of my statement. It didn't take long for him to do just that.

"You went inside?"

"I did. Let's just say being one of Surtr's descendants has its advantages. Even then, I got singed coming out and I sure as hell don't want to risk going back in again anytime soon."

"We will discuss this later, Ripley."

I rolled my eyes. Roderick Drake understood better than most the necessity of not letting the world know some of our more unique gifts. More than that, he knew how important it was not to make public the truth about the ancient gods. The DNA labs wouldn't be able to keep up with the requests for tests if humanity learned the gods of ancient mythology actually existed, at least some of them. Everyone would want to know if they had the blood of the deities.

More dangerous would be those normals and paranormals who wanted what those of us descended from the "gods" had—or what they thought we had. Since the Upheaval, a black market had arisen that supplied paras to those willing to pay the right price. There were those who wanted the "challenge" of hunting and killing a werewolf or similar were-creature. Certain businessmen wanted to know what it was in our blood that let some of us live so much longer than a normal human and why others of our kind didn't suffer from the cancers and other diseases that afflicted so many. Then there were those who wanted slaves to tell them about the next market trend or to cast spells over lovers and enemies.

"I understand your concerns, sir, but I believed it was the best course of action under the circumstances. I made the decision and I'll accept the consequences."

Hopefully, they wouldn't be too serious.

"Mr. Drake, there is something else you should know."

"Go on."

"Young Dani was sent home early from school today. She'd just gotten off the bus and was started toward Red's office when someone hit her and tried to grab her off the street. She managed to fight and break free. The bastard who hit her ran. No ID on him yet."

"You make sure she's all right and do whatever you can to keep her safe." Silence stretched out between us before he continued. "What can the Conclave do to assist, Ripley?"

"You probably need to be ready to intercede if the local or state authorities decide to start a pissing contest."

Which they would, considering not only where we were but what I already knew about the fire. The fact there were deaths involved made that interference all but inevitable.

"I assure you, I'll be closely monitoring the situation."

That should have reassured me, but something about his tone worried me. "Mr. Drake, are the other Zones reporting trouble right now? Anything out of the ordinary?"

When he didn't answer right away, I had my answer. Too bad I didn't know the details. Worse, I had a sick feeling in the pit of my stomach that the only way to get the answers I wanted was to do the one thing I'd been resisting for so long.

"Ripley, I know you don't want to hear this, but it is time for you to reconsider your position." Drake's voice softened and, for once, he sounded almost unsure about how to continue. "I've done my best to respect your decision not to accept the Conclave's appointment to be the region's senior marshal."

I swallowed hard, knowing where this was headed.

"I, as well as the other members of the Conclave, have also appreciated the fact you agreed to work with us as one of our marshal on a case-by-case basis. But there are things you don't know, things that leave me no choice but to ask you to reconsider your decision. You may not have the experience of some of our other marshal, but your parents trained you well. They were the best we've had in generations. I know you will be as well. If what's happening is as serious as I suspect, we need you not just for this investigation but for the investigations to come."

"Mr. Drake." My throat went dry, and my voice broke.

"Please, Ripley. Accept the appointment. Help us determine not only what happened at Red's, but what is happening around the country and who might be responsible."

I lowered the phone and closed my eyes, tipping my face toward the sky. Even though I decided before his call to do as he asked, I hesitated. Once I let them get their hooks into me, life as I knew it would change. I wasn't Mom or Dad. I didn't want to become like them: one dead serving the Conclave and another missing and long presumed dead. But what choice did I have? Agreeing would give me not only the authority to remain involved in the investigation, but it would give me access to information I wouldn't otherwise have.

And if there's one thing I'm good at, it is using information to garner additional information and tracking down the source of whatever I'm looking for.

"Mr. Drake, if I agree, you and the other members of the Conclave must understand that I will continue living my life as I please. I will do my job as marshal, but you and I both know that isn't enough to keep me busy all the time. I'm not going to become someone walking around, badge or credentials showing, scaring folks into behaving just because of my position. If you can't agree to that, we have nothing else to discuss."

"We can and will agree."

I opened my eyes just so I could narrow them in suspicion. That was much too easy, not that I'd argue. There was too much to worry about, more important things to worry about.

"I want to maintain control over what cases I accept and who I work with. I know you allowed my parents that sort of leeway."

"And you'll have it as well."

If possible, my eyes narrowed even more. He agreed too easily. Either things were a lot worse than I suspected or he had an ulterior motive, one that would bite me in the ass sooner or later.

Knowing my luck, it was both.

"Send me a contract for this job as well as one appointing me as the region's senior marshal. I'll look them over and send back any changes I want. We can use both of them as the framework for any contracts going forward." God, I hoped I wasn't making the biggest mistake in my life. Even if I was, I needed to do this to find Red and find out what the hell happened and why. "But I want to start working right away."

"Then consider this your official notification that you are the new senior marshal for the Zone. As such, you are to take control of the investigation into the day's events. The appropriate paperwork will be sent immediately to all local and state law enforcement agencies. I will also reach out to the governor and let him know not only that you have accepted the role as the region's marshal but the rest of it as well. A full briefing package, along with your updated credentials and a new badge, will be sent as soon as everything is pulled together."

"All right. Thanks."

Griffin Starke would have a fit when he found out, but I didn't care. If his fragile werewolf ego couldn't handle working with me, he could just sit this one out.

"Ripley, understand this is your investigation. You are the prevailing legal authority regarding anything dealing with what happened this morning. If the locals have an issue with it, deal with them. Better yet, if they give you problems, let me know and I will deal with them."

"Yes, sir, I understand."

"Good." I couldn't see him, but I had a feeling he nodded in satisfaction. "Ripley, there's something else you need to be aware of. The situation is much more serious than you know. The reason I'm the only one on this call is because the other members of the Conclave are speaking with your fellow marshals around the country. We're activating each of you. The full extent of your authority will be detailed in your briefing materials. Read it and then get back to me with any questions or concerns you might have."

What else could I say beyond, "Yes, sir."?

"Before you ask, we don't know a great deal yet. However, there have been targeted attacks in four of the North American Zones today. All have the earmarks of paranormal attacks. Most have used fire, but one used a magically created storm and accompanying high winds, possibly even a tornado, to destroy an entire block. Each of the attacks took place deep within the targeted Zones. We're still trying to coordinate the flow of information. And, Ripley, there have been casualties, more than what you reported."

Damn it. This was worse than I feared.

I thought for a moment, wondering how much information to push for over an unsecured line. Discretion won out, and I went for general information instead.

"Understood, sir. I do have a question. Who will be coordinating for the marshals?"

We needed to share information instead of working on our own, assuming the other incidents were connected—and my gut told me they were. Hopefully, Drake understood.

"Right now, each of you is to report directly to the Conclave. Once we have preliminary reports from everyone, we will meet and decide who will act to coordinate your efforts."

I didn't like it, but I understood. Until the Conclave knew what was happening, it wanted all decisions to be made with an eye to the big picture instead of the small.

"Yousef is still here, sir. Do you want him to stay, or should I send him to one of the other Zones to help out there?"

"Keep him there for the moment, Ripley. Maybe he can keep you from killing the police chief."

I chuckled, relieved to hear the humor in his voice. Drake understood the rather strained professional relationship I shared with Griffin Starke. It went beyond the fact I could and would, when necessary, not only step on Starke's toes as a cop, but I would also jump into an investigation and take it over.

"He can try." I turned serious again. "Since you mentioned Chief Starke, he may be an issue."

"Don't worry, Ripley. I'll make sure he knows you are now the senior marshal in the region."

Better him breaking the news than me.

"When we send the briefing packet and the rest of it, we'll be including a secure cellphone as well as a sat phone and laptop. Keep them safe."

"Understood, sir. I'll report back as soon as I can." I lifted a hand when Cuellar called to me, letting him know I'd be right there. He nodded and turned his attention back to whatever he'd been studying. "Sir, I need to go. Captain Cuellar looks like he might have some information for me."

"Go. Reports morning and night, Ripley, more often as warranted."

"Yes, sir."

I slid the phone back into my pocket and looked around. Relieved to see Yousef talking with several of the bar's employees across the street, I called to him. If he was going to be around for a while, I might as well put him to work.

"I spoke with Drake," I said without preamble as he joined me.

"I know. He texted while you were talking. Can't say I'm not glad you've signed on. The people here know you and will respond to you quicker than me. I'm still the newcomer."

I nodded. He was right about that. Even though he'd been in town six months, he was a stranger to many who lived here. Hell, he could live here for six years and he'd still be an outsider as far as some of them were concerned. The unfortunate truth, however, was he'd done little to make himself part of the community. He did his job and at the end of the day he went to his apartment. He didn't take part in community activities. He hadn't made many, if any, real friends. He continued to hold himself apart and that attitude meant most everyone in town looked at him as an outsider and always would.

Truth be told, I sometimes fought that mindset as well. That sucked because I needed to trust him without second thoughts if the proverbial shit hit the fan—something I had a feeling already happened.

"Anyway." I waved off his comment, knowing he understood the need to get to the point. "The Conclave's doing a couple of things regarding the situation here. They're letting Starke and Cuellar, not to mention the local pols, know I've agreed to accept a position as the region's senior marshal. Drake also told me to take control of the investigation. He'd like you to stay and help until we get to the bottom of this." I quickly filled him in on the rest of what Drake said. His expression darkened, and then he nodded.

"Now I need to see what Cuellar can tell me. If you're done here, go to the bar and check everything there. It's possible what happened here has nothing to do with the other incidents. You and I both know Red has enemies. However, for the moment, we can't rule anything out."

"Understood. I'll let you know what I find."

"Thanks." I looked back at the building and the flames still visible through the windows. "Did you manage to contact everyone?"

He shook his head. "Here's the list of the ones I haven't been able to reach so far."

I took the sheet of paper and scanned his cramped writing. More than a dozen names, some who were family members of Red's employees living at the warehouse. Others worked at the bar. I mentally marked off the seven in the safe room. That left Red and the others unaccounted for. Were the bodies I found some of those named? I didn't know and prayed they weren't. Justice would be served if the ones responsible for setting the fire lost their lives in it.

"If I'm still held up here when you finish at the bar, talk to the business owners in the area. See if they saw or heard anything that might help us make sense of what happened. Find out if they've received any threats recently. Some of them have security cams. If they point this direction, see if they'll let you review the footage." Assuming, of course, the cops hadn't already confiscated any footage there might be. "Once that's done, one of us needs to contact Gemma and bring her up to speed. We need to know what else she can tell us. Hell, Yousef, we need to give her what information we have so she knows what we need help with."

"I'll keep in touch, Ripley. Let me know if anything else happens here."

I nodded and watched him disappear into the crowd that was not getting any smaller. Then I turned and made my way back to the tent where Cuellar and the others worked to coordinate the best way to fight the flames and find a way into the sub-basement to rescue the survivors.

Time to pull up my big girl pants and do the job I really didn't want.

8

ROCK, MEET HARD PLACE

"Gentlemen."

Cuellar looked up and nodded once before turning his attention back to whatever he'd been studying on his tablet. Starke, however, slid his cellphone into his pocket and pulled himself up to his full height, as if doing so would intimidate me. Standing six-six and built like a linebacker, he did intimidate most people, especially when his usually brown eyes flashed a deep green, showing just how close to the surface his wolf happened to be. Too bad for him that it only pissed me off. After everything that happened, I was in no mood to deal with Griffin Starke when he tried flexing his authority.

Something he should be well aware of.

"I guess I should have expected you'd find some way to poke your nose into the investigation." He snarled, his lips peeling back from his teeth. I swear, in another moment, he might start foaming at the mouth.

Well, he wasn't the first ill-tempered dog I'd dealt with. Too bad I didn't have a rolled up newspaper to smack his nose with. Still, there were other ways to make him heel.

"I didn't ask for this, Starke, but I sure as hell wasn't going to tell the Conclave to fuck off." I made a point of glancing at the pocket where he'd stashed his phone. "I assume Mr. Drake contacted you."

"Is that what you call it?" He barked out a humorless laugh. "He *instructed* me to work with you, whether I like it or not. He doesn't care that you aren't trained for this sort of thing and all you're likely to do is get under foot and fuck up any evidence we find."

Anger, as cold as my flames had been hot, washed over me. Not that I'd let him see it. I wouldn't give him the satisfaction of knowing his insult struck a nerve.

"Starke."

"Not a word. Not one fucking word." Starke frowned and his hands fisted at his side. "I swear to God, Ripley, I'm going to strangle you and then I'm going to hunt down the Conclave and do the same to them. You can't seriously be thinking about taking over the investigation."

I started to respond and then stopped. Satisfying as it might be to tell him to quit taking himself so seriously, we didn't have time for a pissing contest. Instead, I decided to play it by the book. If nothing else, that would throw him off balance.

"First of all, Chief Starke, I suggest you close your mouth and think very carefully before you say anything else. I shouldn't have to remind you that I could take you into custody for threatening not only one of the Conclave's marshals but the Conclave itself. However, I understand you're worried about the current situation, and you're stressed because you don't have the scene under control yet. So, I'll forget the threats, for now at least."

I lifted a hand and shook my head before he could interrupt. "Second, and more importantly, I have information your department and the Glenham Grove Fire Department don't." If that didn't warn Starke he needed to think before saying something he might regret, he was a fool. "The Conclave not only knows what's going on here, but it's also been made aware of other attacks against our people and holdings within four of the North American Zones today. Mr. Drake said it appeared to be a coordinated attack. The Conclave has issued orders that we are to respond accordingly."

I gave him a moment to consider what I said before continuing.

"The Conclave is now in the process of notifying each of the agencies involved in the investigations, as well as the local authorities, that Conclave marshals will take charge of the investigations. Until we know for certain the motive behind these attacks, the Conclave wants to take no chances. You both should understand just how disastrous this could be if it turns out someone wants to start a war with our kind.

"That also means, in this case at least, that I am now in charge of the investigation. I have accepted the Conclave's offer to become the Zone's senior marshal." Another pause, praying I hadn't overplayed my hand. "I want to work with you and Captain Cuellar, Starke, not against you. Our personal feelings don't matter. They can't right now. The only thing that does is do everything possible to find those responsible for the attack before anyone else is hurt.

"Think about this before you blow a gasket, Starke. There are benefits to working with the Conclave and with me. For one, I have every intention of leaving the handling of the media to the Conclave. That keeps the reporters off your back."

And mine.

"If that's not enough to convince you to work with me, think about this. Your investigators will have the full resources of the Conclave and every other agency it feels should be included in the investigation. All you have to do is ask and, if I agree, it will be yours. Same goes for you, Captain Cuellar."

"I can live with that." Cuellar glanced between Starke and me and grinned slightly, picking up on the cop's frustration.

"If you take one step out of line, Ripley." Anger suffused Starke's face, and he took a step closer.

I stood my ground, letting him know he didn't intimidate me.

"You need to stop and very carefully consider what you say next, Starke. I didn't want this position. You know that—or at least you should. You've known me all my life. I may have trained all my life to be a marshal, but after my folks, I didn't want it. That's why I've only accepted a few assignments when the Conclave's come to me. But this is different. Someone attacked people I care for in the middle of our town, in the middle of the Zone. The one place we should all be safe. So, you tell me what I should have told Drake when he asked me to

73

finally agree to become the Conclave's senior marshal in the region on a permanent basis."

I waited, my eyes never leaving his face. When he said nothing, I continued. "Then consider this. I can't step out of line because, like it or not, this is now my investigation. You report to me." I inhaled deeply, focusing on not letting my temper get the better of me. "Starke, I don't like this any more than you do. But it is what it is, and neither of us has a choice. So, let's work together and figure out what the hell is going on."

If possible, his expression turned even colder. A muscle jumped along his jawline. Damn it. I hated this part of him and, unfortunately, it was a very large part of him. Probably came from him being a lycan. They might be pack animals, but lycans were also the most stubborn, self-righteous, and overly confident members of the paranormal community you could ever meet—unless you were unfortunate enough to run into a really old vampire or a few others we did our best never to speak about. Fortunately for all of us, those paras were very few and even further between.

"The choice is yours, Starke. You either work with me or you appoint someone under your command who will." I returned his gaze until he looked away. Then I turned my attention to Cuellar. "Now, you had something you wanted to show me, Captain?"

Cuellar nodded and waited as I moved closer. He swiped a finger across the screen of his tablet. Then he handed it to me. It took a moment before I realized what I held: the blueprints for the building. Better yet, they were updated blueprints, submitted the last time Red made improvements. I thought back, remembering how Red added additional security systems, updated the living quarters, and enlarged the safe room only a year ago.

Now, if only they showed the location of the emergency exit. Surely, Red hadn't been foolish enough to keep that little tidbit of information off the blueprints. But, knowing him and knowing how paranoid he could be, it wouldn't surprise me if he did.

"I don't know enough about how to read blueprints to understand everything I'm looking at, Nico. Do you see anything that might help?" I handed the tablet back and moved to stand behind him so we could both study the display.

"I think this." He tapped the screen and enlarged a section of the display. "This may be what we're looking for. It's not listed as an exit of any sort. According to the notes attached to the plans, it is marked as possible door to a storage area to be built in the future. To me, that means there has to be a void behind the wall because no contractor in his right mind would want to dig out the area after the building was completed, not if they could help it. I'm thinking this is where Red has his emergency exit. That's the good news. The bad is we don't know where it comes out."

I frowned. If Cuellar was right, Red once again proved himself to be a damned idiot. Leave it to him to omit that little bit of information.

I took a closer look at the plans, trying to visualize the area Cuellar pointed out. Then I looked down the street in the only reasonable direction for the tunnel to run. Eyes narrowed, I studied the three-lane road and the buildings that lined it. As I did, I prayed Red's paranoia didn't include having the exit tunnel make unexpected twists and turns before reaching its end.

This part of Glenham Grove tended to older warehouses, many of which had been converted to combination business/apartment buildings after the Upheaval. In those that had been converted, the bottom floor or two housed businesses, shops or restaurants and the upper floors lofts or condos. Almost all were now owned by paras, although a few were still owned by normals who recognized the financial benefit of maintaining ownership in the Zone.

More than that, I knew Red owned several buildings nearby. Closing my eyes, I thought back, searching through my memory for snatches of conversation where he discussed his real estate holdings. I knew Red. He wouldn't risk having the tunnel open into a building he didn't own and hadn't secured. All I had to do was figure out which one of the buildings down the street met the criteria—assuming the tunnel didn't branch off and head in another direction.

"There!"

I pointed to a four-story warehouse almost as old as Glenham Grove itself. For years, it stood vacant. Until recently, there'd been talk about condemning it and tearing it down for "the public safety". That was a holdover way of thinking from before the Upheaval. Now, buildings inside the Zones were often difficult to build. Contractors and their workers needed to be paranormals, or at least people not as sensitive to the energies within the Zones as most normals. That meant rehabbing buildings took precedence over tearing down, especially if the bones of the building were good.

This particular warehouse stood almost a block down and across the street from Red's office. That made it close enough for an easy retreat while still being far enough away most wouldn't give it a second thought if keeping an eye on the converted warehouse where Red had his offices as well as living quarters.

At least not unless they knew Red owned the warehouse. Something I doubted more than a handful of people did because Red bought it through a shell company very few knew he held an interest in.

Cuellar moved to my side. He looked where I pointed and frowned thoughtfully. Eyes narrowed, he studied not only the warehouse but the buildings in between. I waited, praying I was right. If not, our people inside the safe room were screwed.

Instead of saying anything, Cuellar once again activated his tablet. The fingers of his right hand flew across the screen as he typed in a series of commands. His expression thoughtful, a frown drawing his brows together, he studied the screen. Then he stalked off in the direction of a group of firefighters waiting for an assignment.

"I want all the buildings on this block checked. Just because it looks like the fire is confined to this location, let's not risk being wrong."

Heads nodded, expressions just as grim as his.

"Rogers, Broussard, take a team and check out this warehouse." He tipped the tablet so they could see whatever was displayed on the screen. "Search the basement levels for anything that looks like it might connect to a tunnel leading back in this direction. Pay special attention to these areas." He tapped the screen.

Callie Rogers, a witch-lycan hybrid, nodded. Then, with a jerk of her head to Jean-Paul Broussard, JP to his friends, she started off, calling for several others to join them. I watched as they gathered their gear before they moved down the street, shouldering their way through the crowd that continued to gather despite the best efforts of the police to hold them back.

"Are you sure?" Starke looked first at me and then at Cuellar.

"No." I shook my head. "This is Red we're talking about. He tells me a lot, but not everything. But it's the only thing that makes sense."

"Why that building?"

I made a split-second decision. Telling him Red owned the building felt like a betrayal of the trust Red put in me. But I couldn't refuse to answer. No, I needed something that made sense and fit what Starke knew about Red.

"Because it sat empty for so long. Years, if I remember correctly. None of the other buildings in the area have been vacant for more than a few weeks at a time. At least not that I remember." I gave a soft chuckle. "Hell, it wouldn't surprise me if Red didn't figure out a way to convince anyone interested in the building to stay away until he finished whatever he planned to do with it."

Not the entire truth, but close enough the werewolf should accept it. But that wasn't my real concern at the moment. Finding another way into the office was and the warehouse down the street happened to be my only bet at the moment. I turned to Cuellar and made a split-second decision.

"Captain, do you have a spare set of bunker gear I can borrow? I'm going with your people to check out the warehouse."

Cuellar's eyes narrowed once again. Before he could answer, Starke grabbed my arm, his fingers digging in, and spun me to face him.

"What the fuck do you think you're doing?" His voice dropped, the timbre of it warning his wolf lurked just below the surface of a very fragile control.

I made a point of looking at the fingers wrapped around my upper arm before looking back up. He hissed out a breath, surprised and angered, when I did. I didn't need to be a mind reader to know what he thought. How dare I look him directly in the eye? Doing so violated the rules of the pack. He might not be the Alpha, but he was the Beta, the second most powerful werewolf in the local pack. In most other packs, he would be Alpha. Because of that, he was used to others showing submission, especially when his wolf was so close to the surface.

Too bad. I wasn't of the pack.

I never pledged obedience, much less submission, to the pack.

A lesson I'd teach him very quickly if he didn't back the hell off.

"I suggest you remove your hand before I remove it for you." I spoke softly, my eyes flashing. The fact I neither addressed him by his rank nor by his place in the pack was a calculated insult, one I hoped didn't wind up biting me in the ass.

Starke's lips peeled back, and he growled in response. Cuellar showed a good sense of self-preservation by keeping his mouth shut and leaving this to the two of us to work out. When another of the fire-fighters moved in our direction, he gave a quick shake of his head and shot out a hand to keep the man back. Wise man. He didn't want any of his people in the fallout zone should this situation go badly.

Which it could very easily do.

"I asked you a question." Starke ground out the words even as he released his hold on my arm.

"I believe the answer is obvious." I continued looking him directly in the eye. "Now step back."

He growled again and his features blurred slightly before he got himself under control again. "Marshal, you're to remain here. I'll go with the crew."

Before I could object, he spun on his heel and stalked down the street after Rogers and her team of firefighters. I watched, shaking my head. Sooner rather than later, Griffin Starke and I needed to come to an understanding. He might believe he held the upper hand, but he didn't. Not only did I happen to be the Conclave's marshal, but he did not know exactly what I was. If seeing my Surtr aspect didn't warn him there was more to me than he knew—and he was a fool if it didn't —then his skull was even thicker than I thought.

"Rip, I've known the two of you a long time. I suggest you figure out how you want to handle him before he returns." Cuellar grinned and slapped a hand on my shoulder. "That is one unhappy man."

I chuckled softly. "There is no handling him, Nico. You know that. His kind and mine simply don't get along."

"You two have always butted heads, Rip, even when we were kids. But this is different. You know it." He gave me a look my inner child recognized, the same look Mom used to turn on me whenever I did something exceedingly foolish. "At least you should."

I opened my mouth, ready to deny it, and stopped. Cuellar had a point. Damn it. Something was going on with Starke. I didn't know what, but it was impacting how he dealt with both Nico and me, and me in particular. That wasn't good. The potential for it to blow up on our faces was unforgivable now. That meant, like it or not, I needed to act like the grownup I supposedly was.

"Nico, do you have any idea what's going on with him?"

God, I hoped he did. Nico Cuellar was, among other things, an empath. It wasn't his primary talent, but it was probably his most useful one. At least in situations like this. Assuming his very rigid sense of ethics let him tell me what he knew or suspected.

He shook his head. "I've heard some rumblings of trouble in the pack, but that's all it's been. Rumblings."

I closed my eyes and sighed heavily. Trouble in the pack was the last thing we needed right now. The fact there might be issues there meant I needed to look into it. Unless I got Yousef to do it. Everyone knew the danger of a pack going rogue. The para community didn't need that happening, nor did it need the inevitable panicked response from the non-para community should it come to that.

Shit, damn and fuck. I so didn't need this right now.

None of us did. Of all the paranormal creatures revealed after the Upheaval, the lycans were probably the hardest for normals to accept. With vampires, there was a mystique to them, caused partly by the recent surge of books and movies romanticizing their kind. Then there was the whole not being able to go into the sunlight. Most folks figure that made it easy to distinguish who might be a bloodsucker and who wasn't. Of course, the sale of religious crosses and garlic went up dramatically after the world figured out vampires are real.

But werewolves and their kin are a different matter. They look and act human except after they shift. Then they become vicious animals. At least that was the belief of most people, even most paras. The truth is that it takes a combination of strong Alphas and a ruthless set of laws about their kind passed by the Conclave to keep the werewolves and their kind under control. To protect lycans from the rest of the world, legal protections were put into place by the Feds. But, in the end, it still falls to the Conclave to make sure the lycans don't decide to go hunting humans in a bid to become top of the food chain.

As marshal—damn, I couldn't wrap my mind around that and knew it would take time to accept the role and all it entailed—one of my responsibilities was making sure the local pack maintained control of their members and, if not, it was up to me to deal with the problem. I'd seen Mom and Dad deal with problems with the pack and knew it was by far not their favorite part of being a marshal. Especially since it brought them into conflict with Alpha Carson Lewis and, for me, with Griffin Starke, his Beta.

That was a complication I didn't need on top of the fire and Red going missing.

"All right, Nico. I'll talk to him and try to clear the air."

Actually, I'd talk to his sister. If there was trouble, Sophie would let me know.

I hoped.

But that was for later. Right now, I had more pressing matters to deal with.

"What's the latest on the elementals? When will they get here?"

"Last update was the water and air elementals will be here within half an hour or so. The fire elemental is still almost an hour out."

I nodded, wondering if our people inside the building had that long, safe room or not.

9

SOMEONE BETTER TELL ME SOMETHING

The sun had long since disappeared below the horizon before I made my way back to the SUV. Exhaustion dragged at me. The smells of smoke, sweat, and other things best left unsaid clung to my clothes and hair. My stomach rumbled unhappily, reminding me I hadn't eaten since morning. Not that I wanted to anytime soon. Not after everything I'd seen and done since returning from Gemma's and walking into what came very close to being my own personal hell.

What I wouldn't give to turn back the clock twenty-four hours. Maybe then I'd be able to prevent what happened.

But woulda', coulda', shoulda' wouldn't lead me to the person or persons responsible for the attack on the warehouse. I needed to focus on finding them. Then I'd make them pay for what they'd done.

Hell, I'd make them pay for everything they planned on doing from this day until the day of their deaths. Karma was a bitch and I planned on being her uber bitch of a weapon to wield against the bastards who hurt my friends—no, my family.

At least there had been some good news. Cuellar's firefighters discovered the tunnel leading to the office outside the safe room. If we hadn't known to look and if we had failed to take into account Red's highly developed sense of paranoia, they never would have found it.

Even so, finding it and actually accessing it had been two different things. Red had the damned thing locked, sealed, and warded. I spent an anxious hour or more watching the firefighters work to deal with each obstacle put in their way by a man I owed my life to but who I wanted to throttle at the moment.

It took hours to make entry into the passageway and then bypass each of the "safeguards" Red put in place between the entrance and the office outside the safe room. By the time the firefighters reached the office, the fire suppression system had failed. They spent valuable time none of us knew if we had or not, fighting back the flames so they could safely open the door standing between them and the survivors. Then more precious minutes were spent getting the survivors geared up the best they could before bringing them out through the tunnel to where paramedics waited.

I spoke with each of them, hoping they could tell me something, anything, to explain what happened. They all said the same thing. The day had been like most others. Some were working, others on break. One had been on the phone with her husband. Suddenly, the lights flickered, followed by a loud pop! they couldn't identify. A moment later, the power went out. Not even the emergency generators Red installed for the various parts of the building worked. Paranoid bastard that he is, Red had drilled into all everyone what to do in such a situation. They gathered up anything of value within easy reach, found the flashlights he kept at strategic points throughout the building, and headed to the nearest exits.

Except whoever set the fire anticipated that. Flames blocked the exits, driving them back to the center of the building. Each of the survivors said it felt as if they were being herded somewhere, probably toward their deaths. No matter where they turned, they found fire.

Then Red was there. Standing between them and the flames, he ordered them to the center stairwell. They were to go down. Down to the basement and then to the safe room where they were to lock themselves in and wait until someone came for them. Then he all but shoved them down the corridor toward the stairs, reminding them not to use the elevators. The last any of them had seen of him was when he shut and locked the stairwell door behind them. He pounded on it once and then there was nothing but silence.

While the firefighters worked to get the survivors out, the elementals finally arrived. The air and water elementals arrived first. Cuellar sent the water elemental, a sprite of a woman who looked to be nearing her eightieth birthday, to the warehouse down the street to help protect the survivors as they were brought out of the safe room. The air elemental worked her magic to keep any sparks or flames that might escape the building away from the rest of the businesses in the area. The fire elemental began working to get the flames under control, muttering softly to himself as he did.

Then it became a waiting game.

And I hate waiting.

Now, with nothing left for me to do until Cuellar's people agreed to let me reenter the building or until Starke had something to report, I turned to leave. A team of firefighters would remain on the scene overnight, making sure none of the hotspots flared up. I planned to do my own walkthrough come morning, whether Cuellar agreed or not. Before then, I needed to check on everyone at the hospital, report to the Conclave and get some rest. Before that last happened, I needed to stop by Razor's to check on Dani and let her know what I could.

Damn it, Red. Where the hell are you?

I climbed into the SUV and rested my forehead against the steering wheel. It would be so easy to shut down and sleep. Instead, I forced myself to sit up and slid the key into the ignition. The moment I did, my phone pinged, signaling an incoming call. Almost afraid to answer, I tapped my left earbud, praying nothing else had happened.

"Ripley, where are you?" Yousef sounded almost as tired as I felt.

"About to leave the scene. You?"

"Just leaving the hospital. Security's set up here and they know to contact both of us if anything happens. Starke also has several officers here standing guard."

"Good." I scrubbed a dirty hand over my face, rubbing eyes suddenly burning with unshed tears. "How are they?"

"They'll be fine. A few burns from when they made their way to the safe room and the one sprained ankle. They'll probably have nightmares for a bit, maybe some PTSD, and Carlisle discovered she has a pretty bad case of claustrophobia she didn't know about before. But they should be fine. Everyone is worried about Red and the others who didn't make it to the safe room."

"Yeah." They weren't the only ones. "Still no word on Red. So far, only the three I found have been confirmed dead and we don't have IDs on them yet. But there are still several of our people unaccounted for. They shouldn't have been at the office today, but they're in the wind for now. Starke has his people looking for them."

"And you?"

I didn't answer right away. Since he'd just left the hospital, I didn't need to go in tonight. Morning would be soon enough.

"I'm heading to Razor's. He and I are overdue for a talk." I thought for a minute and made up my mind. Youssef needed to know everything I did if he was going to help me figure out what was going on. "Razor had visitors yesterday who might be able to tell us something to help, Yousef. Before I speak with them, I want to get his take, not only on them but also on what they've already told him. I also want to check on Dani and make sure she's okay."

I also needed to see if she remembered anything that might help explain what happened—not to mention finding out what led up to her being sent home from school early.

"What do you want me to do?"

"Go home and get some rest. We need to hit the ground running in the morning and I have a feeling it's going to be a very long day." I thought for a moment. Normally, we'd meet at the office. "Meet me at the café at six thirty. We'll compare notes and figure out what our next moves should be."

"Try to get some rest tonight, Ripley."

"You, too."

I tapped the earbud again, ending the call. Then I reached for my phone where I'd tossed it onto the passenger seat.

Red, where r u? Contact me asap.

I stared at the screen, praying for a quick response but none came. Damn it.

Ten minutes later, I stood at the backdoor to Razor's shop. Darkness cloaked the ground floor. Not even the neon signs identifying the shop were lit. Upstairs was a different matter. Lights shone from several windows on the second and third floors where Razor had his living quarters. Once again, I sent a text, this time to the tattoo artist, letting him know I was there.

The locks clicked, and the door slid open. As I stepped inside, a single overhead light came on, giving off just enough illumination for me to see the staircase to my right. The door slid shut behind me and the locks re-engaged as I started upstairs, lights coming on ahead of me to show the way.

"You look like shit, Ripley." Razor handed me a beer and a wet towel as I stepped into the "great room" that took up most of the second floor.

"Feel like it." I took a long pull on the beer before using the towel to scrub my face and neck. "Dani?"

"Upstairs getting ready for bed." He reached out and stopped me before I could head up. "She's fine, Ripley. Layla is with her. Trust me, my friend, you need to clean up before she sees you or you'll only worry her more."

I didn't like it, but I'd seen my reflection in the SUV's rearview mirror. The wet towel might have helped, but it wouldn't be enough. I needed to wash up and change. But the latter meant going home, and I didn't have that much time. Hell, I wasn't sure I could stay awake that long.

As if reading my mind, Razor led me across the room to the far end of the floor. He opened a door almost hidden in the wall. I knew there was another room beyond the great room, but I'd never been inside. Now I stood in the doorway and whistled softly.

"Damn, Razor, this is nice."

Nice didn't really describe it. I stood just inside what could best be called a mini spa. A massage table sat in the center of the room. Across from the door stood a cedar-lined two-person steam room. To the right, a shower made for orgies took up most of that wall. A two-person jet tub sat to the left, a large video screen on the wall above it. Although no candles were burning, the air was gently scented, and I felt some of my tension easing. This room presented a side of the man I never expected.

"You must never tell anyone about this, Ripley." He growled out the words, but his eyes twinkled.

"No fear about that, my friend. Of course, the cost of my silence will be letting me use this from time to time."

He pursed his lips and appeared to consider my offer. Then he gave me a look I knew too well. He had his own conditions. The question was if I'd agree without too much dickering.

"If you let me do at least one of the protections you keep asking for, but this time in ink. That will make them stronger and easier to recharge when necessary."

Now it was my turn to consider. We'd discussed this before. I trusted Razor not to misuse his power, and I'd seen first-hand just how strong such protections could be. More importantly, Red trusted him enough to let Razor ink a number of sigils and other symbols of power on him over the years. But this was a big step, especially since I hated needles.

"Razor." I didn't whine, but not by much.

"Rip, please. Today's events prove there's something going on neither of us understands yet. The inking will help keep you safe." He scrubbed a hand over a face clouded with more emotion than I'd ever seen from him. "Ripley, that little girl upstairs needs you. We all need you, especially if something's happened to Red."

Damn, but he knew how to hit all the right buttons.

"Tell me what you have in mind while I clean up."

With that, I stepped toward the shower and waved a hand, watching as the glass turned opaque. Razor chuckled softly when it did.

"You're no fun, Ripley."

"And you aren't getting a show tonight, Razor." I stepped inside and closed the door behind me. "Now, what do you have in mind?"

I stripped and tossed my clothes and shoes over the glass enclosure. Another wave of my hand and water streamed over me from above and from the sides. As it did, I groaned in relief. Reaching for shampoo, I listened as Razor spoke, outlining not only what he wanted to do for me but also about Dani and what she'd said and done since I last saw her.

"Thanks." I wrapped a towel around me and stepped out. Razor met me with a floor-length soft robe that looked and felt like cashmere as he wrapped it around me. "How long will the inking take?"

"If we do it all at once—which is what I recommend—about six hours. But you can sleep during it."

Sleep? He had to be joking. No way I could sleep with needles going in and out of my skin as he worked.

He must have read the skepticism on my expression. "Ripley, this is no mundane tattoo. I don't use my machines for this kind of work."

Eyes narrowed, I cocked my head to one side. "Then how?"

He reached for my hand and led me to the massage table. Before I knew what he planned, his hands closed around my waist and he boosted me up. My butt hit the table, and he stepped back. I watched, pulling the robe tighter around me, as he moved to a cabinet next to the tub. When he turned back, he held a leather rolled pack which he set on the massage table at my side.

"These are the tools I'll use, Ripley." He opened the pack, revealing items I'd associate with drawing and not making a tattoo. Then he reached for my right hand and pushed the robe's sleeve back from that wrist. "This is what it will feel like."

I watched as he picked up an instrument that resembled a paintbrush. He "drew" something on my forearm. Unlike the million little bee stings I expected from a tattoo, this almost tickled. Then I felt the kiss of magic against my skin. He might not be "inking" me yet, but he was letting me know how it would happen.

Maybe it wouldn't be as bad as I thought.

"All right. But I want to see Dani first."

"There are clothes in the closet. I'll wait for you in the great room."

With that, he slipped out of the room, closing the door after him.

It didn't take long to dress and make my way upstairs. I stopped in front of the door to the bedroom Razor said they'd set up for Dani and took a moment to prepare myself. Dani would want answers about what happened and why. Hell, I wanted answers as well. But, until I had them, I needed to find a way to reassure her. Knowing I couldn't put it off any longer, I lifted my hand and lightly rapped my knuckles on the door before pushing it open.

"Ripley!"

Dani ran across the small bedroom, straight into my arms. I looked over her head to where Layla Issawi stood next to the bed. She smiled slightly, her expression troubled. When she nodded in Dani's direction, I followed her gaze and frowned. A soft, catlike nub of a tail flicked back and forth under the oversized tee shirt she wore for bed. Running a hand over her head, I felt the tufts of her cat ears. Poor kid. Worried, she forgot to maintain control over her forms.

Not that I blamed her.

"Easy there, kiddo." I gently guided her to the bed and sat, pulling her onto my lap.

"You were gone so long, Ripley." Tears streamed down her cheeks.

"I'm sorry, but I needed to stay in case they needed me for anything." I wiped away her tears and lifted her face so she looked at me.

"Red?"

I shook my head. "I don't know, sweetheart. I haven't heard from him."

"He wasn't there?" Hope filled her voice.

"It doesn't look like it." Not a lie, but not necessarily the truth either. Cuellar's people were still combing the building, looking for any others who might have been trapped inside.

"Then he's okay, right?"

"I'm not going to lie to you, Dani. I don't know." God, I wished I had answers for her. "I'm worried because we haven't heard from Red. That's not like him." I continued to hold her close, doing my best to reassure her. "Here's what I do know. He saved those he could. He made sure they got to the safe room in the sub-basement. I also know that by the time I left, there'd been nothing found to indicate he was still inside."

"You know Ripley's going to do everything she can to find Red and to find out what happened." Layla dropped onto the mattress at my side, her hand rubbing gentle circles on Dani's back. "Knowing Red, he'll be sitting at our breakfast table, drinking a cup of tea, and wondering why we've all been so worried when we get up in the morning."

I prayed the naga was right. But I found it hard to believe. Red might be many things, but a coward he wasn't. Nor was he the type to abandon his people. If he could, he'd be here, making sure everyone was all right and doing everything possible to find those responsible for the attack.

And I had no doubt that's exactly what happened—someone attacked the warehouse, just as someone had attacked the other Zones. But why?

And where the hell was Red?

"I want you to remember what Layla said, Dani, because she's right. Red's going to show up." Alive, I hoped. "Right now, you need to get some sleep."

Her arms tightened around me, and she burrowed her head against my chest.

"Dani, look at me." I waited until she did. "I'm not going anywhere tonight. I promise. I'm going to talk with Razor and then he's going to do some work on me. I'll be here when you wake up. If you're not up before I need to leave, I'll wake you to say goodbye."

"Can't I go with you tomorrow, Ripley?"

I caressed her cheek and smiled slightly. "No, sweetheart. You can't go with me. I'm going to be doing Conclave business tomorrow."

"You and I are going to hang out together, Dani," Layla said. "Don't worry about school. I'll call and get your lessons, so you don't fall behind. After we work on them, I'll help you with your other lessons." She let Dani's sleek tail slide across her palm, a gentle reminder that the girl needed to be more careful with her control.

"That sounds like a good idea." I smiled at Layla in appreciation. "Now get to bed, kiddo. I'll check on you later. Promise." I brushed my lips against her cheek and carefully twisted so I could shift her onto the mattress.

"You won't go without telling me?" She held my hand tightly.

"Promise." I stood and helped her under the covers. "Layla will sit with you until you fall asleep. I'll be downstairs with Razor, promise. Night, sweetheart."

"Night, Ripley."

I walked backwards to the door, watching as she settled down. Then I motioned for Layla to join me. I needed a word with her before I went downstairs.

"Thanks," I said softly as we stepped into the hallway.

"It's my pleasure, Ripley. She is a good girl, and she's been very worried about Red and you."

"Make sure she doesn't leave here unless you or Razor are with her. Something's going on, something bad, and I don't know what might happen next."

"We will protect her as if she was our own," the naga promised and, for one moment, I saw her snake aspect in her features.

"I know. You love her like I do." I'd never leave Dani with her otherwise. "I need you to do something else for me, if you will."

"Of course."

"See if you can get her to tell you what's been going on at school. They sent her home early again. I don't know if they called Red. They certainly didn't call me, and I thought we'd handled the bullying problems the last time something happened."

"Let me see what I can find out. If she doesn't tell me, I'll check with her teacher and a few others I know there."

Relieved, I smiled slightly.

"Thanks. I'll be downstairs with Razor if you need me."

Now to see what he could tell me before letting him work his magic. At least no needles would be involved.

I found Razor waiting for me when I made my way downstairs. He watched, his expression neutral, as I crossed the great room in his direction. Then he motioned me to a seat. As he did, I wondered if I should be worried that he wanted to get to business so quickly.

"Okay, Razor, what's going on? You said we needed to talk."

I settled on one of the leather chairs and watched as he paced back and forth. The shaman no longer made any attempt to hide the fact something bothered him. No, it was more than that. He was worried and that, in turn, worried me. That worry ratcheted up a level when I glanced around and saw no sign of his cousins.

"We do, especially after what happened at Red's."

He dropped onto the chair next to mine and scrubbed his hands over his face. I waited, giving him time to gather his thoughts and decide how best to proceed. Instead of explaining, he tipped up the beer bottle held between his fingers and took a long draw.

"Ripley, I don't know if the two events are related, but I will say this. When Carlos and Antony arrived, I knew it meant trouble." He gave a mirthless laugh. "Trouble follows them like a shadow on a sunny day."

"Why are they here, Razor? From the way you introduced us, I assume you weren't expecting them."

"I wasn't. I would have let you know they were coming otherwise."

I nodded. One of the unwritten rules of the Zones was to inform the local marshal if potential trouble came to town. Fortunately, that didn't happen often. But paras are people, just like normals. There are good ones and bad. Each of us have our own emotional baggage. Even though the Zones have police forces just like the rest of the country, the marshals do their best to keep the cops from having to become involved. Mainly because human laws—not to mention their jails and prisons—still fall short when it comes to dealing with an out-of-control para.

In most cases, all it takes is a carefully chosen word to the newcomer or the person they came to see, reminding them of the price of breaking Conclave law. Sometimes, however, it took more. If it brought a marshal into the picture, the situation had gone past what the local cops had authority to deal with—and that was why Starke and I often found ourselves at odds, even though, before today, I rarely acted as a marshal. He believed the police force was the end-all, be-all of law enforcement in town. Reality was something very different.

And it is what would, sooner or later, bring us into direct conflict and the lycan had no idea what he'd be facing when that time came.

"So, what's spooked you, Razor?" I took another look around, making no attempt to hide what I did. "While we're at it, where are your cousins?"

"I'll answer your second question first. They are staying with Aras."

My mind boggled and my eyes all but popped out of my head.

Aras?

"Razor, what's going on?" I leaned back, not sure I could take many more surprises.

"I don't know and that is the truth of it, Ripley. My cousins came because there is trouble back home and they hoped I might be able to help. Someone, possibly more than one person, attacked our grandmother's compound. It was an arcane attack that could have been fatal to everyone there if my grandmother wasn't as paranoid as Red. From what the cousins said, our people managed to turn back the attack. There were few serious injuries and no fatalities, but Carlos said they have yet to learn who was responsible."

He waved a hand, stopping me from interrupting.

"My abuela is a bruja, Ripley. She taught all of us, but me in particular. She is also the leader of our kind back home. Things are not so formal there as they are here. Partly because the people there have always believed more in the paranormal and the spiritual than most people here in the United States. That is what makes the attack on her home so concerning. There are few so foolish as to attack a powerful bruja."

He took another drink and set the bottle on the table between our chairs. "But that isn't all. Antony told me the local Rift is behaving strangely and has been for some several weeks. It seems to expand at some times and at others it almost disappears. Our people are worried and hoped I might know what's happening."

"Have they spoken with the South American Conclave?"

Razor gave an elegant shrug that said so much without saying anything. They hadn't and I shouldn't be surprised. Nor should I ask too many questions.

I sighed and considered the best way to respond.

"What about the local marshal?"

"There isn't one, at least not local in the way you think of it." He stood and crossed to the kitchen. I waited, knowing he needed a few moments to decide how much to tell me. When he returned, he carried two more beers. He handed me one and then returned to his seat before taking a long pull on his own bottle. "Ripley, things are different down there. marshals are not as prevalent as they are here. Part of it comes from the fact we are suspicious of authority figures. Long before the Upheaval, too many of us dealt with law enforcement officials who were as corrupt as the drug cartels and human traffickers. Having a para, or anyone else, with the authority of life and death over us is not something we welcome easily."

I nodded. Over the years, he'd told me about his life before coming to Texas. To say it was very different there from here is putting it mildly. I understood why they distrusted the legal authority. Even so, his family needed to talk with the South American Conclave, especially if the attack might be linked to what happened here.

If they wouldn't do that, would they talk with our own Conclave?

That was something to discuss with Razor, but later, after he discussed everything with his family.

"Care to tell me why your cousins are with Aras instead of here?"

His smile sent chills down my spine.

"They might be my cousins, but they have yet to tell me the full truth, my friend. They think they can fool me. But they forget I can sense when they try to lie or hide something from me. There is a connection we share as family that ties us together and lets me see into their hearts. While I do not believe they have come to cause trouble, I cannot be sure, and I will not take chances with Layla or with young Dani. I will not risk this town that welcomed me when many would not. Aras understands and will make certain they do nothing foolish before he returns them to me come morning."

"I need to talk with them."

He nodded, understanding. "And so you shall—but after I speak with them again. I promise their tongues will be loose and willing when you do." He lifted his beer and tilted it in my direction, a slight smile touching his lips. Then he leaned back and seemed to relax, at least a little. "I have some ideas about how to do your markings, Ripley. Before we get started, do you want them to be visible or do you want to hide them within an image so no one suspects they are there?"

I considered for a moment. There were those who would ask questions if I suddenly showed up covered with ink. More importantly, if the sigils and spells were visible for all to see, the element of surprise was lost.

"Tell me what you see as the strengths and weaknesses of both, Razor."

He nodded, pleased with the question. Maybe I'd just passed his first test of the night.

"Hidden means those familiar with such things would have to know not only what to look for but where to find them. They would be hidden in the shadings and shapings of whatever image or scene you want me to draw. That gives the advantage to you because they wouldn't know you came prepared for at least certain aspects of trouble.

"The weakness in them being hidden is that it would take longer for you to activate them, at least until you can find the markings within the images through nothing more than muscle memory."

Sipping my beer, I considered. Everyone at Red's and in my rather limited circle of friends knew Razor had been after me to let him ink me. They wouldn't be surprised, at least not too much, if I finally agreed to it. They might even think he took advantage of the fact I'd be exhausted and not willing to argue after the day's events. He'd never do that, but he wasn't above making a pitch when he felt I was more likely to listen—and I was after the events of the day.

"If we go with an obvious inking, what do you have in mind and how big would it be?"

"There are several options. The first is a larger scene, one best suited for your back. The problem with that is you would have issues reaching the sigils to activate them. But it could be done. Here."

He reached for an art pad that rested on the table between our chairs and flipped it open. For a moment, he looked at the page before handing it to me. I studied the image, marveling at the detail in the art and wondering how in the world he planned on doing something like that in a matter of hours. I doubted anyone could do it in less than several days. But then he wasn't just anyone, and he didn't plan on doing a traditional "inking".

"It's gorgeous, Razor." I lightly ran a finger down the jungle scene. "But it is a bit much, even if it would be covered most of the time."

"Flip the page then."

I did and gasped softly. Instead of a large back piece, this time I looked at two—well, three—separate images. One represented a full arm sleeve. Wrist to shoulder covered with images representing Surtr, the Earth and Sun, and even the Tlanuwa. The giant bird of prey, with its metal feathers, soared high in the sky above mountains that lay beyond the grasslands where horses and buffalo grazed. Interwoven in it all were the magical protections I never would have noticed if I hadn't known what to look for.

The other set of drawings were much the same, but this time split between both arms. The "inking" ran from wrist to elbow. It appeared more balanced but not as impactful.

The final set, on its own page, showed only the sigils and other protections. Nothing to hide them. They would be there for everyone to see—and counter if they had the time and the knowledge to do so.

"The full sleeve, I think." I leaned forward, handing back the pad. It was more than I was truly comfortable with, but I preferred not advertising my arcane protections any more than I advertised my mundane ones.

"Then come. This will take time, but it will be well worth it. You have my word on it."

I hoped so.

God, how I hoped so.

10

WHERE'S RED?

I woke the next morning to the enticing smells of coffee brewing and bacon frying. A warm pressure weighed down my middle and two large paws kneaded against my full bladder. Opening my eyes, I looked around, fighting down the momentary panic when I didn't recognize my surroundings. I most definitely wasn't in my own bed, much less in my own apartment. Then the events of the day before came roaring back and, with them, the need to find answers.

Not to mention getting some vengeance if anything had happened to Red.

But first, I needed to reassure the small bobcat trying to make a pincushion out of my belly.

"Dani, you're such a pretty girl in this form, just like you are in your other." I rubbed her ears and then gathered her in my arms as I sat up. "And it's really cool waking up with you keeping me company. But I need to get going."

As if she'd been waiting outside the door, Layla stepped inside the small bedroom. In one hand, she carried a large mug of coffee I really hoped was mine. With a smile, she handed it to me. Then she reached down and took Dani from me. She gave the bobcat a loving pet before setting her on the ground. With a soft pat to the cat's rear, she sent Dani to her room to change back to her human form.

"Razor's already in the shop getting ready to open, Ripley. He asked me to check on you. He said you had a late night and would need coffee and possibly an ear."

"Thanks."

She sat next to me and reached for my right hand. Together, we studied the new "tattoo" sleeve covering that arm. The fingers of my left hand gently traced the shapes, finding the magical symbols and feeling the power of them even as I marveled not only at the artwork but at the fact it didn't hurt. Razor had been true to his word. The inking—No way could I call it a tattoo. Not after witnessing the magic he wove into the work—had been pain free until the end when he bound the last of the protection spells into the inking and then into me. Now I had a piece of artwork most would have paid thousands for.

Not to mention having to sit for hours, possibly even days, for it to have been completed.

More importantly, I had protections no one would expect. Considering my new line of work, that might help keep me alive when things got dicey.

"You can tell him I'm fine, Layla." I held the mug between my hands and inhaled the rich aroma before taking that first fortifying sip. Then I glanced at my watch, trying not to wince at the early hour. The fact she was not only awake but alert and dressed boggled the mind. How the hell did she do it? "And I need to get going. I'll stop back by later this morning to talk some more with him—and I'll probably take you up on the offer of an ear."

"You are always welcome in our home, Ripley." She reached out and gently touched the back of my hand. "I don't have many friends. I count you as one of them. I will always be here for you."

"Thanks, and the feeling's mutual." I covered her hand with mine, letting her see and feel the truth of my words.

"Then do us both a favor, Rip, and see Razor on your way out. He'll worry otherwise and no one wants to deal with him when he's grumpy because he's worried about something."

The idea of the shaman worrying almost brought a smile to my lips before I remembered our discussion from the night before. Besides, I liked Layla too much to make her deal with the man when he was in a mood.

"All right." Another sip of coffee. "Are you sure you don't mind keeping an eye on Dani today?"

Layla smiled, affection lighting her otherwise dark eyes. "Ripley, she's welcome to stay with us as long as necessary. You know we'll keep her safe." Another smile. "If you haven't figured it out, both Roberto and I love that girl like she was our own."

It took me a moment to realize who she meant. Very few called Razor by his given name. Hell, I'm not sure most folks knew his given name. For as long as I could remember, he'd been Razor. We'd known one another more than five years before I knew he had any other name. Still, if anyone would know, it'd be Layla. The two of them had been together almost as long as Razor had been in Glenham Grove.

While her use of Razor's name surprised me, her comment about Dani didn't. Everyone who worked with Red had unofficially adopted her as their little sister. Somehow, she'd managed to find a spot in Razor's and Layla's hearts as well. Not that I blamed them for having a soft spot for the girl. Dani was a sweetheart and as loyal as they came.

"Thanks, Layla." I smiled at her over the rim of my mug. "I'm hoping Red gets in touch with me—hell, with anyone—soon. Until then, I need to try to figure out what's going on and why." I drained the coffee, not caring it was still almost too hot to drink. "Let me know if you hear anything, especially about why Dani was sent home from school early, or if Dani needs me?"

"Of course." She patted my leg and stood, extending a hand to help me to my feet. "I'm afraid your clothes from yesterday are trashed, Ripley. I hope you don't mind, but I borrowed your keys. I went to your place after you came up to bed and got you some clothes as well as a few other things I thought you might need. I put them in the bathroom. There's more in the closet. Roberto and I would be honored if you'd stay here as long as you want." She shook her head, stopping my protest.

"Ripley, take time to consider it. Think about this as you do. Dani's going to feel better if you at least spend the nights here as long as she's staying with us. She loves us but you're the one she looks to for protection. We're the fun aunt and uncle. You're her big sister in every way that matters."

I couldn't fault her reasoning and nodded.

"Thanks."

I looked around, trying to decide where to place the mug. Lessons learned years ago at my mother's knee stopped me from setting it on the beautiful, hand-rubbed wood of the bedside table. Layla saved me and reached for the mug.

"Go grab a shower, Ripley. What would you like for breakfast?"

"As wonderful as one of your breakfasts sounds, I can't." And that hurt. Layla was trained as a professional chef. Turning down one of her meals hurt my soul, at least my stomach's soul. "But I'm meeting Yousef at the café shortly."

"Then we'll expect you for dinner unless you're working."

She didn't explain what she meant by "working". She knew I would drive myself to exhaustion trying to find out what happened to Red and who was responsible for the fire at the office.

"I'll touch base during the day. But I really do need to get going now."

Half an hour later, I settled at my regular table at the far end of the small dining room in Three Sisters Cosmic Café. The moment I did, a mug of coffee floated across the room and settled gently within easy reach on the table. From the kitchen, a hello! sounded. I chuckled softly as the sign on the door flipped to closed and the lock engaged even though no human hand touched them.

"Showing off, Sele?" I turned in my chair to look toward the kitchen.

"Not me, Ripley," the petite blonde answered as she pushed open the kitchen door and stepped into the dining room. "Romy's in a mood," she added softly.

"I heard that!" her sister yelled from the kitchen.

Selena Boucher grinned and winked as she joined me at the table. She glanced at the counter and waved a hand. Leaning back, I watched as the glass dome over what looked like a freshly baked apple pie lifted. It hung in the air as two pieces of pie were sliced and floated to saucers before transporting across the dining room to the table. With a soft clink! the dome returned to place.

"Are you in the pie already, Sele?" Elle Boucher, the third sister, wiped her hands on a white dishtowel as she appeared from the kitchen.

"Ripley wanted a piece."

I grinned and shook my head. This back-and-forth between the sisters was normal and my preferred way to start the morning. No matter how serious the day promised to be, they reminded me I needed to remember to hold onto the good. But that wasn't why I started today there. Besides telling Yousef to meet me there, I wanted to hear anything they might know about what happened yesterday.

"Right."

Elle rolled her hazel eyes and tossed her black braid over her shoulder before joining us. Within moments, pie and a mug of coffee appeared in front of her. One thing about it, having three witch sisters as café owners meant service was rarely slow and then only if you did something to seriously piss them off. If you were smart, you only did so once.

"You might as well join us, Romy." I didn't bother raising my voice, knowing she'd be listening to what we said. "I'd like to talk with all three of you before the morning rush starts."

"How about me?" a voice asked from my feet.

I yelped and shoved back from the table. A very feline chuckle sounded in response. A moment later, one of the largest black cats I'd ever seen leapt onto the tabletop. He padded over to rub his head against each of the sisters before returning to sit in front of me.

On my plate.

Really?

"You're getting no tuna today, Cat."

I grabbed him by the scruff of his neck and lifted him off my plate, relieved to discover one of the sisters managed to save my pie before he sat his fat furry butt down. Sele took him from me, cradling him in my arms.

"I. Am. Not. A. Cat."

It might have been more effective if he hadn't hissed at me at the end of the statement.

"Looks like a cat. Acts like a cat." I leaned forward and smelled his breath, wrinkling my nose as a very fishy odor filled it. "Smells like a cat. Is a cat." I gave him the stink-eye. "You're just lucky one of your sisters saved my pie. Otherwise, I'd haul you to Animal Control and report you as a nuisance."

He swatted at my hand, earning a scolding from Sele. "Behave, Cal. Otherwise, I'll help her take you to Animal Control."

The cat bared his teeth and then wiggled out of his sister's grip. The other two laughed as he stalked out of the dining room, his tail high to show his disdain. As he did, I shook my head. Almost a year ago, Calvin Boucher decided to try a spell he found in some long-forgotten ancestor's book. To say it backfired on him is a massive understatement. He's been a cat since then. Whenever I asked Sele or one of her sisters about what happened, they shook their heads and reminded me Cal always thought more of his abilities than he should. That alone convinced me that at least one of the sisters knew how to help him shift back but were holding out until he admitted his mistake and apologized for not listening to them in the first place.

Still, it was unsettling to have a cat talking to you. Especially one as full of crap as Calvin. Unless I missed my guess, he'd probably use up his nine feline lives long before he figured out all he needed to do to change back was tell his sisters he was sorry.

"Here you go, Ripley."

Romy returned my pie and then sipped her cup of tea. Some unspoken communication passed between the sisters and Elle nodded. Apparently, a decision had been made. Hopefully, it would help me figure out what was going on.

"Before Yousef arrives, we need to talk." Elle looked so serious, worry began churning in the pit of my stomach.

I leaned back, mug in hand. "All right. About?"

"Several things, actually," Sele corrected and glanced at the others. "I'll begin, shall I?"

Her sisters nodded.

"Aunt Gemma called after your visit. She told us about your

conversation and her concerns. She sounded scared, Ripley. We've never heard her like this before and it worries us."

"Worries me too," I admitted.

Especially considering what happened after our conversation.

Sele flicked a glance at her sisters, her expression growing more troubled. "After you left, Aunt Gemma felt dark forces centering on this part of town. That's why she called. She said she was going to try to trace the source. I warned her not to, at least not without one of us coming to shield and ground her. But she refused. She said we'd be needed here, both yesterday and for the next few days and that we were to stay here. That was before we learned about the fire."

I swallowed hard.

The next few days?

"Have you spoken with her since?"

"We've called, but she hasn't answered." Romy shook her head, her expression troubled. "Ripley, we're worried about her."

I understood, but it wasn't out of character for Gemma to let calls roll over to voicemail. If she was busy doing a working of some sort, it even made sense for her to do so. The last thing she'd want was to risk a spell going sideways because she got distracted. Still, it looked like I'd be making another trip out to her place before the morning was over.

"Did she say anything that might help identify who might be responsible?"

"No." Sele held her cup between her hands and stared into it. "I'm worried, Ripley." She looked at her sisters. "We're worried."

"I'll check on her as soon as I can. I promise." I thought for a moment. Part of me wanted to ask one of them to go with me. Then I remembered what Gemma said and my blood ran cold. "I don't want to add to your worry, but what she told you about being needed here the next few days concerns me. I'm going to ask you to do what she said and stay here. I'll have Yousef or someone else go with me to check on her." Possibly even Razor if he can take the time away from his shop.

"Ripley." Sele looked at me, fear and determination reflected in her eyes.

"Please. Gemma's right about one thing. If what happened yesterday was just the beginning, you're going to be needed here. Folks are going to have questions about what happened and they're going to be worried. By being here, by keeping the café open, you not only provide a sense of normality, but you can listen to what they say —and you can let me know if you hear anything that might help get to the bottom of all this."

"Are you speaking as our friend or as the marshal?" Sele asked. "And, before you answer, we know you finally accepted the position the Conclave's been offering you the last several years. Mr. Drake contacted us last night to let us know and to ask us to do everything we can to assist you."

I frowned and then nodded. It made sense. The three headed the largest local coven. The only thing that really surprised me is that Drake didn't tell me about the call. What other little surprises did he have hidden up his sleeve?

And did I really want to know?

"I'm asking as both. The Conclave wants me to take lead here. There's more going on than just what happened at Red's and it isn't limited to North Texas. That's why I'd appreciate it if you'd keep your eyes and ears open. If anything feels off or wrong, I need to know."

Besides, I didn't need them running around where they might get caught in the middle of whatever the hell was happening.

"We'll let you know if we hear anything. You have our word," Romy said.

"Thanks." I took a sip of coffee, thinking for a moment. "You said there was something else you wanted to discuss."

The sisters looked at one another again and I waited. Whatever they had to say, they didn't like it. No, that wasn't quite right. They were uncomfortable, as if they needed to say something and they didn't know how I'd react. Doing my best to hide my worry, I lifted my mug and sipped, the pie forgotten for the moment.

"Here."

Sele slid a thick business-sized envelope across the table to me. She hadn't had it when she sat down, so either one of her sisters handed it to her when I wasn't watching or she'd magicked it there. Not that it mattered.

As I reached for it, I felt traces of magic rising from the brown paper. The energy felt familiar, and I gasped softly as I recognized it. Red. But how?

"Red left this with our mother not long after he took you in, Ripley," Elle said. "He told her to give it to you if anything happened to him. Maman gave it to us when she moved to Chicago to be with Mamé. We spoke with her last night and she agreed Red going missing after the fire qualifies."

I thought back. Isadora Boucher, Gemma's sister-in-law, returned to Chicago to take care of her mother almost four years ago. The sisters stepped up then to take over leadership of the coven as well as management of the café. They'd done a good job with both, much better than their mother in my opinion.

"Do you know what's inside?"

They shook their heads.

"Guess I'd better open it and find out."

I turned the envelope over and studied the seal. At first glance, it looked like any other envelope. But normal envelopes didn't have magical energies dancing around them. They didn't have a subtle protection sigil drawn across the flap. I knew Red was paranoid, but this took it all.

At my touch, the seal broke, confirming it had been attuned to me. I carefully reached inside and withdrew a stack of papers. Several contained the blue backing I associated with legal documents. Others, some stapled together and others loose, rested on top of them. I carefully placed the stack on the table and started reading the top page.

Ripley,

If you're reading this, something's happened. I'm dead or missing. Like it or not, this damned life of ours is a dangerous one. Always has been, but it's been worse since the Upheaval. Before then, being a para meant hiding what we are from friends and family. The Upheaval helped some ways but made it worse in others. While we don't have to hide like we used to, revealing our existence made us some enemies we didn't have before. Enemies who fear us and who want what we have and will do whatever it takes to get it.

Young as you are, you've seen that first-hand. That's why I promised your folks I'd keep an eye on you if anything happened to them. I know I wasn't the parent you wanted or needed. Hell, girl, I never wanted to be a parent. But you've made me proud. I hope I didn't screw you up too badly these years since you came to me.

Whatever's happened to me, there are things that must be dealt with and you're the only one I trust to do them. Your parents were my closest friends, and you know I don't trust just anyone, much less to the degree I call them friend. But I did your Mom and Dad. Ripley, I might not have wanted a daughter, but you've been just that to me, giving me much more than I ever gave you.

Enclosed are documents giving you legal control over all my personal and business holdings. I trust you to care for them and those folks associated with them just as I would. They are our family. I know you understand how important that is.

There's also the paperwork naming you Dani's guardian until she's of age. She loves you and I know you think of her as your little sister. Take care of her and guide her. If something's happened to me, it means trouble has finally found our little part of the world. Do not let it touch her. She's been through so much already.

It's all set up, girl. You have power-of-attorney for everything. It will be revoked only upon my return and upon my execution of specific documents. Copies of those documents have been included. The originals are on file with my attorney. My will, both for the human courts and for the Conclave, is here as well. You inherit everything, except for a trust I've set up for Dani and a few specific bequests for some of our people. I trust you to see they are carried out and to take care of our little family.

You've been the daughter I never had, Ripley girl. Your parents would be so proud of you. Might not have told you before, but I am too.

There's something else I need to give you. It's not with this batch of documents. I couldn't trust it falling into the wrong hands. You'll find it in the safe I had built at the same time as the safe room. Here's what you need to know to get inside. You might even discover a few things in it you can find a use for.

Take care, little one. Stay strong and continue protecting our people. Lean on those who care for you because you can't always do it on your own. That's a lesson I learned a long time ago—and one I forgot until you came into my life.

Redmond

P.S.: Ask Roberto to be with you when you get the documents and other items out of the safe. He'll be able to guide you on the use of some of them. Gemma will be able to with the others.

R.

I blew out a breath and read the note again before glancing at the other documents. None of this made any sense. Between the safe room and the letter—not to mention the legal documents and all the rest—one thing became abundantly clear. Red knew something bad was going to happen—or at least he expected it to.

Why hadn't he said something? Given some kind of warning?

The answer might lie in the safe but getting to it wouldn't be easy. The building was still an active crime scene. Worse, it would be days before the Conclave's investigators—who I'd be calling in as soon as I spoke with Drake—finished checking for any evidence of a paranormal attack. Then there were the local authorities. Cuellar probably wouldn't be a problem. He'd seen my firewalker act the day before. But Starke. . . .

Griffin Starke would be a problem. No doubt about it. His werewolf nature meant he resented my pulling rank where the investigation was concerned. That was bad enough. Worse, his mama raised him to protect the female of the species and he—and his wolf—expanded that to all females. I didn't doubt for a moment he'd do his damnedest to keep me out of the building and "safe" behind the police line.

Too bad I didn't intend to comply, especially after reading Red's letter.

Damn it, Red. What the hell is going on?

"Ripley?" Elle lightly rested a hand on mine, her expression concerned.

"Sorry. Got lost in my thoughts for a moment." I swallowed against the lump of emotion threatening to close my throat. "This changes things." I lightly tapped the stack of papers. "Yousef should be here soon. I'm not going to be able to wait for him. If I leave a note, will you make sure he gets it? Also, I'd appreciate it if you told him what you told me. Let him know I'll be in touch, probably within the hour."

"Of course, Ripley, but shouldn't you wait for him?" Sele asked.

I shook my head. "Red's thrown a wrench in the works that I need to deal with." I tapped one finger against the pages before carefully replacing them in the envelope. Then I slid it into my bag. "While I pull together the note, will you try calling Gemma again?"

"I'll do it." Sele pulled her cellphone from the pocket of her apron and input her aunt's number.

As she did, Romy produced a pad and pen for me. Elle climbed to her feet, telling me she'd get me a go-cup of coffee. I nodded and turned my attention to composing a note for Yousef while also trying to figure out how to get into Red's building without butting heads with either Cuellar or Griffin. Something told me that pulling the marshal card needed to be my last resort.

A few minutes later, I slid the note inside the envelope Romy handed me. After scrawling Yousef's name on the envelope, I blew out a deep breath. How the hell was I going to get inside the building without either Cuellar or Starke trying to stop me?

Maybe Razor would have an idea—assuming he agreed to go with me.

"I need to run."

I stood and pulled several bills from my wallet. Before I could toss them onto the table, Sele closed her hand over mine and shook her head.

"Not this morning, Ripley."

Her sisters moved to stand behind her, presenting a united front before I could protest.

"Thanks." I smiled slightly. "Do me a favor. Send lunch over for Dani and Layla later. Layla and Razor are looking after her for me while I try to figure out what's going on."

"We will."

"Thank you." Now I pressed the bills into Sele's hand, knowing she wouldn't object to me paying for their lunches. "Your aunt?"

She shook her head, her eyes troubled. "No answer."

"Keep trying and let me know if you get through to her." I slid the strap of my bag across my body and accepted the to-go cup of coffee from Romy as well as a breakfast wrap. "I need to talk to Razor and run by Red's. Then I'll head out to her place. I'll let you know what I find, and I'll tell her to call you."

Assuming I found her.

"Thanks, Ripley." Romy leaned forward and gave me a quick hug. "Let us know if there's anything else we can do."

"I will. You three let me know if you hear anything of interest."

Who knows? Maybe I'd get lucky, find Red standing on the street outside the office, and Gemma busy casting a new spell of some sort and ignoring her phone. Then they could figure out who tried to burn the building down around everyone's ears and I could tell the Conclave everything was under control.

And maybe pigs could fly and Hell had frozen over.

11

BACK INTO HELL

What a difference a day makes. The smells of smoke, water and wood burning might still hang thick in the air, but clouds of black smoke no longer billowed skyward. Only a single firetruck, Cuellar's official SUV, and two police cars were parked in front of the renovated warehouse. Their emergency lights flashed a warning to stay away. A warning that instead acted like a beacon calling to the curious like a light in the dark to insects.

A warning that did not apply to me.

From my spot on the sidewalk across the street, I studied the former warehouse where I'd spent so much time over the last decade. Other than broken windows and some scorching from the fire, there was little on the outside to betray what happened yesterday. Any doubts I had that the fire's origin had been supernatural, that put it to bed.

And now it was up to me to figure out what happened and why.

But that was after I found Red's safe and had a look inside.

Which meant dealing with Nico Cuellar and hopefully getting in and out before Starke learned what I was up to.

I sipped coffee from the go-cup Sele pressed into my hands as I left the cafe a few minutes earlier and then glanced at my watch. I had just enough time to talk with Cuellar and make my case before Razor arrived. Then in and out, hopefully without incident and maybe with some answers to the questions the fire raised.

I found Cuellar in the tent that still served as the command post. He sat on a campstool in front of a makeshift table made from several sawhorses and plywood. Several tablets, both paper and electronic, rested on the tabletop. He held his phone to his ear, his expression a mix of concern and exhaustion. Seeing me, he held up a finger to let me know he'd be with me soon. I nodded in return and looked around, spotting a firefighter who appeared to be taking a break.

Leaving Cuellar to his call, I stepped out of the tent and approached the young man. Recognizing him from the day before, I smiled and fished a twenty out of my pocket. Then, thinking better of it, I shoved the bill back and pulled out my phone. A quick text and then I turned my attention to the man—Marcus, if I remembered correctly.

"You eat yet?"

He shook his head.

"Figured." Just as I figured none of the other firefighters still on-scene had. "I just texted in an order for coffee and pastries to Three Sisters. It will be ready by the time you get there. I'll let Captain Cuellar know I sent you."

For a moment, he didn't appear to understand. Then a smile slowly spread across his face and he took off at a jog. Trusting him to get back as quickly as he could, I turned back to the tent, hoping Cuellar had finished his call.

"You look like you haven't been home, Nico."

He gave a half-hearted smile and shrugged. "I wanted to make sure we had things in hand here."

"And?"

"Fire's out, at least for the moment. It started back up three, maybe four times, since you left. Let's just say that the Adepts have earned their fees and then some on this one."

I frowned. His comment meant the fires hadn't been caused by hot spots but by lingering magic. Damn it!

"Where are they?" I glanced around, seeing no one but local first responders.

"See the travel trailer down the block?"

I glanced in the direction he pointed and then nodded. Who could miss the ancient but showroom quality Airstream, its silver skin gleaming in the morning sun?

"They're grabbing some sleep. Keeps them close in case we need them."

Made sense.

"Is there anything else you can tell me, Nico?"

"Only that we haven't found any other bodies, but we're still checking the building. It's slow going between the damage inside and the need to make sure we don't trip any of Red's protections or anything that might trigger the spell that started the fire."

Lips pursed, I nodded. "What about the bodies I found?"

"We got them out a couple of hours ago. They've been shipped to the Dallas ME. Old Doc Hargrove isn't equipped to handle anything like them."

Another nod. "Any idea how long before we get a report back?"

He shook his head and then shrugged. "Your guess is as good as mine, Rip. Between their backlog and the fact the bodies were charred to a crisp, whoever gets assigned to them will have their work cut out for them."

I cursed softly. Delays I didn't need. What I needed was a cause of death and IDs on each of them.

"All right." I blew out a breath. "I sent one of your men to the café to pick up an order for me. I figured you and the others were ready for some coffee and food. You deserve it after the day—and night—you've put in."

He smiled and then narrowed his eyes in suspicion. Yep, he's known me too long.

"While I appreciate the gesture, I have to wonder what do you want."

I tried to look innocent but failed badly judging his expression.

"Ripley, why do I think I'm not going to like what you say next?"

"Nico, how could you?" I grinned at his groan and suddenly we were back in junior high and I was trying to convince him to do something he really didn't want to do.

"I could because I know you." He pushed away from the table and stood. "So, what is it?"

He did know me. Hopefully, he remembered I never dragged him into trouble when we were younger. At least not trouble for the sake of trouble. Even back then, my parents' training meant I looked out for the underdog and knew when I needed backup to deal with a bully or worse.

"I need access to the sub-basement. Specifically, to the safe room and the area around it."

"Why?"

"Another of Red's little surprises is all I can tell you." I stopped him before he could interrupt. "Nico, that's the truth. I don't know what I'm going to find. Red left me a note telling me to check the area. Before you ask, I don't know why. I hope whatever's down there will help us figure out what happened and why."

Not to mention help figure out where Red happened to be.

"I need more than that, Rip."

"Then how about this: I'm the marshal in charge of the investigation and I say so." I didn't want to pull rank on him, but I would if it got me in and out before Starke showed up.

"Ripley." Nico Cuellar dragged a hand through his hair. As he did, he looked at me with eyes dark with exhaustion and frustration. "Do you have any idea what you're asking? Hell, do you have any idea the spot you're putting me in?"

I couldn't argue, so I didn't.

"I'd say I'm sorry, Nico, but I'm not. I don't have a choice. The Conclave put me in charge and I owe it to them, to Red, and to all those who work for him and who live there to find out what happened. I promise I'll do my best not to contaminate any evidence, but I need to do this without wasting any more time."

"I need more if I'm going to sign off on this, Rip, and you need to understand I can't guarantee your safety."

"I'm not asking you to, Nico. Trust me, I understand the potential danger and wouldn't be doing this if it wasn't absolutely necessary."

I was grasping at straws, but what choice did I have? Besides, Red would kill me if the safe's contents fell into anyone's hands but mine. While I'd do just about anything to find him, I wouldn't betray his trust in me. I couldn't, not after everything he'd done for me by taking me in and raising me after Dad died and Mom disappeared.

"All right, but if Griffin finds out, I'm denying knowing anything about this."

I chuckled softly and nodded. I'd do the same thing if our positions were reversed.

"I'll make sure you're clear on this, Nico. If he finds out before I'm done, tell him the truth. I pulled rank and threatened to bring the Conclave in on it if you refused."

It wouldn't make Starke any less angry, but it would give Cuellar an out. That was the best I could do.

"Ripley." He sighed and shook his head. "All right. But be careful and watch your six. Between Red's safety measures—and I use that term very loosely—and the remnants of the spell that started the fires, I don't know what you might come across."

"Understood. I'll touch base when I'm done."

With that, I walked off. The less Cuellar knew right now, the better —for both of us. Besides, Razor should be waiting for me down the street. The sooner I told him what I could about the situation, the better. Hopefully, he might have some explanation for why Red wanted him with me when I opened the safe.

Half an hour later, we stood inside the safe room, staring at a doorway in the far wall that had been hidden by several supply cabinets.

"Did you know this was here?" I didn't look at Razor where he stood next to me. Instead, I studied the heavy metal door with the biometric control panel next to it. How in the hell was I supposed to open it?

He shook his head. "Red told me he had a safe in here, explaining he wanted it to be a secure as anyone inside the safe room. But this?" He waved a hand at the door. "I had no idea."

"How about why it wasn't found when the firefighters were in here yesterday?"

He didn't answer right away. Instead, he stepped closer to the door, his right hand held in front of him. I waited, giving him time to do whatever he was doing. As I did, I looked around, wondering if Red had anything else hidden down here.

Damn it, Red, what have you gotten us all into?

When Razor turned back, his expression told me all I needed to know.

Magic.

"Someone put a look away spell on the door, Ripley. They'd have seen the shelving in front of it but wouldn't even think to look behind it. If they got too close, the spell would activate and they'd suddenly feel as if they needed to look elsewhere. Only those keyed to the spell or those strong against such magic would remain unaffected."

"Who could have set the spell for Red?"

"There are at least half a dozen in town who could have. Of those, only one or two are adept enough, powerful enough to set the spell and leave it without having to come and renew it on a regular basis."

"All right." It was something to follow up on later. For now, I needed to get through that door to see what was on the other side.

Razor said nothing as he studied the keypad and biometric scanner next to the door. Then he punched in a series of numbers. A moment later, I yelped in surprise as he grabbed me by the neck and pulled my head down to the scanner.

Before I could say anything, a click sounded and the door slid open with an almost silent whoosh. An interior light came on. I stepped forward, ignoring the tingle of magic that danced across my exposed skin. Then I stopped just inside the doorway. Disbelief washed over me as I glanced around the "safe". That might be what Red called it, but it was so much more. Almost the size of the safe room we entered through, it contained a mix of tables, display cases, filing cabinets, and so much more.

What the hell?

Behind me, Razor cursed softly. Not that I blamed him. This "safe" was the thing of dreams and nightmares both.

"Razor?"

It would take days, if not weeks, to catalog everything. Who knew how long it would take to determine why Red had all this. Not to mention why he wanted me to find the room and have access to it.

"I knew about some of this." He stepped forward, his expression as stunned as my own. "But I think I know what he wanted you to have, at least part of it."

As he spoke, he moved to a table against the far wall. I watched as he looked over the items carefully laid out there. when he turned, he held several items in his hands. My breath hitched and I swallowed hard. It couldn't be.

It just couldn't.

"Razor."

My hands shook and tears burned my eyes as I reached out to gently touch the weapons he held. As I did, the years rolled back. I was once again a young teen, watching Mom as she prepared to leave on her last assignment for the Conclave. Her hands moved automatically as she checked the guns and slid them into matching thigh rigs. The kukri had been secured to the front of her tactical vest. Other weapons, some arcane and others mundane, were secured as well. Then she turned to me, her expression serious.

Tears tracked down my cheeks and I brushed them away as the memories washed over me. I never saw her again. A week later, Red and several others from town, not to mention members of the Conclave, came to see me. They told me Mom was missing. She failed to report in and none of the other marshals had been able to locate her. I wasn't to give up hope. They would continue to search, and they would find her.

But they hadn't. Days turned into weeks and weeks into months. Now, years later, Mom remained listed as missing, but we all knew the truth. She was dead—or worse.

So how the hell did Red come to have her weapons? Weapons she carried with her on that last mission.

"Razor?"

"I don't know." He said nothing else for a moment. "But I think you should take these."

I nodded. Then I took another look around. My breath hissed out to see a battered leather jacket I also recognized. Without a word, I reached for it, adding it to the weapons that now lay on a table next to me. No way would I leave them behind. Hell, I didn't want to leave any of this behind, not until I knew what it all meant and could confidently say it was not what the person or persons behind the fire were after. But how the hell was I supposed to get it all out? Then there was the little matter of figuring out where to store it.

"Is there any way to ward this room to keep everyone else from finding it and getting inside?"

Razor chewed his bottom lip for a moment and then shook his head. "It can be done, but it wouldn't be easy and it would take time you don't have right now, Ripley. But even if I could do it, there's no guarantee it would keep the room safe if the building came under attack again."

"I was afraid you'd say that."

I considered my options. Each one was thrown out as quickly as the one before it. I simply couldn't leave the contents of the room unguarded and I didn't dare tell anyone else about all this. Talk about being between a rock and a hard place.

I paced into the safe room and then back, thinking hard and not coming up with any answers. Life was so much easier when I was a simple bartender.

"Ripley?" He spoke softly, gently.

"I need to secure all this somewhere I can go through it without anyone stumbling upon it." I looked around again and then scrubbed my hands over my face. "Any ideas?"

He thought for a moment and then nodded. It should have reassured me, but something about his expression told me he had his doubts.

"What?"

"There is a place where you could store all this and keep it safe. The protections around it are as strong as what I have on my own building."

Surprise had my brows lifting as I looked at him, waiting for him to explain. I knew he had arcane and mundane protections on the building that housed his home and his shop. But to know another building had the same level of protection—a level I suspected was even stronger than Red had on the warehouse—brought me up short.

"Where?"

"Your house."

For a moment, I stared at him, not understanding what he meant. Then realization dawned on me. He meant the house I grew up in before Mom's disappearance. The house I hadn't been back to since that terrible day when Red and the others came to tell me about her disappearance. The day I went to live with Red, a man I didn't really know and who didn't want to raise a family, much less a grieving girl. The man who did all he could despite that to be a good parent to me.

"H-how?"

"The Conclave has paid to keep the protections going. Once a month, a service goes in to clean and do any maintenance that might be needed."

"W-why didn't you tell me?"

Why didn't Red?

"I thought you knew and chose not to live there." He looked at me, compassion in his eyes. "Ripley, I honestly thought you knew about the house."

I shook my head. How many more secrets would rise up to ambush me before this was over?

"We can discuss it later. Just tell me this: are you willing to move there for the interim and have these items stored there?"

Going back, knowing Mom and Dad wouldn't be there, would never be there, hurt. But I didn't have a choice. I needed a safe place for all the items Red left in my care. My apartment certainly wouldn't fit the bill. Besides, it gave me a base of operations, somewhere to meet with Youssef and others.

"How do we get all this." I waved my hands at the contents of this so-called safe. "There?"

"I can take care of it. You just need to make sure no one interrupts for the next few minutes."

I opened my mouth to ask how and then snapped it shut. He wasn't speaking to me as Razor, my friend and tattoo artist. At the moment, he was Roberto, the shaman who was as powerful as Gemma

119

in his own way. I might not know how he planned on moving everything, but I trusted him to do as he promised.

"All right. What else can I do?"

"Take whatever you want to keep with you out of the room and then wait out there until I join you."

I nodded and slid into my mother's leather jacket, surprised by how well it fit. Leaving her weapons on the table for the moment, I did a cursory check of the rest of the contents. Several more weapons joined the pile as well as a couple of files containing legal documents I had a feeling I needed to read through. The rest could wait until I returned home.

Home.

I wasn't sure I was ready for that.

Ten minutes later, Razor rejoined me. Exhaustion marked his face, etching deep lines from the bridge of his nose to the corners of his mouth. Shadows bruised the skin under his eyes. Before I could ask, he gave a slight nod and motioned toward the interior room. Stepping around him, I looked through the door and shook my head. The room that had been filled with boxes, display cases, file cabinets and more just a few minutes earlier now stood empty. It boggled the mind.

It also confirmed what I always suspected. There was much more to Razor than the magic he worked with his runes and wards. Seeing it up close and personal not only gave me a new respect for the shaman but it also served as a reminder that everyone in the Zone had hidden talents, something I needed to keep in mind.

"Thanks. I owe you."

"You owe me nothing, Ripley. I did this because you never ask for anything and because it was the right thing to do." He looked at me and grinned, mischief dancing in his eyes. "Besides, Layla would have my head if I didn't do everything I could to help. You are one of the few who accept her as she is, without judging her or being afraid of her."

"You two are family, Razor." As much as Red.

"As are you, Ripley."

He glanced at his watch which reminded me to do the same.

"Let's get out of here before someone decides to come looking for us, Razor."

He nodded and followed me out. We moved quickly, retracing our steps through the corridor leading from Red's building to the second warehouse half a block away. When we emerged into the morning sun, I blew out a breath. Time to let Cuellar know we were safely out of the building and that I'd brief him later in the day. For now, I wanted to have a look at the house I grew up in. But that had to wait until I met Yousef and we figured out the plan for the day.

Then, whether I liked it or not, I needed to have a talk with Griffin Starke.

12

FALLING DOWN THE
RABBIT HOLE

What I wanted to do was go "home" and spend the rest of the day—possibly the rest of the week—going through everything Razor transported from Red's safe. But I wasn't a fool, at least not usually. Returning to my childhood home wouldn't be easy. I hadn't been back since the day Red and the others came to tell me Mom had disappeared. That day, they helped me pack and I moved into Red's. He already had a room ready for me and, true to his word, he made sure I had everything I needed going forward. What I hadn't known, and hadn't considered, was that he kept the house and he and the others had made sure it was kept up in case I ever wanted to return.

Now I had to make that decision, something I wasn't ready to do. At least there were other things I needed to do first before facing the ghosts of my past.

Before that happened, I needed to check back in with Cuellar and Starke. After dropping Razor at his shop, I returned to my SUV and considered how I wanted to set the stage. One thing I knew from my earlier encounters with Starke as a marshal was that I needed to remind him quickly and firmly that I was there in my professional role for the Conclave and not as the girl he went to school with.

And I had the perfect way of doing so.

It didn't take long to secure Mom's thigh rigs in place. Then I checked the matching Ed Brown 1911s, making sure the safeties were on before sliding them into the rigs. With that done, I pulled on Mom's leather jacket. As I did, I inhaled deeply. Even after all this time, the jacket smelled like her and, for that one brief moment, it was as if she was with me. Holding that feeling close, I settled it in place and pocketed my keys. Time to face the devil in his den, so to speak.

And there he was, waiting for me, his expression telling me everything I needed to know. I was about to deal with a very pissed off werewolf and didn't have a rolled up newspaper to swat him on his nose when he inevitably stepped over the line. Silly me for forgetting it.

Griffin Starke paced back and forth inside the command tent, stopping and glaring at me when I entered. "What the hell were you thinking, Walker? You can't just waltz into a crime scene and go blundering around like you know what you're doing. I warned you yesterday. I won't have you disrupting my investigation."

I folded my arms under my breasts and counted to ten, once again wishing for that rolled up newspaper so I could smack the big, bad wolf across his nose.

"I will remind you that this is my crime scene by order of the Conclave, Starke. I wasn't blundering around, as you so kindly put it. "I was looking for something specific, something that might help explain what happened yesterday and why."

Starke's eyes narrowed and he snarled in frustration. "And you didn't think to tell me?"

I couldn't help it. "Oh, I thought about it." I smirked as he sputtered in disbelief. Then I turned serious. "If you'd quit strutting around like you own the town and we should all submit to you like good little wolves, I might have explained before Razor and I went inside."

He twisted his head, lifting his face. His growl rumbled from deep in his chest. "You took Razor inside? Have you lost your fucking mind?" He shoved his hands through his hair in frustration. "Give me one good reason why I shouldn't run you in for being a goddamned fool."

"You mean besides being there in my role as marshal?"

He didn't say anything, just stood there, glaring at me.

"Look, I didn't take Razor inside to go snooping around, if that's what you're worried about. I wanted him to see if he recognized any of the magical energy patterns still present in the building."

There was no need to tell him I also wanted Razor's help with the safe he'd kept secret for so long.

"So, what did you find?" Starke demanded, his eyes narrowing as he took a step closer.

I stood my ground, refusing to back down. "No hotspots for Rico there to worry about." I nodded at Cuellar, silently apologizing for him being caught in the middle of my feud with Starke.

"What else?"

I considered for a moment. If I told him about the safe and its contents, I had no doubt he'd order everything taken into the police station to be "kept safe". Since I had no idea if any of the contents of Red's "safe" dealt with what was going on, not to mention wanting to keep anything pertaining to my mother in my possession, I shook my head.

"That's not how it is going to work, Starke. I'll go through what we found and if it relates to the case, I'll read you in. Otherwise, you'll get no access to it until Red returns and says it's okay." His eyes sparked and his jaw tensed in anger. "Don't push me on this, Griffin. I mean it."

He leaned down, his face inches from mine. "You're playing a dangerous game, Walker. You're not invincible, no matter what you think. You keep messing with my case, and I guarantee you'll regret it."

"That is enough!"

I placed my hands on his chest and shoved. A normal human wouldn't have been able to budge him, not the way he stood all but rooted in place. But I wasn't a normal human, as he well knew. Anger and frustration leant me strength and he stumbled back two steps before he righted himself. His smile as he looked at me sent a chill down my spine.

"That's going to cost you." He reached for his handcuffs in their case on his belt.

"Stop it, both of you!" Cuellar moved between us, shoving us back a step or two. Then he stood there, glaring first at me and then at Starke. "The last thing we need is the two of you getting into a pissing match. If you can't work together, then one of you is going to have to step back and let someone take over for you." He paused, once again pinning Starke with a look that spoke volumes. "And you know who it will be, Griff. She's the fucking marshal. Like it or not, we work for her right now. So, pull your head out of your ass or walk away."

"Rico," he growled.

"I mean it." Cuellar stood his ground, an act of bravery—or foolishness—I respected. When the werewolf dipped his chin slightly, Cuellar relaxed a little. "You know she wouldn't do anything to jeopardize the investigation."

Another dip of his chin was the only response Starke gave.

"As for you." Now Cuellar turned his attention to me. "Quit baiting the ill-tempered werewolf. You know better."

Since I did, I nodded. "How about we turn our frustration with one another into energy better spent trying to figure out what's going on?"

"All right. Just don't keep me in the dark, Walker."

With that settled, I motioned for the men to move further inside the tent. As they returned to the makeshift table and took seats on the camp stools, I pulled my phone from the inside pocket of Mom's jacket. They waited, sporting almost matching expressions of curiosity as I did.

"I just emailed you a video I took of the inside of the safe room as well as the area leading to it, Rico. Still images of the area are next."

He nodded and pulled up the emails as they came in. While he and Starke studied the video and photos, I moved to stare at the front of the warehouse. It still amazed me the fire inside raged as hot and long as it did and there was little to show of it on the outside. That alone was enough to convince me of its arcane nature. Not that I needed any further convincing. Not after everything I'd seen and heard in the last twenty-four hours.

"You're sure Razor didn't see any signs of active hot spots down there?" Cuellar asked a few minutes later.

"I am." I considered for a minute. Best to be completely upfront in case anything else happened. "But we didn't go into the rest of the building. So, there might still be some elsewhere."

Cuellar nodded, his expression thoughtful. "I'll have Aimee check after she rests some more."

"She the fire elemental?"

Another nod. "Is there anything else you can tell us?"

Maybe like what I was really doing down there.

"Red had another room down there, one he had locked down and hidden behind arcane protections. One I didn't know about."

Starke arched a brow. "Then how do you know about it now?"

I considered rolling my eyes but didn't.

"Because Red left a letter for me in case anything happened to him. He told me about the room in the letter."

Now Starke sat up, his eyes alert. "What did the letter say?"

I gritted my teeth and counted to ten—again.

"For your information, Red wrote the letter several years ago. You know him. He always has a backup plan and I'm that when it comes to his business and personal interests. There was nothing in the letter that might shed a light on yesterday's events. He told me about the room because some of the documentation I need to handle things for him until he shows back up was in there."

The camp stool scraped across the pavement as Starke abruptly stood. At the same time, Cuellar rolled his eyes and muttered something about me being foolish enough to keep baiting the foul-tempered werewolf. But my attention remained on Starke as he stalked around the table in my direction.

"What. Did. The. Letter. Say?" He grabbed my arms and hauled me to my feet. "Every damned word, Ripley. Tell me what it said."

Anger surged as he once again drilled a finger into my chest. I'd warned him. But he couldn't let go of his damned werewolf stubbornness and pride. Now he was trying to drill a hole in my chest and, para or not, I'd have bruises come morning. It was past time someone taught him he wasn't the biggest, baddest predator in town.

Without a second thought, I grabbed the hand that continued to poke at my chest. My thumb and forefinger found the pressure points. Bearing down, I twisted my hand, increasing the pressure and sending him to his knees. As he gasped, I bent his hand back even further until he whimpered as I held the wrist near the breaking point.

"Ripley." Cuellar spoke softly. He knew better than to surprise me or try to get between the two of us just then. "Think about what you're doing."

Oh, I was thinking about it. Thinking about it and knowing Starke left me no other option unless I wanted to seriously hurt him.

"This is your last warning, *Chief.*" I released my grip and stepped back as his arm dropped limply to his side. "Do not lay hands on me again."

Starke looked up at me, his eyes wide and his face pale. "What the hell, Walker?"

"I'll put it in terms even you can understand. That was me reminding you to watch yourself," I said coldly. "Remember, there are bigger and badder things in this world than a werewolf and you'd be wise to recognize that I'm one of them."

I stood there, staring down at him, my anger slowly subsiding. Starke stayed where he was, looking up at me, anger and embarrassment reflected in his eyes. Hopefully, I'd made my point, and that he wouldn't make the same mistake again.

"I still need to see that letter and I need to see what was in that room." Rubbing his hand, he climbed to his feet. Wisely, he returned to the table, putting it between us.

"The short answer to both of those is no." I shook my head and stared him down when he tried to interrupt. "The letter was personal. He wrote about my parents and his friendship with them. He asked me to look after Dani and take her in. He wants me to look after the businesses and employees. That is the general gist of the letter.

"As for the contents of the room, there are a number of personal papers and personal items in them. I will go through them and let you see any that might deal with the current situation. But I will be the first to review those items."

"Walker." He looked ready to argue, then his expression softened in resignation. "Ripley, I don't want to fight with you. But I'm the seasoned cop. You need to let me take control of whatever was in that room."

I thought about Red's letter and my mother's things Razor found and shook my head.

"I'll compromise with you. I will go through as much as I can tonight and will brief you in the morning. Sooner if I find anything that connects to the fire or Red's disappearance."

"And I'm just supposed to take your word for it?"

Damn but the man was a stubborn ass.

"Giff," Cuellar warned.

"Leave him be, Rico. He'll either learn or find himself out of the investigation before he knows what happened." Hopefully, Starke decided working with me beat being kicked out of the investigation.

"Griffin, I promise I'll let you know if I find anything in Red's things that might help with the investigation," I said firmly. "But you will never put your hands on me again, and you will never treat me with such disrespect again. Is that understood?"

"Ripley," he growled, shaking his hand at his side.

"I mean it, Griff." Maybe calling him by his nickname would cut through some of his anger. I needed him thinking, not just reacting from his bruised ego right now. "You need to remember I'm part of this investigation because I'm the Conclave's marshal. I'm not just the girl you went to school with," I said, my voice hardening again. "And I expect you to respect my position."

A moment of tense silence stretched out between us before Cuellar sighed and shook his head. "Look, both of you need to calm down." he said, his voice steady. "We're all on the same side here."

I turned to Cuellar, taking a deep breath to calm myself. "You're right, Rico," I said. "And I apologize. To say I'm just tired and stressed is putting it mildly."

"It's alright," Cuellar said with a small smile. "We're all feeling it."

I stabbed my fingers through my hair in frustration.

"Griff, we've spent most of our lives picking at one another. But believe it or not, I do respect you and your position as the town's chief of police. It's just hard to break old habits."

He heaved a sigh and nodded. "Same."

"What's your next step, Rico?"

"Once Aimee and the other Elementals give the all-clear, I'm sending the arson investigators in to see what they find. I also want to send a couple of crews in to make sure we don't have any hotspots waiting to flare up."

"Any idea how long it will be before my people can get inside to retrieve any of their belongings that survived?"

My people.

That's what they were, at least until Red decided to show back up.

Cuellar didn't answer right away. Instead, he looked at the building, his expression thoughtful. When he looked back, I knew I would not like what he had to say.

"I can't say they'll ever be able to get inside, Rip." He waved off my objections before I could even open my mouth. "We need to check the building for structural integrity. We also need to have someone come in to make sure there are no magical traps waiting to be sprung."

I nodded. "Leave that to me." As I spoke, I pulled my phone and sent a text to Drake, asking for help with that. Almost instantly, he responded that he'd see to it and would text me the details as soon as it was arranged. "It's being arranged. I'll let you know when to expect the investigator."

He nodded. Then he gave a jerk of his head, indicating it might be a good idea to make my escape. Since I agreed, I didn't argue.

Before I left the tent, Starke spoke up, his voice still tight with anger. "Ripley, you better not be keeping anything from me. We need to work together on this."

I turned to face him, meeting his gaze. "I've already said I'd keep you informed of anything I find out. If that's not good enough, I suggest you talk to Mr. Drake. Of course, he might not be as nice about things as I've been."

I made no attempt to hide my sneer or my flash of anger. So much for putting the past behind us. Then I turned on my heel and left the tent. The miserable, self-confident, furry, mangy dog could just go fuck himself. I'd had enough of him to last a lifetime.

As I made my way back to my SUV, the weight of the investigation pressed down on me. There was so much to do, and I wasn't sure what to do next. I needed to talk to Dani again to see if she remembered anything else about the man who attacked her. I needed to talk to those who'd been trapped inside the warehouse and rescued later. I needed to go back to Gemma's and check on her.

Then there was everything Razor and I found in the safe room. I'd dearly love a day, maybe even a week—hell, who am I kidding? I'd need a month or more to go through everything. Already I had more questions than I wanted to consider.

Damn it, Red. How did you get my mom's jacket and weapons? What do you know about her disappearance that you haven't told me?

Once safely inside the SUV, I called Yousef and filled him in on what happened.

"What is your next more, Ripley?"

"I'm heading out to Gemma's to check on her. While I do that, why don't you go to Razor's? Talk to Dani about what happened yesterday. See if she's remembered anything else. If Razor's cousins are there, talk to them. You get to be the nice one because I'm going to put the fear of God in them later today."

If that didn't cause them to tell me what the real reason was for them coming to town, nothing would.

"I will let you know if they tell me anything of interest."

"Good." I thought for a moment. "Let Razor know what you plan and that I asked you to talk to them. He can call me if he has any questions or concerns."

"Understood." He paused and I slid the key into the ignition. "Stay safe, Ripley."

"You do the same, Yousef."

I ended the call and dropped the cellphone back into my pocket.

As I pulled away from the curb, I couldn't shake the feeling that things were only going to get worse from here. But I couldn't let that stop me. I had a job to do, and I was going to do it, no matter what.

13

TROUBLE IN THE AIR

Like it or not—and I really didn't like it because of the time it would take—I needed to head back out to Gemma's. I hoped something good came from the trip, namely that she had more of an idea about what her bad feeling meant and why she was having it now. I also hoped she didn't turn me into a frog—or worse—for interrupting her. Hopefully, by leading with the fact that I was returning as she asked and that her nieces were worried about her, I'd avoid that particular fate.

The closer I got to Gemma's, the stronger the sense of dread worming its way into my gut became. The sky turned dark with thick clouds and the air around me sparked with magical energies, more than I'd ever sensed before. These energies drifted out from Gemma's cottage in wisps and tendrils as if they were rising from some great furnace deep inside her home. The sickly sweet smell of rotten meat followed, stinging my nose and making me gag. Memory of yesterday's warnings about magical storms had me considering heading back to town without further exploration of the reality. But I couldn't. A feeling of foreboding came over me. It felt as if an army moved through the woods near her house, invisible to all but me. My hair stood on end and my skin tingled with magic drawn from a distant place.

From the Rift.

My mouth went dry, and my hands had a death grip on the steering wheel. This was so not good. Even as one small part of my brain gibbered at me to turn around and run, I pressed down on the accelerator, picking up speed. Something was wrong. Something that focused on Gemma or her home. Not only did I owe it to her and to everyone she'd ever helped to find out what was going on, but it was my duty as marshal.

Thanks so much for making sure I had a strong sense of duty, Mom.

Sarcasm dripped through my brain as memories of both my parents telling me how important it was to do our duty to those who needed our protection.

Slowly, I peeled the fingers of my right hand from the steering wheel and pulled one of Mom's 1911s from the rig on that thigh. Without taking my eyes from the road, I placed it on the passenger seat within easy reach. Then I tapped my earbud and called Yousef, listening as the phone rang and rolled over to voicemail.

"It's me. I'm almost to Gemma's but something's wrong. The energy out here is off the charts. Not a storm, not yet at any rate. If you haven't heard back from me within an hour, send help and then contact the Conclave. Tell them something's going on with the Rift."

I tapped the 'bud again and ended the call. Once I had, I resumed my death grip on the steering wheel and focused on the road ahead of me, fully expecting a monster from my nightmares to appear at any moment.

And here I thought Tuesdays were better than Mondays. If today was any indication, I'd been wrong all my life.

The moment I turned and saw the yard in front of Gemma's house, I knew things were as bad, if not worse, than I feared. If I didn't know better, I'd swear someone had filmed a fantasy movie here. The scars of fighting were everywhere. Turf torn up, pitted. Trees shattered or toppled. And the bodies. Dear sweet gods, the bodies. If that wasn't bad enough, the fact most were not even vaguely human was.

I parked as close to the house as I could get. Once I had, I twisted around and reached for the duffel resting on the back seat. By the time I climbed out of the SUV, I was armed not only with the 1911s, but also more blades and a Benelli Super Black Eagle 3 semi-auto shotgun. Inside the duffle, now slung cross-body, was additional ammo, a few explosives I shouldn't have, and other "goodies". Hopefully, it would be enough if it came to a fight.

Leaving the engine running in case I needed to make a quick exit, I stepped out. When I did, the stench of death hit me like a punch to the gut. Swallowing against the bile clawing its way up my throat, I scanned the area, searching for any signs of life. My right hand rested lightly on the butt of the 1911 at that thigh. I didn't dare let my guard down. The magical energies in the air were heavy, almost suffocating. As they threatened to overwhelm my senses, I prayed the wards Razor wove into my inkings worked half as well as he promised. If they did, I might get out of here alive.

God, what the hell was happening?

With the 1911 in my hand and held at the ready, I used my free hand to tap my earbud once again. Using the hood of the SUV for cover, I took a longer look at the surrounding area. A shudder ran through me as I recognized the carnage scattered across the lawn, leading outward from the house.

Bodies, too many for a quick count, littered the landscape. Not all of them were dead. They moaned, their cries hurting my ears and setting my nerves on edge. Their injuries, the smell of blood, the sight of the dead around them all meant the survivors would be scared and angry. Worse, in some cases they needed to feed to heal.

And I did not want to become the first course of their recovery lunch.

I tapped my earbud again and cursed when the call rolled over to voicemail—again.

"Yousef, it's me again. You need to get out here now. The shit's hit the fan and I need backup. Come armed and armored."

I rang off and thought for a moment. Hopefully Starke wasn't so angry with me that he ignored my message. If he did, we were all well and truly fucked.

Griff, bad trouble at Gemma's. Looks like a war zone here. Dead and dying out front. Haven't made entry yet. Will do so shortly. Need backup and medical assistance. FYI, paras involved, some that should not be this far from the Rift. Come armed and armored.

I hit send and blew out a breath. I considered calling Sele and her sisters. Then, looking around at the carnage littering the lawn, I decided against it. I might feel better having three powerful witches to help if the proverbial shit hit the fan, but I wouldn't do that to them, not before I found Gemma and had a better idea what happened.

Keeping my eyes on the area in front of the house, I backed toward the front porch. When the heel of my right boot hit the first step, I dared a quick glance over my shoulder, making sure no unwanted surprises waited for me on the porch. Relieved to find no bodies, living or dead, waiting for me, I climbed the three steps, walking backward as I did. I wasn't about to turn my back on the wounded predators slowly clawing their way across the lawn in my direction.

Sooner, rather than later, I'd have to deal with them. Many would need to be put down. Some might be saved if they received medical treatment in time.

And assuming they had not been part of the attack on the house, something I doubted. But that was a decision I'd make after I found Gemma.

Please let her be safe.

"Gemma?" I called as I tried the front door.

Locked.

The easy course of action would be to call Sele and her sisters to bring their key. But every instinct screamed that was not the course to take. Trusting my gut, I stepped back. One deep breath and then another. Big mistake. Bile once again rose in my throat and I fought to keep from being sick. Not daring to do that again, I aimed the 1911 at the lock and looked away, shielding my eyes with my left arm. The shot reverberated and some of the creatures behind me shrieked in fear. Too bad. Sorry, but not sorry. If I was lucky, it would keep them away long enough for me to figure out what the hell was going on.

My right foot kicked the door open. Once inside, I slammed the door behind me and looked around. Unlike outside, the inside of the house looked much as it had only yesterday. Well, except for the hole in the door. I grabbed a heavy chair and shoved it in place in front of the door. It wouldn't stop anyone determined to get inside, but it would slow them down. That had to be enough.

"Gemma!"

Standing in the entry hall, I lifted my head and closed my eyes, letting my senses search for her. There was no mistaking the stink of power, energy and sweat, all of which mixed with fear and determination. That was enough to worry me. But at least there was no stink of blood and other things best left unsaid.

Praying that meant Gemma had not been hurt, I moved slowly into the great room. My breath hissed out and fear raced through me, rocking me back. In the center of the room, almost in the exact center of a circle she'd drawn with salt, lay Gemma. Her athame lay near her outstretched left hand. In her right, she grasped her ritual sword. Barely daring to breathe, I approached the circle, thinking hard about how to get to her if the circle was still active.

The energy of the circle sizzled the closer I got. I might be able to cross through, but I doubted it. Gemma's magic was too strong, and I had little doubt she'd put everything she had into the protective circle to keep her attackers out if they got past her outside defenses. Like it or not, it was time to call her nieces.

"Ripley, did you find her? Is she all right?"

"Sele, don't interrupt. Just listen." Not exactly the best way to keep her from worrying, but I didn't have time to be gentle. "I'm at your aunt's. There's trouble here, or at least there was. It looks like a group of paras attacked the house. Gemma managed to keep them outside. The wards on the house held. She also cast a protective circle in the great room. It's still active and I can't get through it to get to her. I need you and your sisters to come see what you can do."

"Aunt Gemma?"

"Unconscious." At least I could see her breathing and I was holding onto that as good news. "I can't tell more than that."

"We're on our way." She held the phone against her as she told her sisters what I said. "We'll be there as soon as we can."

"Sele, listen to me. You need to be careful. The energies out here are unlike anything I've ever seen. There's something going on with the Rift."

"Understood. Watch your back, Ripley. We'll be there soon."

I didn't say goodbye. Instead, I ended the call and then quickly programmed in Rico Cuellar's number. When he picked up on the first ring, I had a feeling Starke already clued him in about my earlier call. Not that I minded. Hell, I'd accept any and all help right now.

"Rico, don't talk. Just listen. We've got a situation out at Gemma's. Looks like dozens of paras. Most of them are the kind the rest of us don't even want to talk about, much less come into contact with. The majority are dead, but some are still alive. Those are badly injured. They're going to need to be assessed. Do you have anyone certified to do it?"

"I am." He sounded as grim as I felt. "Gemma?"

"Unconscious inside her protective circle. I can't get to her. I let Sele know and she and her sisters are on their way."

"Do you see any injuries?" Gone was the worried friend, replaced by the competent professional.

"No." Thankfully.

"All right. I'm on my way. I'll bring a team with me to help contain the situation. Griffin is already on his way."

"Thanks."

My next call was to Razor.

"Griff filled me in, Rip. What can I do to help?" he said the moment he answered.

"It's worse than you know, Razor. Gemma's place is a war zone. I don't know how many paras--and not the good kind--are dead or injured outside her house. She's inside her circle and the girls are on their way to take it down so we can get to her. I don't think she's injured, just over-extended."

"What else?"

Leave it to him to realize there was more to it.

"The energies out here are going insane. I've never seen anything like it." And never wanted to again.

"And?"

"Razor, I can feel the energies trying to tie into me. No one's going to be able to stay here for long. Not until things settle down. All I can be sure about is it's coming from the Rift, and it scares the hell out of me."

"Do you want me to come out?"

I was tempted to say yes, but I needed to know he was not only safe but in town to protect Dani if anything happened there.

"No, but hunker down at your place. Make sure Dani stays with you. Same with Layla. I can't shake the feeling that things are only going to get worse."

"All right."

"Get the grapevine going if it isn't already. The town needs to prepare for trouble. If someone sent these paras after Gemma, it's possible they are also responsible for what happened yesterday. We need to be ready."

"Already done. Griff sent out the word after getting your message."

"Good."

That was good. Hopefully, it would be enough to keep everyone safe.

"Ripley, let me know when you're on your way back."

"I will. Stay safe, my friend."

"I should be telling you that."

I slid the cellphone back into my pocket and moved to crouch at the edge of Gemma's circle. If there was any safe way to get to her, I would. I wanted nothing more than to load her into the SUV and get the hell out of there. But I couldn't. All I could do was stay alert and wait for the others to get here.

I blew out a breath and climbed to my feet. I'd never been one to sit around and wait for the next shoe to drop. Nor did I particularly like the thought of waiting inside as the monsters outside slowly clawed their way across the lawn and up the steps to the house. No, it was time to go have a closer look at who—and what—tried to get to Gemma.

Maybe I'd even figure out what the fuck happened and why.

But first things first. I needed to make sure the house was clear. Then I could focus on whatever waited for me outside.

14

IS THAT A WOLF WITHOUT SHEEP'S CLOTHING?

For a moment, I stood just outside Gemma's protective circle, unsure of my next move. I needed to head back outside to take control of the situation there. As if I really could if any of those downed paras healed enough to decide to make me their next meal. That meant I needed to make sure they understood the folly of that way of thinking. But I also needed to check the house. I was lucky no "surprises" jumped me while I tried to get to Gemma or while I made my calls. If Griffin Starke knew, he'd rightfully read me the riot act for being every kind of fool.

So, I needed to make sure he never found out.

But only after I checked the house.

After checking the chair was still firmly shoved under the door knob, I cleared the ground floor. Then I went up. Call me foolish or accuse me of being afraid of what I might find, but up beat down to the basement. That would come soon enough. But I didn't mind putting it off as long as I could.

Upstairs, I checked each room, making sure to look out each window as I did. Maybe it was my imagination, but some of the fallen paras seemed a little closer to the house. Not good. It also lit a fire under me to hurry up and secure the house. Then I could go outside and deal with the enemy I could see.

Damn it, I wished I could ask Gemma what happened. For all I knew, some of those paras had been trying to help her. But I didn't dare take the risk of trusting any of them until I knew exactly what happened.

After securing the basement doors, one that had been a coal chute once upon a time and the other the door leading into the house, I checked Gemma one last time. She lay where I left her, the protective circle still active and keeping me out. Trusting she'd be safe there, certainly safer than I would be in very short order, I left. I'd put it off long enough. Time to go take a closer look at what was going on outside.

I slipped the chair out from under the door knob and opened the door. The heat that all but slapped me in the face didn't surprise me. Welcome to Texas. But the stench of death hanging in the air caused me to gag, bile clawing its way up my throat. I swallowed hard against it and pulled the door closed behind me. Standing with my back to it, I pulled the Benelli around and cradled it in my hands, fighting the urge to return inside and hide until help arrived.

C'mon, Rip. You can do this.

For a moment, I considered drawing on the abilities inherited from Surtr. Tempting as it might be—after all, most of the creatures I'd seen so far would have a hard time munching down on a walking tower of fire—I didn't know how the magic I now felt crackling in the air would react to that aspect. The last thing any of us needed was for me in the Surtr aspect to go rogue.

For now, I needed to trust my training and my instincts—and pray for more than a touch of good luck until backup arrived.

Eyes scanning the yard in front of me, my head on a swivel, I slowly moved off the porch. Bodies littered the ground, blood and other things best left unsaid turning the green grass dark. Insects, drawn by the blood and gore, buzzed around the ready feast. I watched, noting the bodies they focused on. Those were dead or close enough it no longer mattered. The other bodies needed to be checked and dealt with.

Those were also the bodies that now appeared to be closer to the house than before. That left me with only one choice. Like it or not, I needed a closer look at the fallen paras. Wasn't that going to be fun, especially since I'd already seen enough to give me nightmares for years to come?

Holding the Benelli at the ready, I blew out a breath and took one and then two steps away from the porch. The world narrowed to the pounding of my heart, the feel of the shotgun in my hands, my finger next to the trigger, the groans cutting the unnatural silence of the day.

Who knew Tuesdays could be as bad as Mondays?

Less than ten feet from the porch, six werewolves lay where they'd fallen. If I had to guess, they'd tried protecting the house. That assumption was confirmed by the sight of two redcaps lying nearby, their throats torn out, chests mangled, their short swords bloodied. A dozen or so ghouls lay with them, ripped to pieces by the wolves.

Further out, more creatures lay. How many, I couldn't hazard a guess. Bodies mangled, body parts strewn across the lawn, they looked as if they'd been caught in a blast of some sort. My money was on them having triggered one of Gemma's wards. That was a mistake they'd never make again.

Good for you, Gemma.

Careful where I stepped, I moved further from the house. To my left, movement caught my eye. A scaley figure, its skin dark and knobby, blood pouring from numerous wounds, lumbered to its knees before falling onto another nearby body. At first, it looked as if the first had simply collapsed. Then it reared back, head lifted, mouth open. Blood dripped from teeth meant to rip meat from the bone. Which he —it—had done judging by the flesh dangling from his mouth.

Oh hell no. The last thing I wanted or needed to deal with was an Átahsaia.

I didn't stop to think. I simply acted. Birds took flight, screaming in protest as the shotgun came to life in my hands. The three shells ripped into the Átahsaia, turning its head into pulp. Still acting on instinct, I closed the distance, dropping the Benelli on its strap and pulling my kukri. Putting my body behind the swing, I chopped through the creature's neck, separating what was left of its head from its body.

Ignoring the gore, I turned to the creature it had attacked, a mountain troll the likes I'd only seen in reference materials. Two shots from one of the 1911s to the head and three swings of the kukri finished it off.

And that was just the beginning.

Time lost all meaning as I moved among the fallen. The occasional cry of pain or whimper of fear reminded me I wasn't alone. The fact any of these poor bastards still lived blew my mind. I'd seen enough to guess at least two sides existed in the battle that took place on the lawn. Some had tried to protect the house and Gemma. Others fought to get inside. The implications scared the shit out of me, but I couldn't let it distract me. I needed to help those I could and dispatch those too badly injured to be healed or those who violated Conclave law by leaving the Rift.

Who I really wanted to get my hands on was the witch whose magic I still felt dancing along my skin like the bites of a million stinging ants. Magic that helped these creatures gain access to the property. Someone with the ability to summon a teleportation circle that allowed them to bypass at least some of Gemma's protections and wards.

Someone with magic strong enough it now worked to heal the fallen so they could renew the attack.

But who—or what—had that sort of power?

I sure as hell didn't and I doubted anyone, even Gemma, in this sector did.

C'mon, Rip. Pull up your big girl panties and see if you can find anything out there to answer some of your questions.

There are times, like now, when I really hate that inner voice telling me what to do.

Mouth tight, kukri in one hand and the Benelli in the other—and thank all that is holy for the strap slung across my chest that helped hold it ready—I went back to work.

Check the fallen.

Make sure the dead are really dead.

Dispatch those with little chance to survive.

Do NOT let any of them touch, scratch, bite, or eat you.

Should be simple enough—not.

My life turned into a of blur of blood, chopping and shooting. One part of my mind chattered away in near-hysteria, more concerned about how all the blood and other bodily fluids would be next to impossible to get out of my jeans and how my boots would never be the same. And, damn it, I really loved those boots. Another part, the one guiding kukri and gun to finish off the wounded monsters foolish enough to grab for me, kept telling the chittering to shut the fuck up. Jeans and boots could be replaced but living and breathing couldn't, and I'd really hate to become some flavor of undead.

Worse, I'd hate to become dinner for any of the paras trying to find food to give them the strength to regenerate amputated limbs or lost blood.

While those two parts of my brain went at one another, the rest of me focused on staying alive and making sure none of the wounded made it to the house. I walked slowly through the carnage, chopping here, shooting there, praying I'd be able to put the images of what I did out of my mind sometime in the future so I could be able to sleep.

You can do this, my baby. Head and heart, those are the two targets. Decapitate and stop the heart. Silver and shot. You know what to do.

I stumbled as my mother's voice sounded in my head. I looked around, praying I didn't find her on the field of the fallen. Then the memory of her putting a knife and practice gun in my hands washed over me. I'd been maybe six at the time. We were in the backyard. Dad tended the grill on the back deck while Mom and I "played". I hadn't realized then that she was actually training me to one day become a Hunter.

I blinked against the tears burning my eyes, remembering another lesson.

Never take your eyes off a wounded para. It doesn't matter if they look like you, Ripley. Some of the worst monsters hide their true natures behind innocent faces.

Well, there were no innocent faces here, but there were more injured than I first thought.

I stepped cautiously through the bodies, careful of where I stepped. As I did, I swept the area with the shotgun. Nerves taut, senses on high alert, everything seemed to be hyper-focused. Then a soft groan sounded from my left and the world came to a screeching halt as I swung in its direction, leading with the Benelli, ready to shoot anything that moved. Questions could wait. Living to see another day was at the top of my priority list just now.

There, no more than six feet from where I stood, lay another a werewolf. It was one of the few lone bodies I'd seen. Most of the others lay in groups, almost like small squads working and dying together. But this one was different. Why?

That question and a myriad of others fled as the wolf groaned. Slowly, its head turned in my direction. Blood ran from its mouth and nose. More blood, too much blood from wounds too numerous to count, matted its dark fur. Its sides rose and fell with each quick, shallow breath. Then its yellow eye focused on me and it growled lowly.

Instinct kicked in and I leveled the Bennelli at its head. All it would take is a single pull of the trigger and I'd blow the top of its head off. The kukri would finish the job. But I hesitated. I needed to know what happened here and this poor bastard might be able to tell me.

Besides, I needed to find out if Starke knew the wolf, especially since this one did not appear to have been helping protect Gemma's house.

"Shift back," I ordered, praying it understood me and retained enough strength to do as I said.

The wolf whimpered once, its eye closing for a long moment before opening again. "C-can't."

I stared at the werewolf in shock, my mind racing with disbelief. How could it speak while still in wolf form? That was impossible. But there it was, a broken and battered creature, speaking to me in a weak, rasping voice. Add to that the glimmer of intelligence in the one eye I could see and the nightmare just got worse. This wasn't your run-of-the-mill werewolf. But what it was, I did not know and I sure as hell didn't want to be around when it recovered enough to do more than pant and whine in pain.

It whined again as it slowly stood. Blood poured from its wounds. Its legs shook and it panted as if fighting for one final breath. But its eyes as it turned to fully face me sent a chill of fear down my spine. No longer yellow, they glowed a red as dark and deadly as the blood matting its fur. It bared its teeth and took a staggering step forward.

"You are too late, Hunter," it rasped. "Ker, the bringer of death, is here. You will make a good addition to her army."

The wolf's words froze me for a split-second. I'm not sure what surprised me more: the way it called me Hunter, the term used for the Conclave's enforcers from before the Cataclysm, or that it said I'd make a good addition to this Ker's army. What the hell did that mean?

Think, Ripley. You must know the name. Mom would have taught it to you. Think.

Another memory, more fleeting than the last. Not Mom this time but Dad.

Ker is a necromancer, Ripley. One of the most powerful. Crazy as a bedbug. She thinks she's a death goddess but she's still human, at least as much as you and I are. She can be killed. She's managed to live this long because she's smart, powerful, and paranoid. She doesn't let anyone close to her without having her magical hooks in them. If she ever targets you, don't try to take her on your own.

Great, just fucking great. If the werewolf was right, I had a crazy wannabe death goddess running around my Sector and fucking with my Rift. The Conclave was going to love this.

Assuming I lived long enough to tell them.

Which I planned to do.

That meant I needed to stop standing there, making a nice big target out of myself.

"Bring her on," I said, my voice low and fierce. "I'll be ready for her."

With that, I leveled the Benelli at the wolf's head and fired.

15

HE SHOOK HIMSELF LIKE THE DOG HE WAS

"**A**re you a fucking idiot?" I demanded as I rose from where I'd crouched behind my SUV at the sound of him speeding up the drive. Even as I recognized the SUV, I held the Benelli at the ready. After everything I'd seen and heard the last half hour, I wasn't going to take any chances. "I almost shot you."

Griff climbed out of police issued SUV with the department's logo on the driver's door. His expression went from anger at my greeting to concern as he took in the mud, blood, and other things staining my clothes and boots. The last of his anger disappeared as he turned and looked at the area around us. The color drained from his face and he swallowed hard. How he managed not to shift was beyond me. The sight of so many bodies and the almost overwhelming scent of blood had to call to his wolf. Instead, he looked as if his ears had been pinned back and his tail was tucked between his legs.

Interesting. I'd never seen him like this before.

But that didn't excuse speeding up the drive without flashing lights or sirens. While he might have avoided issuing a "come to dinner" invitation to the other paras in the area, he'd damned near gotten himself killed. He was so very lucky my parents taught me good trigger discipline. Otherwise, I might have blown his fool head off.

Now he stood there, looking like he'd been hit between the eyes with a two-by-four, and I don't mean a metaphorical one.

"Snap out of it, Starke!" When he didn't speak, didn't even move, I lowered the Bennelli and shook him none too gently. "Griffin, look at me. If you can't handle this, get in your SUV and get out of here. I can't let some scared-assed pup distract me right now."

I'll admit, the insult was deliberate, one aimed straight at his were-wolf—and very male—ego.

He shook himself like a dog shaking water from its coat and then scrubbed his hands over his face. When he looked at me, his eyes were haunted. Understanding, I smiled slightly in reassurance and led him to the porch, turning him away from the bodies littering the yard. I wasn't a werewolf. The carnage affected me differently.

Thank God.

Before either of us could say anything else, the sounds of other vehicles speeding up the drive reached us. The first, an ancient silver sedan, drove past Griffin's SUV and skid to a halt at the end of the drive, its front bumper less than two inches from my rear bumper. Without a word, Sele and her sisters climbed out. They took one look around before racing up the steps to the porch. Sele briefly rested a light hand on my arm before they disappeared inside the house.

Good. They'd take care of their aunt.

Assuming they could get through her protective circle.

That left me to deal with Starke and Yousef who parked behind Sele's car. He looked around without a word. Then he leaned back inside the car, straightening a few moments later, shotgun in hand.

Griffin took one last look around before focusing on me. He still looked a little green around the gills. Not that I'd say anything. How could I when I didn't doubt for a moment I looked the same? That didn't matter. What did was the fact he no longer fought his wolf for control. Better yet, he no longer looked whipped.

"What the hell happened here, Rip?"

Gone was the officious, over-confident ass of a werewolf. A man shaken to his core replaced it. Funny thing, I preferred the overly-confident Griffin Starke to this one.

"Did you do this?"

I shook my head. "No. This is what I found when I got here."

He arched one brow and flicked a glance at my bloody jeans and boots. He didn't say anything, but I knew he wanted an explanation. Hell, he deserved one. After all, he responded to my call for help and he didn't have to.

"Talk to me, Rip. Tell me what happened."

I nodded, shifting positions slightly so I could see most of the yard. The last thing I wanted was for one of the bodies to get up and attack again. I learned long ago that dead didn't mean lifeless, not for certain paras. Until the bodies were burned, the appropriate spells cast, and their ashes scattered—preferably far from here—I wouldn't rest easy.

"There's not much to tell, Griff. Sele and her sisters asked me to check on their aunt because they hadn't been able to contact her. When I got here, I found this." I waved a hand at the carnage.

"Gemma?"

"Alive." I hoped. "Inside a protective circle I couldn't break. I called you and the sisters." Among others. "Then I went back outside to make sure there was no further threat to Gemma."

"The blood?" He indicated the dark stains on my boots and jeans.

"I gave mercy to those too badly injured to recover." Something that would forever haunt me.

"Walk me through it, Rip."

I blew out a breath and closed my eyes. I'd give almost anything to avoid having to relieve the last hour. But he needed to know, not only because he was the police chief but also because of his position in the pack. There were werewolves among the dead. If they belonged to the pack, he had some explaining to do. If they didn't, well, the pack might be in trouble from outside. Either way, I couldn't leave him in the dark.

"The scene pretty much tells it all, Griff. But here's my take. Judging from the way the bodies are laid out, there were at least two opposing groups. The group closest to the house was protecting it and Gemma. I recognize some of them. Loners mainly, paras who have never been comfortable around others but who Gemma made feel at home, like family. Some of the others, I don't know. My guess is they stayed closer to the rift because they are not all human in their appearance."

Griff didn't say anything. Instead, he stepped away from the house. I watched as he moved through the nearest dead. His back was turned to me, so I couldn't see his expression. Not that I needed to when he stiffened or when I heard his quick intake of breath. He'd recognized at least one of the fallen. When he turned, his eyes bled to gold as his wolf fought for release.

Praying I wasn't about to make a really bad mistake, I closed the distance between us. Keeping my hands open and out from my side so I presented no danger was one of the most difficult things I've ever done. It wouldn't take much to force him into a shift. If that happened, he could tear me apart before I could defend myself.

"Griff, listen to me." I spoke softly, my voice sounding more confident than I felt. "We need to work together on this. Trust me when I say there's more going on than either of us realized. If you check further out, you're going to find paras we simply don't see in this region. I found at least half a dozen Redcaps. There are other para species as well, some of whom are not supposed to leave their rifts."

"What else?" he growled.

"These aren't the only wolves and it is obvious some of them were part of the attacking force."

His lips peeled back, revealing teeth starting to elongate. Damn it!

"Starke, get hold of yourself!" I snapped, putting as much authority in my voice as I could. At the same time, I called on my own magic, feeling the welcome warmth of flames as they began dancing around my hands. "You need to maintain or get away from here. Do you understand?"

He threw his head back and howled. Then he turned and stalked several feet away. I waited, dousing the flames around my left hand before resting it on the gun at that thigh. If he turned and did not have his wolf under control, I'd put him down. I wouldn't kill him, not unless he forced me, but I would make him hurt and I'd make sure he couldn't shift back, at least not easily. I could risk him doing something foolish until the situation was under control.

"Do you think I had anything to do with this?" He waved a hand toward the fallen bodies without facing me.

"No." I shook my head. He and I might be at odds more often than not, but I knew he was devoted to the town and to Gemma. He'd rather cut off his own arm than hurt the witch. Risking his anger, I moved to stand behind him and rested a hand on his arm. "No, Griff. I know you didn't have anything to do with this. If you'd been here— hell, if you'd know what was happening—you'd be with those who did everything they could to protect Gemma."

He didn't say anything. Instead, he lowered his head. Whether in prayer or something else, I didn't know. Honestly, I didn't care, not as long as he got his emotions under control and his wolf withdrew.

"Griff, I need you to listen to me." Damn it, I didn't have time for this. "You're not going to like what you find further out. There are more wolves. It looks like they were working with the Redcaps and others as they attacked the house. I need to know if you can check them and the other fallen to see if you recognize them. I need your word that you'll let me know if you do and how you happen to know them. Most of all, I need to know if you can help me figure out what happened and make those responsible pay because this is connected to what happened in town. It has to be."

He nodded and turned. Once again, he looked at the blood staining my jeans and boots. His expression troubled, he reached out and placed a finger under my chin, lifting my face so I looked him in the eye.

"Are you all right?"

I gave a slight shrug. "Not really, but I can't worry about that right now. We need to deal with this." Now it was my turn to wave a hand at the fallen bodies. "And we need to see what Gemma or Sele and her sisters can tell us. Whatever's going on, it's escalating. I don't want to think about what might happen next."

He nodded and then frowned. "Where's Yousef?"

Surprised, I glanced around. Not seeing him, I pulled one of the 1911s. Before either of us could do anything else, a shot sounded from behind the house. Well, that explained where he was. He was making sure no danger presented itself from that quarter.

I hoped.

Griff drew a deep breath and then slowly exhaled. As he did, I watched the change come over him. Gone was the man shaken by the scene around us. Gone was the wolf quivering inside him, wanting to hide from the predator responsible for the carnage littering the land around us. In their place stood the confident, cocky man I knew and all too often butted heads with.

Thank God. That was the man the situation needed, especially when he learned the rest of it.

"Are any still alive?"

"Some." Mostly among those who appeared to have been fighting to protect Gemma. "I gave mercy if they were injured too badly to heal themselves."

He didn't need to know I'd done the same with others who might have been able to survive their wounds. Those were the ones who, by leaving the area closest to the Rift, left themselves open to an immediate death sentence under Conclave law. Their magic, not to mention their very natures, made them too dangerous—to humans and to paras —to be allowed out of the area closest to the Rifts. I'd have nightmares about the last few hours, but that would be later. For now, there was still work to do.

"Ripley, what aren't you telling me?"

He waited, his hands shoved in his pockets. Maybe he understood he asked a question I didn't want to answer. Maybe he figured he wasn't going to like the answer. Whatever the reason, he didn't push.

"Nothing really. But you need to see the dead and injured. You need to tell me if you recognize any of them and from where."

He didn't like it, and I didn't blame him. But there was no way to avoid it. He needed to see the werewolves scattered among the other bodies. I'd leave the one I'd spoken with until last. By then, maybe we'd have an idea about what happened and why.

Without another word, I motioned for him to come with me. Together, we walked the area in front of the house. I remained silent, giving him the chance to study the bodies and assess the conditions of the few survivors we came across. Whatever he thought, he kept it to himself.

As I guided him toward first one and then another and yet another fallen werewolf, his expression turned hard. His jaw clenched. He didn't have to tell me he recognized at least some of the dead. Everything about him telegraphed it. His spine stiffened. His jaw firmed. A growl escaped from behind clinched teeth. Anger, frustration, and more than a touch of fear turned the energies around him almost black. To his credit, he held firm control over his wolf.

Most telling of all was the fact he recognized the bodies without them having shifted back into their human forms. Did that mean they were part of his pack? I knew the pack members as humans, but most of their wolf forms were unknown to me. Even as my right hand itched to reach for the gun at my thigh, I stood ready in case the situation blew up in my face.

"H-have." He cleared his throat and tried again. "Have you contacted the Conclave?"

I shook my head. I couldn't delay much longer but I wanted to know what he had to say first.

Then there was that nagging voice in the back of my head reminding me I hadn't received any additional information from Drake about the other attacks he'd mentioned when I first called to let him know about the attack on Red's place. Suspicion built on paranoia that was built on more suspicion kept me from reaching out. Until I knew more about what happened, I'd keep this to myself.

"Not yet." I nodded to the two carcasses a few feet from where we stood. "You recognized them."

It wasn't a question. It couldn't be. I wasn't the girl he'd gone to school with and who had known me all my life. Not right now. Now I was the Conclave's marshal, its enforcer and its hunter of those paranormals who broke our laws.

"I'm not sure." He didn't look at me.

I sighed and shook my head.

"Griff." I reached out and once again rested a hand on his upper arm, turning him so he faced me and not the bodies. "I need to know."

He nodded, but he didn't like it. His eyes flashed angrily, and one hand fisted at his side. Instead of reacting, I waited. I understood how torn he was in that moment. He had a loyalty to his kind. That's something I understood. He also had a loyalty to the oaths he took as a police officer and the loyalty we all felt to Glenham Grove and those living there.

Finally, he huffed out a breath and spun on his heel, stalking several feet away. Then he turned, his face completely devoid of expression.

"You need to let me handle this where they're concerned, Ripley." He ground out the words, his voice dropping almost half an octave as his wolf pushed for release.

Shit. He wasn't going to make this easy, not that I expected him to. We hadn't had an easy relationship since junior high. But this wasn't the two of us doing our best to push the other's buttons. This wasn't him picking on me because he couldn't figure out what I was and, by default in his mind, that put me lower down the predator scale than him. Well, that wasn't going to happen this time, not when we stood in a field of bodies, some of which he recognized.

It was past time for me to shift from someone who might be considered a friend, at least on a good day, to my professional persona—and I didn't mean the bartender everyone knew.

"Chief Starke, I'm not asking."

His brows winged upward in surprise. A moment later, the surprise disappeared. His eyes narrowed and his upper lip lifted into a snarl. Whatever he knew or thought he knew, he didn't plan on sharing it. At least not yet. Like always, he expected information to flow *TO* him and not the other way. Well, that wasn't going to fly. Not after yesterday and sure as hell not when we stood in the middle of a field of bodies today.

"This is pack business, *Marshal*, and will be dealt with as such." He ground the words out.

"This--" I waved at the sea of bodies, at the pitted ground, before looking him square in the eye. "This makes it my business. I suggest you take a step back and take a deep breath and don't make it worse than it already is." I looked him in the eye, something few dared do to one of the pack. "I am not one of your wolves, Starke, and you certainly aren't my alpha. So consider your next words carefully because, where this is concerned, I am the alpha, not you."

"Ripley." My name rumbled deep in his chest.

He stepped toward me, his expression as dark as I'd ever seen. His eyes glowed and I knew his wolf looked out from them. Part of me wanted to back down. It had been years since I pushed him this hard. I learned then how foolish it was to push a werewolf too far. Luckily, Red had been nearby and he stopped our fight before it got out of hand. Now, with the memory of that time fresh in my mind, I considered backing down. Then my own back went up. I wouldn't back down. Not now. Not ever.

"You have no clue who or what you are dealing with, Starke."

Instead of stepping away from him, I stepped forward, all but chest bumping him. His growl turned into a gasp of surprise when he realized I could suddenly look him in the eye. Either he'd shrunk almost half a foot or I'd grown those six inches and he growled again when he realized it was the latter. My eyes glowed golden and my own wolf aspect—a gift that came direct from the Morrigan and not from her servants the werewolves—flooded his senses. Gone was his growling and snarling. In its place, he whimpered once before shaking his head and struggling to regain control of his wolf.

"I told you long ago that you didn't know everything about me, Starke." My voice sounded rougher, deeper than usual. His eyes widened in surprise. "Perhaps one day you will push me far enough to understand that you have spent your entire life underestimating me. You might even earn the lesson that will come that day. For now, we have other matters to deal with. However, you need to understand that you and your kind are not at the top of the food chain. There are paras out there you don't know about, some you do but that you don't know all they are capable of. Then there are those like me who you think you know. The truth is that you don't really know who and what I am."

I stepped back and drew in a deep breath, holding it for a moment before releasing it. "For now, you need to remember this is MY investigation. I want to work with you, but I will not abdicate my duties and responsibilities to you. Now get your head out of your ass and start talking to me or my next call will be to the Conclave. I promise you will not like the action it will take because you failed to cooperate."

He stared at me for a moment, almost as if I'd grown a second head.

"W-what are you?"

I smiled, without humor or affection. It was the smile of a predator before pouncing on its prey.

"You haven't earned the right to ask that question, Starke."

He blinked, surprised by my response.

"Griff, you know every para has reason to protect our secrets. Your pack doesn't tell those outside the pack your secrets. I can guess some of them, but that's because I've grown up around you and because my parents worked with your kind and they believed in making sure I knew what to look for. But I haven't betrayed those secrets and won't, at least not without good cause. Can you say the same? Can you promise your allegiance to the pack won't cause you to betray me and mine?"

"Ripley." He tilted his head back, almost as if praying for patience. "I'm making a mess of this and I apologize. But this is pack business. You need to understand that."

"What I understand is that what happened here, especially in light of what happened in town, goes much further than the pack. Your kind isn't the only para species represented here." I moved away and pointed to a fallen werewolf and then to a fallen elf one I'd never seen before. Nearby lay a partially disarticulated Tsuchigumo. The giant spider-like creature came straight from my nightmares and I considered putting a few rounds through it just to make sure it was dead. "I'll give you a few minutes to pull yourself together and decide how you want to do this. I hope you agree to work with me. We don't have to be at odds on this." I paused and ran a hand over my face, letting him see my frustration. "Griff, we need to work together. If we don't, we risk more than just our friendship. We risk our town and the people we care for."

I turned and stalked off. Yes, stalked. My wolf aspect remained close to the surface and she was very proud of herself for metaphorically swatting the stupid lupine on his nose. She even sent me an image of a rolled-up newspaper that had me snickering in a way I knew Starke would not appreciate. Still chuckling, I pulled my phone and texted Yousef, telling him to finish securing the rear of Gemma's property before reporting back to me.

As I neared the house, Nico Cuellar met me. He cocked his head to one side and arched a brow. That was enough to let me know I was still "more" than I usually am. I sighed and closed my eyes, concentrating on the human aspect of my very screwed up genetics. When he chuckled softly, I opened my eyes and shook my head, my mouth quirking into an amused smile. Then I joined him on the front porch.

"You done scaring the poor wolf?" A smile twitched at the corners of his mouth.

"Hopefully." I prayed it was enough. "What about Gemma?"

"Before we talk about her, let me give you some other information."

I frowned, surprised. Then I nodded.

"I brought Ephraim with me. He's had a *look* at the wards. Said he saw enough out here to be worried about them."

That made two of us. Gemma's wards should have kept everyone but those she approved or keyed the wards to out.

"And?"

"He said it looked like the wards had been overloaded. That means someone as powerful as Gemma attacked them or a group of witches or elementals did. He's done his best to reinforce them but the rest needs to be done by someone keyed to them."

Bile churned in my stomach at the thought of someone as powerful as Gemma moving against my town. "Can he tell me anything about who it might be?"

Cuellar shook his head. "No, but he said Gemma might be able to."

"How is she?" It worried me he was out here instead of inside helping Sele and the others with their aunt.

"Stable. Sele and her sisters brought down the circle and I checked her out. She overextended herself and is going to need to rest and recharge her energies."

"Can I talk to her?"

"Not yet. Give her a couple of hours. Right now, I'm not sure she'd make much sense."

I didn't like it, but I understood. If things were as bad as I feared, I didn't dare do anything that risked her recovery. We were going to need her at her best. The sooner she recovered her strength, the better.

"What else?" He looked worried enough I knew there had to be more.

"Sele's insisting on taking her back to town where she and her sisters can care for her."

"And?"

"She needs to go to the hospital."

"Nico, be honest. Does she need to medically or are you wanting her to just to be safe?"

He shoved a hand through his hair. "Both?" He sighed and leaned against the side of the house. "Ripley, she's overextended herself more than is safe. Yes, she's strong and she's taken good care of herself. Yes, Sele and the others are more than able to make sure she doesn't do anything else to tax her system. But she isn't young any longer. I can't guarantee she won't suffer any complications. Her heart, her brain, there are so many things that could go wrong."

I nodded, understanding. But I also understood why the sisters were adamant about taking their aunt home with them.

"How about a compromise?" I considered various options before continuing. "Let them take Gemma home with them and I'll make sure someone you approve checks on her a couple times a day." I knew several nurse practitioners who might agree and there were always EMTs I could ask.

"All right." He glanced beyond me to the carnage littering the lawn. "She doesn't need to be here while your people deal with this."

Hell, I didn't need to be there, not that I had any choice.

"I'll tell Sele and the others they can take Gemma on. We can set up the rest of it later." He inhaled, almost as if bracing himself. "Then I'd best see if I can do anything to help the survivors."

"Thanks, Nico. I'll check with you before I leave."

For now, I needed to see if Griffin had come to his senses yet. If not, life was going to become even more difficult than it already was.

16

I LOOKED LIKE I WANTED TO COSPLAY

I didn't think the day could get any worse. After all, what could be worse than spending hours moving among the dozens of dead and dying paras, offering mercy to those who had no hope of recovering from their wounds and dispatching those who never should have left their rifts? By the time I was ready to head back into town, all I wanted was a long, hot shower and my bed. Unfortunately, neither would happen any time soon. Someone—probably Layla—had put a go-bag in the SUV, so I had a change of clothing. Dreading the thought of driving back to town covered in blood and worse, I stripped out of my clothes and washed down with the hose outside Gemma's house. I might not be truly clean, but at least most of the gore no longer clung to me. Reminding myself a shower waited once home, I dragged on the spare set of jeans and tee shirt, pulled my boots back on, and headed to the SUV.

Sitting behind the steering wheel, I stared out the windshield, watching as Griffin slowly crossed the yard to his own SUV. His shoulders slumped and his feet dragged against the grass. In that moment, he looked like the weight of the world rested on his shoulders. In a way, it did, by his choice. I'd offered to speak with the pack alpha about what happened. As the Conclave's marshal, it fell within my official duties to do so. But Griff's pride reared up and he said he'd take care of it. I could talk to Lewis later if I wanted. When I tried to argue, he simply waved a hand at the carnage around us and said I had other things to worry about. He was right, but that didn't mean we wouldn't discuss his easy dismissal of my needs as marshal.

I watched as Griff climbed inside his SUV and then tapped my earbud before calling him. I waited, hoping he answered.

"What?" He ground out the word, a sure sign his temper was fraying.

"One quick question before we both get the hell out of here. Have you seen or heard from Yousef recently?"

Silence. I waited, the only thing letting me know he hadn't hung up was the sound of his breathing. Then I heard the faint sounds of his fingers drumming against the steering wheel. I didn't need to see him to know he frowned. Of all the things I could have asked, this probably ranked near the bottom.

"Not for the last several hours. Why?"

I leaned my head against the headrest and blew out a frustrated sigh.

"Something's going on and I don't know what." One thing I did know, I didn't like it. "I called him half an hour ago when I couldn't find him. He wouldn't tell me where he was. All he said was he was following a lead. Then he hung up on me."

To my surprise, Griff didn't laugh to learn someone had the audacity to hang up on me. Instead, he growled deeply. He didn't like this any more than I did. Unfortunately, that did not reassure me. Not that much could right now, short of having the heads of those responsible for what happened raised on pikes outside of town.

I waited, wondering what was going through Griff's mind. I didn't have long to wait. The driver's door opened, and he climbed out of his SUV. I watched as he stalked down the drive to where I waited. I thumbed the control and the driver's side window lowered as he neared.

"He hung up on you?" Griff looked like he couldn't believe it.

I nodded. Instead of saying anything else, he looked down the drive. A number of vehicles still lined it. Some belonged to the police department. But there were also several ambulances and a firetruck. Sele and her sisters left two hours earlier, taking their aunt with them. Nico would remain, along with Griff's chief of detectives, a Berserker who happened to be one of the kindest, most gentle people I knew— until riled.

"Yeah, and he did so before telling me where he was."

That bothered me even more than the fact he hung up on me. How the hell was I supposed to back him up if he ran into trouble?

"When did you notice him gone?"

"About an hour and a half ago." I thought for a moment. "That's not quite right. I'd noticed before, but figured he was around back or on the side of the house and I just didn't see him. Honestly, I was too focused on what needed to be done to keep track of him."

Which had been my mistake. One I didn't plan on repeating.

"His car?"

"Gone." I nodded to the space where he parked earlier.

"Want me to ask my cops to keep an eye out for him?"

I considered for a moment. Then I shook my head. Until I had a better idea what Yousef was up to, I didn't want to tip my hand. Still, I needed to know where he was and what he was doing.

"Is there one of your wolves you trust to look for him and keep their mouths shut?"

For once, Griff didn't take insult at the question. After the day's events, I doubted he even considered doing so. Not when the bodies of more than a dozen lycans littered the area around the house, more than half of which showed signs of being part of the attacking force. He'd assured me more than once that only two or three of those we suspected of attacking the house came from the pack, and two of them hadn't been part of the pack for months. Still, the knowledge rocked him, and I trusted him to make sure whoever he chose to look for Yousef was loyal.

"I'll ask my sister. You know you can trust her."

I should hope so since we were best friends. Instead of saying anything, I gave him a nod. Then, not liking the pain and anger reflected in his dark eyes, I reached through the open window and lightly grasped his arm.

"Griff, don't." I waited until he looked at me, really looked at me and not at the memory of the last six hours. "I know you had nothing to do with what happened—here or in town. I trust you to make sure the pack is loyal—you and Sophie, not the alpha. I also trust you to do everything possible to protect Gemma and the town."

"And Yousef?"

I closed my eyes. I didn't want to doubt Yousef. Not when the Conclave initially sent him here because I hadn't been ready to formally take up the position of Conclave marshal. That decision haunted me now. Could I have prevented what happened at Red's, what happened here, if I hadn't kept refusing the Conclave's offer?

None of which answered Griff's question.

"I don't know, Griff." I hated admitting it, especially since he knew me well enough to understand why I had doubts about Yousef.

"Good." He surprised me by giving a decisive nod. "Something's off with him, Rip. You know it even if you haven't wanted to accept it. Marshals are supposed to become part of the town or region they're assigned to. That's an important part of gaining the trust of those who live there. Yet, he's made no attempt to get to know any of us, even you."

Like it or not, he was right.

I motioned for him to step back so I could get out of the SUV. Once he had, I slid out. For a moment, I said nothing. He waited, giving me the time I needed to gather my thoughts.

"I know," I admitted. "That's one of the reasons why I finally agreed to step up after what happened at Red's. His attitude didn't matter as long as nothing was happening. But I'd be lying if I didn't admit something's felt off about him since the shit hit the fan." I shoved my hands into my pockets, frustration returning.

"Explain."

"You know what it's been like these last couple of days. I doubt you've gotten any more rest than I have."

He gave a nod.

"I also bet your people, your cops and the wolves you trust the most, have been doing everything they can to help."

Another nod.

"I can't say the same where Yousef's concerned. Instead of taking the initiative, he waits for me to tell him what to do. When I do, he doesn't keep me in the loop. I have to ask for an update and then it's like pulling teeth. Maybe he resents the fact he's no longer in charge. I don't know and I don't really care. What I do care about is the fact I can't rely on him, and I don't trust him, not right now."

His expression darkened and a frown tugged at the corners of his mouth. Part of me hoped he told me I was overreacting. I didn't like doubting Yousef, especially since the Conclave sent him. Worse, I didn't like the doubts I felt toward the Conclave, Drake in particular, because of Yousef's actions.

"Trust your gut, Ripley," Griffin said. "If you feel something's off about Yousef, keep him on a short leash and limit what you tell him. There are others you can trust, folks who have your back and who will go to the wall with you. You know that."

He was right. But it was hard not to question my decisions. Hell, it was hard not to question everything and everyone right now.

"Thanks." I smiled slightly. "Tell Sophie I'll check in with her as soon as I can. But it's going to be a while."

"Will do. I'll let you know what Alpha Lewis says."

"Thanks. I'll keep you in the loop as well."

Gee, listen to us. We were acting like responsible adults. That's not how Griff and I dealt with one another. Maybe this really was a nightmare and I'd soon wake up.

I took one last look around before climbing back inside the SUV. Time to get back to work.

Unfortunately, the day's surprises weren't over.

Half an hour later, I pushed open the door to Razor's shop and stepped inside. From where he sat behind the counter, Aras looked up, frowned, and climbed to his feet. A moment later, he slipped past me to lock the door and flip the sign from open to closed.

"Aras?" My eyes narrowed as worry mixed with suspicion.

He frowned once again and then jerked his head toward the rear of the building.

"Trouble," he hissed. "Not sure what, but Razor said to send you back as soon as you arrived."

I closed my eyes and considered making a run for it. I was too tired and too stressed to deal with anything else. But I didn't have the luxury of hiding beneath the covers until the world returned to normal, no matter how tempting it might be. After a deep, bracing breath, I opened my eyes.

"Tell me what you can, Aras."

His lips peeled back, exposing pointed teeth that always sent a shiver down my spine. He opened his mouth and then snapped it shut as he finally took in my appearance. For one of the few times in our acquaintance, he looked worried. Then he turned on his heel and moved to the merchandise case. I watched, unsure what he was up to. A moment later, he shoved a tee shirt sporting the shop's logo and a pair of running pants in my hands.

I guess the hose at Gemma's hadn't been enough, even with a change of clothes, to hide what I'd been up to for much of the day.

"Thanks." I started toward the changing room and then stopped, turning back to the elf. "Dani?"

His expression softened. "She's upstairs. Layla kept her busy today, but she's worried about you and wants to know if there's been any word on Red."

That didn't surprise me. If only I knew what to tell her.

"I shall let her know you're back and will be up as soon as you finish your business with Razor." He turned serious again. "I do not know all that has happened today, Ripley. But Razor is angry, more than I have seen in a very long time, and it goes beyond what happened at Gemma's. You should also know Layla is barely maintaining control. I believe she would have shifted long ago had it not been for Dani and the need to keep her safe and reassured."

I closed my eyes and counted to ten. The last thing we needed was the naga letting her anger take control and shifting. She could lay waste to this part of town in short order and I did not want to have to be the one to deal with her, potentially in a fatal way. Especially since I wasn't sure which of us would survive the encounter.

"If you would wait with Dani, I'd appreciate it, Aras." I considered for a moment. There was something else he could do to help. Hopefully, he agreed. "After I speak with Razor, I need to talk to you about what happened at Gemma's. You may be able to identify some of those involved."

"I will do what I can." He bowed his head, almost as if giving an oath. "You and I might not be what most would call friends, Ripley, but I trust you and I respect you. You have never treated me differently because of who or what I am. But it goes beyond that. Gemma is a friend, as is Red. I will do all I can to help discover who is behind the attacks, I will do it. Just as I will help bring those responsible to justice."

I had a feeling his idea of justice might be different from mine, but I wasn't going to turn aside any offer of help.

"Thanks." I closed the distance between us, stopping two steps in front of him. Holding his gaze, I lifted my right hand to chest level, palm up. Then I bowed over it, lowering my gaze to show I trusted him. A moment later, I looked up. "Aras, there are few I trust as much as I do you, especially where Dani is concerned. You are family."

"You honor me, Ripley. Know I feel the same." He paused and tilted his head to one side, listening. "Change and see what Razor wants. I'll go sit with Dani. Know this, however. She needs to see you to be reassured right now."

I nodded, understanding. I felt the same way.

"I'll be up soon." I stepped away and then looked back at him. "Aras, I'm trusting you to keep Dani safe and to help safeguard everyone here, including Razor. It's important."

"You have my word and my pledge."

I nodded once, knowing better than to reply. A dark elf's pledge, especially this dark elf's, was as close to an irrevocable bond as possible. Those few words meant he would lay down his life to protect Dani and the others. I prayed it never came to that. I'd seen enough death today to last a lifetime. Hell, I'd caused enough it would haunt me until I drew my last breath. I did not want to add his death to the tally.

A few minutes later, my clothes stuffed inside a garbage bag and hidden behind the door until I could reclaim them, I left the room. As I did, I caught sight of my reflection. I didn't know whether to laugh or cry. I looked like a discount store version of a video game character—running pants and tee shirt, my mother's leather jacket thrown over one shoulder, her 1911s strapped to my thighs because I didn't know what else to do with them—I sure as hell didn't want to leave them lying around—and the shotgun in one hand. Oh, and tac boots. Yep, I very definitely looked like I was unsuccessfully trying to do some cosplay.

At least Aras gave me running pants and not a pair of the shorts I knew Razor also sold.

Any humor I felt disappeared the moment I stepped inside what Razor euphemistically called his conference room. It was basically a large room at the rear of the building. Inside were a cafeteria-style table and chairs. A battered coffee maker sat on top of a card table against the far wall. Four very pissed off people appeared to be waiting for me. Razor and Layla stood on one side of the long table and Razor's cousins on the other.

But that wasn't what caught my attention, although it was enough to warn me I'd gone from one trouble spot to another. Even the energies swirling around the room, dark and angry, mixed with fear and something else, barely registered. Not when my attention focused on Layla. She stood there, as close to shifting into her snake form as I'd ever seen without her completing the shift. I took one look at her eyes with their slitted pupils, at the way her neck flared to the sides like a cobra's hood, at the scales forming on her face and hands. If she opened her mouth, I didn't doubt for a minute that she'd have a forked tongue and fangs.

This was so not good, especially not after what I'd seen at Gemma's.

"Someone care to tell me what's going on?"

I stepped further inside and closed the door behind me. Razor and Layla looked ready to kill—or worse. And, yes, there are things worse than death in this post-Cataclysm world of ours. The cousins looked as if they wanted to flee and the only thing keeping them where they were was fear of what their cousin and his wife would do if they tried. Layla might scare the shit out of them, but it was Razor I worried about. Razor, no longer the easygoing tattoo artist, stood with arms crossed and an expression I was glad wasn't aimed at me.

I paused at the head of the table, my gaze sliding over the shaman and the naga before settling on the cousins. Silence dragged out, putting my already frayed nerves on edge.

"Razor?"

Power unlike any I'd felt from him before radiated off of him. His tattoos glowed with magical energy. Some of them seemed to come alive, moving and rippling across his arms and neck. It wouldn't surprise me if several pulled free from his skin and took corporeal shape. Heaven help us if that happened.

What the hell had been going on in my absence?

As I waited for someone to say something, anything, I wished I could turn the clock back forty-eight hours. Maybe then I could make sure the last couple of days didn't happen. But wishes weren't reality, no matter how much we wanted them to be. Now I had something else to deal with. Until I knew what caused the current standoff, I remained at a distinct disadvantage.

Damn it.

"Talk to me people before I start knocking heads together."

"Marshal Walker, these *fools*." Layla all but spat out the word. "Have not been entirely truthful with you or with their cousin. They withheld information that possibly could have helped you stop the attack at Gemma's. Instead of delivering their grandmother's message to their cousin, they chose to hide certain facts from him. Because of that, our town and our people have suffered."

I gritted my teeth, closed my eyes, and counted to ten. My hands fisted at my sides. If they knew something that could have prevented the attack on Red's or at Gemma's they'd never see South America again. If I had my way, they'd never see another day of freedom.

Hell, they wouldn't see another minute of freedom.

"Explain." I ground out the word, not caring if I sounded harsh.

"I spoke with our grandmother before your return, Marshal," Razor said, his voice so deep and dark I inhaled sharply. He was pissed, not that I blamed him. "She sent these two with very specific instructions, instructions they failed to obey."

This just kept getting worse and worse.

"In what capacity did she do so, Shaman?" Since he and Layla were being formal, so would I. Let the cousins see I knew Razor's real title and respected him and his power. "And does she have a request of my office or of the Conclave?"

"She sent them as the bruja of our clan and as an equal of any member of the Conclave." He glared at his cousins before looking back at me. "She instructed them to formally present themselves to you and they failed to do so. Just as they failed to pass along her message to you and to Red."

A spate of Spanish from both cousins all but exploded before I could say anything. Razor's eyes flashed dangerously as he slashed a hand in front, silencing them. Both looked like bullies on the school-yard, doing their best to save face even as their knees knocked and fear gnawed at their bellies because someone dared stand up to them.

"You will keep your mouths shut until Marshal Walker wishes to hear from you and then you will speak only in English."

"Roberto," Carlos whined.

"Silence!" Layla hissed out the sibilants, her cobra aspect becoming more pronounced as she swayed in place.

I glanced at Razor, worried. He simply returned my gaze and gave a slight nod. Hopefully, that meant Layla maintained full control over the naga part that always lay just below the surface. If not, I'd be the first out the door when she lost control. I had no desire to tangle with a supernatural snake bigger than I am.

"Shaman, I wish to hear from you and Madam Issawi before hearing what these two have to say." I pointedly turned my back to the two cousins, insulting them by showing no fear of anything they might attempt. "My only question for now is if they should be confined immediately or if I should wait to hear what is said."

"And I would ask in return if you would take them into custody or if you would turn them over to Chief Starke and the local authorities."

"They would be in my custody." Which meant they would be confined to a special cell in Griffin's jail, one designed to nullify magic and hold shapeshifters in place. Razor knew of the cell, but I was betting the cousins did not. "A necessary move since I don't know what they can do, and I will not put anyone else in danger. It appears these two have caused enough trouble as is."

Razor's cousins hissed in protest but made no other sound as he shot them a quelling look. They glared back but otherwise made no attempt to object. Good. Maybe that meant they'd finally explain what the hell they thought they were doing by disobeying their grandmother.

"Shaman, they are your people, your family. Who do you think should deal with their betrayal?"

Razor's lips twitched and one of the cousins inhaled sharply. The strong scent of fear filled the room. Interesting. Who were they most afraid of and how could I leverage that fear to my benefit?

"Our grandmother. She suffers fools even less than you do, Marshal."

Layla chuckled almost evilly and nodded when I glanced her way.

"Then I will leave them to you. They are not to leave this building. If you feel it necessary, secure them in the holding cell. I will make sure Chief Starke knows you have my authorization to do so." I turned slightly so I could watch the cousins' reaction to what I said next. "Please contact your grandmother and request a teleconference between the three of us. I would discuss this situation with her, not only to learn why she sent these two but also to discuss what has happened both in your homeland and here."

"Of course, Marshal. It would be my pleasure." He cracked his knuckles and his cousins paled even more.

"Until we have dealt with these two and they are on their way back to your grandmother, both you and Madam Issawi are acting as my agents."

"You honor us, Marshal," Layla said. "I assure these two will not leave this room."

"Thank you." I gave a slight smile before sobering once again. "As for you two, you have failed to do as your bruja instructed. You have failed to comply with known Conclave law by not presenting yourself to me upon your arrival in town. You have withheld information that might have prevented the deaths of more than two dozen paras in this region and a great deal of property damage. That alone is enough for me to take you into custody and make sure you are confined for the next decade or two at one of the Conclave's prisons. Count yourself lucky I don't have the time to deal with you personally.

171

"However, you are here illegally. Because you failed to follow your instructions from your bruja and because you violated our laws, I have no choice but to confine you to this room. You may only leave if Razor and his good lady are with you. Do not try to take advantage of their good will. I assure you they will inform me if you cause any trouble or if you try to leave. If you manage to get outside without permission, I won't hesitate to issue a kill order because I will assume at that point you are part of what's been happening here. Do not make the mistake of doubting my word."

"You need not worry, Marshal." Razor's voice rumbled deep in his chest, his anger palpable in the room.

"Shaman?" Worry once again gnawed at the edges of my control.

"Roberto, no. It is family business." Antony fell silent when Layla hissed, showing her fangs.

"It was before you disobeyed our bruja, our abuela. I won't address your foolishness for violating our laws." He turned away from them, his expression cold, anger blazing in his eyes.

"Our grandmother's message might have helped prevent at least this morning's events had these two fools followed her instructions." Razor inhaled deeply and rubbed a hand over his face. "The attack on our family's compound was very similar to what happened to Red's warehouse. Unfortunately, we lost people in the fire before our own elementals were able to get it under control."

I frowned and glared at the cousins where they continued to stand defiantly on the other side of the table.

"What else?"

"My older brother has disappeared. Like Red, he was last seen in the building the attack targeted. His was not one of the bodies found. The last anyone saw of him, he was telling those with him to get to safety while he tried to hold back the flames. That is when my grandmother sent word to Red to be alert. Then she sent my idiot cousins with more information."

Information they kept from us.

"Why would she warn Red and why send these two fools instead of directly contacting me or the Conclave?"

"That I do not know," Razor said. "I will find out."

I chewed my lower lip, thinking hard. We were missing something —I was missing something—and I worried it would bite us in the ass before we figured it out. As marshal, I needed to make sure that didn't happen.

Praying I wasn't about to step in it with Razor and Layla, I decided to make a very point, one neither of the cousins could ignore.

"Shaman, would you please call your grandmother now and find out everything she can tell us? I agree what happened there and here must be connected. I don't want to waste any more time waiting for these two—" I jerked my head in the cousins' direction—"decided to finally give us her message."

"Of course. Perhaps she has new information since they left home."

"Thank you. Lady Layla and I will remain. I believe it is time these two understand how much trouble they've landed themselves in."

Razor's lips rose in a slow, almost evil smile before he nodded once. I watched as he didn't give his cousins so much as a glance before leaning close to Layla and whispering something in her ear. She grinned and a chill ran down my spine. Whatever he said, the naga approved.

That did not bode well for the cousins, especially since I was in no mood to put up with their crap.

"Gentlemen," I said as the door closed behind Razor. "Sit your asses down. Don't move unless we tell you to. Now!"

Layla stepped closer to me and shook her head as they remained standing. "Stupid males." She shook her head as she sneered at them.

I lifted my left hand and inhaled deeply. A moment later, flames danced around my hand and up my arm to the elbow. Pain washed over me and was gone as Surtr added inches to my frame. Not that I let them see the agony of that small transition. I wouldn't show weakness, not to them, now or ever.

"Do you know fear?" I asked, voice rough, flames dancing above my upraised palm.

"They are foolissssh, Marssssshal," Layla hissed, swaying back and forth as she became more reptile than human. "Let me hunt them, teach them mannersss." Her words hissed out and both brothers paled, swallowing hard.

"Not yet." I lifted my left hand and watched, my head tilted to the side, as flames grew from my fingertips to elbow. "Tell me what you know before I let the good Lady Layla have her fun with you. Or perhaps I'll hunt you myself. Your actions are enough to sign your death warrants already."

Sweat pricked out on their foreheads. They looked at one another and started speaking in rapid Spanish, their voices sharp with panic. The stink of it filled the room.

"Quiet!" I thrust out my right arm, almost as if throwing a baseball. Except this time a ball of fire left my hand and smashed against the floor between them. They leapt back, shrinking against the wall. "You are fools. Even if I let you go, what do you think your grandmother will do to you when she learns you failed to do as instructed and that failure cost her son and others she cares for their lives? And what about Roberto? There is a reason he is called Razor. Do you really want to learn why first-hand?"

"Y-you don't scare us," Antony said.

"I should." I gripped the edge of the table and shoved it out of the way. The screeching of its legs as it slid across the floor filled the air. Layla hissed and her neck thickened, broadened as scales replaced skin and hair. "Understand this. What happens next is on you. You have been given opportunity after opportunity to tell us why you came and why you did not do as instructed. Your cousin vouched for you and that is the only reason I didn't arrest you and boot you out of town when we first met. What I do now, I do in my role as the Conclave's marshal.

"Look at me. Do you have any idea what I am or what I can do? You see only one of my aspects. One. Of. Them. I could finish transitioning to this aspect quicker than you realize. How would you deal with a walking, talking, thinking pillar of fire."

For a moment, neither said anything else. Then, with one last look at Layla swaying at my side, they couldn't talk fast enough.

17

MAYBE YOU CAN GO HOME AGAIN

"Yousef, I need an update. Call me as soon as you get this."

I frowned and tapped my earbud, ending the call. Where the hell was he and why wasn't he answering his phone? I hadn't seen or heard from him for hours and part of me worried something might have happened to him. My gut told me otherwise. Whatever he was doing, he did on his own and to piss me off. Something I realized he'd been doing since the day he arrived in town. Not once had he been obviously disrespectful of my role as marshal, but there had been a number of small insults and snubs, all aimed at showing he was more qualified, more experienced, and better suited for the role of senior marshal.

Which, in truth, he was.

But that didn't erase the fact the Conclave asked me to take up the position and I'd finally agreed.

Now I needed to find out what the hell he was up to and I prayed it didn't come back to bite me on the ass.

"Call Griffin Starke." I turned the key in the ignition and carefully pulled away from the curb as I waited for the call to go through. Hopefully, he wouldn't send me to voicemail like Yousef. Of course, he knew how foolish that would be, especially right now. There really were benefits to having known one another as long as we have, even if we spend as much time wanting to beat sense into the other as we do trying to get along.

"Has something else happened?" Concern thickened his voice.

"Razor's cousins might not be directly involved in what happened either at Red's or at Gemma's but their decision not to follow their grandmother's instructions, to tell Razor what's been going on back home, and their basic stupidity added to the problem. I've left them with Razor and Layla and they have twenty-four hours to tell him everything and then get the hell out of town. When I left, Razor was still talking with their grandmother and Layla was half-shifted, standing guard."

Griff growled, not that I blamed him.

"But you're sure they had nothing to do with what's been going on here? Their arrival lines up with them being involved."

"I am." I considered for a moment before continuing. "I made sure they understood how foolish it would be to continue holding out. They are scared of both Razor and Layla. Let's just say they learned how foolish it is to underestimate me. By the time I left, they were begging to tell everything they know."

The growl turned into a chuckle.

"I should probably remind you how a defense attorney would react to what I think you did, but I won't."

"Good, because they won't go through the human courts if they fail to comply with my instructions. I've already informed them their crimes rise to the level where I can issue a death warrant for them."

Griffin said nothing for a moment, then he chuckled softly. "They piss their pants?"

Now I chuckled and wrinkled my nose at the memory. "Let's just say they were begging Layla to ask Razor for some dry clothes."

"I'll touch base with him when I finish up here. What's next for you?"

"I have a stop to make and then I'm tracking down Yousef."

He didn't say anything. He didn't need to. His silence spoke volumes. He no more liked what was going on than I did. He also didn't understand why Yousef suddenly disappeared.

"I talked with Sophie. She said to tell you she'd have some of the wolves looking for him. They know to report to you if they learn anything."

"Thanks, Griff." I stopped at a four-way stop and checked for traffic before turning. "Is there anything on your end I need to know about right now?"

"No. At least not yet. I've let the alpha know we need to talk and am on my way to the compound now. I'll check in with you when I'm done."

"Thanks."

And thank goodness he wasn't going to be a hard ass about it.

"Shall we meet up when I'm done?"

I blinked once and then shook my head, a bemused smile on my lips. Amazing what a crisis could do to make us forget our rivalry and more than our fair share of bad blood.

"Sounds good." Hopefully, one of us would find something useful out. "Call when you're headed this way. I'll meet you at my parents' house."

He didn't say anything for so long I wondered if he'd hung up. Then he coughed softly. For once in our lives, I'd said something he didn't know how to respond to. He knew me well enough to understand I wasn't joking. He also knew me well enough to know this was something I never expected to happen. I hadn't stepped foot in the house since the day Red and the others came to tell me about Mom.

"Ripley, are you all right?" He spoke softly, his worry clear.

"I am. I'll explain when I see you."

I ended the call before he said anything else. If I was a better woman, I'd lay good odds on him contacting his sister. I couldn't worry about that right now.

Five minutes later, I climbed out of the SUV and looked across the broad front lawn at the house I'd grown up in. My feet felt glued to the cement as I stared at the two-story Victorian, the rosebushes in the flowerbed in front of the wide porch, and the well-kept lawn. It looked almost exactly like it had the day Red and the others came to tell me about Mom.

My breath hitched and I forced one foot in front of the other, slowly walking toward the house. Memories of that washed over me. That day, I stood on the porch running the length of the front of the house, watching Red lock up. My backpack was slung over one shoulder and a duffle rested on the porch at my feet. The others stood back, giving the two of us some privacy as Red promised to take care of me until we found Mom. Little did either of us know it would be the last time I stepped foot in the house in years.

But he'd kept his word, even though I didn't doubt there were times when he wished he hadn't taken me in. I wasn't easy to deal with those first few weeks and months. But he stuck with it, and he believed in me and in keeping his word to my parents. Now I needed to do the same.

I needed to find Red and make sure he knew how much I appreciated all he'd done for me.

But first I needed to go inside, check out the house and see if Razor was right to suggest basing out of here until I got to the bottom of what happened.

I pushed open the gate in the short stone wall that lay just beyond the sidewalk and stepped through. The lawn was well-cared for as were my mother's flowerbeds. Memory of her spending happy hours working in the beds, telling me how important it was that we helped things grow in the Zone and brought some beauty into the chaos that followed the Cataclysm, washed over me. Tears burned my eyes and I swallowed hard against the emotion tightening my chest.

I could do this.

I needed to do this.

My hands shook as I climbed the three steps to the front porch and approached the door. The keys Razor gave me earlier slid effortlessly into the locks and the door swung open almost on its own. For a moment I stood on the threshold, steeling myself to take the next step. When I did, I'd be stepping back in time even as I took a step forward.

There was no smell of disuse or mustiness one would expect when entering a house that hadn't been lived in for more than a decade. Instead, the faint smells of lemon oil and something else I couldn't immediately identify filled the air. The entryway looked much as it had the terrible day I learned Mom disappeared. Someone had picked up the shoes I'd kicked off the day before. They'd also done something with the jackets that hung on the hooks just inside the door.

What else had they done and was I ready to see?

You can do this, Rip.

I moved further inside. Emotions continued to wash over me and with them came memories of good times with my parents. If I closed my eyes, for a moment it was as if these last years without them hadn't happened. This was still the house I grew up in. It might be a little tidier than the day I left, but it was home.

Home.

My eyes burned with unshed tears and the fingers of my right hand traced across the top of the table near the door with the basket where my parents always left their keys. Part of me halfway expected to smell an apple pie baking in the kitchen at the rear of the house or hear my mother singing as she cleaned. She might have been one of the Conclave's best marshals, but she was also a homebody. She loved spending time here and doing things for Dad and me.

I missed her so much.

I reached up and dashed away a single tear and sniffled. Then I screwed up my courage and stepped further inside. Ready or not, I needed to look around, decide if I could stay here and, if so, what I needed to make the place livable for the immediate future.

I walked through the first floor, my fingers trailing across tabletops and the backs of chairs. In the kitchen, I paused and shook my head. It seemed Razor had done more than just magic the contents of Red's safe room here—and I needed to find where he'd stashed them. The pantry and refrigerator were stocked with my favorite foods as well as a few healthy options. He—or more likely Layla—even laid in a supply of my favorite coffee, beer, and wine.

Because it had to be after five somewhere in the world, not to mention the fact I really needed it, I grabbed a beer and headed upstairs. My bedroom looked exactly as I remembered, with the exception that someone had made the bed and tidied up some. Mom's room, with the familiar furniture and the family photos, did me in. I sank onto the edge of her bed and cried. I cried like I hadn't since learning she was missing. I cried until my nose was plugged and my chest hurt.

God, I missed her.

I'd give anything to have her here today, to let her know how I'd done everything I could to become a woman she'd be proud of. To have her brain to pick about what was going on because I sure as hell was in over my head.

I left the room, closing the door behind me, and fished my phone out of my hip pocket. A moment later, I waited for Razor to pick up.

"Well?" I asked without introduction.

"They will be gone come morning. My grandmother is even less amused by their actions than we are, my friend. Trust me, they will be in the literal doghouse when they get home."

I nodded even though he couldn't see me. He also confirmed my suspicion that the cousins were shifters, probably weres, and not strong enough to be trusted with more than errands for their grandmother and their pack.

"Be sure to tell your grandmother I send my thanks and that I will do whatever I can to help with the problems there once I get a handle on what's happening here."

"I will and she sent you much the same message." He gave me a moment before continuing. "Where are you now, my friend?"

"At the house." Which he probably already knew. I didn't doubt for a minute that he had his own wards on the house, wards that would have warned him the moment I stepped onto the property. "I take it I owe you and Layla for stocking the kitchen."

"Layla," he said. "I was dealing with my idiot cousins."

"And the things from Red's safe room?"

"In the basement. You should have no trouble finding where they are. But, should you need help, call."

"Thanks. What else did your grandmother say?"

"It is best we have this conversation in person, Ripley. The situation back home is much like what we have seen here. She is sending me additional information, including some video of the attack on the compound, in case it helps."

"And Red?"

"It seems the two of them have been discussing shared concerns for some time now. That is something else she is supposed to send information on."

"All right." I didn't like waiting, but he was right. This was a discussion best done face-to-face. "Anything else I need to know?"

"No, my friend. We are safe here. Layla and Aras are with Dani. My cousins are confined in the basement where they will stay until Aras and I take them to the airport. I've already arranged for room in the hold for them."

My brows winged upward. "The hold?"

"It is more than they deserve, but it will be pressurized. I will not pay for two tickets inside the cabin for those curs." He spat out the last word. "They have shifted and are caged like the dogs they are. They will remain in this form until our grandmother decides what to do with them."

I blew out a breath, glad I hadn't made the woman mad. To be powerful enough to enforce a shift over any length of time was beyond anyone I knew except, perhaps, Gemma. The thought of two witches— or witch and bruja—with that much power sent a chill down my spine. Thank goodness they were on our side.

Here's hoping to them staying that way.

"All right. I'm going to finish up here and then I need to talk with Sophie and try to track down Yousef."

Razor hissed out a breath, stopping me from saying anything else. His reaction surprised me. Wondering at it, I made my way downstairs to the first floor. I'd been too focused on being back home for the first time in so long, I hadn't locked up behind me. I wanted to correct that oversight before heading down to the basement.

"Razor?"

"I am sorry, my friend. This is another conversation to be had once you return here. Perhaps I am simply on edge after talking with my grandmother. But do me a favor. Watch yourself and watch your back. There is more to what's going on than we understand right now."

That had to be the understatement of the year, perhaps of the decade.

"All right. I'll be back as soon as I can."

"Be careful, Ripley." Before I could respond, he muffled the phone.

The soft murmur of voices came through, but I couldn't make out the words. "My apologies. Layla said to tell you to check in once an hour. Otherwise, she will come looking for you."

I rolled my eyes. Serious as the situation was, Layla on the hunt would only make things worse.

"Is she still mid-shift?"

"No. She didn't want to worry Dani."

That, at least, was good news.

"Tell her not to worry." God knows, I was doing enough worrying for all of us. "I need to get going Razor. I'll be here a little longer. Then I'm going straight to Sophie's office. If anything changes, I'll let you know."

We said our goodbyes and I slid the phone back in my hip pocket. Time to find the things from Red's.

Standing at the foot of the basement stairs a few minutes later, I shook my head. The basement was much larger than I remembered. Mom's and Dad's safe room was still there, the seals Mom put in place the day she left still active as were those Red added at the request of the Conclave. But beyond the small storage area and the safe room was another area, finished out but unfurnished. At the far end was a wall I knew hadn't been there before. In the center of the wall was an innocuous door and I had no doubt it could withstand anything short of a direct missile strike.

Hell, who am I kidding? Knowing Razor, it could withstand even that.

I cocked one eyebrow when the door slid open almost silently as I approached. Razor must have attuned to me. I'd need to ask him to add some additional safeguards. But that could wait. I needed to take a look at what was here.

Feeling like a cross between a kid about to be let loose in a candy store and a criminal soon to face a firing squad, I stepped inside, wondering what I'd find and if there'd be anything that might help explain where Red had disappeared to or what happened at the warehouse.

18

YOU WON'T LIKE IT IF YOU MAKE
HIS SISTER MAD

An hour later, I stepped outside. Much as I wanted to spend more time going through Red's files or revisiting memories of my past in the house, I didn't. I had too much to do. Not that it stopped me from taking a quick look at everything Razor magicked to the house. Nor did it stop me from grabbing a quick, and very much needed, shower. I made a mental note to thank Layla for making sure I had clothes to change into. I'd bring more of my things from my apartment later. For now, I had a great deal to do and the sinking feeling I didn't have much time in which to do it.

But that wouldn't stop me from returning tonight.

For the first time in more than a decade, I'd sleep in my own bed in my own room.

I knew she wouldn't like it, but Dani would stay with Razor and Layla until the danger was over. In the meantime, I needed to talk with Sele and her sisters about reinforcing the wards on the house. I didn't doubt Razor planned on adding his own protections.

Thank goodness.

"You are screwing up her schedule—again," the blonde sitting behind the desk opposite the door said as I stepped inside the law offices of Starke and Starke.

In this case, the Starkes were mother and daughter, Griffin's mother and sister. The blonde happened to be a cousin and member of the pack. We had a long history, one going back to grade school. One where Callie Kunhardt joined other pups from the pack in tormenting me. Even back then, Sophie stood up for me. More than once she pinned her cousin's ears back, figuratively and literally on at least one occasion. Even now, Callie continued trying to prove her dominance over me.

Perhaps today was the day to teach her the error of her ways.

"Enough, Callie!"

The blonde hunched her shoulders. On the desktop, her hands fisted. I smiled slightly, nodding at the tall redhead standing in the doorway. Sophie Starke's green eyes flashed in anger as she stared at the receptionist and then she turned her attention to me. Before I could say anything, she held up a hand, stopping me. Then she stepped further into the reception area, making sure the blonde not only knew she was there but also looked at her.

"Both my mother and I have warned you about your attitude, Callie. The only reason you still work here is because you promised to improve your attitude. Whether you want to admit it or not, there are those both inside the pack and out of it you should show submission to. The marshal is one of them. You will apologize and you will not try to fuck with her ever again. Not if you want to continue working here."

Callie lifted her head. Her lips peeled back, baring her teeth. Before she managed to say anything, Sophie acted. She closed the distance between them. Her right hand closed around Callie's throat, lifting her to her feet. Leaning in, Sophie growled long and low.

"You have no other choices," she drawled.

"I will speak with the alpha about this."

Sophie threw her head back and laughed before releasing her hold on Callie, letting her drop back onto her chair. "Do it and see how far that gets you." She shook her head, her red hair brushing her shoulders. "Or do you want to meet me at the next pack meeting to prove which of us is stronger?"

I almost winced. There were no females in the pack who could best her in a fight, fair or not. I doubted there were more than one or two males who could, her brother being one of them. The only question was if Callie's ego would let her back down.

"You're still too proud for your own good, Callie." I sighed. Nothing had changed since middle school. "I guess you didn't learn your lesson then. Obviously, you need to learn one now. Tell you what. I'll discuss the matter with the alpha and set up a time when the two of us can meet on the field and settle this once and for all. I'll even agree that you can fight in your shifted form."

Her eyes glittered in excitement. Fool. Did she still believe I was only human, even after the events of the last few days?

"But, if you do, I will be allowed to call on any of my special talents."

She paled sightly and Sophie chuckled almost evilly.

"I'd think very hard before answering the marshal, Callie. Just because she never used her abilities on you when we were kids, don't make the mistake that she can't wipe the floors with both of us—assuming I ever did anything to piss her off enough to fight me."

Silence fell and we waited, watching the blonde weight her options. Because she needed a push, I lifted my left hand and repeated my performance from earlier at Razor's. Flames slowly enveloped that hand, dancing in the air above my upraised palm. Then the flames moved up my arm, stopping just before reaching my sleeve. More color drained from Callie's face, and she swallowed hard.

And we waited.

"I apologize."

She didn't spit out the words, but I didn't doubt she wanted to. Instead of calling her on it, I nodded once. Then I turned my attention to Sophie. We'd already wasted too much time on her and her foolishness.

"Bring us some coffee, Callie. Then you may leave for the day. Use this time off to reconsider your priorities. I expect you to explain to me in the morning why my mother and I should continue employing you."

Sophie turned on her heel and all but marched to the door leading to the inner area of the office. She paused, holding the door, until I stepped past her. then she cursed softly and let the door close behind us.

"Sorry about that. She's never figured out it's past time to grow up."

"Don't worry about it. She was right in a way. I am messing up your schedule."

"I don't mind." She smiled and motioned me to one of the leather wingback chairs in front of her desk. "I mean it, Rip. You never ask for favors. So when you text and say we need to talk in the middle of a business day, I know it's serious."

I nodded. "It is and I'm worried it is going to get worse before it gets better."

She settled on the chair next to mine and turned to face me, her expression serious. "What can I do to help?"

Before I could answer, a soft tap sounded at the door. Sophie raised a finger to make sure I knew to say nothing else. Then she called for Callie to enter. We waited in silence as she placed two mugs of coffee on the desk in front of us. Insolently, she turned to leave without saying a word. Sophie rolled her eyes and silently climbed to her feet. I leaned back, crossing my legs, wondering how she planned to deal with this latest insult from our former classmate.

It never failed to impress me how fast a werewolf could move, even in their human form. One moment, Sophie stood in front of her chair. Then next found her standing between Callie and the door. Feet shoulder width apart, arms loose at her sides, she bladed her body, ready for however Callie might respond.

Great. The last thing I needed was a fight for dominance between these two right now. Normally, I'd pay to watch Sophie wipe the floor with Callie. But I didn't have time for it.

Sighing, I shoved to my feet and hurried to Sophie's side. As I did, I dug my badge and ID out of my pocket, flipping the leather case open before holding it up so Callie could see. Then I placed a hand on Sophie's arm, a single jerk of my head indicating that I had this.

"This is your only warning from me, Callista."

Her nostrils flared and anger sparked in her blue eyes at the use of her full name. A name I knew she hated.

"Your behavior since my arrival has been questionable, to say the least. You have disrespected me and my office. You have also disrespected someone higher in the pack than yourself. Someone we both know can not only beat you in a fight, fair or not, without breaking a sweat. Someone who could bring your disrespect to the attention of the pack alpha with a request that he deal with it. If she should do so, I will support her claims and, as marshal, my word has influence, even with the pack."

Callie flushed and, for a moment, she looked ready to shift and attack. Then she looked, really looked, at us. Her gaze dropped to my hands, no doubt checking to see if I'd called fire yet. Then she dipped her head slightly, not a show of respect and certainly not of submission. More like a promise that she knew better than to start something she couldn't finish.

Not that she wouldn't do just that later, probably when Sophie or I were alone.

"My apologies."

Sophie relaxed slightly and motioned her out. As she followed Callie to the door, I returned to my chair, trusting her to make sure the blonde left the building.

"Well, that was fun." Sophie grinned as she returned to her seat a few minutes later.

"Your idea of fun is as strange as ever, Soph."

"What can I say? I'm a wolf, remember."

I shook my head and leaned forward to reach one of the two mugs on the desktop. I held it under my nose and sniffed. Who knew what little "additives" Callie might have slipped into the coffee. I doubted she'd try to poison either of us, but after the last couple of days, I wasn't taking chances.

"Now that's out of the way, what can I do to help the Conclave's marshal?" Sophie asked.

Even though I planned to be as open and honest with her as I could, I didn't answer right away. I wanted to protect her because she'd be as upset by what happened this morning as her brother. I only hoped she'd be more open with me.

"I assume you've talked to your brother, Soph. Did he tell you what happened at Gemma's?"

Her mouth tightened and she nodded once.

"How much did he tell you?"

"Not a lot. He said it looked like a war took place in her front yard and you found Gemma inside her protective circle. It took Sele and the others to get through the circle to get to her. Said he'd explain the rest of it later when he saw me."

"That's the bare gist of it." I pulled my phone from my back pocket and rested it on my thigh. "The condensed version is I went to Gemma's because Sele and her sisters were worried because they couldn't get in touch with her. After everything that's happened, they asked if I'd check on her. Since I needed to talk to her anyway, I did. Unfortunately, I didn't get there soon enough to make a difference."

"Ripley, you're worrying me now."

"Good, because I'm scared shitless right now. Things are going on I don't understand and I'm terrified I'm not going to be able to stop it."

"Tell me."

"All right, but first, I need you to understand I'm here as the marshal but also as your friend. I need your help, Sophie. You have not only your brother's ear where the pack is concerned but also the alpha's. Hopefully, you know me well enough to know I would never ask you to break their confidence without good reason. Remember that when I ask the hard questions."

She stiffened slightly, not that I blamed her. She owed loyalty to the pack, first and foremost, under pack law. But this went beyond the pack and could mean all of our lives or deaths if I didn't play this right.

"When I got there, I found the yard and the field beyond it littered with bodies. Your brother was right when he said it looked like a battle had been fought there. It was bad. Dead and dying all over. Parts of the yard looked like bombs had gone off. There was enough blood and other things to make even your brother look away when he got there.

"I made my way inside the house to look for Gemma and found

her there, inside her circle. She lay on the floor, unresponsive. I couldn't get in, so I sent for help: your brother, Yousef, Sele and her sisters, some others as well. Then I cleared the house, making sure no threats remained inside before I went out to see what I could find out."

She listened silently as I described moving among the bodies, helping those I could and giving release to others. She paled to learn of the different para species involved. When it came to telling her about the wolves, I paused. I needed to do this, but how did I tell my best friend that she might know some of those who broke our laws and lost their lives in the process?

"Sophie, I wish I didn't have to tell you—"

"Werewolves were involved." She spoke softly, her voice flat and emotionless.

I nodded and lifted my phone in one hand. I opened the folder containing the pictures I'd taken at Gemma's. For a moment, I hesitated. Then I gathered my courage and handed the phone to Sophie. I didn't say anything. Instead I waited as she thumbed through the images, the color draining from her face even as her anger at what she saw grew.

"Rip." She paused and cleared her throat before trying again. "Dear God, Ripley. This is our worst nightmare come to life."

"Yeah." I reclaimed my phone and found the picture I wanted to ask about. "Do you know him?"

"Him" was the wolf who threatened me with Ker.

She shook her head before handing back the phone. I took it without a word and found a series of photos I wanted to ask her about. Then I leaned forward, elbows on knees and chin on fists. Time to ask the hard questions.

"Sophie, the questions I'm about to ask, I'm asking as marshal and I really wish I didn't have to. One thing my parents taught me was to stay out of pack business unless it started violating Conclave law. I only know of one time they had to go to the alpha because of something a pack member did. I've been happy to stay out of pack business because the alpha and your brother kept your wolves under control."

"But that's changed after what happened at Gemma's," she said.

I nodded, grateful she seemed to understand.

"I'd like you to look at these photos again and tell me if you recognize any of them."

I handed back the phone and watched as she swiped through the pictures of the werewolves, those still shifted and the very few who had shifted back before dying. For the most part, her expression never changed. That reassured me because it meant she didn't recognize them. Then, as she neared the last of the photos, her expression changed from neutral to shocked followed by cold fury.

"Soph?"

She closed her eyes and I waited as she fought for control. Her featured blurred, wolf to human to wolf and back again. Leather creaked under her grip has her fingernails morphed into claws, piercing the leather, shredding it as she clutched at the chair arms as if they could stop her shift. When she looked at me, her eyes turned more gold than green. I remained motionless in my chair. Anything could force her to complete the shift and I really didn't want to have to fight her.

Not today.

Hell, not any day.

It was over as quickly as it started. She slumped against the back of the chair, her chin dropping almost to her chest. She drew in a shaky breath before scrubbing her face with her hands. When she looked at me, fear reflected out of her eyes.

"Ripley."

"Stop." I shook my head even as I reached over and placed a hand on her arm. "You have nothing to apologize for and I don't blame you for your reaction. I did much the same in my own way. Besides, I need to know what upset you enough to almost force you to shift."

"I need to say this first, Rip." She held up a hand to stop anything I might have said. "I appreciate the way you and your family have always treated the pack with respect and have not tried to interfere in our business. So does my brother, even if he is too hardheaded to admit it most of the time. But this." She indicated the photos on my phone. "*This* changes things. You don't have a choice but to ask the hard questions. More than the interests of the pack are involved."

I nodded.

"So, yes, I recognize some of the wolves."

She turned her attention back to the photos, swiping through them until she found the one she wanted. The first showed a wolf laying near the front porch steps. His tawny-colored coat stained red from too many wounds to count. Blood framed his mouth, a testament to how he'd died fighting. His position between the porch and another group of wolves told me he'd died trying to protect Gemma.

"That's Tommy Baldwin." Her breath shuddered and her eyes shone with unshed tears. "Nineteen years old. His parents were killed in a car crash about five years ago and the pack fostered him. He was a good kid, going to college, doing anything he could to help around the compound. He had the potential of being an excellent second to a strong alpha when he got older."

She wiped her eyes and then looked at me, anger replacing the sorrow, at least for the moment. "Who did this to him?"

"I don't know for sure, Soph." Now it was my turn to stop her from interrupting. "I don't, but I can make a guess that they paid dearly for it. He gave his life protecting Gemma. That's what that picture tells me. Just as it tells me he stood against three other wolves and a redcap. He honored your pack and our town with his sacrifice."

One I planned to avenge.

"Who else did you recognize?"

"Two of the three wolves who fought him. They used to be pack, but they left a year or more ago. Before you ask, I don't know where they went or the full story about why they left. Trust me, I plan to find out and I will let you know what I learn."

"Thanks." Silence settled around us for a moment as we both tried to make sense of what happened that morning. "Sophie, did you recognize anyone else?"

She shook her head. "It's harder with them in wolf form, Ripley. If I could see them in person, get their scents, I might be able to tell you more. But like this, wounded, covered in blood and more, I can't see the distinguishing features we all have. At least not enough to ID them."

"I understand." Even if I didn't like it. Just as I didn't like what I had to ask next. "Soph, is there trouble in the pack?"

"Ripley."

"I wouldn't ask if I didn't have to."

"I know." She leaned forward and stared at her hands where they hung between her knees. "I need your word that what I'm about to say stays between us."

"I can't, Sophie, and you know it. But I will promise not to say anything to the Conclave unless I absolutely have to. I don't want to cause your pack trouble. But I have to do whatever it takes to protect the town, all of it, including the pack."

"Thanks." She climbed to her feet and moved to stare out the window. Without turning, she began to speak. "There have been a few incidents that concern me: rumblings of discontent among some of the pack members, that sort of thing. Nothing that becomes overt rebellion against the alpha, but enough to make things uncomfortable right now. Up until now, all that the alpha has done is scold those involved and hand down a slap or two in pack meetings."

"But?"

"My gut tells me it goes deeper than that. I've spoken with the alpha, but he isn't convinced there's anything to worry about. I don't agree. There is a part of the pack who wants to see someone else as alpha, someone who isn't as concerned about obeying Conclave law."

I frowned, not liking what I heard. Like Niko Cuellar, Sophie possessed certain empathic abilities. That made her special among werewolves who rarely had a second talent. The two combined made her a powerful ally. I most definitely did not want to find out what she'd be as an enemy. If she said the pack was unsettled, I needed to look closer. It might have nothing to do with everything that happened the last few days, but I had to be sure.

"Have any of the pack actually challenged the alpha?"

"If you challenge to a fight for dominance, no. However, there have been at least two attempts that I know of to try to call for a vote. Both failed by solid margins. But it's enough to start causing others in the pack to question how things are being done—whether it is how the alpha runs things or because he didn't take the challenge straight to a fight to put the idiots in their place."

Damn all of them. Alpha Lewis needed to take the pack in hand. If that meant dealing with those challenging him, he should do so. The last thing we needed was the pack being unsettled and the town getting caught in the middle of a battle between werewolves.

As for Griff, he should have told me even if the alpha didn't. As the town's police chief, he swore oaths that went beyond loyalty to the pack. I needed to have a serious talk with both of them.

Something I did not look forward to.

Damn both of them. I did not need this on top of everything else.

Frowning, trying to rein in the frustration and anger boiling up inside me, I punched the wall next to the window. To my surprise, the sheetrock buckled, the plaster shattering. Beside me, Sophie hissed out a breath. Surprised, I turned my head to look at her. She paled, much as her brother had earlier. But this time I didn't have clue one about why.

She stared and shook her head as she looked me up and down. As she did, I could smell her confusion, an almost mischievous humor, and worry. What she said next surprised me.

"Griff told me about your little show of power at Gemma's. I'll admit, I didn't believe him." She actually grinned. "After all, I've known you all my life and you've never done anything close to what he described. At least not that I knew. Now it seems I owe my brother an apology."

Frowning, unsure what she was talking about, I cocked my head and looked down at her.

Down when normally I looked her in the eye.

My stomach did a slow roll and I cursed softly. Morrigan was playing games again. Wasn't it enough that I had to deal with being one of Surtr's descendants? Now I had Morrigan making sure I remembered her claim to my bloodline.

"You've been keeping secrets, more than I suspected." She smiled again, this time in understanding. "I don't blame you. As marshal, you need to keep your talents as much to yourself as possible. Doing so could save your life or the lives of others. Just as I don't advertise my ability empathic abilities. But, damn, girl, you're better at hiding what you are than I ever expected. Not once did I suspect you are one of

Morrigan's and, unless I'm badly mistaken, you are one of her true children, unlike those of us she made.

"But this does change things, at least where the pack's concerned. You could stop all the crap going on within it by simply establishing your dominance over all of us. Something I don't doubt you'd easily do, at least if you're half as powerful as I suspect."

"Sophie, no." I shook my head and concentrated on returning to my normal height and build. "I'll admit that it's tempting. I don't want to worry about the pack right now, not with everything else that's happening. I also don't want to have to explain to the Conclave why I interfered in pack business."

Her eyes widened and she gasped softly. "They don't know."

"They don't and I'd prefer to keep it that way."

She said nothing for a moment. Then she grinned like a kid in a candy store.

"I won't say anything, promise." She held out her pinky, waiting until I wrapped mine with hers, much as we had as kids making a promise to one another. "Now tell me what I can do to help right now."

"Talk to your brother, make sure he's all right. What we dealt with this morning shook him. I suspect he knows, or at least thinks he knows, more about those involved than he let on." I continued before she could interrupt. "Soph, I don't think he's trying to keep me out of this. Nor do I think he's involved in what happened. But he's the pack's second. He takes those responsibilities seriously, as he should. Seeing wolves he knows, wolves he's lived with and hunted with, among the dead and knowing some of them at least were part of the attackers, threw him. I want to make sure he doesn't try to deal with others on his own."

"I'll talk to him."

"Thanks." I thought for a moment. "I'd also appreciate it if you and mother checked with your sources, and I don't care how legal they might be, to see if you can find out anything. See if anyone's been trying to buy up property in and around Red's warehouse. Same with Gemma's place. Check with other packs near the North American rifts to see if they're having problems as well. What happened at Red's wasn't an isolate incident."

"I'll brief Mom as soon as she gets back from court."

"Thanks. Let's touch base this evening. Maybe one of us will have some news by then."

I left her office a few minutes later with more questions than answers and that was really starting to really piss me off.

19

HARD QUESTIONS AND HARDER ANSWERS

I slid in behind the wheel as my cellphone sounded. A quick glance had me shaking my head at the name displayed on the screen. Griffin Starke. It didn't surprise me. No doubt Sophie called him the moment I left the office. As I decided whether to answer or not, two things dawned on me. First, it didn't surprise me one bit Sophie called her brother right away. The fact I worried about him was enough to make her do it. Besides, after seeing the photos from Gemma's she'd want to check on him and there'd be no way to avoid telling him we'd spoken. Second, I was glad. Her talking to him and letting him know how worried we both were made it easier all the way around, especially since I wanted to talk to him before doing anything else.

"We need to talk," I said in lieu of a greeting.

"I think that's supposed to be my line."

I relaxed some to hear a hint of humor in his voice. "Seriously, Griff, we need to talk. Can you meet me now?"

"I need ten to fifteen, but then I'm free."

"Thanks. How about meeting at Three Sisters?"

"Sounds good, Rip. See you then."

He ended the call and I sat there. Part of me wondered if I'd fallen into an alternate universe. Another part simply accepted that Hell had frozen over and for the first time since we were kids, we were getting along. Who knows? Maybe all the crap going down would bring about a better relationship between the two of us. Not that it mattered as long as we weren't at one another's throats until we figured out what was going on and where Red was.

I sent Sele a text, asking if we could use the café's private room. The last thing I wanted was someone overhearing our conversation. I barely sent off the text before she responded, telling me the room was mine to use whenever I needed it. She and her sisters discussed it earlier and they all agreed to keep it open for me. All I needed to do was call ahead and they'd have coffee and food ready for us. I sent a quick thank you and a promise to explain when I got there. Hopefully, my conversation with Griff would go as well.

Hell, I'd be happy if it didn't end up with us coming to blows, something we'd done on more than one occasion.

Griff waited for me outside the café when I arrived. His appearance surprised me. He looked pale and dark shadows bruised the skin under his eyes. He'd changed clothes since we last saw one another, but that did little to mask the impact of the scene at Gemma's on him.

"I need to say something before we go inside, Ripley."

"Okay."

"I should have told you about the problems in the pack. I knew Lewis hadn't even though we'd discussed it. I should have brought the issue to you right then. But I excused myself from doing it because you hadn't accepted the position as the lead marshal. Even after what happened at Red's I didn't say anything, this time because my pride was hurt when you took over the investigation." He continued, not letting me say anything.

"Ripley, you were right to do so. What I saw at Gemma's proved that to me in a way I doubt anything else could have. So let me say this again. I'm sorry and I hope you trust me enough to let me do whatever I can to help understand what's been happening."

What the hell was going on? Griffin Starke never apologized, at least not to me.

No doubt about it. His sister called and read him the riot act.

Thank you, Sophie.

"Griff, don't. We were both at fault. I've avoided taking up my position as senior marshal for too long. Part of it's because I blame the Conclave for what happened to my mother. Part is because I'm terrified I'm not good enough to keep the sector safe. One thing I've never doubted is your dedication to the pack or to this town. I'm asking for your help now because I can't do this by myself."

"I say we try working together instead of against one another. Who knows?" He gave me a cocky grin, one I knew all too well. "We might actually like it."

"Well." I drawled and grinned back at him. "I wouldn't go that far."

He chuckled and reached over to open the door for me. I stepped inside and lifted a hand in greeting as Sele called a greeting from behind the counter where she manned the cash register. She told us to head on back, promising to be there shortly with coffee. Griff asked for a burger and fries as well. Since it had been too long since breakfast, I asked for the same. Then I led Griff through the diner to the private room next to the kitchen.

"Any word from Yousef?"

I shook my head. "No, and I left a message before heading to see your sister. You?"

"Nothing. I've told a couple of my cops to keep an eye out and let me know if they see him or his vehicle. Figured I'd go by his apartment when we finish up here and see if he's there."

"Thanks." I leaned back in the booth across the table from him. Sele slipped in with water and coffee for us before slipping out again, closing the door behind her. "I may be reading more into all this, but I can't help asking myself if he's up to something. If not, why did he disappear from Gemma's and why isn't he answering his phone?"

"I know it might be too much for you to handle, Rip, but I agree with you."

I rolled my eyes. "How about we put our cards on the table, Griff? No holding back. People we care about have been hurt. I don't know about you, but I don't want to give whoever's responsible another chance."

"Sounds like a plan." He lifted his mug and carefully sipped. "Where do you want to start?"

The million-dollar question.

"The way I see it, there are four, maybe five things to focus on: the attack on Red's, the one at Gemma's, the corresponding attacks at the other North American zones as well as at Razor's grandmother's, and Dani's attempted kidnapping. Then there's whatever the hell is going on with Yousef."

"Any or all of which might be related."

"Griff, they have to be related. Nothing else makes sense."

"Okay, cards on the table. You want to start or should I?"

"Why don't we do it in chronological order?"

He nodded. For a moment, no one said anything. Then I started. After all, as far as the two of us were concerned, everything started with Gemma's call the other morning asking Red to send me out to see her.

"She said something that I keep going back to, Griff," I said after going over my conversation with Red and the first few minutes after my arrival at Gemma's. "When she told me about how whatever she sensed reminded her of her experiences before the Cataclysm. She'd warned the Conclave then but didn't this time. Instead, she wanted to talk to me, to put the responsibility of contacting them in my hands. That's not like her. I didn't think to ask why."

"That's not like her."

"I know. When we're done here, I'll check with Sele. Hopefully, I'll be able to ask Gemma about what's been going on."

"I'd like to be there if you can."

"Good." I managed a smile. "I was going to suggest it."

For the next hour, we talked about everything that happened, first at Red's and then at Gemma's. Like it or not, we came to the inescapable decision that the attacks here, as well as the attack on Razor's abuela's compound, had to be related. Until I got more information about the attacks in the other sectors, I assumed those attacks were connected as well.

The attempt to get Dani might not be related. Neither Griff nor I could figure out why anyone would want to kidnap her. We needed to find out more about her family. I'd never felt comfortable with the investigation into the car crash that took her parents' lives. Maybe it was time to look deeper.

And that was something Griff could do easier than me.

"Can you get copies of the accident and investigation reports?"

"I can try. But I need to open an investigation into the attempt to take her." He looked at me, one brow arched in question.

"Do it. I've got the legal paperwork appointing me her guardian in Red's absence." Along with a lot of other legal paperwork to handle his affairs.

"Thanks." He reached across the table and rested his hand on mine for a brief moment before moving it. "Can you look through Conclave records to see if there's anything there that might help us?"

"On my list of things to do tonight."

He made a quick note and then sat back. "Guess it's my turn now."

I nodded and waited.

"This isn't easy for me, Ripley. When it was just what happened at Red's, I knew what to do. The job was simple. Investigate the fire, make sure you and the rest of Red's people were all right, find Red, and make any arrests necessary. I'll admit, I behaved badly when you came in, waiving your creds as the Conclave's marshal. Let me begin by thanking you for not trying to actually take over, for wanting to work with me even when I was being an ass."

I grinned and cocked my head to the side. "Griff, we've spent much of our lives doing our best to piss one another off. I know I need your help with this. We don't have to work against one another just because we both have egos."

His grin, a combination of cocky and seductive, made me laugh softly and shake my head.

"That is *not* going to happen, Griff, and you know it." Even if I'd spent a good part of my teens lusting after him. But a wolf and me, with my weird mix of talents and insecurities, would never make it last. Besides, I don't share, something wolves loved to do. "But it would be nice if we weren't always at one another's throats."

"I can live with that." He extended his hand across the table and I took it, sealing the bargain with a shake.

"The pack?" I prompted a moment later.

He blew out a breath and stared into his mug for a moment. Then he lifted his face, his expression troubled.

"As you've probably guessed, I did recognize some of the wolves at Gemma's."

He didn't look at me. He didn't need to, not when his frustration, anger, even pain were there to read in his scent and posture.

"I figured as much before we left. You got too quiet."

He nodded, his fingers playing with his mug as he drew circles with it on the tabletop.

"I should have told you then."

"Griff, look at me." It took a moment before he did. "Neither of us were at our best there. Hell, I was so focused on not losing my break-fast—or dinner for that matter—that I could barely function. I was operating on instinct alone much of the time there. You were the same. You had to process what you saw, what you scented, everything not only as the police chief and as someone who cares for Gemma as much as I do, but also as a member of the pack and the alpha's second. I'm not going to hold that against you."

"Thanks."

"But I do need to know the rest of it. We said we'd lay our cards on the table."

He sighed and nodded.

"I'll start by saying Sophie called after your visit and ripped me a new one. She also told me she identified Tommy Baldwin."

"She did."

"I should have given you his name earlier and, again, I apologize. I think seeing him is what rocked me the most. He was a good kid, a quick study, and dedicated to the pack." He huffed softly, his eyes going golden as his wolf pushed against his control. "I liked him, Rip. He was the little brother I never had. He wanted to go to college and get his degree. Then he planned on returning here and joining the force."

Tears burned my eyes as I listened. The raw emotion in Griff's voice rocked me. Instead of pushing him to continue, I gave him the time he needed to regain control.

"We'll find the ones responsible for what happened and make them pay, Griff."

Even if it was the last thing I ever did.

"Anyway." He shook himself, much as his wolf would if shifted. "I recognized several of the wolves that didn't shift back in death. Sophie's identification of the ones closest to Tommy was correct. But there were others, further out in the yard. I'll pull together files on them and send them to you. Know this, all but two were no longer associated with the pack. Those two were and, unfortunately, they also had the ear of our alpha."

My breath hissed in between my teeth. Since coming upon the carnage at Gemma's and seeing the wolves among the dead or dying, I'd prayed the pack wasn't involved. Griff just confirmed one of my worst nightmares. If he was right about the two pack members and if they had more than the alpha's ear, the pack might need to be put down under Conclave law.

And there was no way I wanted anything to do with that.

"Have you talked to Alpha Lewis?"

Griff shook his head.

"I wanted to get as much information about what happened and who was involved as possible before doing so." He paused, his eyes all but pleading with me to understand.

Damn it, I did. But this wasn't something either of us could put off much longer.

"Griff, I give you my word, I'm not taking this to the Conclave without a hell of a lot more evidence. I will not risk your pack being condemned because of the actions of a few malcontents." I stopped him before he could say anything. "But that doesn't mean I won't carry out the execution order for any or all of those involved once we have proof of their crimes."

"Rip." Voice deep, rough, he sounded like he was either about to shift or cry.

Maybe both.

"I mean it, Griff. Someone or something somehow managed to not only call paras that would never be near one another together. That someone gave them orders to attack Gemma's and maybe Red's. Those orders coincided with attacks in other sectors. This goes beyond our town or your pack. But the fact there were pack members involved makes me wonder if whoever is behind all this is trying to discredit, if not destroy, it."

"Will you give me until morning to do some digging and to talk with Alpha Lewis?"

I closed my eyes, fighting the doubt raised by his request. Damn it, I didn't want to question where his loyalties lay, but I had to. Whatever was happening went far beyond the two of us. This town and the people living here had been attacked, not once but twice. I couldn't let my feelings for Griff or for Sophie stop me from protecting everyone else.

"Griffin, you're asking me to do more than trust you. You're asking me to continue trying to figure out what's been going on and why without knowing information you have. That puts me at a disadvantage, one that could cost people we love their lives—or worse. Are a few hours worth the risk?"

"I believe so." He shoved to his feet, the legs of his chair scraping against the floor. "Ripley, I'm giving you my word right now that I will tell you everything I find. I also promise that, should I discover anything showing Lewis has been involved in what's going on, I will challenge him for leadership of the pack. He won't live to cause us or our town any more trouble."

"All right." God, I hoped I wasn't making a mistake. "But I need you to keep me in the loop with regular reports until then."

I'd also be talking with Sophie again, making sure she knew where I stood with all this.

"Thank you, Ripley." He returned to his seat across from me. "I know how much I'm asking."

"Then be completely honest with me, Griffin. Are you asking me to wait only because of what you saw at Gemma's or is there trouble in the pack you want to deal with before I step in and bring it to the Conclave's attention?"

"You always did see too much, Rip." He tipped his head back and stared at the ceiling, almost as if asking for heavenly inspiration. Good luck with that. "But I promised to be honest and it is both. This is my pack, my family. I'm asking you to remember that and to give me time to make sure they aren't getting caught up in something they had nothing to do with."

As much as I wanted to argue, I couldn't. Not when I'd do the same if our roles were reversed. Still, he needed to understand he didn't have much time. We had to get to the bottom of this before something else happened.

"You have until morning. But, like I said, I'm asking you to keep me in the loop between now and then."

"I will." He sipped, grimaced, and then shoved aside his mug of now cold coffee. "What are you going to do about Yousef?"

Cards on the table. That was the agreement.

"I need to find out what he's been up to since he disappeared from Gemma's. Then I need to check with some of my sources to see what they can tell me about him." I might never stop kicking myself for not doing that sooner. "I don't want to think he's part of this, but it is clear he is working his own agenda right now. It might be he's pissed I finally accepted the Conclave's offer to be the sector's senior marshal. He might still resent the fact he was sent here in the first place.

"Other than having folks keep an eye out for him and call if they see him, how are you going to find out what he's been up to?"

"I'm going to call in a favor."

Hopefully, Aras would agree. Since Dani was involved, I didn't doubt he would. Still, I wouldn't know until I asked and I wanted to do that in person. That meant I needed to get on my way. There was a lot to do before I'd be able to find my bed tonight.

20

MOM, WHERE ARE YOU WHEN I NEED YOU?

I t was almost sundown by the time I made it back to Razor's. Aras stood at the front door, waiting for me. Without a word, he stepped aside, letting me in. Then the door shut behind me. The click of the lock sliding into place let me know we wouldn't be disturbed. Fine with me. After the day's events, I wanted to take care of a few things, including talking with the dark elf, before checking on Dani and then finding my bed. I didn't even care if I ate.

Aras placed a gentle hand on my arm and led me through the shop to Razor's office. He eased me onto a chair in front of the battered desk. Then he stepped back, head cocked to one side as he studied me, the intensity of his gaze sending shivers down my spine.

"Wait here, Ripley. We need to talk."

I nodded. Without another word, he slipped out of the office, closing the door behind him. I leaned back and closed my eyes. Exhaustion dragged at me. So did doubt. Doubt I didn't dare let take hold.

Doubt about Red.

About Yousef.

Even about the Conclave itself.

Doubt about too many people and their actions.

"Here, drink this."

Aras handed me a mug of fragrant tea. I sniffed and then cautiously sipped. I didn't want to add a scalded mouth to everything else that happened the last few days. Almost instantly, a warmth spread through me and some of the exhaustion fell away. I sipped again, then cradled the mug between my hands, and watched as the dark elf leaned against the edge of Razor's desk, his eyes dark with concern.

"Thanks." I managed a smile that deepened as he relaxed. "I mean it, Aras. This helps." I lifted the mug slightly.

"A recipe of my people. You looked as if you needed it."

"I did." Why lie when he had eyes to see my exhaustion and the way recent events weighed on me? "And I'm glad you're here. I'd like to discuss something with you."

"Of course."

I sipped again. "Aras, I want to start by thanking you. I'm able to do what I need to because you're looking after Dani. I know you will do everything possible to keep her safe."

"That is what I wanted to discuss with you, Ripley." He boosted himself up so he sat on the desk. "I do not disagree with you wanting her to stay here while you are investigating what happened. She is as safe here as she would be anywhere, probably safer. But safe doesn't mean secure. She is scared and she needs to know you are all right and she needs to see you for more than a few minutes at a time."

I didn't sigh, but I wanted to.

"How bad is it?"

"She has been partially shifted all day." He gave a small shrug and a rueful smile touched his lips. "We both know it doesn't help that Layla has been on edge partially shifted most of the day."

"I can't be here and do what I need to, Aras." Much as it pained me.

"And I am not asking that." He waited until I nodded in understanding. "I am asking that you spend the evening with her. Help her with her homework. Layla made sure the school sent it over."

Now I did sigh. The school was something else I needed to worry about. I still didn't know why it didn't notify me they sent her home early, putting her in danger by doing so.

"I'll do my best, Aras. Promise."

"That is all I ask."

I glanced around the office. Even though no one else was present, I felt uncomfortable. He waited, knowing me well enough to understand this wasn't easy.

"Aras, I'm not going to insult you by suggesting you don't know everything that's been going on. I don't doubt Razor and Layla have kept you filled in. That's something I'm glad about."

One dark brow arched but otherwise he gave no indication of how he felt about my comment.

"Still, you need to understand just how serious the situation is. There have been other attacks than the ones here and at Razor's abuela's. There have been other attacks on towns or compounds near rifts around the country. Everything I've seen so far tells me the attacks are somehow connected. Add in the attack and Gemma's and it's obvious something or someone is targeting our kind."

Expression grim, he nodded. "But there is more that worries you."

"There is," I said. "I know of two people who have gone missing in the attacks: Razor's brother and Red. But it was almost three."

Aras bared his teeth, the sharp points reminding me how different he was from the elves of movies and most fiction.

"Dani." He ground out her name and now it was my turn to nod.

"I need to know why someone would want to take her, especially now."

"I do not know, but I will do everything I can to find out." He shoved off the desk and started to the door, suddenly stopping and turning back to me. "There's more still, is there not?"

"There is."

I needed to trust my gut and that gut told me I could trust the dark elf. That's certainly more than it said about Yousef.

"Answer me one question before I explain. What are your thoughts about Yousef?"

He didn't relax, but he did return to the desk and leaned against it.

Arms folded, He appeared to consider how best to answer. The fact he hesitated only added to my worry.

"He hides too much, Ripley."

My eyes narrowed. That simple statement held too many connotations. I needed him to be more specific.

"Explain."

"Perhaps I have lived here too long. But I remember how it was with your parents and even with you, even though you did not want to accept the responsibility of being the sector's marshal." He continued before I could interrupt. "Your parents were fair but firm when it came to enforcing the laws. But they made sure everyone in the sector knew we could come to them, no matter what. They made the effort to get to know us, even those who, like me, aren't the easiest to trust or get to know. We learned they would back us unless they found evidence proving our guilt. Even then, they would look to motivation. They stood for us as much, if not more, than they stood for the Conclave. It helped this place start to heal and to grow as a community after the Cataclysm."

"And Yousef?"

"He is the opposite. He's been here long enough to start integrating into the community and yet he holds himself apart. He does nothing to become one of us, to get to know us, our needs or our desires. He uses his position as marshal to his advantage."

I inhaled sharply, suddenly alert.

"What do you mean?"

"He has used his position to avoid his bills, to make sure he never has to pay at most stores or shops. He has abused his position with some of Chief Starke's officers to avoid the human laws as well. Until you took up the position as senior marshal, he had no one to keep him in line. He owes many in the sector and he has tried, more than once, to force himself on some of our females."

My chair skid across the floor as I surged to my feet. Anger once again filled me. Tired as I was, my control slipped. Flames danced from my fingertips and my eyes glowed gold as I struggled to keep from doing something exceedingly foolish.

"Why didn't you—hell, why didn't anyone—tell me?"

Had I failed others as I'd failed Gemma and those who fought to protect her?

"Because you weren't ready to accept the role." He gestured for me to be seated. "Ripley, we are all right. Any one of us could have dealt with him if it came to that. For now, we've been content to let him tie his own noose. We weren't going to force you into a role you didn't want and weren't ready for. Just as you've made promises to each of us and to Red, we made promises to him and to your parents."

Now he smiled and a shiver ran down my spine.

"But you have proven to us and to yourself that you are ready to accept the role you were born to. My question for you is what I can do to assist?"

I scrubbed my hands over my face and blew out a long breath. Too many forces were at play, some for more years than I could wrap my mind around.

"I need to know where that son of a bitch is and what he's been up to since leaving Gemma's this morning."

One brow winged up as the dark elf looked at me in surprise.

"Something is going on with him, Aras, something I don't know about and I don't like it. Between what I've seen the last couple of days and what you just said, I don't trust him. Hell, I'm wondering if he's not involved in what's happened. That would certainly explain why he hasn't reported in and why he won't take my calls."

"This is something I can help with."

"Thank you." I leaned back, feeling a hundred years old. "Aras, if you or your sources find him, do not approach. Let me know where he is and keep eyes on him. Leave him to me."

"All right." He didn't like it. I saw that much in the way his eyes flashed and his jaw clenched. "Wait here, Ripley. I will be right back."

I nodded and watched as he left the office, closing the door behind him. Once alone, I pulled my phone and called the café. As I waited for one of the sisters to answer, I considered what Aras said. If he was right, and I had no reason to doubt him, then things just got a great deal more complicated.

Damn it, I really wished Red was here. He'd know who I could talk to without risking any of our necks in the process.

"Three Sisters Café."

"Sele, it's me." In the background, I heard the sounds of Romy working at the stove and the muted conversations from the dining room. "How's your aunt?"

"She is resting. She seriously depleted her energies protecting herself and the house."

"Has she said anything about what happened?"

"No. She's still sleeping. That is the best thing for her right now."

I knew she was right, but that didn't help right now. I needed to talk with her, to find out what she could tell me about what happened. But I wouldn't risk her health, not when she'd looked so ill as the sisters tended to her at her house.

"All right. Let me know when she wakes and I can speak with her."

"I will." She fell silent for a moment. I waited, understanding. Gemma was like a second mother to her and her sisters. Their first reaction to what happened would be to do everything they could to protect her. "You should be able to see her in the morning. If she's up to it sooner, I'll let you know."

"Thanks, Sele." I lifted a hand as Aras returned, letting him know I was almost done. "Sorry. I thought I'd check on Gemma while you were gone," I added and he nodded in understanding.

"How is she?"

"Sele said she's resting." I gave a small shrug.

"She would tell you if you needed to worry." He extended a hand and helped me to my feet. "I will do what I can to not only keep Dani safe, but to also find where our wandering marshal happens to be. In the meantime, I have something for you. It served me well when I was younger and it served your father well before his death. He left it with me before his last assignment, asking me to prepare it for you for the day you took up the mantle of marshal."

He extended a wooden box about a foot and a half long and six inches wide and deep. I took it from him, the fingers of my right hand lightly tracing the intricate design carved into the smooth oak. Power tingled up my fingers to my arms, warning me the box had been charmed. Not that it surprised me. The dark elf took few chances, especially with things he valued.

Not that I blamed him.

Inside, resting on a cushion of velvet the color of blood, lay what looked to be a wakizashi. A very old, very beautifully forged wakizashi. One that also pulsed with power coming from the runes etched into the blade.

One I remembered my father practicing with and carrying with him whenever he left home. Why hadn't he taken it that last time?

"Aras." Voice choked, tears burning in my eyes, I closed the fingers of my left hand around the hilt.

"I will teach you the history of the blade another day. But know it has come down your father's bloodline for the last five generations. They used it to protect our kind long before the Cataclysm. He always planned for it to go to you when you were ready. Had he and your mother not been lost, it would have come to you sooner, I believe. But it is yours now. Use it as he did. Use it to protect our home and our friends."

"I will."

The circle begun when I discovered my mother's guns at Red's was now completed with my father's wakizashi.

Now if I only knew who the enemy was and where to find them.

21

A WEREWOLF AND A TROLL CAME STUMBLING IN

"Ripley."

Dani didn't whine, not much at least. Instead, she looked up at me from where she lay in bed, her expression both pleading and mulish. How she managed that combination—and so effectively—I didn't know. Not that I planned to change my mind. Like it or not, she was staying here, where I knew she'd be safe.

"Sweetheart, it's just for another night or two. I promise."

Hopefully, that was a promise I wouldn't have to break.

"But you're going to stay there tonight." Yep, the whine was winning.

Before I could respond, Layla spoke up.

"Dani, you know better." She gave the girl a firm look. "Ripley wants you with her, but she needs to think about your safety right now."

"But if the house is safe enough for her, it's safe enough for me."

I considered beating my head against the wall. With my luck, I'd break the wall.

"Dani, look at me." I settled on the edge of the mattress and waited until she did. "I think the house is safe but I can't be sure. Not until I spend some time there."

"I don't understand," she admitted.

"There are protections set on the house and the property around it that have been keyed to me. But these protections are old, set when my parents were still alive and I wasn't as old as you are. I don't know how the passing time may have impacted the protections. They may be weak enough not to be of much help if trouble finds the house."

"But—"

"But," I continued. "Even if those protections are still at full strength, they will need to be attuned to you before you can stay there for more than a few hours."

"If they're not as strong as they used to be, you won't be safe, Ripley." Fear lit her eyes.

"Dani, Ripley knows, just as she knows staying there tonight is a calculated risk. But she also has ways of protecting herself, ways you don't know about yet." Now Layla grinned at me, mischief dancing in her eyes. "We need to trust her to do what's best not just for you but for all of us."

"Dani, I don't want you to worry about me." I reached out and gently cupped her cheek with my right hand. The fire and Red's disappearance weighed on her and I doubted any of us understood how much. "The protections are still active. I felt them when I was there earlier. That means even if they're weakened, they will still warn me of trouble. I also plan to set up my own protections once I return." Protections that would be both mundane and arcane, but she didn't need to know that right now.

"But I have to be realistic. I can't rely on the protections to give me much warning if trouble does come to the house. That means I have to be able to react instantly to any threat. I won't be able to do that if you're there right now." I shook my head, stopping her before she could interrupt. "If you're there, I'm going to worry about making sure you're safe—and that is exactly how it should be. But, if you're here when something happens at the house, I can react to the threat and maybe even find out who's been hurting our friends."

She thought about it for a moment before nodding. She didn't like it, not that I blamed her. In her position, I'd feel the same. Hopefully, she understood that much as I wanted to stay with her, I needed to do this, for me and for everyone else. I couldn't shake the feeling that something in Red's files that now rested in the basement of my parents' house held the key to what happened to Red, what happened at Gemma's, and possibly even what happened to my mother.

"But," I said, grinning down at her as I dug a finger into her ribs, tickling her. "That doesn't mean you're getting rid of me. Unless something comes up overnight, I'll be back for breakfast, assuming Layla and Razor don't mind feeding me." I looked over my shoulder and grinned at Layla.

"I think I can pull together some toast and coffee for you," the naga chuckled.

"And I'll come back every evening to have dinner with you and to help with your homework. Hopefully, in another day or two, you can move into the house."

For the first time since we came upstairs after dinner, Dani smiled. "Can I live with you?"

"Of course." I leaned down to hug her. "Until everything gets settled and we find out where Red is, you're stuck with me. Hope you don't mind."

She shook her head, her hair whipping around her face.

"We'll talk some more in the morning." I looked around, spotting her cellphone on the bedside table. "Call me if you want to talk or if you need anything."

"Promise you'll be back."

My heart broke to hear the fear in her voice.

"I promise." Another hug and then I stood. "Get some sleep now. I'll be back before you know it."

I hoped.

Layla took my place next to the bed, her hands gentle as she tucked Dani in. I watched for a moment before leaving the room, closing the door behind me. I made it almost to the stairs before I sank to the floor, back to the wall, knees pulled up. Tears burned my eyes as I dropped my forehead to my knees and fought for control.

"You okay?" Layla asked as she sat next to me, leaning in to bump my shoulder with hers.

"Yeah." I scrubbed the heels of my hands over my eyes and then gave her a shaky smile. "She got to me."

"Me too," the naga admitted. "But you are doing the right thing, Ripley. More than that, you explained it in a way she understood. That helps her understand not only how serious the situation is but also that you aren't going to be taking unnecessary chances."

I dipped my chin in agreement.

"But she is scared. She had finally accepted her parents won't be coming back. Then the fire happened and Red disappeared. That was bad enough. But the thought something might happen to you terrifies her. As much as she loves Red and looks at him as an uncle, you are the one she feels closest to. You're her foundation."

I closed my eyes and drew a long, shaky breath. To hear it put into words drove it home. It also drove home the fact I needed to do everything I could to deal with those responsible for everything going on the last few days without getting myself killed in the process.

"And that scares the shit out of me." To put it mildly.

"Use it as a reminder that you have people who care for you and who will be hurt if you let anything happen to yourself." Another shoulder bump. "Now, breakfast will be at seven. If you don't object, I'm going to take Dani to school long enough in the morning to meet with the admin, get her assignments and arrange for her to do classes online for the next few weeks. That should give time to figure out what's been going on, reassure her that everything's going to work out, and find out what's been going on there."

"Thanks." I said nothing for a moment. "Layla, I want the names of those she is supposed to have fought with. Look into them and their families. Make sure the school understands that I will take any and all necessary steps to protect her, especially if it appears they have been turning a blind eye to bullying or anything of the like."

"You leave this to me. It's the least I can do for the two of you."

"Thanks." I climbed to my feet and reached down to help her up. "I'd best get on my way. Let me know if she needs me?" I nodded in the direction of Dani's room.

"I will, as long as you promise to let me know if you need anything."

"Deal." I smiled, confident I was leaving Dani in good hands. "I'll check on her later."

Gods above and below, I hoped I was making the right decision.

The moment I parked the SUV in the drive and stepped out, I felt a difference in the wards. Razor warned me earlier in the evening that he'd been by and had worked on them, strengthening them and attuning them even more deeply to me. The hint of welcome I felt earlier now felt almost like an embrace. Letting my eyes go out of focus, I studied the energies that appeared to wrap the yard and house in a protective cocoon. Smiling slightly as some of my worry slipped away, I climbed the steps to the front porch and made my way inside.

Two hours later, I sat on the floor in the den, surrounded by papers and notepads. Lifting my arms over my head, I straightened my back and stretched until my spine popped. Red was nothing if not a compulsive note-taker, something my search of his files confirmed. But so far at least, I'd found nothing that seemed connected to what was going on. I'd also come to the inescapable conclusion that it was going to take more than just me to go through everything, at least if I wanted it done in less than the next month or three.

Not that it stopped me from looking at some of the information he'd gathered about my mother's last mission. It didn't shed much light onto what happened to her. I had a feeling there might be more somewhere in the files but it, like the rest of the man's records, needed more than just me going through them.

With a yawn wide enough to pop my jaw, I climbed to my feet and made my way to the kitchen. As I studied the contents of the refrigerator, I silently thanked Layla for stocking it for me. After grabbing a beer, I stood there, staring out the window over the sink. Memories of standing there, doing the dishes with Mom washed over me. I had so many good memories in this house, memories I'd all but suppressed after Mom disappeared. Now I had a feeling those memories would be returning, probably at the most inopportune times, knowing my luck.

Beer in hand, I returned to the den and dropped onto the sofa, propping my feet on the low coffee table in front of it. Then I dragged my phone from my pocket.

"This had better be good, Rip. I was about to enjoy a tall glass of wine and a bubble bath," Sophie all but growled.

"I know I don't hold a candle to that, but I thought you might help me go through some paperwork Red left for me."

"Can't it wait until morning? It's been a really long day."

Worried, I considered how to respond. Sophie, unlike her brother, never whined. That she was now confirmed her comment about how long the day had been. Unless I missed my guess, it had also been a rough one. Considering how my day had gone, I almost told her to forget about it. Then I grinned, knowing one thing that would get her here without further objection.

"Enjoy your bubble bath. I would appreciate it if you'd meet me at my folks' place in the morning."

I waited, counting slowly to ten. I made it to three before she sputtered out her response.

"Your parent's house?"

I had her attention now.

"Yep. I'm sitting in the den, surrounded by some of Red's files, trying to make sense of everything."

"You'd better not be shitting me, Ripley."

"I'm not." I activated the camera on my phone and sent her a picture of me sitting there before following it up with one of the stacks of files on the coffee table and floor.

"I'm on my way. Have you eaten?"

"I have."

"I'll bring dessert then. Be there soon."

She rang off before I could respond. Smiling, I sat back, dropping the phone onto the cushion at my side. Hopefully, two sets of eyes would be better than one.

Sitting there, I considered calling her brother. After all, if two sets of eyes were better than one, three sets had to be even better. But I'd agreed to give him until tomorrow to do whatever he needed with regard to the pack. Besides, normally, I'd call Red or Razor. Red was who knew where and I wanted Razor to stay with Dani.

That left Yousef.

Except I didn't trust him.

Sipping my beer, I considered my options. Mom and Dad taught me to keep my enemies close, especially if I managed to convince them I trusted them. I wanted to believe Yousef thought I trusted him, but I couldn't. His own actions told me he either didn't trust me or he was actively working against me. Either way, I didn't want to invite him inside the house's protections and I sure as hell didn't want him seeing all the information Red collected over the years.

But I did need to reach out to him again. It had been hours since my last time checking in and I had yet to hear back from him. I didn't know if it made me a good person or not to hope the reason he hadn't responded was because he was hip deep in trouble.

I took a moment to steady myself and then texted him, telling him I was about to call it a night but that I wanted him to touch base. I was worried because he hadn't checked in and I hoped it meant he'd been following a hot lead. I ended with a note that I'd be forced to contact the Conclave if I didn't hear from him by morning.

If that didn't light a fire under his ass, I didn't know what would.

And, to be honest, I didn't want to know.

Sofie arrived ten minutes later, bearing the promised dessert as well as beer. As I stepped aside so she could enter, she whistled softly and shook her head. Then she stood as if rooted in place as she looked around. I wondered if she was remembering all the good times we'd had here as kids. She spent as much time here as she did at home, especially during the summers. My parents, especially Mom after Dad died, were like her own. I'll never forget how Sofie stood with Mom and me during Dad's funeral, her hand holding mine, hurting almost as much as I did.

"Care to tell me what's going on?" she asked softly as we made our way to the kitchen.

"Let's say Red's been keeping too damned much to himself. Of course, Gemma and Razor were in on this." I wave a hand to indicate the house. Then I told her what Razor said about the Conclave, Red and others keeping the house for me.

"I always wondered why it hadn't been put on the market." She gave a small shrug and I nodded. "I have a feeling there's more to why you asked me over than just this."

"Much more." I stowed the beer in the fridge after grabbing one for her. As I did, she checked the cabinets for plates. A moment later, she slid a slice of apple pie onto two plates and grinned as I all but licked my lips in anticipation. "Did your brother happen to mention my little foray back to the safe room at the warehouse?"

She narrowed her eyes in displeasure as she shook her head.

"Before you blow your top, I took Razor with me. Neither of us were in any danger." At least not too much. "And it was worth it. I knew Red had a safe down there. What I didn't know was the damned thing was as large as the safe room and filled with files and other things."

Since the easiest way to convince her any danger presented by returning to the warehouse paled in comparison with what we found, I motioned for her to come with me. Together, we descended the stairs to the basement. Her only reaction as we moved through the area she remembered into the newer parts was a sharp inhalation. She said nothing as I deactivated the wards in place on the safe room and waited for the door to swing open.

"Ripley, what the hell?"

She stood next to me, her head moving as if on a swivel, as she took in the file cabinets, the long tables filled with more files, boxes and weapons. I didn't answer. Instead, I made my way to the leather chair behind the battered desk. My hands almost reverently lifted Mom's jacket from the chairback before pulling her 1911s from the drawer where I'd secured them.

"How?" She spoke barely above a whisper as she reached out to lightly run a finger down the leather of the jacket before looking at the guns. She recognized them. "Where did you find them?"

"Red had them. Most of what you see here was in his so-called safe. I've been going through his files but there's too much for me to do by myself."

"So you called me."

I nodded.

"What are we looking for?"

That's one of the things I love about Sophie. She didn't ask unnecessary questions. She knew I wouldn't ask for help unless I needed it.

And damn but I needed it now.

"Several things." I quickly filled her in on Razor's grandmother being in contact with Red. "I'd like you to look at the legal documents he left me. I want to make sure everything's in place so I can not only take care of things regarding the warehouse and our people until we find him but, more importantly, that I have all legal authority to handle anything that comes up regarding Dani."

"No problem. But that's not why you asked me over. You could have brought those to me tomorrow morning."

I blew out a breath and gathered up a handful of files before motioning for her to head back upstairs. She gave me a long look before agreeing. Good friend that she is, she didn't push for an explanation as she waited for me to re-secure the room. Instead, she took some of the files from me, balanced her plate with its slice of pie on top of them, and headed upstairs.

"All right, Rip. Tell me what's really bothering you," she said as she took a seat at one end of the sofa. After kicking off her shoes, she curled up against the arm and got comfortable.

"Part of me is hoping you're going to tell me I'm seeing problems that aren't really there." I took a bite of pie to give myself a moment to think. "Sophie, before I answer your question, answer one for me. What do you think about Yousef?"

She blinked once, surprised by the question. When she didn't answer right away, I waited. Was she trying to figure out how to tell me I'd lost my mind by questioning the man or that I should have figured out he was bad news long ago?

"Honestly?"

I nodded.

"I don't trust him."

Crap.

Why the hell hadn't she said something then?

Probably for the same reason Razor hadn't.

"Let me guess. He hasn't tried to become part of the community. He doesn't know us, and he doesn't really care about us. Oh, and you didn't say anything to me because you didn't want to put any additional pressure on me to finally accept the Conclave's offer to become the Zone's senior marshal."

She ducked her head, a sure sign I'd hit that one on the nose.

"Damn it, Soph, does everyone in this town think I'm so fragile you have to hide the truth from me?"

She stared at me like I'd lost my mind.

"No!" She shook her head again, her dark ponytail bobbing back and forth as she did. "But you have to look at it from our point of view, Ripley. To us, especially to those closest to you, you are very much like Dani is to you. We've watched this crazy world of ours rip apart your family and your life. We knew you would step up when the time was right, but we were determined to let you have time to be just you. Not our marshal and sure as hell not the Zone's senior marshal where your sense of responsibility would make you take on all our problems as your own."

I didn't know whether to thank her or scream in frustration.

"Next time, don't be so damned noble." I reached for my beer and took a long swig. "We'll discuss that later. But know that I'm having more than a few doubts about Yousef right now. He disappeared from Gemma's without a word this morning and hasn't done more than a quick text telling me he'd talk to me later since then. Hasn't returned my calls and sure as hell hasn't updated me on where his part of the investigation is going."

"What are you doing about it?"

Now I grinned and, judging from the way her brows winged upward, I probably looked at least half-feral.

"I've asked Aras to see what he can find out."

Sophie blew out a breath and then laughed. She knew exactly why I'd asked the dark elf, just as she knew he would do everything possible to help if it kept Dani safe.

"And us?"

"We get to work. I'd like to make some headway in all this." I indicated the files scattered around the room. "I'd even like to get at least a little sleep tonight."

"Then let's get to it. Where are the legal papers you want me to have a look at?"

I motioned to the stack of files on the end of the coffee table in front of her.

"One more thing, Soph. Have you talked with your brother since we spoke this afternoon?"

"Only long enough to know you guys talked and he's both pissed off and worried and, for once, it isn't about you." She gave me a cocky grin before sobering. "Ripley, we're both worried about what's happened and about some things going on in the pack. I promise he'll let you know what he finds out come morning."

I hoped she was right. I did not want to have to deal with a pack coming unglued while trying to deal with everything else that was going on.

"Then let's get started." I forked up another bite of pie. "And thanks for this. Don't tell Elle, but you make the best pies in town."

She grinned and reached for a file. Time to get to work.

Yawning, I picked up my phone and glanced at the time. Five after three and I felt every hour I should have been in bed and wasn't. Not that sleep would come that night. At least Sophie managed to get some rest. She'd crashed on the sofa a couple of hours ago. I'd paused long enough to cover her with an afghan before returning to the files. As for Yousef, I still hadn't heard from him. He continued to make it difficult for me not to contact the Conclave and report his actions.

I yawned again and carefully climbed to my feet. When Red finally showed up, he owed me more than an explanation. Maybe I was seeing similarities between what happened to Mom and current events because exhaustion had turned my brain to mush. But right now, those similarities—including making sure the marshal sent to investigate her disappearance was little more than a raw rookie, something I didn't doubt they thought of me as—stood out and waved red flags.

My phone pinged, interrupting my thoughts. It pinged a second time, signaling someone or something had set off the motion detectors outside. By the time I reached the door, gun in hand, Sophie was by my side, ready for trouble. To my surprise, she held a gun in one hand and her eyes bled to gold, showing how close to the surface her wolf happened to be.

Ready? I mouthed silently.

Sophie nodded and moved to stand to the right of the doorframe, gun in her right hand. My hand closed around the knob. With a warning nod, I pulled open the door.

And gasped to see Red, more than a little worse for wear, stumbling onto the front porch, weighed down by Griff who looked more dead than alive.

2 2

WHEN NIGHTMARES BECOME REALITY

S hock rooted me in place as the world seemed to come to a crashing halt. The sight of Red, battered and bruised, sent my mind reeling. But it was the sight of Griff, looking more dead than alive, that left me stunned and motionless. Then the sounds of Sophie calling Sele, telling her we needed a healer ASAP, punched through the disbelief and I dragged in a shaky breath.

"I don't give a damn, Sele. Throw your sisters and your aunt into your car and get here." Sophie ground out the words, her voice harsh with the effort to maintain control. "We've got two badly injured men here who need you."

She didn't say anything else. Instead, she ended the call and slid her cellphone into her front pocket. Then she looked at me, her expression enough to get me moving.

With Sophie at my side, I rushed outside. I dragged Griff's right arm over my shoulders, taking on much of his weight. That changed a moment later when Sophie took his other side, moving Red out of the way. But not before she grabbed the closest thing I'd had to a parent in a decade and all but shoved him inside the house.

The moment we stepped inside, the door shut behind us, the lock sliding into place. It did little more than register that none of us had touched it. In the back of my mind, I realized the protections on the house were stronger than expected. I really needed to talk with Razor about them, but that had to wait.

Just like so many other things.

"Downstairs guest room," I said before Sophie could ask. "Don't," I added, seeing Red turning back to the door.

He closed his eyes for a moment and then nodded before following us down the hall to the guest room off the kitchen. Sophie and I held Griff on his feet while Red moved around us to pull back the covers. Then, without me having to ask, he disappeared into the adjoining half-bath to get what we needed to treat the werewolf until Sele and her sisters got here.

"Red, what the hell happened?" Sophie didn't look at him as she carefully cut away her brother's shirt using a pair of scissors she'd found in the bedside table.

It might not be the question I wanted answered, but it was probably the most important one right now. Not that it would get Red off the hook. He still needed to explain what happened at the warehouse, how he got away, and why he hadn't told anyone he was all right. But that could wait until we took care of Griff and found out what happened to him.

"Easy," I said softly as I placed a gentling hand on Sophie's shoulder. The last thing we needed right now was a pissed off female werewolf out for blood.

She blew out a breath before looking at me and nodding once. Before either of us could say anything else, my phone buzzed. I checked the display, relaxing some. Sele and her sisters were on their way and they were bringing Gemma with them. Good. I'd feel better with them here, especially since I had a feeling the protections here were as strong, if not stronger, than at their flat over the café.

But that left several others I cared out of the loop. It might still be hours before sunrise, but I didn't want to risk any of them. I sent a quick text to both Razor and Layla, giving them only the barest of details before asking them to bring Dani and join us here. It was time to gather our forces and come up with a plan.

And, whether he liked it or not, part of that plan meant getting the truth out of Red.

A second text, this one to Aras, followed. I asked him to meet us here for breakfast. Hopefully by then he'd know something about Yousef. Hell, we might get lucky and he'd have some insight into who attacked Griff and why.

"Sophie?"

I swallowed hard as she finished removing most of her brother's clothes. Even unconscious, pain etched deep lines in his face. Cuts, bruises, and what could only be bite marks and knife wounds marked him. That meant more than one person—hell, many more unless I missed my guess—attacked him. But where and why?

More important, how the hell was Red involved?

"Go." She didn't look back at me.

I nodded, understanding. Her anger wasn't aimed at me. No, she wanted the same answers I did. Who hurt Griff and what was Red's connection?

And there was only one person just then with the answers we needed.

Without a word, I crossed the room in three long strides, closing the distance between me and Red where he stood in the doorway. My hand closed over his upper arm. Before he could protest, I dragged him out of the room, closing the door behind us.

Ignoring his demands I let him go, I dragged him to what had been Mom's study. Whether he was surprised by my manhandling of him or I was closer to losing control of my para abilities than I thought, I easily shoved him inside and onto a chair. Then I closed and locked the door behind us. He and I were going to have a conversation, whether he liked it or not.

"You're forgetting yourself, Ripley."

He placed his hands on the arms of the chair, muscles gathering. I shoved him back down, my glare matching his. I was tired, worried, and pissed off and not necessarily in that order. I most definitely wasn't in the mood for games. Not when yet another person I cared for lay injured in one of the guest rooms.

"Don't."

I said nothing else. I didn't have to. His eyes widened in surprise, and he swallowed hard. Then he seemed to almost fold in on himself. Gone was the bluster of a moment ago. Sitting before me now was an old man, one in pain both physical and mental. Worry tugged at the back of my brain. I'd never seen Red like this and it scared me.

"You have a lot of explaining to do, Red." I leaned against the edge of Mom's desk. Exhaustion once again dragged at me. I pushed it back. I didn't have time for it. I could rest later, after he told me what happened after our last conversation. "But let me start. After the fire and your disappearing act, I accepted the Conclave's request to become the Zone's senior marshal. It was the only way I'd have the authority to do what needed to be done to protect our people." I looked at him, surprised when he was the first to look away.

"That includes Dani, Red." I all but ground out the words. "Did you know someone tried to kidnap her at the same time the warehouse was going up in flames?"

He paled and shook his head. Score one for the home team. I'd chosen the right weapon to loosen his tongue—I hoped.

"Now tell me what the hell has been going on? Start with explaining why Razor's grandmother sent two of his too stupid to live cousins to warn you of trouble. Then tell me how long the two of you have been sharing information. While you're at it, explain why you never said anything to me or anyone else?"

Before he could answer, a knock sounded at the door. I shot a warning look at my foster father, letting him know I wouldn't take kindly to him getting up, much less trying to leave. A moment later, I opened the door. Razor stood there, looking as worried and angry as I felt.

"I let Sophie know we were here and she let us in. Layla is settling Dani in your old room. Sele and her sisters are settling Gemma in one of the guest rooms upstairs. Then they'll help Sophie with her brother," he said softly as he looked beyond me to where Razor sat.

"Your cousins?"

"Gone. My grandmother will let me know when they arrive."

I nodded and stepped aside so he could enter. Then I closed and once again locked the door.

"Red was just about to tell me what the hell's been going on." I motioned for Razor to take the seat next to Red before returning to lean against the edge of the desk. It was a shit move and I knew it. But I wanted Red to understand I would and could react to any attempt to leave before he made it to the door. "So?" I looked at him and waited, praying he understood I was in no mood for games.

He remained silent long enough for me to wonder how best to force him to answer. Then he sighed and dropped his head into his hands. I'd never seen him look vulnerable before. Now, in the last few minutes, I'd seen it twice and it not only worried me, but it also scared me. Red had always been the protector, not just for me and for Dani, but for all those who worked for him or looked to him for leadership and guidance. The Red sitting before me looked not only tired and hurt but also close to broken.

"It started about a month or so ago." When he looked up, regret filled his eyes. "Razor, I've known your grandmother for many years now. She's a good woman and devoted to your people. When she first contacted me four, maybe six weeks ago and said there was trouble, I listened."

"And?" I prompted.

"Her village has its own version of Gemma. She went to Anna, Razor's grandmother, because she was worried. She had a series of dreams that closely resembled her visions from before the arrival of the rifts. Then there were reports of creatures venturing away from their lands nearest the rift in that sector. Farms were attacked and people started going missing."

He exhaled and looked at me. I recognized his expression. He wanted—no, needed—to pace but was wise enough not to get out of his chair without permission. I might still be pissed at him for leaving us in the dark, but I needed to trust him. I nodded and watched as Razor shifted slightly in his seat so he could keep an eye on Red.

"Go on," I said.

"There is more to what she said, but the short version is that a lot of what Anna told me reminded me of your mother's last assignment. Especially when she said Razor's brother had been sent to check out the latest reports of trouble and they hadn't heard back from him."

Razor hissed out a breath. His hands fisted on the arms of the chair. But other than that, he didn't react. I had to give it to him. I'd probably be pounding on Red for an explanation.

Hell, that's exactly what I wanted to do.

"Are you telling us his brother disappeared before the compound was attacked?" I asked.

Red nodded.

"And?"

"We were still comparing notes, talking at least once a day as we tried to figure out what was going on." He turned to look outside, and we waited until he was ready to continue. "By then, I was hearing similar reports in our Zone and in some of the others in North America. Then I got word Anna's compound was attacked. That's when I contacted the Conclave."

"You what?"

I couldn't believe it. He contacted the Conclave? Why hadn't he told me before sending me out to see Gemma? Hell, why hadn't Drake told me? That's what made no sense. As my contact on the Conclave, Drake should have told me about Red's concerns, especially once I agreed to become the Zone's senior marshal.

Half an hour ago, I didn't think things could get any worse. I didn't know if that was naivete or foolishness, especially since it now seemed that whatever all *this* was, it was somehow connected to what happened to Mom.

"Ripley?" Red turned, his expression concerned as he looked at me.

"Do you know why Drake wouldn't tell me about your call?"

He shook his head. When I glanced at Razor, he simply shrugged.

"We'll come back to that. Keep going."

"You know most of the rest of it. The next day, Gemma called. She told me about her visions and asked me to send you to her."

"There's still a lot you haven't told us, Red."

I tilted my head back and closed my eyes. Exhaustion, information overload, anger, fear, and so much more all of it combined to make thinking straight hard. But I had to push through. If I didn't, who knew what might happen next.

"Red, this isn't the time to hold out." Razor spoke almost gently. "I know you want to protect us, especially Ripley and Dani. But there is too much at risk for secrets. You know that."

For a moment, Razor hesitated. Then he gave a small, apologetic smile.

"You're right, my friend. There have been too many secrets already, not just from me but from others who should also have known better."

Hopeful, I moved around the desk and sat in my mother's chair. I leaned forward, elbows on the desktop, and waited. As I did, I prayed he knew something to help bring this nightmare to an end. Still, it wouldn't hurt to give him a nudge.

"Red, I know you, just as you know me. There's one thing the two of us can agree on: it is our duty to protect those we care for. That starts with Dani. I need to know what happened to you and why. Knowing that might help me understand why someone tried to kidnap her the day of the fire."

His anger rumbled deep in his throat at the thought of someone trying for the girl. Then he blew out a breath. What he said next surprised me even as it confirmed some of my conclusions about the fire.

"We'd just finished our last conversation when the wards on the warehouse went down, Ripley." His right hand fisted and banged against the chair arm, over and over again in an almost military-like rhythm. "I don't know how or who was responsible. But it damn near tossed me on my ass when it happened. By the time the secondary wards snapped into place, it was too late. Fire already had a foothold in several parts of the building. All the exits that should have been safe, were blocked. I told everyone there to get to the safe room. Then I went hunting."

"And the three dead I found?"

He smiled grimly. "Sent in to make sure the job was done. The first two made the mistake of trying to kill me in a fair fight."

I couldn't help it. I chuckled softly, both at Red's disgust anyone would try to fight without cheating and at the fact he was insulted anyone thought they could beat him, fair fight or not.

"And the third?" Razor asked.

"He either knew better or he learned quickly. He tried taking me down with a gun. Managed to get one lucky shot off before I dealt with him."

"What else?"

"That one admitted before he died that they were supposed to keep our people in the building. Whoever sent them knew I'd stay as long as the others were in danger. With those three dead, I made sure the others got to the safe room. Then I went to the one place I thought I'd be safe: Gemma's."

My lips peeled back as my anger spiked. If he made it there, why hadn't either he or Gemma let me know?

Which is exactly what I asked.

"Watch yourself, girl." His eyes flashed as anger flared.

"Can it, Redmond. I've spent the last couple of days trying to figure out what happened at the warehouse, making sure our people—your people—are all right, and looking for your sorry ass. You could have saved me a lot of effort and even more worry by simply calling and letting me know you were okay."

Razor lifted a hand, stopping me before I could say anything else. Then he turned his attention to Red, his expression colder than I'd ever seen. For his part, Red stared at his friend and then lowered his gaze. He might not be cowed, but he did appear to recognize he'd screwed up.

At least I hoped so.

"You're right. I should have gotten word to you." He rubbed a hand over his face before looking up. "I wasn't in any shape to do so that first night. Between the fire, the fight, and my injuries, I couldn't. Gemma hid me and patched me up. That's why she didn't answer your calls after that first one when you warned her what happened."

"Where were you when her place was attacked?" Razor asked.

"And are you the reason why they attacked her?"

If he was. . . .

"I left that night. She didn't want me to, but I thought it best to leave before whoever is responsible for attacking the warehouse thought to look for me there. The last thing I wanted was to bring trouble to her doorstep." He cursed softly and looked like he wanted to do even more before continuing. "I thought by leaving, I'd keep her safe."

He failed, something I didn't need to point out.

"Red, you know both of us respect you and all you've done to help our kind. You've stood as protector for so many of us over the years. You dealt with the Conclave after Mom disappeared when it wanted to come in and do what it called housekeeping simply because we're a bit too independent for some of their comfort. Does any of what happened then have anything to do with what happened?"

"I don't know."

Frustration once again roughened his voice. When he looked at me, I saw the truth reflected in his eyes. He didn't know, although I had no doubt he had his suspicions. A quick glance at Razor convinced me he felt the same way. Now I needed to figure out how to respond, not only to Red's suspicions but my own?

"Red, what did the Conclave say when you reported your concerns after talking with Razor's grandmother?"

This time when he stood, neither Razor nor I made any move to stop him. Whatever caused him to want to flee earlier was gone. Whether he accepted we were fighting the same battle, realized he needed help with whatever was going on, or he just needed to talk it out, I didn't know and frankly didn't care. Not as long as he told us the truth, all of it.

He didn't say anything right away. Instead, he moved to stand before one of the bookcases lining the wall to my right. Books, pictures in various sized frames, and small collectibles lined the shelves. He studied the pictures for a moment. Then he picked one up and turned around. A moment later, he handed me the picture. Seeing the photo, the last one taken of my parents and myself before Dad's death, choked me up. Tears burned in my eyes and blinked against them.

Red obviously thought this helped answer my questions. Unfortunately, I had no idea why he thought so.

"Red?" Razor's brow knitted as he looked between us.

"I took that picture."

"I remember." I gently traced a finger across the glass protecting the image. "Dad left a couple of hours later."

Red nodded, his expression grim.

"Before he left, he told me to look out for you and your mother. He had a bad feeling about the assignment." He frowned, as if remembering that moment, before returning to his chair. "It wasn't the first time the Conclave asked him to deal with a para who left the area around a rift. Your dad was one of their best hunters and, unlike others, he killed quick and clean. He didn't believe in drawing it out, especially since he felt most of the paras confined to the areas closest to the rifts couldn't help what they'd become. He also knew some of them could be assimilated at least into our own settlements if given the chance. But the Cataclysm was still too fresh of a memory and fear, from the humans and from our kind, was still too high.

"He argued against the death warrant for the basilisk he'd been sent after. He knew there had to be a reason it left its territory. But the Conclave ignored him and told him to either accept the assignment or they'd find someone else to do it. One of them even suggested ordering your mother to do it if he didn't."

I winced. The one way to convince Dad to do something he didn't want to was to threaten either Mom or me. Of course, he also had the reputation of making sure those responsible learned the error of their ways as soon as possible. I had no doubt he would have done the same thing this time had he come home.

"Do you believe it was a set up?"

Red nodded and then shrugged, the implication clear. He believed someone, probably someone on the Conclave, set Dad up but he didn't have proof.

"How does that relate to what's happening now?" Razor asked.

"I'm not sure it does. All I've got is my gut telling me everything that's happening now goes back to then, if not to sometime before then."

Red slumped in his chair. For the first time, I realized how pale he happened to be and how carefully he moved. We'd all been so focused on Griff when they showed up earlier, none of us realized how badly Red was injured. Cursing, I shoved out of my chair and hurried to where he sat.

"One more question." Or maybe two. "And then we're getting your injuries treated, Red."

He tried waving me off only to stop when he realized I wasn't in the mood to argue. Instead, he dipped his chin. The fact he agreed so easily confirmed my fears. Damn it. I should have paid closer attention.

"I'll explain after your injuries have been treated and we've all gotten some rest." I sat back on my heels, holding his hands to let him see how serious I was. "But right now I need you to be completely honest with me because I'm having my own doubts about certain members of the Conclave and their agents. Tell me this: do you believe there could be a traitor among its members, someone who is willing to put personal goals or money or power or whatever the hell they might value above the oaths they took and above the rest of us?"

Red looked me straight in the eye, something as paras we normally didn't do. Not when there were those of our kind who could use such contact to influence the other person.

"Just as I can't prove someone set up your father and caused his death or was behind your mother's disappearance, I can't say for certain there is a traitor on the Conclave."

He might not say it, but everything about him convinced me he believed it to be true.

"But you believe there is the possibility," I said and he nodded. "Is there anyone in town I should be wary of? Someone who might be working with the person or persons on the Conclave who have abandoned their oaths?"

Another nod.

I waited, then rolled my eyes when he remained silent.

"Red, I need to know." I huffed out a rueful laugh. "Hell, if it's who I think it is, you don't have to worry. I'm already keeping them at arm's reach."

"Yousef."

Part of me wanted him to name someone else. Hearing him name the other marshal, all I could do was blow out a long breath. I released Red's hands and climbed to my feet. I felt his eyes, as well as Razor's, on me as I turned and moved back around the desk and took a seat.

Then I leaned forward, forearms on the desktop, anger burning deep inside me.

"That's who I have questions about," I said. "I've asked Aras to try to locate him. Griff and Sophie have wolves from their pack, wolves they trust, looking as well. He's been AWOL since the attack at Gemma's."

"Has he seen the records from the warehouse? Does he know what they include?" Red sounded worried.

"No. He knows I returned to the warehouse, but not what I found or that the files have been moved here." I waved off Red's objections before he voiced them. "They are safe here."

And that brought me to my questions about how he happened to have my mother's jacket and the weapons she'd taken with her on that last assignment. But they could wait until someone treated his injuries and he got some rest.

"Razor, will you help him upstairs. Put him in one of the other guest rooms on the second floor. I'll get Sele or one of her sisters to have a look at him. Red, you're to do what they tell you and get some rest. You're safe here and the protections are set. I'll know if anyone tries to enter the property."

"Thanks, kid." He managed a slight smile as he levered up to his feet. "You look like shit, Ripley. Follow your own advice and get some rest."

"Planning on it."

Just as soon as I spoke with both Sele and Sophie. Hopefully, they could tell me something to help make sense of this mess we found ourselves in.

23

WHEN DID I BECOME THE ADULT OF OUR GROUP?

M orning came all too soon. The three hours of sleep I managed weren't enough, but it beat the alternative. For a few moments, I lay in the middle of the bed, eyes closed. As long as I didn't open them and look around, I could deny the events of the last few days. I wasn't in my mother's bedroom, sleeping in her bed. Red and Griff hadn't shown up mere hours earlier, beaten and worse. The house I'd grown up in hadn't become a base of operations as we tried to figure out who wanted any or all of us dead—or worse.

Like it or not, I couldn't put off getting up and returning to the real world.

I sat up and slid my legs over the side of the bed. I needed coffee. Lots and lots of coffee. More than that, I needed a shower. Hopefully, the two would be enough to jumpstart my brain.

Less than ten minutes later, dressed in jeans, a tee shirt and barefoot, I made my way to the kitchen where I started coffee before going to check on Griff. The door to the guestroom opened silently and I slipped inside. I nodded slightly to see him sleeping. It looked as if he hadn't moved more than an inch or two all night. Sophie sat in a chair by the window, laptop open and her fingers flying across the keyboard. She looked up and smiled wearily. Then she set the laptop to the side and climbed to her feet. I waited, figuring she wanted to talk but didn't want to disturb her brother.

"How is he?" I asked as we moved several feet down the hall away from the doorway.

"Better. Sele worked on him last night and healed the worst of his injuries. It's still going to take him a week or so to fully heal, but he's no longer in danger."

Relief filled me. Griff and I might have our differences, but I never wished him ill—at least I never really meant it when I did.

"I'm glad to hear that." I rested a hand on her arm, noting how tired she looked. Dark shadows bruised the skin under her eyes. Her clothes, the same ones she'd worn last night, were rumpled. Despite her reassurances, worry gnawed at me. "Has he been awake?"

"A couple of times, but not for long." She scrubbed her hands over her face. "He couldn't tell me much, Rip. Sele said he'd remember more after he rests some."

That didn't surprise me, but it was a disappointment. Still, if he'd told her anything that might help. . ..

"What did he say?" I hated asking, but right now every bit of information helped.

"Like I said, he doesn't remember much. He'd been on his way to meet with Alpha Lewis. He was on his way to the compound when he came on what looked like a crash. He parked and got out to see if anyone needed any help. When he did, he neither scented nor saw anything to warn him there was trouble. The next thing he knew, something hit him, throwing him back against the car. He lost consciousness almost immediately."

I frowned, not liking what she said. The crash smelled of a set up. The fact Griff hadn't scented anything to warn him of trouble most likely meant a witch was involved. Neither of which reassured me. If that was the case, we needed not only Sele and her sisters but Gemma at their best.

Damn it, I did not want Glenham Grove turning into a war zone.

"Soph, you know I want you to stay with your brother."

"Don't." She shook her head before I could continue. "I know you're about to tell me you want me to stay with Griff but that I need some rest. I don't, but not yet. I'll catch a nap later. For now, we both have work to do."

I arched a brow, inviting her to explain. I felt sure she had something in mind I hadn't considered yet.

"Griff told me he'd let Lewis know he was coming to see him. Maybe Lewis isn't behind what happened, but he must have told someone about Griff's call."

Since I agreed, I said nothing.

She slid down the wall, to sit on the floor. I joined her there and waited, giving her the time she needed to gather her thoughts and decide what to tell me. Much as I wanted to remind her she could trust me with anything, I understood the thin line she walked. Until I made it an official request, she had to respect pack law and pack dynamics.

"Rip, I need you to give me a little leeway here. I've been checking in with my sources with the other Conclaves and some of the other packs. I'm not liking some of what I'm hearing. I'm asking you to let me make some more calls before asking what I've found out. I promise I won't keep anything from you, but I need to be sure. Right now, I'm getting too many conflicting reports and there are too damned many unanswered questions."

"Sophie, I'll give you as much time as I can. I trust you. You're my sister by choice. But you've got to promise to clue me in if you hear anything that might impact us here."

She didn't say anything. Instead, she reached over and grasped my hand, giving it a quick squeeze that expressed not only her gratitude but her understanding as well.

"You need to promise me something, Rip. Promise to watch your back. Don't leave the house without being armed and armored. I know you've got some really nasty tricks up your sleeve, but it takes time for you to call on them. We both know that. Just like we both know you're vulnerable during your changes, just like I am when I start a shift."

"I will so long as you take your own advice. Something's going on and I have a feeling it's part of a conspiracy that goes back years, maybe even decades."

Something that went back to Mom's disappearance and possibly even further back. Worse, it could be much wider than I thought.

And that scared the shit out of me.

"Get back to Griff and let me know when he wakes again." I climbed to my feet and leaned down, extending a hand to help her up.

"What are you going to do?"

"Talk to Red and Gemma." Whether they wanted to or not.

"Start with Red. Sele was in a few minutes before you. She said her aunt was still sleeping."

I thanked her and promised to send in breakfast and coffee. Then I headed upstairs. If my luck held, I'd be able to corner Red in his room before he even thought about trying to slip out of the house. Not that he'd get far. I doubted the wards would let him leave, at least not without warning me first.

"Gotta say, Red, I've seen you looking better."

I leaned against the doorframe, arms folded under my breasts. He sat on the edge of the bed. Everything from his posture to the light sheen of sweat covering his face screamed his pain. Worried, I waited, fighting the urge to go to him. He wouldn't appreciate it. Pride, among other things, prevented him from asking for help. Something I knew all too well. But, seeing him wince as he bent to pull on his boot, broke my resolve. Wordlessly, I crossed the room and took the boot from him. Kneeling, I carefully pulled it onto his foot before reaching for the second boot.

"Thanks." Voice gruff, he rested a hand on my shoulder, and I knew that was all he'd say about it. But it was enough. "Of course, I could say the same about you, kid."

"I've been better." No use denying it. "We both have been."

He nodded and leaned forward, arms on his thighs and his hands dangling. "Starke?"

"He's going to be all right. I just checked on him."

Interesting he asked about Griff first. Under normal circumstances, he'd be wanting a report on what went on during his absence.

"Good, that's good." He blew out a breath and stared at the far wall. "Ripley, he saved me last night. If Starke hadn't shown up when he did, those bastards would have had me. I hate to say it, but I owe him."

If Red admitted he owed Griff, things had been worse than I

thought. Still, there might be a silver lining to it all—if Red would finally open up about what happened. Starting with telling me where he was when Griff found him.

"Where, Red? Where were you and who attacked you?"

For a moment, his expression turned mulish. Then he dropped his head into his hands. He hated asking for help almost as much as he hated being unable to help those he cared for. But this was bigger than his ego. I prayed he realized it.

"I was out at the old cabin on Black Snake Creek."

I sat back on my heels and blinked in surprise. I knew exactly where he meant, and my blood ran cold. The cabin was less than five miles from the Rift, far too close for comfort. The wild magics in the area corrupted and changed anything there for too long. The only problem was no one knew exactly how long too long was.

"Red," I hissed. "Have you lost your mind?"

He shook his head. "I hadn't been there more than a couple of hours."

I frowned, not liking the implications. His attackers either followed him there or had the cabin under surveillance. But why? Why would they be watching the cabin unless they expected him to go there?

Damn, this kept getting worse and worse.

"How long have you been using the cabin and what were you using it for?" I climbed to my feet and crossed my arms under my breasts.

"I haven't."

He held up a hand before I could interrupt. His eyes flashed for a moment, anger and something else flaring. Well too bad. This was more than wanting to know what he was doing when I wasn't around. Our friends, people we cared for, had been hurt because of secrets he'd kept. I was tired of it. Like it or not, he needed to come clean.

"Red."

He snarled, a clear indication of his temper. Instead of backing down, I waited. Silence worked better than arguments when he was in this mood. I'd learned that lesson not long after moving in with him.

"All right." He didn't throw his up his arms, but he might as well have. "I go there several times a year. Why isn't important."

"Damn it, Red, quit being stubborn. The events of the last few days should prove exactly how wrong you are."

He nodded once.

His story was simple. The cabin became the place he went when he wanted to do something, whether it was nothing more than making calls he wanted to make sure no one overheard to activities he didn't want the Conclave learning about, without interruption. It was also where he and Gemma would meet from time to time. Seems the two of them had an entirely different relationship than I suspected. Part of me cringed at the thought of two people who stood in as parents for me after Mom's death being involved in *that* way.

But it explained how his attackers might know where to find him. If he'd been under surveillance for as long as I was beginning to suspect, they knew about the cabin.

After the attack at the warehouse and once he realized staying with Gemma painted a huge target on her back, he decided the cabin was his best bet to stay safe while he figured out what was going on. Unfortunately, someone else had the same idea.

"What happened?"

"I was stupid." The disgust in his voice matched his expression. "I didn't think anyone would be foolish enough to follow me that deep into the area around the Rift."

Understanding dawned on me with all the subtlety of a meteor strike.

"Damn it, Red!" I paced the length of the room to stand in front of the window. But, instead of looking outside, I turned back to him, not caring what he saw in my expression. If I understood him correctly, he'd not only been foolish, but he'd also come damn close to committing a fatal error. "You didn't set any wards on the place?"

Looking miserable, he shook his head.

I blew out a breath and closed my eyes, counting to ten. Once satisfied I could speak without yelling, I looked at him and arched one brow. He arched a brow in return and the staring contest began. This time, however, I was determined not to be the one to look away first.

"You're getting too good at this," he grumbled. "Don't get cocky, kid. I'll admit it. I didn't think it through. I was hurt, exhausted, and needed time to rest and figure out my best course of action. I didn't think they'd try for Gemma once I was gone. I sure as hell didn't think they'd follow me that close to the Rift."

Tempting as it was to argue—or remind him yet again that he'd been a fool—I didn't.

"Tell me about the attack."

"Not much to tell. It happened after I fell asleep. I woke to the howls of wolves and then something crashed into the side of the cabin. I knew better than to let them trap me inside, so I bailed out of the back."

I closed my eyes again and prayed for patience. That was the last thing he should have done. Instead of leaving the safety of the cabin, he should have holed up inside, barricading the doors and securing the shutters on the windows. But noooo. Not Red. Not that man who thought he was indestructible.

Damn him!

"How many and what species?" I dragged a chair over to sit at the foot of the bed. "I assume there were more than wolves involved."

"At least three wolves, a red hat, and I suspect a witch. There were others but I didn't get a good look at them."

I narrowed my eyes, not believing him.

"Red, tell me. I'm going to have to go out there to see what I can find, and I'd really appreciate not walking into a trap."

"You need to stay the hell away from there, Ripley!"

"That's not going to happen, Red. So, tell me what else was out there."

He frowned but nodded. "I'm not sure but I saw what I believe to be a hodag. I can't be sure, but there were at least a dozen creatures there. They were attacking from all sides. But in the dark, I couldn't get a good count."

"And Griff?"

"He came racing up in wolf form and took down the first two wolves before they knew what happened. That's when everything went South. Whether it was the Rift, or the witch, or everything in conjunction, the energies went wild. From the shadows, gunshots rang out. We were both injured, but we managed to drive off the attackers. Once we did, Griff shifted and we came here."

"All right." None of it made sense, but then nothing about the last few days did. "I want you to stay here, Red. No bullshit now. I want you here because you need to heal but also because your presence will reassure Dani who is upstairs sleeping as well as help keep the others from doing anything foolish. Can I trust you to do as I ask?"

"I don't like it, Ripley."

"I really don't give a damn it you like it or not, Red. Live with it." I leaned back and sighed. "Sorry. I'm tired and I'm worried. You staying here eases more than one of my concerns."

He said nothing for a moment as he studied me. "All right. But you need to be careful."

"I will." I stood and, to his surprise, bent and lightly kissed his rough cheek. "Thank you. I'll let you know when I'm ready to leave. Right now, I need coffee and I want to see if Gemma's up to talking to me."

"Be easy with her, kid." Affection softened not only his expression but his voice.

"I will and I'll talk to you later."

2 4

STOP CATTING AROUND

S ele stepped into the hallway as I approached Gemma's room. As
she did, I stopped, worry building. Dark circles, so dark they
looked like bruises, shadowed her eyes. Her shoulders drooped and
exhaustion clung to her, real and palpable. Then she saw me and her
expression hardened as she placed herself between me and the
bedroom door.

Hands out to my side, doing my best to project nothing but
concern, I moved closer. Before I could say anything, the bedroom door
opened once again. This time, both Romy and Elle stepped into the
corridor. They looked between me and their sister. Neither said
anything. They didn't have to. Not when they looked as tired as Sele.

"Not now, Ripley," Sele said.

Tears gathered in her eyes. I inhaled sharply, concern ratcheting up
to fear. Before I could reply, Romy placed a gentling hand on Sele's
arm. For a moment, they looked at each other. Whatever unspoken
conversation transpired between them, Sele nodded once before she
seemed to shrink into herself.

"How is she?"

I didn't know what else to ask. Besides, their answer would dictate
what I said and did next.

"Ripley, please. Let her rest." Sele all but begged.

That was enough to convince me the older woman needed more time to recover. Unfortunately, I needed to talk to her. Hopefully, she knew something to help me figure out what's been going on.

"Sele, you know I wouldn't bother her if I had any other choice."

"But—"

Romy placed a gentling hand on her sister's arm. "Ripley, we know. It's just that she's not well. She over-extended herself badly trying to protect the property yesterday. She needs to rest and not get upset."

"But," Elle took up. "We know you need to talk to her, and she's already said she needs to talk to you." She looked at her sisters and shook her head before Sele could protest. "All we ask is you try not to upset her. She really is stretched thin right now."

"I promise." The last thing I wanted was to do anything to jeopardize Gemma's recovery. "There's more going on than we know and I have a feeling your aunt can help me understand at least some of it."

"Ripley, can't you wait a few hours at least?"

I shook my head and led them to the window at the end of the hall. I waited as they followed. They I pointed to the north, in the direction of the Rift. Dark clouds swirled, alive with energies that went beyond normal atmospheric phenomenon. Lightning warred with wild magics inside the clouds. Whatever was happening, the Rift was involved and the last thing any of us needed was for it to go wild again. If it did, I didn't know if our town and everyone in it would survive.

Even if we did, would we want to? We'd already seen what changes a wild Rift could do to the world around it. We weren't ready for another Upheaval.

At least I sure as hell wasn't.

Elle gasped and reached for her sisters' hands. For a long moment, they studied the scene in the distance. Feeling something weaving between my legs, I glanced down. Cal, still in his cat form, rubbed against me, almost as if trying to reassure me. Then he moved to weave in and out of his sisters' legs. Maybe he wasn't as much of a screw up as I thought.

"She's got no choice and neither do we." Sele closed her eyes. A moment later, she straightened her shoulders and drew a deep breath before looking at me. "We're trusting you with our aunt, Ripley, and we're trusting you to tell us what we can do to help. This." She swept an arm in the direction of the window. "Terrifies me."

"Me, too," I admitted.

I returned to Gemma's room and opened the door. She sat up in bed, looking out the window, her expression troubled. Then she looked in our direction and smiled slightly. Before anything could be said, Sele and her sisters hurried to the bed. Gemma accepted their kisses and queries about how she felt. When she assured them she felt better, the three looked as if they didn't believe her. Not that I blamed them. I didn't believe her. How could I when she looked older, more tired and worn than I'd ever seen? Worse, the exhaustion and pain reflected in her eyes betrayed just how much the day before had taken out of her.

"Ripley." Voice soft and still weak, she extended a hand in my direction. "Are you all right?"

I took her hand and bent to kiss her cheek much as Sele and the others had a few moments earlier.

"I'm fine. You did all the hard work yesterday. All I had to do was a bit of cleanup." Hopefully, she wouldn't ask what I meant. I didn't want to think about the deaths I'd had a hand in, no matter how much they deserved it.

The look Gemma gave me told me she knew better. But she didn't push. Instead, she patted the mattress and waited for me to sit. Then she looked up at her hovering nieces and smiled almost gently.

"You can quit hovering, girls." She lifted her hands and shooed them to the door. "Go. I need to speak with Ripley and then I want to rest some more."

"Aunt Gemma."

"Selena, I am going to be all right and it is important I speak with Ripley." The look she leveled at Sele left no doubt she meant it.

"Ripley."

Sele said nothing else, but her meaning was clear. I was not to do anything to push Gemma's recovery back. I dipped my chin, glad she understood I didn't have a choice right now. Apparently satisfied, she led her sisters out of the room. I didn't doubt they waited in the hallway just outside the door. Not that I blamed them. It's exactly what I'd do in their place.

For several long moments, Gemma and I sat in silence. Then she sighed and nodded. Time to talk.

I only hoped she could tell me something, anything to explain what happened yesterday.

"Ripley, is Red?"

She didn't finish. Instead, she looked at me, her worry plain to see. If Red hadn't admitted the full extent of their relationship, I'd never have guessed. All I saw in Gemma's expression was worry for a friend. I wondered if Sele and her sisters had any idea their aunt and my foster father were more than friends.

"He's going to be all right, Gemma."

Relief had her sagging against the pillows someone had carefully placed behind her so she could sit up in bed.

"What happened to him? The girls wouldn't tell me."

I shook my head. Of course they wouldn't tell her. Maybe if she and Red hadn't been so closed mouth about their relationship. At least I could answer her questions and maybe it would be enough to loosen her tongue. I hoped so. I was tired of being the last one to know what was going on.

"After he left your place, he went to the cabin near the Rift."

From the way Gemma hissed out a breath, she knew about the cabin and approved of him going there about as much as I did.

"That man is a stubborn fool." She shook her head and her mouth formed a thin line of disapproval.

"You'll get no disagreements from me, Gemma." I gave her a moment before continuing. "He got careless once he was there. He didn't set additional wards. The cabin was under attack before he could prepare. But he did get lucky. I haven't had a chance to talk with Griff yet, so I don't know how he wound up in the middle of every-thing. All Red said was he saved the day. I'm not going to lie, though. Griff's hurt badly. If he was human, I don't think he would have made it."

"The girls said it was bad but promised he was going to be all right."

I nodded, taking comfort in what she said.

"Redmond is truly going to be all right?"

"He is. I wouldn't like about that." Hell, I wouldn't try lying to her about anything. Not only would she know it, but I didn't doubt for a moment she'd make sure I never tried anything so foolish again. "Gemma, I hate to ask, but I need to know what happened at your place and why you didn't call for help."

"Before that, let me tell you why I took Red in after the fire."

I almost asked if she meant beyond the fact they had a relationship I doubted anyone knew about, including her nieces. Then I thought better of it. Instead, I nodded and waited, giving her time to decide how to begin.

"He showed up two hours or so after you warned me about the fire. I've seen him hurt before, but never like this. The signs of the fire were there but so were signs he'd been in a fight. I brought him inside and treated his injuries. Once I had, he finally told me a little about what happened. Unfortunately, Redmond is as stubborn as he is loyal and he didn't tell me everything. I knew it but I thought there would be time come morning to hear the rest of it."

Except, unless I missed my guess, he was gone by morning.

"What else did he tell you?"

"Not as much as either of us would like." She sighed wearily and closed her eyes for a moment. When she did, she looked every one of her years and then some. "He told me the magic wards in the warehouse felt different after you called him. Before he could investigate, the first fire broke out. Then all he had time to do was get the others to safety and get out. He admitted the intruders managed to surprise him, especially the last one. Once he dealt with them, he knew he needed to find a place to lay low, heal up, and figure out who was responsible. I tried to convince him to call you, but he felt you were safer not knowing he was alive. I didn't like it and told him he had one day then he had to contact you, Ripley. If he didn't, I was going to tell you everything I could about what happened."

Unfortunately for all of us, everything went to hell before the end of her timeline.

"I take it he left the house the next morning?"

She nodded, her expression a mix of misery, frustration and anger. "He did and his only explanation was he was trying to protect me."

"Gemma, I need you to remember how you felt when he said that. Remember and understand I will like it even less than you did if you're trying to figure out how to protect me right now."

She chuckled softly and nodded. "All right." She took my hand in hers and gave it a quick squeeze. "I sometimes forget you're a grown woman, every bit as talented and capable as your mother. You must forgive me for wanting to protect you, Ripley. You are every bit as much a part of my family as Sele, Elle, and Romy."

"Love you too, Gemma." I smiled and leaned forward, briefly pressing my lips to her cheek. "So what happened next?"

Angry at Red—and herself for giving her word that she'd wait a day before coming clean with me—she decided to set her magical circle and see if she could *See* anything. What saved her from being overrun were the wards around the property. The moment the outer-most one activated, she reacted instinctively. She reinforced the protective wards, especially those closest to the house. With that done, she activated a new set of wards. They controlled offensive magical spells. At least that explained the areas outside where it looked like bombs had gone off. With that done, she added an extra layer of protections around her magical circle and texted Red on the phone she'd given him, one I hadn't known about.

Damn it! Why hadn't he let me know what was happening? That was something else we'd be "discussing" later, after I saw the cabin and had a better idea about what we were facing.

"Before you ask, I didn't call you because I didn't have time. The attacks on my wards were coming from all directions. It was all I could do to keep them up while I reinforced the others. I won't lie, Ripley. I was scared, more scared than I've been since the Cataclysm. My only real goal at that point was to hold out as long as I could so I could leave clues for you to find in case I didn't survive."

I swallowed hard, fear wrapping a cold fist around my heart. What the hell were we dealing with?

"I promise I'll do everything I can to keep you and the others safe." I didn't know how, only that I'd do it. "What else can you tell me?"

"I didn't expect a direct attack. The magical attack made sense, but not the attack by the wolves and other paras. Now that I have time to think about it, I'm reminded about what happened to your mother."

Frowning, I asked what she meant.

"How much has Red told you about your mother's disappearance?"

Obviously not enough, but I didn't say that. "Not much."

"When she didn't return, he went looking for her. You know that much."

I nodded.

"He located the site of her last fight. It's there he found her jacket, weapons, and other items. It was enough to convince him not only that they were hers but that she'd probably met her death that day. Not that he didn't try to find her. He wanted closure, not just for himself but for you as well." She paused and gave a wry smile. "He also wanted vengeance. Your parents were among the few he saw as family."

"What happened?"

"He saw enough at the site that he knew he needed to get back to town and report to the Conclave. What he found went beyond your mother finding herself in a situation she hadn't expected. She'd been ambushed. She fought back, killing a number of the creatures that attacked. But she was overrun."

"T-tell me."

"Werewolves, kobolds, even a redhat and more."

I inhaled sharply, the scene I found outside Gemma's house making a warped type of sense now. There was a connection between what happened to Mom and what had been happening the last few days. But what? More importantly why and who the hell was responsible?

"There's more, isn't there?"

Gemma nodded. For the next ten minutes, I listened as she described the last time she saw Mom. The day before leaving, Mom went to her. According to Gemma, she'd been uneasy, worried. The Conclave wanted her to investigate an increase in activity near the West Texas Rift. According to what little the Conclave told her, paras confined to the area by Conclave edict were leaving and wreaking havoc on the surrounding area. They wanted Mom to investigate and deal with the problem.

Except the problem dealt with her and I once again wondered if that hadn't been the plan all along.

"Do you know who gave her the assignment?"

Gemma nodded. "Drake."

I bit back a curse. Another tie, another coincidence—and I didn't believe in coincidences.

"Did she have backup?"

"I don't know."

"All right." I drew a deep breath, held it for a moment and then exhaled. "Is there anything else you think I need to know?"

"Just watch yourself, child. I feel the danger is only beginning and it's going to focus on you."

Great. Just what I needed—not.

"I have every intention of it." Unfortunately, I couldn't rely on Yousef, not until I knew what the hell he'd been up to the last twenty-four hours. That meant I needed someone else watching my back and my options were limited. "I want you to make me a couple of promises, Gemma."

She narrowed her eyes as she looked at me. A moment later, she nodded.

"I want you to stay here until we know more about what's going on. The wards here have been reinforced. But that's not all. Not only are Sele and her sisters here, but so are Razor and Layla as well as Griff and Sophie. Aras will be here as soon as he finishes checking something for me. You'll be safe here."

At least as safe as she would be anywhere else in town.

"All right."

"Thanks." I smiled and climbed to my feet. "Get some rest now. You've had us worried."

"You be careful. I don't understand what's going on, but trust no one outside of those you named."

"Promise."

While she settled back in bed, I left the room. The moment the door closed behind me, Sele and her sisters appeared. With them, winding through their legs, was their brother. I shook my head and bent, grabbing him by the scruff of his neck before he could react. When he raised a paw, claws extended, to take a swipe at me, I gave him a shake and held him at eye level.

"Enough," I growled. "I don't have time for your stupid tricks, Cal. We're in trouble here, something you should have realized when your sisters brought Gemma back to town yesterday. You've had your fun playing the cat, but it's time to step up and help your sisters. If you won't, I'm tossing you out and you can fend for yourself."

He opened his mouth and hissed, then jerked in my grasp when I popped one finger firmly against his dark nose.

"If you need help changing back, your sisters will help you. Just ask them. But quit hiding behind your pride and quit thinking it's cute being a cat and slinking around all over the place." I spun on my heel and carried him down the hallway to the window looking out in the direction of the Rift. "*That* is only one part of what we're facing right now. So get with the program or start figuring out where you're going to hide when it all goes south on us."

I dropped him and he landed heaving on all fours. Instead of running off, he sat there, looking between me and his sisters. The fact he hadn't tried to flay the skin from my shins meant I'd at least put the fear of God into him. I hoped it also knocked some sense into this hard —and furry—head.

"I mean it, Sele. He gets his act together and shifts back or he's out of here. He's a liability in this form."

"Rip's right." Romy bent and grabbed Cal before he could run and hide. "I'll remind you, big brother, Sele's the nice one. Elle's the smart one. I'm the one who will skin you, paint your furry butt yellow and kick you out before Ripley can."

He hissed and she simply cocked one brow at him. When she did, the cat seemed to deflate.

"We'll make sure he changes back, Ripley," Sele said as she gently took their brother from Romy. "What are you going to do now?"

"I need to go check something out. The wards should keep everyone here safe. Don't try to take them down for anyone until I come back. There are things going on right now I don't understand and I'm worried our enemy might be closer than any of us think."

"Do you want one of us to go with you?" Elle asked, her eyes clouded with concern.

"Thanks, but no. Stay here and keep an eye on the others. That way I won't worry about anything else happening."

At least not too much.

25

CHECKING IN WHEN ALL I WANT IS TO GET OUT OF THIS HANDBASKET TO HELL

Three hours later, I sat in the SUV and stared at the remnants of the cabin. It had never been anything to write home about but seeing it like this left me wondering how the hell Griff and Red managed to escape. Whoever was behind the attack, they wanted no evidence left about what happened. Unfortunately for them, they miscalculated.

No, they didn't miscalculate. They underestimated Red and they hadn't planned on Griff's unexpected arrival. The two might have had the crap beat out of them in the ensuing fight, but they'd left bodies behind, a warning to others who might follow.

The carnage didn't come close to what I found at Gemma's, but the similarities were too strong to dismiss. Werewolves, several who died in the middle of shifting and others still in their wolf forms, one kobold, the arm of what I guessed was now a very pissed off redhat, and more littered the ground in front of the ruins of the cabin.

Unlike Gemma's, however, there were no survivors. Either the attackers took them off when they retreated or they killed them. It might mean no survivors to question, but it also meant I didn't have to worry about something bigger and badder than me, at least while I was in my human form, rising up to try to eat me.

What I couldn't quite fathom was how the cabin with its stone walls and metal roof had been turned into a pile of rubble. No explosion did it. Instead, it looked as if the walls had been pushed inward until the cabin collapsed in on itself. Either the attackers had their very own pet giant, not something I wanted to consider, or more magic had been involved.

As if there wasn't enough magic in the air as it was.

I remained inside the SUV with its protective wards as I studied the area. Even with the wards, the hair on my arms stood on end and I felt the rogue magics battering against the wards. Fear turned my mouth dry. The last thing I planned on doing was getting out. Who knew what this level of magical energy would do to me? Fighting the urge to throw the transmission into reverse and get the hell out of there, I picked up my phone from where it lay on the passenger seat and opened the camera app.

Ten minutes later, I sped away from the cabin and the mind-numbing rogue magics of the Rift. The sooner I made it back to town and had Sele or one of her sisters check me out, the better I'd feel. Then I needed to see Griff and Sophie. The fact wolves kept showing up at scenes like this worried me. I might trust the two of them, but I didn't trust the pack, especially since it had yet to offer to help deal with the current round of trouble.

But first things first, I needed to see if there'd been any word from —or of—Yousef.

"Anything?" I asked the moment Aras answered my call.

"Only things that make me ask more questions. We need to meet."

I bit back a curse and focused on putting more distance between me and the cabin. "I'm on my way back to town. It will take at least an hour. I'll call when I'm closer and we'll meet up."

"It will take me that long at least to get back. Watch your back, Ripley."

"You do the same." I considered for a moment before making up my mind. "Aras, I'm going to try calling him one more time. I'll let you know if he answers."

"Understood." Now it was his turn to pause and I could almost see his forehead furrow in thought. "Ripley, is everyone safe?"

"They are. I left them at the house and the wards are up. No one's getting in until

I'm back."

"Back from where?" A hint of suspicion roughened his voice.

"Red told me where he'd gone after leaving Gemma's. I needed to have a look."

"And?"

"It's bad. Much like what we found at Gemma's."

He needed to know if for no other reason than to understand how dangerous our situation was. His curse confirmed he understood. Good. That meant he'd take no unnecessary chances. At least I hoped so.

"Aras, I'll let you know when I'm almost to town. It's time we sit down with everyone and figure out what we know and don't about what's going on."

"Just watch yourself, Ripley. If this is as bad as we both fear, whoever is behind it won't hesitate to harm you if you get to close."

I assured him I planned on being as careful as possible. Then I ended the call. Even though I needed to try one again to reach Yousef, I hesitated. Until I put miles between me and the Rift, I didn't want anything else distracting me, something the call definitely would. Besides, I needed to think—about what happened the last few days and about what I'd seen at the cabin.

Halfway to town, I slowed and glanced in the rearview mirror. The Rift no longer filled the mirror. But there was no mistaking the fact something was wrong. Clouds continued to build around it, dark against the sky. Lightning flashed, clashing with the rogue magics arcing toward the ground. Praying those magics settled before we found ourselves facing another Cataclysm, I pulled over. Ready or not, I needed to try yet again to reach Yousef.

When my call rolled over to voice mail, I frowned. Then I shot off a quick text, making no attempt to hide my frustration and concern with the situation.

Yousef, where are you? Report in. Otherwise, I will inform the Conclave you are awol.

I hit send and dropped the phone back onto the passenger seat.

That was all I could do until he either checked in or I spoke with Aras.

———

"WELL?"

I met Aras in front of the house. He said nothing. Instead, he nodded toward the gate. Understanding, I concentrated on the wards, seeing the magical energies surrounding the property, forming a protective shell that dipped below the ground. A moment later, a gateway shimmered and opened almost directly in front of the gate across the front walk. The moment it did, I motioned Aras inside. I followed, turning back to make sure the wards returned to their prior state. It might be overkill, but after everything that happened recently, I was in no mood to take any chances.

"I found where he's been but not where he is now."

We moved slowly down the walk toward the front porch. I paused and looked at him, waiting for him to explain. Then I realized there was another question I wanted answered before finding out where he'd been. No, I wanted to know who he'd seen.

When I asked, Aras' expression darkened.

"After leaving Gemma's he disappeared for much of the day. Several of my contacts confirmed seeing him heading away from town but could not follow without being seen. They offered to try to shadow him, but I said not to. I assumed you did not want to tip your hand."

He waited until I nodded. I didn't like it, but he was right. Until I knew what Yousef might be up to, I didn't want him knowing I had my doubts about him. But I'd give almost anything to know what he did after leaving Gemma's. With every passing hour, worry turned into suspicion. I didn't want to doubt him, but he was making it damned hard.

"What else?"

Please let there be something else.

"He showed up at the pack compound late afternoon and, from what I've learned, he was there an hour or so before leaving. From there, he went south. None of my contacts know where he went then."

"Do you know who he saw when he went to the compound?"

He shook his head. "I have my suspicions."

I arched one brow as I leaned against the porch post. "Care to share?" "There is trouble within the pack. I assume you know this." I nodded.

"My guess is that your marshal met with the alpha. But whether it was to discuss the wolves you found at Gemma's or to recruit him for some reason, I know not." "All right." I pushed a hand through my hair.

That put a new spin on things, one I didn't like. One that made it all the more important I talked with both Griff and Sophie before I did anything else. But how the hell was I supposed to ask them if their alpha, if their pride, was about to go rogue?

"I need to check on a couple of things. Go on in and let Razor know what you found. If anyone asks, I'll be back shortly. Until I am, no one leaves the house. The wards will protect you."

I hoped. After what happened at the warehouse, at Gemma's, and at the cabin, my confidence in magical wards wasn't as strong as it had been.

"Where are you going?"

From anyone else, the question would have rankled. Not from Aras, not now. Not when I recognized his concern.

"I'm going to The Red Dragon. Drea and Jayden are opening today." Assuming I remembered the bar's schedule. "I need to have a word with them."

"All right." He studied me for a moment. Then he reached out and lightly rested a hand on my arm. "You watch yourself and that temper of yours, Ripley. We need you thinking, not just reacting. I do not understand what is happening, but something tells me you will be the key to making sure no one else is injured."

I didn't like it, but I nodded. Then I motioned him inside the house. Once he complied, I hurried across the lawn to where the SUV waited. The sooner I talked with the bar's managers, the sooner I could get back and, hopefully, figure out how to end this nightmare once and for all.

The moment I entered the bar, I relaxed. Someone, probably Razor, had reinforced the wards since my last shift. The magic danced across my skin and buzzed inside my head. Most wouldn't feel it, at least as long as they did nothing to trigger the wards. Hopefully, it would be enough to protect the patrons once the doors opened for business in a couple of hours.

Standing behind the bar, Drea and Jayden, a mated pair of shapeshifters. The closest I'd come to naming Jayden's species, and he was exceptionally closed mouth about what his species happened to be, was Garuda. I'd seen him shifted once, not long after he came to work for Red. A drunk werewolf tried tearing the bar apart. Jayden shifted with an ease that surprised me. One moment, the slim, unassuming man with blond hair and blue eyes stood behind the bar. The next, he sported the head, wings and legs of a very large eagle, complete with a very dangerous looking beak, to go with his human body. To say he made very short work of the drunk is putting it mildly.

Drea, on the other hand, never tried hiding what she is. She didn't flaunt it, but it was hard to ignore the three fox tails that sometimes peeked out of her clothing. The Kitsuné was quicker to anger than her mate, but she much preferred the shotgun Red kept under the bar or a liquor bottle up side the head if someone got too handsy during one of her shifts. When I asked about it once, she simply smiled and said she didn't want to do anything to damage her pelt. In a way, it made sense. When she fully shifted, she was much smaller than many of the other species who frequented the bar. The shotgun made a great equalizer and who was I to argue?

"You look like you could use this, Rip." Jayden slid a mug of coffee across the bar in my direction.

"Thanks." I took a sip and sighed. He made excellent drinks but his coffee was to die for.

"Red?" Drea looked at me in concern as I hooked a stool and took a seat.

"Safe." I nodded as the two almost sagged in relief. "I'm not going to say much more than that right now."

Jayden's expression darkened, not in anger but in worry. "The rumors are true then, aren't they?"

I might not know exactly what rumors, but I could take a guess. I also needed to trust these two, not only to run the bar but to protect its employees and any patrons who showed up. Considering everything that happened the last few days, I had no doubt the bar would be packed with people wanting to know what was going on.

"The short version is someone, and more likely a group of some-ones, attacked not only the warehouse but also Gemma's place yester-day. Gemma's going to be all right, but she overextended herself trying to protect the house and land around it. As for Red, he's been in hiding, needing to recover from his own injuries. I've seen them both and know where they are. So I know they're as safe as possible right now."

"What can we do?"

"Business as usual but with a few twists." I prayed I wasn't making a very big mistake, one that put them in danger. "Open up on sched-ule. But call in extra help. I'm authorizing it. Not just bar, kitchen and floor help. I want additional security as well. At least two on the door, checking everyone who comes in. If they aren't known to you, they don't get in. I want a list of any newcomers trying to get in and any of our regulars who seem off in any way."

"You got it, boss." Jayden grinned as I scowled at him. "What else?"

"The wards stay up. Don't tone them down any. We're taking a big enough of a chance opening up."

"You going to be here?" Drea asked.

I gave a small shrug. "I don't know. That's why I want extra securi-ty." The question was who. "Call in Juan, Gena, and Alex. They aren't on the schedule, but they're the best we have."

"No, you're the best we have," Jayden corrected. "But we also understand you have to worry about the big picture right now—Marshal."

"Thanks for understanding. I'll be here if I can, but I don't want to promise. As for the others, I'll authorize overtime as long as they're here and they're ready for trouble." I caught my lower lip between my teeth, thinking hard. "Hell, everyone who works tonight will get over-time. I'm not going to ask you to work, not knowing what's been going on, without making it worth your while."

And Red could bitch all he wanted when he wanted, but he left me in charge. So he'd live with it, like it or not.

"Ripley." Drea drew out my name, but her protest died when I shook my head. "All right. What else can we do to help?"

"Call me if anything, and I don't care how minor it seems at the time, feels off. If you can't get me, call Razor or Sophie."

That had them both looking at me in surprise. Instead of objecting or asking any of the questions reflected in their eyes, they nodded. I smiled, finished my coffee and stood. For a moment, I looked around. The bar looked different in the light of day. Tables with chairs stacked on top of them until someone mopped the floor filled the room. The bar gleamed in the light. The liquor bottles on the shelves behind the bar caught the light and sent it cascading out in million little motes of color. Thanks to spells Red paid a fortune for, none of the cigarette and cigar smoke from the night before remained. Instead, it faintly smelled like a freshly mowed lawn. It wouldn't last once the door opened, but I'd take it for now.

"Rip, how worried should we be?" Jayden asked.

"I don't know." I couldn't lie to them. "My gut tells me that whoever's behind this isn't going to try anything else so soon. But let's not run any risks. If you feel something's wrong, clear the bar out and close it down. You know where the safe room is?"

Fortunately, Red is as paranoid as a cat in a room filled with rocking chairs. Each of his buildings had either a safe room or a secret exit. Some had both.

"We do. Red showed us after he promoted us."

"Use if it you need to. Just let me know." I really didn't want to have to walk through fire again to find out if any of my friends had been killed—or worse. "I'll check in when I can."

"You get some rest. You look like you're running on fumes." Drea looked at me in concern.

"That's the plan." Just not anytime soon, unfortunately.

To reassure myself no surprises lay hidden inside the bar, I did a walkthrough. Satisfied, I waved a quick goodbye to Drea and Jaylen and headed out. Time to get back to the house and compare notes with the others. Hopefully, they had a better idea about what our next move should be than I did.

26

WHO WAS THAT WITCHY WOMAN?

G ravel crunched under my boots as I crossed the parking lot. My
SUV was one of three vehicles present. That much, at least,
hadn't changed while I was inside. I dug in my pocket, reaching for
my keys. Then the world pitched before slamming to a stop. Magical
energies hit me, almost dropping me to my knees. My head whipped
up and I scanned the area. The keys fell to the ground, forgotten.

Bracing myself, I dropped into a protective stance. Flames danced
around my hands. My eyes bled to gold as both of my aspects pushed
forward, fighting for release.

One part of my brain laughed almost hysterically as it pictured an
eight-foot-tall wolf clad in flames going on the hunt. With my luck, my
fur would catch fire and I'd incinerate myself.

Low growls passed my lips as I tried to identify the source of the
attack. That was all it could be. Nothing and no one else appeared
impacted by what happened. That meant someone, or something,
targeted me. Well, they'd soon learn what a serious mistake that had
been.

"Show yourself." I spoke softly, assuming whoever was behind the
attack had to be near to make sure it didn't go astray.

I waited, every sense heightened. A scrape of leather against the pavement gave me a location. I turned in time to see a small, slim, pretty woman of indeterminant age step around the corner of the building nearest the bar. Her blonde hair was pulled back into a simple tail. She wore a sundress and scrappy sandals. Her blue eyes and cherubic face made her look as if she couldn't hurt a fly. But every instinct screamed that her appearance was deceiving. Any doubts I might have had disappeared when she spoke.

"Such an easy target. You are lucky I only wanted to get your attention." She spoke softly, but the evil behind her words wrapped around me in an oily embrace.

"Not so easy, as your little pets can tell you," I said, reminding her of the dead at Gemma's.

"So young and full of yourself. Just like your mother."

I refused to react to the obvious bait. Instead of responding, I narrowed my eyes and relaxed my stance. As I did, she cocked her head to one side, her brows drawing together in a mix of frustration and curiosity. I wasn't reacting as she expected. Interesting. Who told her what to expect?

"Thanks. My mother was a very special woman." I smiled, not letting her see the questions and doubts running through my mind. "But you have me at a disadvantage.

You are?"

She blinked, almost as if she couldn't believe what she heard. Interesting.

"Your worst nightmare."

I tossed my head back and laughed. When I stopped, I made a show of looking her up and down, a sneer on my lips.

"That would be easier to believe if you didn't look like a poor imitation of a certain doll with too much boob and ass and not a brain in her head."

Her hands fisted at her side and she actually stomped her foot like a petulant toddler. Interesting. Then, eyes blazing, she looked at me, doing her best to appear intimidating.

"Then let me do this properly." Her voice dropped. Gone was the slight lisp I hadn't noticed until now. "You are supposed to have been well-trained by your parents. So you should recognize my name."

I yawned, feigning boredom. "And that is?"

"Ker."

I wanted to gasp, maybe even turn tail and run. If she spoke true, this was the woman the werewolf at Gemma's named. She was the para my father warned me about so many years ago. Ker, the death spirit. Unlike some of the myths surrounding the Keres, Ker could and did kill, usually in the most gruesome way possible.

Shit, damn and fuck.

"Big talk for such a little lady."

She remained where she was, never moving closer. I prayed that meant she wasn't going to attack. But, for all I knew, she was simply biding her time, waiting for an opening. Well, I didn't plan on giving her one. In fact, if I could bluff her into leaving I would, starting with calling on my aspect of Surer to add not only height but bulk to my person.

I only hoped I didn't need to do more because I wasn't sure I could transform into either of my dominant aspects quickly enough to counter anything the woman sent at me.

"You would be wise not to underestimate me." Ker smiled slightly. "I so wanted to see you for myself. You are the first in a very long time to try to stand against me."

"Maybe if you didn't hide in shadows, Ker."

"But the shadows are so much fun and little humans are afraid to look too deeply into them." Her little girl laugh sent a chill down my spine. Then her expression hardened and the evil lurking beneath the surface shone through. "I may respect the fact you want to protect those you care for, but that is weakness. One I will exploit for my bene-fit. So listen closely, Ripley Walker. Turn over Redmond Oakley and the girl if you want to save this shithole of a town and everyone who lives here. You have twelve hours to comply."

I didn't say anything. I couldn't. Even though she didn't name Dani, I knew who she meant. What I didn't know why she wanted Dani. Not that it mattered. I wouldn't give either of them up, not without a fight.

And I was one hell of a fighter.

But I was also smart enough to know this was neither the time nor the place for a fight. So I did the one thing Ker didn't expect. I laughed. I laughed so hard, tears ran down my cheeks. I laughed until I had to bend over in an attempt to draw a breath. At least that's what it looked like. Instead, it was my chance to grab my backup gun from where it rested in an ankle holster. Ker stared at me for a moment in surprise as I straightened, gun in hand. Then she simply disappeared in the blink of an eye.

Damn it!

Unless I missed my guess, she'd never really been there. I doubted it was even Ker. No, my money now lay on it being someone projecting her image, using it to hide their own identity. All I knew for certain was whoever it was had to be nearby. Of course, that could mean anywhere from a block away to miles, depending on the ability level and strength of the person casting the spell.

But they'd made their point. This round went to whoever was pulling the strings. But it wasn't a complete win. Ker, or whoever it was, might be smart, but she'd made a mistake. She tipped her hand. Now I had a solid direction of inquiry, one I planned on following without any further delay.

———

"Rip, drink this."

Drea placed a glass of whiskey on the desk near my right hand. For a moment, she studied me, making sure I was all right. I knew better than to try to reassure her. When I ducked back inside the bar after Ker disappeared, both Drea and Jaylan saw me shaking in reaction. While Jaylan escorted me back to the office, Drea went to pour me a drink. Now they both watched, waiting for an explanation.

"We're not opening." I croaked it out and reached for the whiskey, tipping it back with a flick of my wrist.

"Ripley, what happened?" Jaylan asked.

"Let's just say someone wanted to make a point in the parking lot and they got my attention." I carefully replaced the glass on the desktop. Then I dropped my head into my hands. They waited, giving me time. "I think it was just a projection, but it was enough to scare the shit out of me. I'm not going to risk any of you or our patrons. The bar is closed tonight."

"Are you all right?" Drea asked.

"I will be." Given a year or two. I pushed away from the desk and stood. Tempting as it was to stay there, hiding away from the world, I couldn't. Ker, or whoever they were, started the clock ticking. I didn't have time to waste. "Text when you're on your way home and when you get there. Otherwise, I'm sending someone to check on you."

"Ripley, you're starting to scare me," Drea admitted.

"Good. Because I'm not going to let anyone else I care for get hurt." Then, seeing their concern, I sighed. "Sorry. My little encounter shook me. I don't think you have anything to worry about, but I am not willing to take the risk."

"All right." Jaylan looked at his mate and she nodded, her expression troubled.

"We'll contact the rest of the staff. What else can we do?"

"That's it for now. I'll let you know if I think of anything."

Drea gave me a hard hug before letting me leave. She and Jaylan stood in the doorway, watching me cross the parking lot to the SUV. Before climbing in, I turned and waved. Then I slid in behind the steering wheel, locking the door after me.

"Ripley, where are you?" Sophie asked the moment she answered my call.

"Heading to the house. There's been a complication."

"Are you all right?"

"Yeah." For now, at least. "Do me a favor. Make sure Dani's okay. Then tell the others we need to talk when I get there."

"All right. Time?"

"I'm leaving the bar now."

"We'll be waiting."

"Any word from Yousef?" Red asked as I joined everyone except Dani and Aras in the dining room fifteen minutes later.

I shook my head, my expression grim. "No, but I'll come back to that shortly. Something happened while I was out that we need to discuss first."

It didn't take long to tell them about Ker or whoever it was. No one said a word as I described what happened. Their expressions ranged from deep in thought to anger to worry. But it was Red I paid the most attention to. The fact Ker mentioned my mother, and in a way that made me think she knew Mom, worried me. It also reminded me there was still a great deal about Mom's last assignment I didn't know. Things I started to wonder if Red knew.

"Do you think it was really her?" Griff asked from his place down the table.

I glanced at him, relieved he felt well enough to be out of bed. Not that he looked all that much better. Pain reflected in his eyes and drew deep lines in his face. He held himself carefully, as if his ribs hurt a great deal. Worried, I looked at Sophie who simply shook her head, her meaning clear. She didn't think he should be up yet and he overruled her.

"My gut tells me no, not that it helps much." "I don't understand," Layla admitted.

"We're basically fucked if Ker is really involved in what's going on. She's a death deity and from what my parents taught me, the reality is much worse than the myth. She wouldn't hesitate to kill any and all of us for the fun of it." I looked around the table, letting them see how worried I was.

"And?" Razor prompted.

"She didn't make any attempt to kill me. She didn't make a move against me. Instead, she seemed curious about me and was testing how I'd react to an implied threat. When that didn't work, she told me I have twelve hours to turn over Red and

'the girl'."

"The girl?" Sophie's brow knitted.

"Dani," Gemma said grimly.

I nodded. Then I turned my attention back to Red. "Why does she want the two of you?"

"I don't know." When none of us said anything, he frowned. "I really don't."

"All right." I didn't believe him. How could I when he'd been keeping so many secrets? Secrets about my mother, probably secrets about Dani, and who knew what else. "Then tell me how what happened to my mother ties in with everything that's been happening. Too many people have been using her as a way to warn me off this."

"Ripley, you have my word that I don't know. All I can say for sure is your mother was not comfortable with that last assignment. It felt off to her. But she couldn't pinpoint why."

"Why didn't you tell me you went to her last known location and found her things there? And why did you keep them instead of sending them on to the Conclave?"

Several of the others gasped. All eyes were on him. Instead of trying to deny it, he slumped in his chair. Every year of his age, every ache etched on his face.

"I knew your mother would want her guns, her jacket and other things I kept to go to you. I gave the Conclave what they needed and nothing more." His eyes glistened with an emotion so deep it surprised me. "They deserved nothing else of hers. They'd already taken your father. They took her life as surely as if they ordered her death themselves. I wasn't going to let them take the rest from you."

I heard the truth and nodded. "Thank you." Nothing else needed to be said.

"So what do we do now?" Gemma asked.

I glanced at my watch. An hour had passed since my encounter with Ker.

"I need your help, each of you. We don't have much time and I'm not going to turn anyone over to that bitch." That was one thing I was certain of.

It didn't take long to hand out assignments. Aras would continue looking after Dani. Layla would help. Gemma and her nieces would contact other witches to see if they knew anything that might help. Red and Razor would talk with Razor's grandmother to see if she could tell us anything else. Then they'd contact their own sources in the other sectors. That left Sophie and me to deal with the rest of it, starting with the pack.

But after I made a couple of calls.

"You said we'd discuss Yousef," Gemma reminded me.

"For now, he is considered persona non grata." I shook my head before anyone could interrupt. "He's not been in contact since he left

Gemma's yesterday. Aras tried locating him and all he learned is that he showed up at the pack compound hours later yesterday. He was allowed in and there is no indication of where he went afterward."

"Is he involved in what's going on?" Razor asked.

"We have to assume he is. That means no sharing of information with him, no matter how inconsequential it might seem, without my approval. Understand?" Everyone nodded.

"Griff, do me a favor and contact Nico. Let him know what's going on and see if he has any ideas. Also let him know what I've decided about Yousef."

"Consider it done."

"Thanks." I smiled slightly. "Sophie, I shouldn't be too long."

With that, I climbed to my feet. Time to make my calls and see just how deep the shit was that we'd fallen into.

27

ON THE TRAIL AGAIN

"Care to tell me who you called?" Sophie asked as she pulled away from the house.

For a moment, I considered refusing. Then I changed my mind. She needed to know if she was going to help me with what I had in mind. Beyond that, I needed a sanity check. With everything that happened recently, I didn't trust myself not to be jumping to conclusions.

"I made several calls actually," I admitted. "The first was to the senior marshal near the southern border. Then I contacted one of the marshals in Tennessee." Both of whom I knew fairly well and both of whom admitted there had been odd things going on in their Zones as well. "They confirmed the Rifts closest to them are also acting strangely and that they've had trouble in the Zones."

"Same sort of trouble?"

"Not exactly, but similar enough to worry them once I told them what had been happening here."

"What's going to happen?" She stopped at the intersection and glanced across at me.

"They're contacting some of the other marshals to see if they've had any trouble and report back later. They're also sending me all they can about what they're dealing with."

"I assume you're returning the favor."

I nodded and motioned for her to drive on. "I am."

"Who else did you call?"

"Jeanette O'Connor."

Sophie whistled softly. "The Conclave Chair?"

"Yeah." And my knees were still knocking from it.

"What did she say?"

"Before or after wanting to know why I wasn't going through Drake?"

"Both?"

"She wasn't happy. Even after I explained about Yousef's disappearing act and the fact Drake hadn't done what he promised regarding sending me information from the other Sectors that reported trouble the day of the fire, she tried deflecting me. It wasn't until I told her what Ker, or whoever it was, said about my mother that she listened. She still wasn't happy, but she finally admitted I wasn't out of line for contacting her."

"And?"

"She admitted the Conclave isn't sure what's going on. There was the implication at least some of them are worried one of their own might be working against the Conclave."

"Damn."

"Yeah." I tipped my head back, closing my eyes. "She knows we're on the clock here and said to keep her in the loop."

"And Drake?"

"She said to act as if nothing's wrong if he contacts me."

"You watch yourself, Rip. He's not going to take kindly to you going behind his back."

"Then he should do as he promised. I'm tired of being three steps behind and having to navigate what's happening blind." Anger roughened my voice.

"Okay."

Silence fell as we drove on. It didn't take long to reach the pack's compound on the south side of town. Most of the pack lived here, partly because the pack owned the land and buildings inside the compound and partly because werewolves are pack animals and need contact with others of their kind. Sophie and her brother were the exception, choosing to live in town for reasons of their own.

Reasons I probably should have discussed with Sophie before coming here.

"You know better than to bring an outsider here, Starke," the male wolf snarled as he stopped us at the gate.

As he postured, Sophie sat there, all but looking through him as if he was below her notice. Then she looked at me and winked, her smile telling me she knew he couldn't see. Before he could say anything else, she jerked a thumb in my direction.

"Do you really want to challenge me, Rufus?" Humor filled her voice. "She is no outsider. She is the Zone's senior marshal and she has business with the alpha. Take it from me, you do not want to stand in her way."

He bared his teeth and tried to up his posturing. Instead of intimidating either of us, all he did was make me want to smack his nose with a rolled up paper.

"He said nothing about expecting you."

"And I'm sure he tells you everything." It was out before I could stop it. His jaw dropped and I took advantage of his surprise to climb out of Sophie's Jeep. "You have two options, Rufus. You can stand back and let us through or you can explain to your alpha why I was forced to leave and return, but with other marshals as backup and why I had to report to the Conclave that the pack refused to cooperate with my investigation."

He snarled, his eyes bleeding to gold, a sure indication his control over his wolf was slipping. Instead of agreeing, I climbed back in the Jeep and glanced at Sophie. She looked calmer than I felt but then I saw her fingers drumming against the steering wheel. She was pissed but she wasn't going to let Rufus—and could that really be his name know.

The moment he disappeared from view, loping into the trees to the right of the drive, she slid the Jeep into gear. As we drove further into the compound, I arched a brow in question. Not expecting an answer, I considered our greeting and the lack of respect the wolf showed her. His attitude surprised me, especially since I knew how strong Sophie's wolf was and didn't doubt she could easily defeat the man, in either form, if it came to a fight.

"Is that an indication of what I can expect?"

She nodded without taking her eyes from the drive.

"What about Alpha Lewis? Is he going to be trouble?"

"I don't know." Exasperation and frustration filled her voice. "He's been different the last few months. His temper shorter, his respect for the Conclave lessening. I don't know what's going on with him but it's not good for the pack and it's not good for the town."

"All right. I want you to stay with the Jeep. Let me deal with him." I didn't want her getting in trouble with her pack. We had enough to worry about without adding to it.

"Not a chance in hell, Rip." She pulled into a parking space outside the one-story building that housed the alpha's office. "I promise not to start anything, but I will have your back."

I didn't have time to argue. Instead, I once again climbed out of the Jeep. As I did, the front door of the building opened and Alpha Carson Lewis stepped outside. What was it with the wolves and how they immediately started posturing in an attempt to intimidate us?

Lewis slowly climbed down the three steps to the parking lot, his black boots all but silent on the concrete. His dark hair swept across a broad forehead and kissed the top of his collar. Flecks of gold lightened his otherwise brown eyes. But it was the anger reflected in those eyes that put me on my guard.

Four other wolves exited the building after him and took up protective positions at his back. My own wolf aspect growled softly, not in anger but in anticipation. She wanted to *play* with them and I had no doubt they would not find it nearly as entertaining as she did. As enticing as the thought of beating them at their own game happened to be, I didn't dare give in to temptation. Not when I felt more eyes on us from the safety of the nearby buildings.

And certainly not until I knew where the rest of the pack's loyalty lay.

Lewis slowly closed the distance between us, his eyes narrowing to see a gun at each thigh and the badge clipped to my belt. This was the first time I'd ever come on pack land in my official capacity. Hell, as far as I knew, it was the first time a marshal had been here in their official capacity since before my mother's disappearance.

"What do you want?" Lewis did not try to hide his disdain.

"I came out of respect for the pack." Not really, but he didn't need to know that. "Several dead werewolves have been found at different crime scenes over the last few days. I wanted to see if you recognize them and, if you do, I need to know what you can tell me about them."

"My pack is accounted for." Seeing Sophie standing behind me, he frowned for a moment before giving her a predatory smile. "With one exception."

"Really?" I leaned against the Jeep's front end, doing my best to appear unconcerned. "Because several of the wolves have already been identified as either past or current members of the pack. So care to try again?"

His upper lip peeled back and the gold flecks in his eyes became more predominant. Then he seemed to think better of retorting. Instead, he turned his attention to Sophie. Praying things didn't go south, I waited to see what he did next.

"Get your ass over here, Sophia," he ordered.

My brows winged skyward. Sophie hated the more formal version on her name, something anyone who'd known her more than a few minutes knew. To call her Sophia was tantamount to calling her out.

"With respect, Alpha, I think I'll stay where I am. The marshal asked for my assistance and I agreed because it is the right thing to do for not only the town but for the pack."

Lewis threw his head back and howled. As he did, the wolves ranged behind him began growling, their features blurring as their control slipped. To my surprise, Sophie remained unmoved. She stood all but motionless, her expression impassive. Whatever was happening, she was unmoved. Any other time, I'd be impressed. But with the situation about to blow up in our faces, I wanted to stop things before the situation devolved into chaos.

"I remind you that you are a member of this pack at my sufferance, a female who should know her place." Lewis waved a hand, calming the wolves at his back for the moment. "You broke pack laws by bringing this *outsider* into our territory without permission. Unless you want to be foresworn and outcast, you will get on your knees and submit *now!*"

Before I could stop her, Sophie stepped around me. For one moment, I worried she would do as the alpha said. Then, as she stopped, I knew this was much worse. She was ready to challenge the alpha and I couldn't risk that. I didn't need the pack going rogue—or worse—right now. I sure as hell couldn't risk her getting injured. Griff would have my head if anything happened to his baby sister. If all that wasn't bad enough, Sophie would skin me alive if I stopped whatever she had in mind.

But I couldn't just stand there, letting everything go to Hell in the proverbial handbasket.

"Tell me, *Alpha*. Where is your second?" I put as much disgust into his title as possible as I pointed to the redhead standing behind and slightly to his right. The man who looked like he couldn't be more than twenty-five and who was much too thin without too little muscle definition for a werewolf. Interesting. It was something I needed to discuss with Sophie when we got out of here. "Do you know where Griffin Starke is? Or perhaps I should ask if you care."

"Pack business does not concern you, woman." His eyes flashed angrily and turned a deeper gold as his features shifted, blurred.

"There you are wrong." I stepped up to stand shoulder-to-shoulder with Sophie. "I am the Zone's senior marshal. I've waded through the blood and gore of current and former members of your pack. Members you should have informed me had been cast out and members you should have informed me were missing.

"I also know exactly where your second is. A man who is supposed to be your friend, your brother in all but blood. I know he was injured by the same people who attacked the town and who attacked Gemma. You may not care about the town, but Gemma has been a friend to the pack since before you became alpha."

Two of the wolves at his back faltered, looking between their alpha and me when they heard Gemma had been attacked. But it was the unhappy murmuring behind me that caught my attention. The pack members I'd felt watching us were not happy to learn about the attacks. Lewis heard it as well and snapped his teeth together, not nearly as effective as if he'd done it after shifting.

"It is clear from what I've seen since arriving that there is trouble either in or with the pack. That is bad enough. Worse, you haven't informed the Conclave of trouble even though it is clear to me it could impact our relationship with the normals. Unless you have a very good reason for keeping this information to yourself, you and I have a problem."

I didn't know where the words came from, but they were out before I could stop them.

"You have no authority here, Marshal." His words slurred as his teeth elongated and his facial features began morphing from human to wolf.

All right, Morrigan, you wanted out to play. So let's play.

Lewis wanted a fight. Too bad he wouldn't get one. Morrigan would see to that.

Without taking my eyes from him, I removed my weapons, making a show of it and of my disdain for him and his wolves. Sophie took them, a slight smile curling up the corners of her mouth. Without a word, she secured the guns at her thighs, much as I had. Then she accepted my mother's jacket from me, softly promising to make sure nothing happened to it. I gave a quick nod before turning my attention back to Lewis.

"Do you really think you can force me to do anything I don't want to?" I threw it out like a challenge. When he said nothing, I laughed. "There's my answer. You're a coward. How the hell have you managed to control the pack for as long as you have without having the balls to stand up to a mere female?"

Sophie chuckled. She knew exactly what I was trying to do. After making sure I was ready, she stepped to the side. Others of the pack slowly appeared from the homes and offices where they'd been watching. The air around us came to life with anticipation, curiosity and something else I'd have to think about later, after this was over.

"Perhaps it's time for me to contact the Conclave and tell them this pack needs a new alpha for its continued survival?"

Lewis howled in protest a moment before he leapt in my direction.

As he did, the last of his control over his wolf slipped and he began to transform. I stood my ground. This was the moment of truth, a truth I needed to accept as much as he did. Between one moment and the next, I stopped fighting the pressure that had built in my chest from the moment we neared the compound. Power rushed through me as Morrigan's gifts sprang to life.

Sophie's sharp intake of breath was almost instantly echoed by others at our backs. Whines filled the air and the sounds of people dropping to their hands and knees followed. The corners of my mouth lifted. The pack recognized the power flowing through me and that was all I needed.

Now to see if Lewis did as well.

"Stop!"

I didn't raise my voice. I didn't move from where I stood. I simply watched as the brown wolf with silver highlights obeyed. He whimpered, his claws scraping the concrete of the parking lot as he dropped to his belly. I held him there and simply arched a brow at the men still standing behind him. They swallowed hard, fear filling their expressions. Then they slowly dropped to their knees. It was an act of submission I hadn't asked for, but one I wouldn't discount either. Now to deal with the alpha.

"I gave you a chance, Lewis. Now shift back."

Whining, he did as I said. It wasn't quick, certainly not compared with how quickly he shifted from human to wolf, and it wasn't painless. But I didn't care. It was the act of submission I needed even if it destroyed his place in the pack.

"Now, you are going to answer my questions. Understand?" I asked once he knelt before me, as naked as the day he was born.

"Y-yes." His muscles quivered as he tried to force himself to his feet only to fail. "W-what are you?"

Before I could answer, Sophie stepped forward, placing herself between me and her alpha and his followers. She stared them down for a moment before turning to face the rest of the pack currently present.

"You ask what she is, but can't you feel it? Don't you recognize the touch of Morrigan, the mother of us all? Do you not feel it through the ties of our blood?" Murmurs of surprise and wonder were her only answer.

"Marshal Walker is so much more than we are. She is no mere wolf who answers to Morrigan, the mother of us all. She is from Morrigan, a direct descendant. She calls to us and we answer. We can no more fight her than we can fight our own inevitable deaths." She paused for effect before continuing.

"Now ask yourselves this: why has she not made herself known to us in this form before now?"

If that wasn't my cue, I didn't know what was.

"I didn't because that is not our way." At least it wasn't my way. "Morrigan wanted you to be free, not to be my pets, answering to my whim. I wanted you to prove yourselves on your own, without the threat of what I could do if you failed."

"That is the way. It is as written in our lore," someone said from behind me.

"But your alpha has failed you, just as he has failed Morrigan." I pointed in his direction. "All he had to do was answer a few questions. Instead, he tried to punish a member of the pack for following the laws. He turned his back on his second who was badly injured while trying to protect each of you as well as those who live in town. He left me no choice. What happens next depends on him and on each of you." "W-what do you want?" Lewis asked.

Such a simple question. Why couldn't he have asked it earlier?

I asked my questions, starting with the wolves at Gemma's and ending with the trouble with the pack. It took time. Too much time. But, in the end, I had answers that, like it or not, led to more questions. Lewis wanted to return to the old ways where the pack could hunt any prey, including humans. He wanted open hunting grounds, unrestrained by city limits or human laws. Even more telling, he wanted a return to a time when the wolves could hunt and change anyone they wanted, regardless of if the prey agreed to being made a werewolf.

The Conclave refused, recognizing the danger Lewis' request presented. That is when Lewis began looking for allies in his quest to return to pre-Conclave ways.

"Carson Lewis, you have violated pack and Conclave laws. The only way to save your life is to answer my final questions. Failure will see you dead by my hand as this sector's marshal. Do you understand?" "B-bitch," he whined.

"You have no idea."

I extended a hand, trusting Sophie to understand. A moment later, she handed me my weapons. Once I'd secured them back in place, she moved to help me into my jacket. Then she took up her place at my side, ready to react if danger presented itself.

"Yousef Asghar was seen entering this compound earlier today. Why was he here?"

Lewis' face contorted as he fought the need to answer. I waited, wondering if he understood his attempt to remain silent spoke almost as loudly as anything he might say would.

"Very well. You have sealed your fate, Lewis. You are no longer alpha of this or any other pack."

"Y-you can't!"

"I can. As senior marshal, I have the authority to as granted by the Conclave. But I am not doing this as their representative. I am doing this as Morrigan's heir. You have failed her."

Almost as one, those gathered gasped. I had no doubt if I turned, those behind me would have taken at least one step back. Lewis might be too shocked to understand the full impact of what I said, but they weren't. The only question was if I could do what I alluded to.

"Sophie Starke, I task you with naming those loyal to your formal alpha and who will not support the pack's next alpha."

She hissed out a breath but nodded. Then she quickly named not only the wolves who stood with him as he tried to confront us, but also Rufus and several others. I nodded and called them forward, waiting until they ranged out on either side of Lewis, on their knees and as helpless as he.

I nodded and moved to stand behind the men, looking out on the rest of the gathered pack members. As I did, I prayed I was doing the right thing. But what other choice did I have? I needed to take control, even if only temporarily, to ensure the pack's survival.

Morrigan, this needs to be done. I hope to hell you understand.

"These men do not deserve to share Morrigan's gifts, and gifts they are. But they are gifts that come with responsibilities." I let my gaze go from one end of the gathering to the other. "My question to each of you is if you are willing to step up and fulfill those responsibilities or if you will follow these men down the path to ruin?" No one spoke in their defense. Good. At least so far.

"Carson Lewis, you and those with you have failed your pack, your kind and those you should have protected. You have ignored Morrigan's teachings and laws. You do not deserve to enjoy her gifts and protections. In her name, I rebuke you, each of you."

They cried out, a mix of pain and anguish, as Morrigan's touch withdrew from them. At the same time, those gathered turned their backs. They did not move off nor did they offer any solace or sympathy to the former wolves. From this day forward, none of those kneeling before me would be able to shift into their wolf forms. They would be cut off from their wolf aspects in all ways. It was harsh, but at least I carried no more blood on my hands.

"Sophie, choose six you trust to take these *men* into custody. They are to be marked as outcasts and foresworn. Their holdings within the compound and any holdings procured with pack funds are forfeit. They are to be detained and allowed no contact with others of the pack until morning. Then they are to be driven from pack lands and removed from the Zone. If they return, they are condemned without recourse. So says Morrigan."

"It shall be done."

I nodded and moved through the crowd toward the Jeep. I'd wasted enough time here and for what? Nothing. I was no closer to finding out who was behind the attacks than I had been.

DANGLING THREADS AND UNRAVELING THE PAST

"What the hell, Rip?"

At least Sophie waited until we were halfway home before losing her cool. To be honest, it surprised me she managed to hang on that long and I was grateful she did. The last thing any of us needed was for the pack to see one of the two I appointed as interim pack leaders losing her temper, especially until Griff was able to assist her.

"Don't, Sophie. I had to do it."

"I get you had to deal with Lewis and the idiots kissing his ass. But the rest of it? Surely you could have figured something else out." She lifted her right hand from the steering wheel and dragged it through her hair. "Do you have any idea what you've done?"

I understood how she felt. I'd turned pack hierarchy upside down and inside out. I wouldn't blame her if she thought I'd lost my mind. Hell, beneath my very tenuous control, I was screaming and really wanted to run for the hills. This was not what I signed on for when I agreed to be the Zone's senior marshal. Unfortunately, fate didn't seem to care.

"What else was I supposed to do?"

She pulled to the side of the road and parked. I waited, taking a bet with myself over whether she'd beat her head against the steering wheel or kick me out of the jeep. Even money said she would do both. Instead, she turned in the seat enough she could look me in the eye.

"I don't know." She blew out a long breath. I waited, knowing she was still trying to come to terms with what happened. "Rip, are you going to take over the pack?"

"Not a chance in hell, Sophie."

Taking over leadership of the pack was the last thing I wanted or needed. It was also the last thing the pack needed, especially after today's events. When I said as much, she relaxed. Curious, I waited for her to explain.

"Rip, no one can deny who and what you are, especially after today's performance. But you aren't a wolf, at least not a wolf like us. We'd follow you, but it would be through fear for most of the pack. Your reality would be that there would always be someone, be they a member of our pack or another, looking for a chance to overthrow you. None of us needs that."

I nodded in complete agreement.

"Trust me, Soph. I know."

"Then who are you tapping to act in your stead? I assume you have someone in mind for Griff and me to help pave the way for."

"No one, at least not permanently. The closest thing I'll do to appointing someone as the new alpha is having you and your brother run things for the pack until all of you can decide on a new alpha."

She glanced at me before turning her attention back to the road. "I know you, Rip. What aren't you telling me?"

I didn't deny it. The only reason I hadn't said something before now was because I didn't know how she'd react.

"There is." At least we were parked. That meant we wouldn't wreck out when I told her. "I know how the pack worked under Lewis. To say it was more than a bit misogynistic is putting it mildly. That said, it's clear you are as well-respected as your brother, if not more. I also know you are at least as strong as he is and I've always suspected you could be an alpha in your own right if you wanted."

She looked at me, her eyes narrowed. Instead of saying anything, she carefully eased back onto the road.

"And?" she drawled a few moments later.

"My choice to lead the pack would be you, with your brother acting as your second, if I had to put someone in as alpha. For one, I know Griff will always have your back. Whoever is chosen as the new alpha will need a strong second as well as several others he or she can trust implicitly.

"But there's another factor in my choice, if I were to make one. We need Griff to remain as police chief and I don't think he could do both, at least not for the immediate future, if he became the new alpha. He'd try but both positions would suffer because he couldn't give either his full attention and, frankly, right now the pack needs someone who can devote their full attention to it.

"Finally, you are a natural leader. The others respect you and listen to you. More than that, you will make sure the women in the pack are treated fairly, something I doubt has been happening under Lewis."

"I don't know if the pack will accept me as alpha."

Surprised, I did my best not to let her see it. I expected her to argue. Instead, her reaction told me she'd considered it before today's events. Just how bad had things in the pack been?

And why the hell hadn't Sophie or Griff said something?

I almost snorted at the idiocy of my own question. I knew the answer. They hadn't said anything because I hadn't been ready to step up and accept the role as the Zone's senior marshal. How many other problems had I caused by that act of rebellion?

"Stop it, Ripley." She didn't look at me but her tone spoke volumes.

"Stop what?"

I didn't need to see her face to know she rolled her eyes.

"Stop blaming yourself for whatever you're feeling guilty about."

"How?" Frustration roughened my voice. "If I'd realized what was happening with the pack, I might have been able to prevent today's events."

Just as if I'd realized why I never fully accepted Yousef—hell, I'd never really trusted him—I might have a better idea about what was going on. I couldn't shake the feeling that he was involved. How deeply and to what extent, I didn't know.

And I needed to find out, sooner rather than later.

"Then blame Griff and me because we didn't tell you there was trouble. We didn't think it was as bad as it was. We didn't think we needed someone from outside of the pack to shut it down." She glanced at me, her eyes flashing with an anger I knew was aimed at herself.

"And you didn't know I'd be able to put an easy end to it if necessary."

That was a lesson I'd never forget. If they'd known my connection to Morrigan, they might have come to me with their suspicions and concern.

"Ripley, we both made mistakes. But remember this. I haven't said I'd agree with your suggestions about the pack. It's something I need to talk to Griff, and probably our parents, about."

"I need to have a word with your brother as well."

She nodded and we fell silent for the rest of the drive to the house.

"Ripley!" Dani threw herself at me, wrapping her arms around my waist, the moment I stepped inside.

"Hey, kiddo." I hugged her, looking past her to where Layla stood at the foot of the stairs. Relief filled me when she shook her head and then smiled. "Have you been good for Layla and Aras?"

"She most certainly has," Layla assured me. "You okay?"

"Just tired." I watched as Sophie slipped past me and climbed the stairs to go check on her brother. "Something smells good."

"Layla's cooking dinner." Dani let go of me long enough to grab my hand and pull me in the direction of the living room.

"Dani's been helping," Layla said as she fell in behind us. "You have about an hour before everything's ready."

"Thanks." I tipped Dani's face up so she looked at me. "You finish helping Layla. I need to make a couple of calls and then talk with the others."

"But you'll be here for dinner?"

"I most definitely will." I gently brushed my lips against her cheek. "Run on."

"Two things, Ripley," Layla said once we were alone. "Roberto is meeting with Nico and should be back soon."

I frowned, worried he'd left the safety of the house and its wards.

Not that it surprised me he'd been able to. After all, he set most of the newer wards and, unless I missed my guess, most of the older ones as well.

"Anything I need to worry about?"

She shook her head. "I don't think so. Nico said he had some information about the fire. Since you weren't here, he said he'd go."

"What else?"

"Yousef called."

I blinked, surprised. That was the last thing I expected her to say. Then the implications hit. He'd called but he sure as hell hadn't called me.

"Who did he call?"

And why them instead of me?

"No one."

"I don't understand."

"He called here, Ripley. He called the landline."

I hissed out a breath. It wasn't exactly a secret I'd been to the house. Glenham Grove was small enough it didn't take long for gossip to spread and me moving back here would be big news, especially after the fire. But for Yousef to know and to have discovered the land line I'd forgotten about did not reassure me. I doubted anyone from town would share the news with him unless he specifically asked and I doubted he would—at least not without an ulterior motive.

"What did he want?"

"No clue. When I told him you weren't here, he hung up before I could ask to take a message."

"When was this?"

"Maybe an hour and a half ago."

After I reached the werewolves' compound. Had someone warned him I was there? Or was there another explanation?

"Thanks for letting me know." I considered for a minute. "I hate to ask, but I need to meet with the others and I don't want Dani overhearing. Can you keep her busy? I promise to fill you in."

"I can, but wait until Roberto gets back. He might have some information to help make sense of what's happening."

I nodded. She was right. Not that it made waiting any easier. But it did give me time to talk with Griff.

Who was already in a deep discussion with his sister when I found him on the back porch. Seeing me, they nodded but kept talking. Taking that as an invitation to join them, I did just that. After all, it was my house and I had no doubt Sophie was telling him what we found at the compound.

"Well?" I arched a brow as I looked at Sophie.

"I have two questions." Griff placed a gentling hand on his sister's shoulder and turned his attention to me. "First, did Sophie understand you correctly? You want her to be our new alpha and me as her second?"

"No offense, Griff, but I do." I motioned for them to take seats at one of the slate tables. "If what's been going on has taught me anything, it's that we need you as police chief. You've managed to keep the town calm and your cops have been working their cases even as you've been helping me figure out what the hell's going on. Your pack needs a constant and steadying hand right now. Not only because this change in leadership has not followed the usual process but also because I have a feeling there's been a great deal happening with the pack I don't know about." He nodded, not denying it.

"What's your second question?"

"What other secrets have you been keeping from us?"

I chuckled softly and shook my head, a smile playing at the corners of my mouth. "You know a lady never reveals all, Griff."

He threw his head back and laughed. Then he gasped in pain and grabbed his ribs. All humor fled at the reminder of how badly he'd been injured. That goodness he wasn't human. Otherwise, he'd probably be fighting for his life right now.

"Another time, if I dared call you a lady, you'd try to beat my ass." Humor sparkled in his eyes.

"True." I leaned back and relaxed for the first time in hours. "As for your question, you have seen my main aspects and have a pretty good idea what I can do. If there's anything else, I don't know about it."

Which wasn't exactly the truth. From their expressions, neither Griff nor Sophie believed me. But they didn't press.

"If Soph and I agree to your plan, can we count on your support?"

"You can, but it will be as your friend, as a resident of Glenham Grove, and as the Zone's marshal. I will not step in again as one of Morrigan's unless there is no other alternative."

"Sophie?" Her brother looked at her, his expression letting us both know the decision was hers and hers alone.

"All right." She blew out a breath before sitting up and straightening her shoulders. "But we will do this right, Griff. You were Lewis' second, which means you will be the one to issue word to the pack of my desire to step up. Make it clear pack law will be followed. Any challenges will be met according to our ways."

I hissed out a breath but didn't say anything. I couldn't, not if I meant what I said about staying out of pack politics. But I didn't have to like it. What Sophie suggested was accepting any and all challenges to fight for the right to be alpha. I prayed no one stood against her but had a sick feeling in the pit of my stomach there would be more than one wolf who couldn't stomach being ruled by a female, by a bitch. "I will not interfere, but I want to be there."

Griff stopped any protests his sister might have with a slight shake of his head.

Then he looked at me, his gaze steady and measuring.

"Why and in what capacity?"

"The first is simple and ties directly with the second. I want to make sure no one tries anything unexpected." I would have Sophie's back, even if I wasn't a member of the pack. "As for the second, I will be there as friend and as the Zone's marshal. Nothing else."

Fortunately for me, there was precedent for a Zone's marshal to be there when a pack needed a new alpha.

"With that understanding, agreed." Griff reached across the table to shake hands. "What else?"

"We're waiting for Razor to get back. Layla said Nico called with news about the fire." I glanced back at the house, watching Layla and Dani working side-by-side in the kitchen and made a decision. "After dinner I'll have Layla take Dani upstairs. I want to see what everyone has to say. Ker's deadline is going to be here before we know it and I have no intention of turning either Red or Dani over to her." Especially not Dani.

"Before that happens, I need to return to the compound and get things rolling there." Now it was Sophie's turn to stop her brother from saying anything. "No, Griff. You can't go with me, not until you're healed up some more. I won't risk anyone challenging you right now. I need you at my back, not laid up in bed—or worst."

He bristled at the suggestion he might not be able to defeat anyone who challenged him. But, instead of arguing, he dipped his chin in agreement. I breathed easier when he did. Sophie was right. She needed him watching her back until the pack settled and accepted its new alpha—hopefully, her.

"Do it from here, Soph. I made it clear the transition was to be made under the direction of you and Griff. Until we get through tomorrow, I don't want our forces split." She didn't like it, but she agreed.

Before anything else could be said, Layla rapped on the window over the kitchen sink, letting us know it was time to come in. I stood, watching as Sophie hovered protectively at her brother's side. If his wince of pain earlier hadn't convinced me he still needed time to heal, that did. Hopefully, he'd have the time he needed, even if my gut said differently.

An hour later, Romy surprised me by volunteering to take Dani upstairs and sit with her while the rest of us discussed what we'd learned. Before Dani could protest, the witch grinned and whispered something in her ear. Dani blushed and grinned, throwing her arms around Romy's waist. Then she gave me a hug and ran upstairs, calling for Romy to follow.

"What did you say to her?" I asked with a laugh.

"I told her I'd teach her how to call the wind. She's enough magic to be able to do that."

"I'll come too." Cal pushed his chair away from the table and stood. "We'll keep her busy until you can come tell her goodnight, Ripley."

I thanked them and leaned back, looking around the table at my friends, my family. This might be a council of war, at least it felt that way, but they were still the people who meant the most to me. People I would do everything possible to keep safe.

"We don't have much time. Ker, or whoever the hell it was, gave me twenty-four hours to turn over Red and Dani. I have no intention of doing so. That means we need to figure out what the hell's been going on, who's responsible, and deal with them before anything else happens."

"Before we go any further, Aras and I checked the area around the bar as well as security video captured by the bar's cameras and other cameras nearby," Sele said. "You were right, Ripley. It was a projection. A good one, but a still a projection. Whoever did it had to be nearby. That's why we wanted to check the video from nearby businesses."

My heart beat a little faster. "What did you find?"

"One thing's for certain, no matter what you were told, that wasn't Ker or any of her sisters."

I almost sagged with relief to hear that. It was bad enough dealing with a witch powerful enough to create the projection I'd faced. It was much, much worse to be forced to deal with one of the Kere. Hopefully, this meant things weren't as bad as I'd feared.

"Then who was it?" Razor asked.

"Her name is Alicia and the last Aunt Gemma heard, she was working with the Conclave."

My stomach turned over. If the Conclave was behind what happened...

"More specifically, she worked with Drake," Gemma said.

That made more sense. First Yousef and now this Alicia. Who else would crawl out of the woodwork before this was over.

"Red?" I looked down the table to where he sat. "You know more than you've told us."

"That's the problem, Ripley. I don't know anything you haven't already figured out for yourselves. I have more than a few questions and suspicions, but no proof of anything."

"I assume you share these questions and suspicions, Gemma."

Sele and Elle looked between their aunt and me in question, not understanding what I meant. Instead of explaining, I waited, wondering who would break first: Gemma or Red.

"I do," the witch confirmed. She reached for her cup and delicately sipped her tea before continuing. "This goes back years, Ripley. It started with your father's last assignment. I didn't feel good about him being sent after the basilisk. When we spoke a few days before he left, he admitted he worried about the assignment. Not because he felt it more than he could handle but because he felt as if he wasn't being told everything about the situation. That wasn't the first time he felt information was being withheld. But it was the first time he had a feeling that it could lead to trouble he might not be able to handle. He asked me to watch over you and your mother should anything happen to him."

"And?" I didn't trust myself to say much else, not when my temper was spiking.

"I tried asking him why he felt something might go wrong. That wasn't the way your father thought about anything. He took precautions, yes, but he wasn't fatalistic. I knew your mother was worried. I could see it when she didn't think anyone was looking.

"Before leaving, he came to see me. He wanted additional wards, something no one else knew about. That's when he told me there was something about how his assignment was being handled that didn't sit right with him. He had minimal information about what was going on and why the Conclave issued the kill order for the basilisk. He also said a witch he didn't know but one he took an instinctive dislike for was in on the briefing with Drake. Something about her sat wrong with him and he didn't trust her or, for that matter, Drake. He had nothing concrete to pin it on, only a gut feeling."

Something Dad always trusted, telling me more than once that his gut saved him more times than he could count. The fact he ignored it this time, and that Drake seemed to have been involved along with this witch seen near my encounter with

'Ker' set off all my alarm bells.

"Tell me, who else around this table has concerns about the Conclave or any one member in particular?" I sat there, forearms on the tabletop, fingers twined to keep from hitting something—or someone.

"I think it safe to say we all do now, Ripley," Razor said. "As for before we found ourselves in our current position, all I can say is I have been uneasy for some time without knowing why."

Layla nodded as did Aras. Interesting.

"We knew there was trouble, but thought it limited to the pack." Sophie looked at her brother who nodded in agreement.

"All right." I scrubbed a hand over my face, thinking hard. "We're all exhausted. I know time is running out but we won't be able to do anything if we don't get some rest. Before we do, I want to make sure we are all on the same page."

I stood and moved to stare out the window set in the far wall. Outside, darkness had fallen. In the distance, clouds swirled near the Rift, the rogue magics escaping lighting them with reds and purples and the occasional white and green. When I turned back to the others, they watched me, their expressions concerned.

"You need to understand that what I'm about to do could be seen as active disloyalty to the Conclave, at least to the representative assigned to this part of the country. If you don't want to be involved, I won't hold it against you. I thank you—more than you know—for everything you've already done. But if you can't accept what may happen moving forward, you need to leave now."

I waited, unsure whether I should be relieved or not when no one made a move to leave. I appreciated their willingness to help, their loyalty, but I didn't want them getting into trouble with the Conclave because of me. Except this, whatever *this* was involved much more than me. Glenham Springs and its continued survival headed the list. Then there were their own families. There was even my family, not the least of which were my parents and what happened to them. Like it or not, the trouble we faced now had a long history and it was past time to deal with it.

But there was one more question to be answered before I knew how to proceed. "Thanks." I smiled and returned to my chair. "Red, I get why they might want to get their hands on you. So many people in town see you as their protector. You've been the public face for the town, especially for those who needed help. You are also a planner and it would be natural to assume that taking you out of the equation would seriously impact our ability to respond to whatever they have in mind. What I don't understand is why they want Dani?"

And that worried me. My gut told me it went beyond believing they could use her to control Red or the rest of us.

"If I knew, I'd tell you." Red looked as perplexed as I felt. "You have my word." That was good enough for me. Red's word was his bond. It always had been.

"All right." I thought for a moment. "I no longer trust Yousef. I am not asking you to violate pack secrets, Sophie, Griff, but do you know why he was at the compound earlier today and do you know if he's had other meetings with Lewis or anyone else there?" "If he's been there, no one said anything to me," Griff said.

"He's been there a couple of times I know of. Until today, I thought he came at your request." Much as I did earlier, Sophie pushed away from the table and moved to stare out the window. "The only reason I know is Lewis and some of the other males never saw me as anything other than a bitch to torment and sniff around as if I was in heat."

Griff growled, his hands fisting on the tabletop. I glanced at him and shook my head. The last thing we needed was him losing his temper. Jaw clenched, he dipped his chin in understanding.

"They will be dealt with, Sophie." I waited until she turned and some of the anger in her stance eased. "What did they say?"

"Only that Lewis and Yousef had been meeting under Conclave orders."

That brought a growl from me. Like it or not, I needed to find out what the fuck was going on.

"All right. Everyone get some rest. We'll meet again for breakfast at five thirty." Hopefully, that was early enough Dani wouldn't be up.

"What are you going to do?" Griff asked, watching me closely.

"I have a couple of calls to make and then I'm going to crash." Then I'd hunt. Those who plotted against my town and my people would soon learn just how foolish they'd been.

29

GOING OVER HIS HEAD

"I expected a report by now, *Marshal.*"

I rolled my eyes and fought the urge to tell Drake what I thought about him and his expectations. It was too early and I'd had too little sleep to deal with him this morning. Fortunately, sanity prevailed and I didn't say what was on the tip of my tongue. Instead, I swung my legs over the side of the bed and sat up. One deep breath later, I once again lifted the cellphone to my ear.

"My apologies, sir. I assumed my interim report yesterday would be enough for the moment." I winced, hoping he didn't hear the insincerity in my voice. "To say things have been happening fast down here is putting it mildly. I was up most of the night dealing with new information."

"Explain."

I began my carefully excised report. The last thing I wanted was for him to realize what I suspected. He listened as I spoke, occasionally asking a question. When it came to describing the events at the compound yesterday, he stopped me. I waited, knowing what he said next would answer some of my questions and wondering if those questions would confirm my suspicions.

"You'd better have a damned good explanation for interfering in pack politics, Walker."

The anger in his voice didn't surprise me. Instead, it answered at least some of my questions about his role in everything. Instead of asking why I took the actions I did, he went straight to the attack. That meant only one thing. He approved of the way things were under Lewis and did not want that particular boat rocked. Well too bad. I'd not only rocked that boat, but I'd managed to sink it to the bottom of the proverbial ocean.

"I believe I had more than adequate cause to do so, sir." Not that he agreed. "I will be forwarding my written report some time tomorrow. I am still tying off a few loose ends here and I'm sure you want the full picture instead of only a partial one."

Besides, I hoped to have everything settled one way or the other by then—including discovering the full extent of his involvement in what's been going on.

"I want an explanation now, Walker. There might still be time to smooth over any trouble you've caused with this ill-advised move."

"Mr. Drake, you might be my Conclave contact, but you do not have the authority on your own to override my decisions as the Zone's senior marshal." I didn't need to see him to know my answer rankled. Too bad. I'd do the same thing again given the circumstances. "The situation at the compound negatively impacted not only the pack but everyone in this Zone. The only way to ensure everyone's continued safety was to take action. I will gladly forward my report to the entire Conclave once my investigation is finished. Until then, I have better things to do with my time than jumping through political hoops of your making."

"Walker, I can revoke your appointment."

"You can try, sir, but I doubt the rest of the Conclave will agree, especially when they learn the other marshal you sent to ride herd over me has not only refused to report in for the last twenty-four hours, but has been conspiring with the former pack alpha to not only destabilize the Zone but to actively violate Conclave and human laws."

I waited, knowing I'd said too much but not caring. I didn't have time to play nice with him or anyone else.

Silence stretched out so long I wondered if the call had dropped. Instead of saying anything else, I climbed to my feet and crossed to the closet. Might as well start getting ready for the day. One way or the other, the proverbial shit was going to hit the fan. The only question was if I'd manage to dodge it or get buried by it.

"I knew taking you on as marshal was a mistake. You're too much like your mother." He spoke softly, menace filling his voice.

"I'll take that as a compliment, sir." I smiled even though he couldn't see it. "And I plan to handle this situation exactly as she would have."

"This is not over, Walker."

He ended the call. It would have been much more effective had he been on a land line and could have slammed down the receiver. Chuckling softly, knowing that round went to me, I carried my clothes into the adjoining bath. I needed a shower to clear my head and clothes because there were simply too many people in the house to go around nude. Then I had another call or two to make before heading out.

A few minutes later, I sat at what had been my mother's desk and pulled up my contacts list on my phone. Finding the one I wanted, I hit the call button and waited, wondering if I was doing the right thing or signing my death warrant.

It was fifty-fifty of it going either way.

"Ripley, I didn't expect to hear from you this morning," Isabel Mankowitz, chairperson of the Conclave, said a few moments later. Her soft Southern drawl put most people at ease. I couldn't afford to be one of them today.

"I appreciate you taking my call." I needed to keep this businesslike so she understood the seriousness of the situation. "I assume you are aware of the situation we're facing down here."

"I know a little, but not much. Drake said you and Yousef have it well in hand." I cursed softly. No wonder she said she was surprised to hear from me.

"I wouldn't say that, ma'am, not if I'm being honest."

"Oh?"

"Ms. Mankowitz, the situation here is far from settled. There have been two direct attacks by paras against first Redmond Oakley's warehouse in town and then against Gemma Blackrock at her house outside of town. The paras included not only werewolves, at least a couple of whom belonged to the local pack and others who had been members of the pack, but also redhats, goblins, and more. They also tracked and attacked Red at the cabin he took refuge in after the warehouse attack. I have also received a threat that if I don't turn over Red and his ward, young Dani, that they will attack the town again."

She hissed out a breath, stopping me. Her reaction alone told me she had not been kept in the loop. Yet another reason to assume Drake was involved somehow.

"I think you'd best tell me everything, Marshal, and I do mean everything." The Southern drawl turned hard and I knew better than to disobey.

It didn't take long. I started with Gemma's call to Red, asking me to come see her. Mankowitz's listened. Unlike Drake, she didn't interrupt. Instead, I heard her pen scratching across a pad as she took notes. Whether to remind her of questions to ask or actions to take, I didn't know. It didn't matter. I was doing what I needed to protect my town and the people I cared about.

"I wish you'd consulted with me before acting with regard to the pack, but I trust you felt you didn't have the time."

"I don't believe I did." I thought for a moment, trying to choose my words carefully. "We already had proof the pack, or at least certain members, were involved in the attacks. The pack's second had been injured helping Red escape the second attack on him. The fact the alpha did not act to prevent such actions needed to be addressed.

That decision was reinforced once I arrived at the compound and learned more about what was going on within the pack."

"And Yousef?"

I exhaled heavily. "That is the million dollar question." And then some. "In the time he's been here, he has done little to nothing to fit in and get to know the townspeople, much less those living outside of town but within the Zone. He certainly hasn't gained their trust. Since the attack at Red's he has kept even more to himself and he left Gemma's without telling anyone and has not been in contact since then. All I know for certain is that he has been to the wolves' compound, meeting with Lewis."

"Did you report this to Drake?"

"I sent a preliminary report and he called earlier this morning. Let's just say he doesn't agree with my actions."

"I see."

And I had a feeling she did. At least I hoped so.

"What did he say?" When I didn't immediately respond, she sighed softly. "Ripley, this is important and I will explain later. But I need to know what he told you."

"I can send you a digital file with our conversation." Something I doubted Drake considered I'd make. "But the short version is he did not approve of me interfering with the wolves and he all but threatened to remove me as the Zone's senior marshal."

"He did what?" She ground out the words.

"He threatened to remove me," I repeated. "I'm not proud of it, but I reminded him that he didn't have the authority to do so on his own. I also said I would send a full report on my investigation tomorrow, after I tie up some loose ends."

"I will deal with Drake, but that has to come after we take care of several things first."

I wished I could see her because I didn't have a clue what she meant and that worried me.

"Where are you right now, Ripley?"

"At my parents' house. Razor suggested I set up here, since the warehouse is toast." Literally, at least on the inside.

"Excellent. By any chance are Gemma and Razor there with you?"

"Yes, ma'am." I decided honesty was the best policy, for the moment at least. "Dani is here as well. So are Razor, Layla, Red, and Gemma's nieces."

"Good. Very good." She sounded as if she approved. "Tell Gemma and Razor that we need to meet and ask them to make the appropriate preparations. I will join you in half an hour."

I blinked, unsure what she meant. When I called, I assumed she was at home in Tennessee. Was she close enough to get here in thirty minutes?

"I will let them know." And hope one of them had an answer.

"Good. I will see you soon."

With that, she ended the call. For a moment, I sat there, trying to make sense of our conversation. Then I pushed away from the desk and climbed to my feet. Time was ticking and I needed to get a move on. Hopefully, when Mankowitz got here, she'd have some answers for me.

Half an hour later, I stood outside the protective circle cast in the basement by Gemma and Razor. Standing at the ordinal points outside were Sale and her sisters as well as Layla. I was the proverbial third wheel, watching as witch and shaman called to their magic, creating what could only be called a doorway in the center of the circle. The primal part of me wanted to run and hide. This sort of thing wasn't supposed to happen, not even in this post-Cataclysm world of ours.

Magical energies rose inside the circle. The doorway shimmered and seemed to become almost solid. A few moments later, Isabel Mankowitz stepped through. She nodded to Gemma and Razor before shaking hands. As she did, I noticed the gloves she wore. They didn't look out of place with her dark slacks, white button down blouse and riding boots. What did look out of place was the black leather briefcase she carried. She said something, her words obscured by the magic contained in the circle. Then she brushed a lock of red hair off her brow and waited as the two dismissed the circle.

"Quit looking like you're going to run for the hills, Ripley." She smiled, humor dancing in her emerald green eyes.

"Sorry." But not sorry. What did she expect? "This is a bit much, especially after being surprised by the projection of someone claiming to be Ker yesterday."

"Of course." She nodded to the three sisters and motioned for me to lead the way upstairs. "We don't have much time, but I wanted to do this in person."

Not knowing what to say, I led her to my mother's—I guess now my—study. After closing the pocket doors behind us, I motioned for her to take one of the seats in front of the desk. Instead of taking the second chair, or even sitting behind the desk, I moved to lean against the desk, waiting for an explanation.

"May I?" She lifted her briefcase and nodded at the desktop.

I nodded in return.

She thanked me and placed the briefcase on the polished wood. I waited, watching as she opened it and reached inside. My brows drew together in a frown as she produced a thick file, a brown envelope that obviously contained something inside, and a leather folio. She laid them on the desktop before closing the briefcase and settling it on the floor next to her chair.

"To start, you need to know that before our conversation this morning, the Conclave had not officially approved you as the Zone's senior marshal. It was to be voted on at our next regular meeting."

My jaw dropped and I looked at her in surprise. I didn't understand. Why would Drake lie and tell me I was the new senior marshal if the Conclave hadn't agreed yet?

"However, we have corrected that oversight." She reached for the leather folio and opened it before handing it to me. "This makes it official. All you need to do is agree and then sign." She extended a pen and waited patiently as I tried to wrap my mind around what was happening.

"I really don't understand."

"Neither do the rest of us, but I have a feeling you're going to figure it out soon." She smiled and watched as I flipped to the second page and quickly scrawled my signature at the bottom of the page. "Before you ask, this is something we've wanted these last few years. You've proven yourself time and again as being more than capable of doing the job, not only in the way you've carried out assignments from the Conclave but also with your work for Red." She reached for the envelope.

"Those are your official credentials, naming you as the Zone's senior marshal, as well as your new badge. You are now licensed to carry both arcane and mundane weapons not only in this state but throughout the country. You report to the Conclave as a whole and not to any single member. Your point of contact with the Conclave will be me, at least for the time being. Understand?"

"Yes, ma'am."

What else could I say?

I fingered the leather of the badge case I now held in my hands before looking at the badge. It was much more substantial than what Drake sent. Studying it, I should have realized there was something wrong with the other badge. I had seen my parents' badges enough times to recognize the difference.

What else had I missed?

"Relax, Ripley." She smiled at me and I nodded. "You've done nothing wrong. You trusted our representative for the Zone. If there anyone is to blame, it is myself and the others on the Conclave. I'm here to correct that problem and make sure you have all the legal authority necessary to do your duty to this town, the Zone and then to the Conclave."

"And Drake?"

"We are adding to the scope of your investigation. You are to determine if he has been involved in what happened here or what happened in other Zones that have seen problems of late."

"And Yousef?"

"He has been relieved of all duties as a marshal. It had been our understanding he was here only temporarily and had moved on to his next assignment. If you find him, he is to be taken into custody and held until he can be transferred to Mesa Ridge."

I swallowed hard and nodded. Mesa Ridge was the black site where the Conclave sent paras who committed the worst crimes against our kind. There they were held or executed, depending on the severity of their crimes. The federal government not only knew about the site but demanded we maintain it to protect the non-para community from the worst of our kind.

"Understood."

"Ripley, you are ready for this. It is our fault—my fault—for not doing this sooner." She reached over and rested her hand on my forearm. "Now, I need your full report. I know you are still trying to get to the bottom of what's been going on, but I want to know everything up to this point. I'll report to the other members of the Conclave so we can be ready to act if needed."

I slipped my hand into my pocket. My fingers closed around a thumb drive. For a moment, I considered. Then I made up my mind. I needed to trust someone and Mankowitz was doing everything she could to reassure me, something Drake never had.

You can trust her, Ripley. Trust her and trust yourself.

Mom's voice was as clear as if she stood next to me. Unfortunately, she didn't. It was my imagination. But it was enough to reassure me.

"Here. Everything I've learned is on this." I handed it over, praying I wasn't making a mistake.

"And here is what we know about the other attacks." She handed over her own thumb drive.

"Thanks." I slid it into my pocket. "I do have one question."

"I doubt it's just one." She chuckled and I grinned in response. "What can I help you with, Ripley?"

"Drake's commented several times recently in a way that makes me believe he had a problem with my mother, maybe even with both my parents. Do you know what was going on between them?"

She sighed and closed her eyes. When she looked at me a moment later, her expression was troubled. Worried, I waited, wondering what she had to say.

"He had been appointed to the Conclave a few years before your mother's last assignment. We set him up as this Zone's representative because your parents, and then just your mother, kept things safe here. We had so few problems, we thought it a good place for him to start learning his duties. We had no reason to be concerned until your mother disappeared. That's when we discovered he'd been sending her on unsanctioned missions, including that last one."

"What. The. Hell. Do. You. Mean?" I ground out the words, fighting the urge to go hunting Drake.

"The Conclave didn't authorize that mission, Ripley."

"Then why wasn't Drake dealt with then?"

"Because we were idiots." She didn't try to deflect my anger. "We didn't want to see what was happening. How could one of us be actively working against the Conclave or one of our marshals?"

"And now?"

"You build the case and you have my personal word he will face the full justice of the Conclave, not just for what happened here but for what happened to your mother and any others he caused harm to." I'd settle for that—for now.

"Any limitations I need to be aware of?"

"You know our laws, Ripley. You have in the folder the contract for your current assignment. Review it and if you have any questions, let me know. However, the quick answer is the only limitations you are operating under now are our laws and even those can be flexible given the right circumstances—which you will confirm with me."

"And if I learn Drake is involved and he takes exception to my investigation?"

"Treat him as you would anyone else who violates our laws. The same goes for Yousef." She checked her watch and climbed to her feet. "You have an arrest warrant for Yousef. If you find enough evidence to charge Drake, a warrant for him will be issued as well. For now, you are the Conclave's senior marshal with all the power and responsibility that entails. I trust you to do the job with as much dedication as your parents before you."

"Thank you." I walked with her to the door. "And thank you for coming to tell me in person."

"It is something I should have done long ago." She stepped into the hallway and paused, turning to look back at me. "If you find any evidence tying either of them to what happened to your parents, do not wait for written authorization. Arrest them. I will make sure the others on the Conclave know I have given my verbal authorization for you to take whatever action is necessary to bring them to justice."

"Thank you." That one comment did more to reassure me than anything else she could have said. "I hate to ask this and I hope you understand, but can you trust the others not to warn either Drake or Yousef?"

"I can. You have your ways of dealing with things and I have mine."

In that moment, I knew I never wanted to cross her. Something told me she was a bigger, badder, and much more dangerous para than I thought.

"May I ask one more question, ma'am?"

She smiled almost gently and nodded. "You can ask anything you want, Ripley. I might not always be able to answer, but I will always do my best to let you know why if that's the case."

"Do you know why whoever is behind all this wants Dani?"

She shook her head. "Unfortunately, no. But I will look into her family tree when I get back to the office."

"Thanks." I joined her in the corridor and led her downstairs. "I'm assuming you're leaving the way you came, Ms. Mankowitz."

"Isabel," she corrected. "I've known you all your life and your mother was one of the few I called friend. Except in formal situations, I'd like it if you used my given name."

"Thank you—Isabel."

"You watch yourself, Ripley. I want daily reports. If you need anything from the Conclave, let me know."

"I will."

Now to figure out my next move and how the hell I was supposed to keep Red and Dani safe once the deadline passed and Ker, or whoever she was, decided to try something else.

3 0

A-HUNTING I WILL GO

Instead of heading back upstairs where most of the others waited, I dropped onto the bottom step and cradled my head in my hands. I'd been a fool in more ways than one. I'd trusted Yousef because of his role as marshal and because he'd been sent by Drake. I hadn't taken the basic precaution of checking into him or even checking into why Drake might want him here. At the time Yousef arrived, Glenham Grove hadn't reported any trouble to the Conclave. I'd been acting in the role of marshal when necessary and between Red and Griffin, things were usually kept under control.

Damn it, my stupidity played a role in what happened.

Cursing, I pushed to my feet and climbed the stairs. When I reached the first floor landing, Sophie saw me. I shook my head before she could say anything. I needed another few moments to consider what I'd learned. Then I needed to decide how best to proceed, starting with those in the house and then with the pack. The last thing I needed was the situation with the pack blowing up in my face while trying to track down and deal with Yousef and quite possibly Drake.

Ten minutes later, I stood before the mirror and studied my reflection. The black I wore matched my mood. Black tee shirt, black jeans, black belt and boots. My badge, the new one Isabel gave me, was secured to my belt. Mom's leather jacket trailed from my right hand. My hair was now secured in a French braid. I looked the part of the Zone's senior marshal. Now to see if I could act the part.

Because I sure as hell hadn't been.

And that lay squarely on Drake's shoulders.

"Wow, Ripley."

Dani's comment as I descended the stairs had everyone looking in my direction. I smiled as she ran to give me a hug. But my attention was on Sophie as she stood. From the seriousness of her expression, she knew something happened. I gave a slight nod before turning my attention to Dani. She had to come first, for now at least.

"You look different, Ripley." She kept her hold on my hands as she stepped back and looked at me.

"Oh?" I had a feeling she meant more than just my clothes.

"You look like you're about to go hunting."

"I am." I draped my arm around her shoulders and looked at the others. "Any chance there's breakfast?"

"More than a chance," Layla said with a smile that didn't quite reach her eyes. "Dani helped me while the rest of you were busy. It's ready if you are."

"I need a minute with Sophie, Red, Razor, and Griff and then we'll be in."

"Don't take too long or it will be cold."

I told Dani to go with Layla, promising to be there shortly. Then I led the others to Mom's study, closing the doors behind us.

"You know, Dani's right, Rip. You look pissed and like you're about to go on a hunt —and I mean a hunt like Griff and I do." Sophie didn't sit even though she motioned her brother to a chair. "What's going on?"

"More than we knew."

I quickly related my conversation with Isabel. Their expressions as I did told me all I needed to know. They were as surprised as I was— and as pissed.

"What are you going to do?" Razor asked.

"I'm going to ask for help from each of you."

I'd be a fool not to.

"What can we do?" Sophie asked.

"Since you asked, I'll start with you and your brother." And pray I wasn't about to make a mistake that could cost any or all of us our lives. "I need you to take control of the pack now. We can't wait for the regular pack meeting. If Drake and/or Yousef have been messing with your wolves, we need to shut it down now."

"Rip." Sophie frowned as she struggled with reconciling what I asked with her vows to the pack and to its laws. "Are you sure?"

I nodded.

"Sophie, I wouldn't ask if I wasn't. It is obvious those two were setting all of us up for something and I think we've had a pretty damned good indication of what after the fire at Red's and the attack at Gemma's. I need to know not only that the pack is under control but also that it is loyal to Glenham Grove and to the Conclave and its laws."

"We'll do it," Griffin said before his sister could respond. "She's right, Soph, and you know it. Don't let your reluctance to step up as Alpha cloud your judgment. This is what we've both trained for."

"Griff."

He smiled gently and climbed to his feet. Then he limped to Sophie's side and pulled her into a one-armed hug. He would always be her big brother but, just then, he was a wolf recognizing her dominance and accepting it even as he pledged his support. As if reading my mind, he looked at me and nodded. We all watched as he carefully, painfully dropped to his knees in front of Sophie, tilting his head to one side and baring his neck.

"You are my alpha. I pledge my support, my arm and my life to you and the pack."

She closed her eyes and breathed deeply. We waited, watching as she struggled with the decision. I didn't blame her. It was a lot to ask. I hoped she understood I wouldn't ask her if it wasn't necessary.

"All right." She reached out and helped her brother to his feet. "But to do so, we need you to make an appearance and give what you want legitimacy. Not as the senior marshal but as one of Morrigan's blood."

I didn't like it, but I'd expected it. Besides, it made sense. As one of

Morrigan's descendants, I shared her ability to control the wolves. They were mine in a way. While I wouldn't order them to accept Sophie as their new alpha, I would make it clear she had my support.

"Unless something else comes up, we'll go immediately after breakfast."

Griff nodded in approval and sent a quick text that I assumed was to the rest of the pack, telling them to be at the compound when we arrived.

"And what would you ask of me, Ripley?" Razor leered and I laughed, exactly as he wanted.

"I'd like you to talk to your grandmother again. See what else she can tell you about what they've been dealing with. Find out who her Conclave contact is and if she's had any dealing with Yousef. I don't care how far back it might go. I want to know everything she can tell us. Ask Layla to check with her sources and her people. If they know anything that might help us, I need to know. Tell her to assure them they will have the gratitude and assistance of this Zone's senior marshal should they ever need it."

"I'll let her know."

I nodded my thanks before turning my attention to Red.

"You've got the same look in your eyes your mother did when she was about to cause me no end of trouble," he groused.

"Then you should know better than to try to snow me about anything, Red." I waited until he sighed softly and nodded. "I'm going to ask one last time. Why would anyone be interested in Dani, especially to the extent they'd torch the warehouse, attack Gemma's place, and then track and attack you?"

He shook his head, a frown pulling down the corners of his mouth.

"I don't know. Her parents weren't particularly powerful paras. Both were shapeshifters, her father into a fox and her mother into a cat. As far as I know, there was no history of para talents in their family lines before the Cataclysm. All I know for sure is they were one of the families who lived near the Rift and they were caught in the first magical wave that hit when the Rift emerged."

Which told me nothing. That description fit almost half the town.

"All right. I want you and Aras to stay with her while we're gone. No one is to be allowed in the yard, much less the house until I get back. Promise me."

He nodded, for once not arguing about being told what to do. That alone convinced me he was as worried as I was. That did nothing to reassure me.

"What about Gemma and the girls?" Razor asked.

"I'd love to keep them here where I know they'll be safe." Or at least as safe as anywhere else, not that it meant much after the attack at Gemma's. "But I need the sisters back at the cafe where they will hear any gossip going around. Gemma can stay with them. I know they will do everything they can to keep her safe. Cal will help." Or turn himself back into a cat.

"When do we start?" Sophie didn't look as shell-shocked, but she still didn't look happy.

"After breakfast."

"And what are you going to be doing?" Red arched one brow at me, once again looking like my boss and not someone I'd been ordering around a few minutes earlier.

"After I finish at the compound, I'm going to Yousef's apartment. It's time to have a look around."

"Not by yourself." Griffin didn't growl, but he made his displeasure clear.

"I'm doing exactly that." I stopped him before he could interrupt. "I want you with your sister. We don't know how all the pack will react this morning. You need to be there to present a united front and to help her deal with any dissenters. Besides, I want you to make sure Lewis and the others being banished are dealt with."

"Then you will remain at the compound with us until that's done," Sophie said firmly. "I mean it, Rip. We can't risk anything happening to you right now."

I didn't like it, but she was right. Damn it.

"Then let's get going. I don't want to drag this out any longer than necessary."

"We'll have breakfast first," Red said as he climbed to his feet. "You watch your back, girl. If things are as bad as we think, Isabel just painted a huge target on you."

I nodded, not liking the fact he was right. But better to have the target on me than on someone else.

31

A FLASH FROM THE PAST

"Ripley, I don't want you to go."

Dani threw her arms around my waist and clung to me. I hugged her, wishing I could stay. The last thing I wanted as to worry her. But what choice did I have? I had a duty—to her, to the others with us, to the town—to deal with whoever targeted our town and loved ones. I also had a duty to my mother to find out if my suspicions were right and this somehow tied in to what happened to her. But that didn't make it any easier to leave Dani.

Not when the way she held onto me reminded me of the last time I said goodbye to Mom.

"Sweetheart, look at me."

I placed a finger under her chin and applied gentle pressure until she did as I said. Worry filled her eyes and it broke my heart. How was I supposed to reassure her when I knew I might not return?

"Dani, I have to do this. I made a promise to protect you and everyone else in Glenham Grove when I agreed to be a marshal. Even if I hadn't accepted the offer, I'd still try to find out who's been trying to hurt you, Red and the rest of our friends. But I promise you this. I'm going to be careful. I'm going to do everything I can to come back home safe and sound."

"Promise?"

I leaned down and kissed the top of her head. "Promise."

Dani held on a moment longer before turning to Sophie and Griff. "You make sure she comes home."

"You have my word that we'll do everything we can to make sure she does," Griff said.

Dani sniffled once before running to where Red stood. He wrapped her in his arms and held her close, softly reassuring her. When our eyes met over her head, he nodded once. He understood even if he wished I didn't have to go.

"Ripley." Aras spoke softly as he approached. "Take this. I have a feeling you will need it."

He extended my father's wakizashi in its simple sheath. I nodded and lifted it from his extended hands. He watched as I tried to figure out what to do with it. Then he stepped forward. A moment later, the wakizashi and sheath were secured across my back. He adjusted everything until I could easily draw the blade.

"Thank you." I gave a slight bow which he returned. Then I turned to Sophie and

Griff. "Ready?"

"Ready," Sophie said.

Even though they protested, I followed Sophie and Griff to the compound in my SUV instead of driving over with them. Even though I'd promised to stay with them, I might not be able to. Depending on what we found there, they might need to stay and I didn't dare put off going to Yousef's apartment any longer than I already had.

Unfortunately, that age-old adage about the best laid plans of mice and men seemed in full force this morning and nothing went as planned. Why should it when the last few days had been nothing short of a nightmare, one I couldn't seem to wake up from?

At least it wasn't all bad. Who would have thought dealing with the pack would be the easiest part of my morning?

The moment we arrived at the compound, Sophie sent word for everyone to gather. Then she led Griff and me to what would be town square anywhere else. At the end of the street, where a park and gazebo might be if we were anywhere else, a circle of packed dirt surrounded on two sides by bleachers stood.

Less than fifteen minutes later, Sophie left Griff and me standing at the edge of the circle. She walked to its center and stopped. Then she slowly turned, taking time to study those gathered, letting them see she not only was in control but that she feared no one. I scented her determination, and a slight smile touched my lips. This was going to be interesting.

"Hear me!" She spoke without the aid of a microphone, but her words carried. Everyone present fell silent, their eyes on her, watching and waiting. "Today the Glenham Grove pack returns to the laws of our kind and of the Conclave. We will be the guardians not only of our town and Zone, but we will work to assist Marshal E. Ripley Walker in any way she requires. This is the role we were made for. This is the role we accepted when the Conclave was formed and we vowed to support it and its laws. This is the role we strayed from under the leadership of our previous alpha. It is the role we will return to. If anyone here does not agree to abide by my decision, they are free to leave the pack now. Or they can meet me here and prove they will be a better alpha than me."

"If anyone wants to stand against Alpha Starke, they must go through me first!"

I turned, searching for the source of the challenge. Making his way down the bleachers to my right, a man who looked like he could rip the trees from the ground, roots and all, scanned the crowd. His dark eyes glowed and his smile sent chills down my spine as he dared anyone to accept his challenge. For a moment, I couldn't place him. Then I gasped slightly. I knew him. But the last time I'd seen him, he'd been a skinny band geek in high school. My what a difference a few years and a lot of time working out could do.

"And before you get to CT, you have to go through me!" An athletically built blonde, Annie Barker, quickly joined CT Mathews in the center of the ring just behind and to either side of Sophie.

"You two don't get to have all the fun. Let them try to get past their elders," a man with greying hair said as he stood.

"Don't forget that we're their betters as well, dear." The brunette beside him grinned and I fought the urge to laugh.

When had Sophie's and Griff's parents gotten back in town? The last I heard, they were in Tulsa, assisting the local pack with some problems the pack's new alpha couldn't handle on his own.

"No one gets to challenge my sister without going through me first." Griffin didn't move from where he stood next to me, not that he needed to.

If that wasn't my cue, I didn't know what was.

I stepped forward, turning so everyone present could see I meant business.

"I am here as the Zone's senior marshal. Your former alpha forced me to step in and put a stop to his actions that violated your own laws as well as Conclave law. By my authority, I supported Sophia Starke as the pack's new alpha. In that same role, I now ask you to confirm her appointment or to issue formal challenges. The leadership of this pack will be decided now."

"Are there any challenges?"

Sophie waited, looking more relaxed than I knew she was. Those standing with her scanned the crowd, looking for anyone foolish enough to take challenge her.

Or worse, someone willing to try something from afar.

When no one spoke up, Sophie nodded once.

"What say you then? Will you follow me as we once again show the town and the Zone and the world the value of our kind?"

The pack howled and cheered in response and I relaxed. At my side, Griff did as well. Now it was down to the formalities as Sophie once again pledged to serve and guide the pack in accordance with their laws and the laws of the Conclave.

The rest didn't take long. In short order, she officially named Griff as her second. Their parents, as well as CT and Annie, filled out her inner circle. They had her trust and the authority to act in her name. More importantly, at least from my point of view, they had her back just as she had theirs.

I couldn't ask for anything more and hopefully it would be enough to reassure the Conclave.

"Marshal, do you have anything you'd like to add?"

She turned to me, her expression confident as long as I didn't look too closely. Then I saw the uncertainty in her eyes.

"Only my congratulations to both you and the pack." I grinned, knowing that wasn't what she expected. "You have chosen wisely. Alpha Starke will be a strong leader but will temper that strength with wisdom and care. She has the support of my office and of the Conclave and we will do whatever we can to assist the pack as you assist us.

"Alpha, I leave the pack in your hands. I know there is much you need to do. I request an update on the situation with Lewis and his followers at your convenience." I didn't need to tell her that meant as soon as possible. She understood the seriousness of the situation. "I will leave you and your wolves to the rest of your business."

Sophie's eyes narrowed and she frowned. Then she simply looked at her brother who nodded once. Like it or not, her intent was clear. Griff was to go with me or there would be hell to pay. Then she neatly boxed me in, using my own words to keep me from objecting.

"Marshal, you have charged us with assisting your office and protecting this town and Zone. So let me begin by sending my brother with you. If you need more assistance from my pack, all you need to do is ask and you shall have it."

Unless I wanted to undermine her authority and everything I'd said this morning, I needed to keep my mouth shut. Instead, I nodded once, a silent promise that we'd be discussing this later. Then I excused myself and led Griffin to my SUV. Sophie could handle things here and I had other things to deal with.

Hopefully, I'd get some answers along the way.

It didn't take long to get there. The parking lot had seen better days, but so had most of this part of town. For several long moments, Griff and I studied our destination. The apartment building suited the cracked and pitted parking lot. Before the Cataclysm, it had been a two-story motel. People stayed here even though we were almost an hour outside of Dallas because of our location. We were close enough for them to enjoy the benefits of Dallas while being far enough away to feel like they were in the country. But the Cataclysm changed all that.

Afterwards, most people didn't want to travel so close to one of the

Rifts, much less stay there. As a result, the owners defaulted on their loan. For several years, the motel sat empty, like so many buildings in the area. Between neglect, the occasional magical storm, vandals, and more, it fell into disarray. That's what Red had been waiting for. He bought the property at a discount and converted it into apartments. They were serviceable, but far from luxurious.

"Ready?" I asked Griff as I unlocked my door.

He checked his gun and then nodded. "Ready."

He climbed out of the SUV and hurried around the front of it to join me at the driver's door. I checked the ease I could get to each of my weapons and then drew a deep breath. Any other time, it might have been bracing. But not this time. This time I wanted to make sure I didn't scent anything that might reach out and bite my ass.

We didn't speak as we crossed the street. Nor did we stop by the manager's office. If Yousef happened to be there, I didn't want anyone warning him of our arrival. If he wasn't, I didn't need the manager to let me in. I had a master that should do it easily. The only problem was I didn't know if I wanted him to be home or not. Angry as I was about everything that happened the last few days, I wanted satisfaction and I doubted I'd have any problem taking it from him.

"Stop!"

Griffin reached over and grabbed my arm, pulling me back as I lifted a hand to pound on the door. Snarling, I looked at him. Had he lost his mind? Then, as he nodded at the door, I felt the unmistakable tingling of a magical ward and cursed softly. If I'd been paying more attention instead of focusing on my anger, he wouldn't have had to stop me. Fortunately, he possessed more common sense than I did.

"Well, that's interesting." I stepped closer to the door, no longer trying to touch it. Instead, I inhaled deeply, trying to scent anything that might be behind the magical wards. "Can you tell anything?"

He shook his head. "I was hoping you could."

"Nope." I could do a lot of things, but dealing with magic like this was beyond me. "Do we call Sele and her sisters or risk it ourselves?"

"It's your call, but I say risk it."

I considered his recommendation. I didn't like playing with magic I knew nothing about, but I agreed. It was possible the wards would fry us up like a couple of strips of bacon, but I doubted it. There was too great a chance someone passing by could activate them. Hell, a stray dog or cat could. Since I didn't think Youssef wanted to explain why his neighbor's pet lay dead on his doorstep, I hoped the wards were set to warn him only.

Unfortunately, there was only one way to find out for sure.

"Stand back."

He stopped me before I could reach for the doorknob. "Ripley, Sophie will kill me if anything happens to you."

As if she wouldn't kill me if something happened to him. But I took the hint. He needed to do this because of her declaration before the pack. That didn't mean I liked it. Which was something I would make sure they both knew when this was over.

Before I could say anything, Griff took the master keycard from me and slid it into the lock. As he did, his jaw firmed and he hissed softly in pain as the wards came to life. Then the lock clicked and the door swung open. The moment it did, the wards fell. Interesting. I wasn't about to complain. Instead, I stepped inside, Griff on my heels, his gun at the ready.

Not that it was needed.

The apartment was empty. Oh, the furniture was still there. From the kitchen to our right, I heard the low *hum* of the refrigerator. But there was a stillness to the place that said no one had been there for at least a couple of days. The layer of dust on the coffee table in front of a well-worn sofa confirmed it. Still, we needed to be sure.

"Well?" I looked at Griff, trying to judge his thoughts by his closed expression.

"We're not going to find anything."

"Agreed, but let's take a look anyway. Maybe he got sloppy." And maybe I'd finally learn how to fly.

While I searched the living room and kitchen, Griff took the bedroom and bath. Hopefully, he'd find more than I did. The living room showed signs of use: the remote control for an ancient television tossed onto the cushion of a battered armchair. A few pieces of paper, no larger than my thumbnail in the cushion cracks of the sofa, as if he'd been sitting there when he tore something up. But not much more and certainly nothing to tell me where he was right now.

The kitchen produced even less, unless you counted the fact he seemed to be addicted to a sugary cereal most people quit eating once they hit adolescence. An open half gallon of milk, well past its best by date, and some wilted salad makings were the only things in the refrigerator. The freezer, however, was a different matter.

"Griff!"

He came running, gun in hand, as I hauled the first of some carefully wrapped objects from the freezer above the refrigerator. Each of the six packages were wrapped in heavy white paper like Mom used to call butcher's paper. Then they were taped with clear packing tape before being sealed in plastic.

"Doesn't look like how I store my frozen meat," Griff said as he put away his gun.

"Me neither. Shall we?" I pulled a knife from my pocket and flicked it open. When he nodded, I slid the tip very carefully under the plastic, cutting it away. "Your turn." I arched a brow and held the knife out to him.

"Step back. We don't know what's in here."

I didn't argue. I'd had enough surprises the last few days to last a lifetime. I didn't want any more.

Griff made quick work of the packages. The first two left me wondering if we'd been wrong. Instead of some form of contraband, they contained two really nice looking roasts. But the other four? Oh, opening them opened a can of worms we never expected.

Griff carefully laid out stack after stack of hundred dollar bills, the contents of three of the four remaining packages. Either Yousef had been taking bribes—or worse—or he didn't trust banks. Naw, who was I kidding? He didn't want to risk the government finding out and hitting with taxes for his ill-gotten gains. The country, and the world, might have lived through the Cataclysm, but some things remained the same, including the IRS.

"Ripley, you need to see this." Griff looked up from the last package as he pushed aside the heavy paper wrapping it.

I stepped closer. Unlike the other packages, this one rested inside a metal lock box that had then been wrapped, taped, and sealed in plastic. I studied it, noting the lock and frowning. Needless to say, Yousef hadn't been kind enough to leave the key for us. Not that we needed one. Between the two of us, Griff and I could figure out how to open the box.

"I assume protocol would be for you to wait for a warrant to open it."

He nodded.

"I have Conclave authorization to do whatever it takes to get to the bottom of what's been happening. Isabel also sent warrants for Yousef's arrest and the search of this place. That includes this box. I'm asking you to open it in my capacity as Marshal."

"That's all I need, Rip."

He grinned and pulled a leather case from his jacket pocket. When he opened it, I recognized a set of lock picks. He studied them for a moment before pulling one from the case. Then he bent over the lock box and carefully maneuvered the pick, moving it this way and that, until we both heard the soft *snick*.

He straightened and stepped back. Before I could reach for the box, he stopped me. My brows drew together when he did. Without a word, he handed me a pair of nitrile gloves. I nodded in appreciation and pulled them on. Then I carefully lifted the lid and looked inside.

"What is it?" Griff asked as I pushed aside what looked like a piece of sheet or pillowcase.

"I-I'm not sure."

Inside were several smaller packages. They weren't sealed as carefully as the lock box or packages of money had been, but they were still wrapped. I chose the largest of the three packages and peeled away the wrapping. A short time later, a leather case, similar to a wallet or credit card case, rested in my hands. The black leather was stained with what I suspected was blood. But it was what rested inside that had my own blood running cold.

"Rip?" Griff sounded as stunned as I felt.

I looked down at a badge and ID I recognized. My fingers trembled as they lightly traced the badge before moving to the ID. Tears burned my eyes as I studied my mother's picture. This, like her guns, jacket and other items, had been with her on that last assignment. It had not been something Red recovered when he tried finding her.

I couldn't say anything. The words stuck in my throat, choking me. I simply held the badge case out to him. He took it, his expression worried, as he looked at me. Then he looked at the case, hissing out a breath as he realized what he held.

"Ripley, if you want his head, I will get it for you. If you want his balls, I'll cut them off and bronze them so you can hang them from your rearview mirror. If you want help dealing with him in any way, you have it. I promise he will not get away with this."

Whatever *this* was.

"I want answers. Then I want his head." I ground it out, taking the badge case back from him.

"You'll have both. My word on it."

I shook my head, holding the case between my hands.

"Don't, Griff. Don't make promises we both know you might not be able to keep."

He simply looked at me, his expression as serious as I'd ever seen. "This is one promise I will keep. You have my word." He rested a hand on my shoulder, giving it a squeeze.

I nodded once, determined to see this through. I didn't care what happened so long as I got answers and that meant finding Yousef.

"Let's go find that bastard."

3 2

SOMETHING WICKED CAME A-
KNOCKING

Leaving Griff to deal with the packs of money, I turned on my heel and left the apartment. He called out to me, telling me to wait, but I ignored him. I couldn't wait. Two hours ago, I knew Yousef was involved with everything that happened the last few days. Now I knew he was also involved with what happened to my mother. He'd played me and everyone else in town, setting us up for who knows what. But no more. If it was the last thing I did, I was going to stop him. . . with prejudice.

I pulled my phone and programmed in Isabel Markowitz's number as I continued to my car. I'd have Yousef's head, but I'd do it with the backing of the Conclave if possible. Even though she'd given me the go ahead earlier, she needed to know this latest information and, hopefully, she might even be able to shed some light on what it meant.

"Ripley, I didn't expect to hear from you so soon," the head of the Conclave said when she answered my call.

"There have been some new developments."

I quickly explained what we found in Yousef's apartment. As I did, Griff joined me, a trash bag I assumed containing the money and other items from the lock box, in one hand. He looked at me, concerned, but said nothing. Apparently satisfied with what he saw, he gave me a nod and continued to the SUV to safely lock away the bag and its contents.

"You're sure the badge is your mother's?" Isabel asked.

"I am." I closed my eyes, struggling not to snap at her. Of course, I was sure it was Mom's. Didn't she realize I'd recognize it instantly? "Isabel, it's not just the badge. It's her badge case, badge and ID."

She didn't say anything for a moment and I waited, knowing she needed a moment to process what I said.

"And he had it hidden away along with a cache of money?"

"Yes, ma'am. All neatly stacked, banded, wrapped, taped, and hidden in his freezer."

"Was there anything else with your mother's badge?"

I cursed softly, realizing I hadn't checked. When I saw the leather case and realized what it was, everything else ceased to matter. Stupid, stupid, stupid.

"There was but I didn't take time to check it. I should have."

"Stop, Ripley. You can check later. What you found was important and I appreciate you contacting me right away."

"Isabel, he's in the wind. For him to have left this much money behind means he knows I'm onto him." Or he had a pretty damned good suspicion.

"Do you think he's left the Zone?"

I considered for a moment. "No." I shook my head even though she couldn't see.

"He has an agenda and he'll try to see it through."

"Then stop him, Ripley. Your authorization on how to deal with him has been expanded. Take him into custody if you can do so without putting yourself or others at risk. But if he resists, if he tries to harm you or anyone else, you are authorized to take whatever action you feel necessary to stop him. I will transmit the kill order as soon as we get off the phone."

"And Drake?"

"The same orders. If possible, I would appreciate you consulting with me before executing the fool, but do not think this is a requirement."

"Thanks."

I'd prefer not killing either of them. I wanted the Conclave and everyone they ever betrayed to know what they did and see them receiving justice. Of course, I also wanted that to happen at my hand, especially if they were involved with what happened to Mom.

"Be careful, Ripley. There is more going on than we know right now." On that, we could agree.

"I need to run, Isabel."

"Report when you learn more, Ripley."

I assured her I would and used the key fob to unlock the SUV. Then I shoved the cellphone in my hip pocket. With Griff on my heels, I hurried across the parking lot, my mind already on what our next move should be.

"Ripley!"

A wave of magical energy hit me like a two-by-four, sending me to my knees. With it came a wave a nausea to rival the worst night of over-drinking I'd ever experienced. The stench of rotting flesh filled my nose and mouth, causing me to gag. Eyes watering, breath coming in ragged gasps, I fought for control.

"Ripley, talk to me."

Griff's voice sounded so far off, too far off.

The sigils, Ripley. Use the sigils.

My right hand moved slowly to my left arm and the fingers touched the activation points, almost as if of their own accord. Razor's sigils flared, a sudden light against the darkness that seemed to envelop me. As the darkness began to recede, I touched the sigils on my arm. The stench eased. But the oppressive feeling remained.

"Damn it, Rip, say something!" Griff's voice sounded rough, as if he was close to shifting.

"S-stay back. I'm okay." I hoped.

I pressed my right hand to the cracked concrete and carefully pushed myself upright. It felt as if I moved through molasses or quick-sand. But I moved. Better yet, I could breathe easier. The protections woven into the sigils came to life and countered the magical energies of the attack.

Just as quickly as the attack began, it ended. I slumped to hands and knees, head hanging low. Instantly, Griffin was at my side. Hands gentle, he carefully helped me first to my knees and then to my feet. His arm around my waist steadied me and I leaned against him, grateful for the support.

"Thanks." I blew out a long breath and reached up with a trembling hand to wipe my face.

"What happened?"

"Not sure. Felt like an attack."

"I'm calling Gemma."

I shook my head, straightening. "No. I'm all right."

"The hell you are."

Before I could argue, my phone and then signaled incoming texts. I dragged mine out of my hip pocket and stared at the display in disbelief. It couldn't be. Damn it, not now.

House under attack. Wards falling. Send help.

Neither of us said anything. Hell, I'm not sure we could say anything. Instead, I dove for the driver's door of the SUV. Grif jumped, sliding over the hood like some action hero. By the time he slammed the passenger door behind him, I'd started the engine and threw the transmission into gear.

"Hang on."

The SUV bucked like a wild horse as I drove over the curb and onto the road. The tires squealed in protest as they fought for grip on the slick street. When had it rained? It didn't matter. Nothing mattered except getting to the house.

"Call the Conclave," Griff said, hanging onto the chicken strap for dear life as I took the corner so fast the car rocked as if it might flip.

I bared my teeth but stopped before saying anything. He was right. This was definitely the sort of thing Isabel needed to know about. I reached up and tapped my right earbud. It beeped and I nodded to Griff without taking my eyes from the road.

"Call Isabel."

"Ripley, is everything all right?" Isabel asked as soon as she answered the call.

"No." I wrenched the wheel to the right, turning onto Main Street. "Red just texted Griffin and me. My house is under attack. He's there with Aras and Dani. We're on our way now."

"Do whatever it takes to protect them, Ripley. You're authorized to take any and all action to do so. Do you need backup?"

Next to me, Griffin was calling his sister, Razor and Sele. They were all the backup I needed or wanted until I had a better idea about what was happening.

"Not yet. I'll let you know after I get there and see what I'm up against."

"Keep me informed and keep safe."

I tapped the earbud again to end the call. As I did, Griff assured me the others were heading to the house now. I nodded but didn't slow. We couldn't wait for them. Not if the wards were failing.

I sped down the street toward home. As I did, Razor's truck raced up from the opposite direction. A moment later, Sele's car appeared behind the SUV. Glad to have the backup, I turned into the driveway, barely registering the fact the gates swung open in front of us.

"Griff, you're with me," I said as I turned off the engine and pulled the keys from the ignition. "Find out where your sister is."

"She just pulled up."

I glanced over my shoulder in time to see her Jeep parking just far enough up the drive to let the gate close. The outside world was now beyond the protections of the stone walls. But was it too little, too late?

Everyone piled out of their cars. Layla took a Quick Look around before shifting. I watched as the monster-sized cobra slithered across the lawn, its tongue tasting the air as she began her search.

"Ripley, here!"

I turned to find Sele. She knelt in the grass near the front porch. In front of her someone lay. I didn't need to see their face to know who it was. I'd recognize the dark pants and scuffed pants anywhere. My heart skipped a beat or two and my breath rasped out. Not again.

"How is he?"

I dropped onto the grass next to her, doing my best to ignore the blood seeping onto the ground from a wound at my foster father's left temple or the number of cuts and what looked suspiciously like bite marks that marred his arms, chest and abdomen.

"R-Ripley." Red's voice rasped as he tried to speak.

"Shh, Red. Let her see to you." I ran a gentle hand over his brow, watching as Sele worked, chanting softly, to stop the bleeding through both mundane and arcane means.

"Need to tell you. Yousef and others. Witch took down the wards. Don't know how."

"I'll find Yousef and the others and I'll find out what they did. Promise."

He closed his eyes, his breath shuddering as Sele continued working. Worried, I looked at her, silently pleading for reassurance. Red was the closest thing I had to a parent. If Yousef took him from me too.
. .

Hell wouldn't be far enough for him to run to. I'd find him and kill him.

I looked up when someone placed a gentle hand on my shoulder. Seeing a very pissed off Sophie standing there, my jaw firmed and I nodded once. Then I did my best to smile in reassurance to Red.

"Take care of him for me, Sele." I climbed to my feet and followed Sophie around the corner of the house to the side yard. "Tell me," I said once we were out of sight of the front yard.

"It's bad, Rip. Aras fought some of them back here, near the back porch. He's hurt badly. Elle's working on him now."

"And?" There was more to it. I could see it in the way she held herself and in the way her wolf fought for release.

"He managed to give much more than he got. We've got bodies: several wolves, a man who looks human but was probably a witch, and a troll."

I whistled softly, impressed. Then I turned serious again. Wolves meant this directly involved the pack and Sophie as its alpha. The only question was if the wolves were part of the pack or interlopers on its territory.

Or some brought in by Yousef and, more than likely, Drake.

"The wolves?"

"I didn't recognize them."

At least that was good news.

"Get photos and prints if they shifted back to human. We need to ID them. Griff can help."

"He's already on it."

"Good." I thought for a moment. "Aras?"

"By the porch."

I had to ask. I'd avoided it so far, knowing the answer and not wanting to make it real by having someone give voice to it. But I couldn't put it off any longer.

"Dani?"

She shook her head.

Anger, fear, clutched at my chest. Fire suddenly danced around my hands and the wolf I'd kept leashed all my life threw her head back and howled. Even though I made no sound, Sophie and her brother looked at me in concern, as if they could sense what I felt. Hell, for all I knew, they could. We were tied by our bonds through my heritage as one of Morrigan's descendants. For all I knew, the entire pack just got a dose of my anger and fear.

The pack.

"Sophie, will you ask your wolves to start searching for Dani? They can cover more territory than we can and I still need to learn what I can from Aras and from the scene."

"I will, but only if you promise not to leave without the rest of us."

Even though that is exactly what I wanted to do, I nodded. She looked at me for a moment, weighing whether I told the truth or not. Then she nodded. I watched as she pulled out her cellphone and began making calls. Relieved the pack was going to help,

I nodded. Even if I wanted to go haring after Yousef and whoever helped him, I couldn't. Not until I knew more about what happened. Certainly not until I knew what happened to Dani. Even though Sophie seemed to believe she wasn't here, Dani was smart. She could be hiding. I prayed she was hiding. The alternative not only terrified me but it meant there was still a very large piece of the puzzle we were missing.

Hell, who was I kidding? We were doing well to know there was a puzzle. We didn't have any of the pieces except one battered piece that might go in the center.

Get a grip, Ripley.

I took one last bracing breath and jogged around the corner into the back yard. The scene that greeted me was surreal. Bodies littered the yard like fallen statuary, including Aras. Unlike the others, however, the elf still lived. He leaned against the trunk of an ancient tree, one hand pressed against a wound in his side that bled too much.

He held a sword in the other.

Well, that accounted for the decapitated wolf near his feet.

"Aras." I dropped to my knees at his side, relieved when his eyes fluttered open.

"Find her, Ripley." He released his hold on the sword and grabbed my hand in a surprisingly firm grip. "She's the key."

"I will. You have my word." I didn't care if it was the last thing I did. I'd find Dani. I'd find the bastards responsible for the carnage here. When I did, they would pay dearly for going after my family. "Can you tell me what happened?"

"Not sure. The wards activated. Red shouted for me to protect Dani before he went out front to stop whoever it was. I knew he wasn't strong enough. But I gave my word to protect her."

I nodded, holding his hand between mine. He loved Dani as much as any of us did. Even knowing Red was still too hurt to fight for long, he would do whatever he could to protect Dani. Seeing the dead who littered the yard told me he'd done his best to do just that. Unfortunately, it hadn't been enough. Dani was gone. Otherwise, she'd be here with him.

"I failed, Ripley. I failed to protect Dani. I failed to keep my oath to you."

With a bloodstained hand that shook from the effort, he lifted his sword and held it out to me. For a moment, I didn't understand. Then I cursed once. Gently, I took the sword from him and placed it once more at his side. I'd spill blood for what happened here, but not his.

"Aras, you didn't fail me or Dani. You fought for her. You killed for her. You shed your blood to protect her. I don't require your death for doing everything anyone could ever ask of you to protect her. What I do require is for you to heal. Then you can help me deal with those responsible for what happened."

Assuming any of them still lived because I was going hunting and, thanks to Isabel, I had the authority necessary to execute anyone who took part in the attack on my friends and my home.

"Ripley, let me see to him." Romy knelt across from me and placed a bag of supplies on the ground at her side.

"One or two more questions first." I looked at Aras, worried to delay his treatment but needing to know as much as he could tell me.

"Ask," the elf rasped.

"How did they bring down the wards?"

"Magical attack. It knocked both Red and me off our feet. Knocked Dani out." He coughed, blood frothing at his lips.

"Easy, Aras." I gently wiped his mouth, doing my best not to let him see the blood now staining my fingers. "What else?"

"The witch managed to break the wards. Attackers rushed the house. Told Dani to hide and I did what I could to keep them outside."

"Did you recognize anyone?"

He dipped his chin. "Yousef."

Anger flared and I pushed it down. Instead, I smiled gently and cupped the elf's cheek with my hand. His skin was clammy, his breathing becoming more labored. Glancing at Romy, I saw her concern.

"Rest now, Aras. You did good, better than any of us could have asked." I bent and gently pressed my lips to his cheek. "Rest now and let Romy help you. Dani's going to need you when I bring her home."

He closed his eyes and nodded one more time.

"Whatever he needs, Romy." I scrubbed my hands over my face, ignoring the blood on them. "Call Isabel Mankowitz from the Conclave if you need anything. Tell her I told you to."

"I will. Now go. Bring our girl home."

"That's the plan."

33

HELL HATH NO FURY AND I WASN'T THE ONE SCORNED

Sophie met me as I shoved the door open and stepped inside the mudroom off the kitchen. Her eyes glowed, her wolf close to the surface. But the fury I'd sensed earlier had lessened. I waited, hoping that meant she had news.

Instead of speaking, she motioned for me to come with her. I followed her through the kitchen into the main room. It amazed me to see how normal everything looked inside when compared to the scene outside. Somehow, Red and Aras kept the fighting out of the house. Not that it saved Dani. She was gone. I knew it. I could feel it. The only questions were if she still lived and who besides Yousef would pay with their lives.

Waiting for us were Griff, Razor and Layla, now back to her human form. All looked as angry and worried as I felt. Before I could say anything, Layla hurried to me, wrapping me in a hug and leaning in, whispering that we would get Dani back. They didn't care about the Conclave, the laws—human or para. Nothing mattered but getting her back.

Since I agreed, I nodded.

"Red?"

"Upstairs. Sele and Elle are working on him now."

"Good." That was good. "Razor, will you go out back and help Romy get Aras upstairs? He's hurt badly."

The shaman nodded once and left, moving quickly to do as I asked.

"What can you tell me?"

It wasn't much and nothing I didn't expect. Dani was nowhere in the house. Someone had kicked in her bedroom door. There was evidence of a struggle but nothing to indicate Dani had been injured, at least not too badly. I grabbed onto that and held it close. Now to figure out where Yousef took her.

Once she was safe, I'd teach that bastard what it meant to piss me off.

"We need to remember that. Despite the scene outside, it's clear they wanted Dani alive. Why? I don't know and, honestly, I don't care. Not as long as they do nothing to hurt her."

They nodded in agreement.

"Aras was still conscious when I got to him." I quickly told them what I could, watching as their expressions went from disbelief to relief and then to anger to hear he confirmed our suspicions about Yousef. "My guess is they left here about ten minutes before we got here, no more than that."

"So they can't have gone far," Layla said.

"No, but we need to find them."

"The pack is already hunting for them, Ripley," Sophie said.

"And my cops are looking for them."

Like it or not, all we could do was wait and pray. In the meantime, we'd prepare. Starting with making sure everyone was armed and ready to go as soon as we had a location.

The next half hour was spent preparing for the upcoming battle. I called Isabel, letting her know what little I could. I watched as Griff made sure his sister and the others had the mundane weapons they needed to go along with their arcane protections. I spoke with Razor, trying to figure out how Yousef and his witch managed to break the wards on the property and house. He had no explanation but several suspicions. We might never know and that worried me more than I liked.

But I couldn't think about that right now.

"You okay?" Sophie asked softly as she joined me in front of the bay window in the sitting room at the front of the house.

"No." Why lie? I was anything but okay. "Anything?"

"Not yet, but the pack's still looking. They're out in both human and wolf forms." She slipped her arm around my waist and leaned her head against my shoulder. "We're going to find her, Rip."

I nodded, unable to say anything.

"I checked on Red and Aras. Sele and Romy said they should recover, but it's going to take time."

Time and luck.

Maybe a little prayer.

"Ripley."

I glanced over my shoulder at the sound of Griff's voice. He stood just inside the door, his cellphone in hand. My heart skipped a beat at the look on his face. Gone was the worry that had been there the last time I saw him. Determination and excitement replaced it. No doubt about it, he knew something and my pulse pounded as I waited.

"We have them."

A feral smile touched my lips. Relief washed over me. With it came a determination to make Yousef pay for his betrayal. They why of it could wait until I'd extracted a pound of flesh for every bruise, every cut, every tear he caused Dani.

"Where?"

"A strip mall the other side of town." He reached out and stopped me when I tried to push past him. "Hold on a minute. I have cops watching from a safe distance away and members of the pack are heading there now to assist. We need to go into this smart, not acting only on emotion."

I hated it, but he was right.

"Get everyone together. We need someone to stay with Aras and Red. I want Sele, Elle and Romy with us."

"Gemma's already here," Sophie said. "She can stay with them. She and Razor have also reset the wards, adding new protections to them."

"All right." I drew a deep breath, forcing myself to think and not just react. "We meet in five. I want everyone going with us ready to leave as soon as Griff briefs us."

"We'll be ready." Sophie squeezed my hand and then left the room to let the others know.

"Griff?"

"We got lucky, Rip. The strip mall is usually closed on Sundays. That's what first caught my cops' attention. They set up surveillance and saw Yousef exit one of the storefronts and cross to a car parked out front. He got something out of the car and went back inside. That's when they called me."

It wasn't much, but it was enough.

"Thank you." I didn't say anything else. I didn't need to. He understood I meant for more than his officers' report. "Let's get this party going."

"Ripley, are you all right?"

I nodded. For the first time in my life, I understood what my father meant when he told me there would be times when nothing mattered more than helping the helpless. It didn't matter the personal cost. Some things were worth the sacrifice.

And Dani's life was one of them.

34

SOMEONE SHOULD HAVE
LEASHED THEIR SHAGGY BEASTS

Two blocks from the shopping center, I pulled over and parked. Leaving the SUV idling, I sat there, gathering my thoughts. If I was wrong about all this, people I cared about would pay dearly for my mistake. But I wasn't wrong. I couldn't be. I felt it in my bones that this was not only the right decision, but the only one given the circumstances.

By all that's holy, don't let me be wrong.

"Marshal, we've got movement," one of Griffin's cops reported.

I reached up and tapped my earbud, removing it from mute. "Tell me."

"We're set up down the street, on the roof of the old Myers Building. It gives us a clear view of the front of the center."

I waited, wishing he'd hurry up and get to the point.

"Chief Starke has two more watching the back."

"She knows that, Ben," Griffin said, reminding me we were on a conference call. "Get to the point."

"Sorry, Chief." He paused for a moment before continuing. "We had two more cars pull up. The first one parked in front of the center storefront. Two people were inside. The passenger got out. Male, midforties looking but my guess is he's much older. My partner's a wolf and he said he smelled of shapeshifter. He went inside. His car and driver remained where they were and the other car drove off."

"Do you have eyes on the second car?" Someone's head would roll if they didn't. I wanted everyone even remotely involved with what happened identified and dealt with, even if I had to do it myself.

"Yes, ma'am. One of our reserve officers is following on his beater of a motorcycle and we've also got a drone on the car." Good. That was good.

"Do you have an ID on the man who went inside?" Griffin asked.

"A tentative one, Chief. He had on a ball cap that he pulled low over his face. But my guess is he's the one you told us to be on the look out for." *Who?* I texted Griff.

Drake. Before you blow a gasket, Ben is the mate of one of our pack and as loyal to us and to the Conclave as you'd ever want.

'k

"Call, keep an eye on the front of the building. If the driver makes a move to get out of the car or to leave, let me know. I'll be on-scene shortly with reinforcements." "Do as the marshal says, Ben," Griffin said and we ended the call.

Sitting there, I beat the steering wheel with the heel of my hand. Anger rose, but so did the lust for the hunt. Everything was coming together, for good or for ill waited to be seen. My money was on the good, but then I refused to consider any other outcome. Not when Dani's life lay on the line.

I glanced in the rearview mirror as a car pulled in behind me. A moment later, a black SUV, almost the twin of the one I drove, parked in front. Soon, two more joined them and I switched off the ignition. Time to move.

"Well?" Sophie asked as she joined me at the rear of the SUV.

"Let's wait for the others." That way I only had to say it once. Hopefully, I'd only have to argue with everyone one time as well.

"All right, Ripley. What can we do to help?" Razor asked as he and Layla joined us.

Soon Griff, Sele, Elle, Romy, and Cal joined us. All looked as determined, and as worried, as I felt.

"None of you need to be part of this." Much as I wanted their help,

I wouldn't demand it. They had their own families and lives to consider and every instinct told me this wasn't going to end peacefully.

"Can it, Rip. We're here because we want to be," Griff said and Sophie nodded in agreement.

"Thanks." Now I smiled, glad they were part of my life. Even Griff who more often than not drove me up the nearest proverbial tree. "But you need to be sure. If you help me, you'll be going against a member of the Conclave. Even though Isabel had given me full authority to act, I don't know how the rest of the Conclave will react if I take Drake into custody." Or worse. "This could backfire on us badly."

"It will be worse if we don't help," Layla said simply and the others nodded.

"She is right, Ripley." Romy reached out and instantly her sisters took her hands.

"Aunt Gemma said as much when we told her we were coming with you."

I rubbed my eyes, wishing I would finally wake up from this nightmare.

"What else did she say?"

Who knows? Maybe she said something that might help me figure out how to proceed.

"She said we all needed to play to our talents and work together. But she reminded us that we are to follow your lead. Whatever's happening, you are the focal point right now?"

"Did she have any idea why they took Dani?"

All three sisters shook their heads. Then I noticed the large black cat weaving in and out of their legs. Cal. I didn't know whether to sigh or laugh. Instead, I decided to make use of him. If he wanted to be a cat, he could go hunting the rats for me.

"Cal, you're going to be our eyes and ears until we get inside. I want you to scout the area around the center. Will you do that for me?"

He sat on his haunches and sat tall and regal. In a move that was all human, he nodded once. Then, with a flick of his tail, he stood and ran off. Romy didn't wait for instructions. She said she'd keep an eye on him and jogged after him. As she did, Griff contacted the cops at their vantage places to let them know we had people moving in. Then he slid his phone into a pocket on his tactical vest and nodded once.

Showtime.

"All right. We're going to do what Gemma said. We're going to play to our strengths." I gnawed my lower lip, thinking hard. "Layla, if you partially shift now, how long will it take you to finish the shift if you need to?"

"She can do it almost instantaneously if needed," Razor said and she nodded.

"Good. Then do whatever you need to get ready. I'm trusting you to decide how much of the shift you need to do before we head out. Sophie, Griff, at least one of you needs to shift."

"I will," Sophie said. "Griff, she's going to need backup and that's you. We're all trusting you to keep her safe." "Sophie," I growled.

"She's right, Ripley," Sele said. "We won't keep you from doing what you need to, but we will make sure to watch your back."

"All right."

I moved to the rear of my SUV and opened the hatch. While I began gearing up, the others did as well. Some claimed weapons and protective gear from my stash and others followed Griff to his SUV to do the same. It didn't take long. As I made one last check of my weapons, I said a quick prayer to any deity that might be listening. So much rested on what happened in the next few minutes.

And so much could go wrong.

"Is everyone ready?" I asked as I closed the hatch and used the key fob to lock the SUV.

"We are," Griff answered for everyone.

"You know what you're to do?"

They nodded. The plan was simple enough. Around the corner from the strip center, We'd split up. I'd go in first, Sophie and Razor with me. The others could follow. Layla and Griff keeping the sisters between them. Once inside, all bets were off and we knew it. So we'd play it loose and smart—I hoped.

Especially when, as we neared the corner, Layla shifted into her reptile form and slithered away. Razor shrugged and didn't look particularly surprised when I glanced at him. I watched as she disappeared around the corner, debating whether to hurry or give her the chance to deal with everyone on her own.

Damn it.

Without waiting for the others, I jogged after Layla. Even though the thought of a cat and a cobra taking on who knew how many paras with unknown abilities worried me, I had faith in them. Cal might act the fool, but his sisters assured me he was a strong witch, almost as strong as them. He was also very much a cat, whether in human or feline form. That meant he was sneaky, deadly, and always ready to get into trouble. Hopefully, that was enough to get all of us through the next few minutes.

"We have a visual on you, Marshal," Ben said through my earbud. "No movement from inside."

I slowed to a walk. "The driver?"

He didn't say anything for a moment. "Let's just say I never thought I'd see a cat and a snake bigger than me working together. The coroner's going to have to scrape the pieces up with a spatula."

I swallowed hard. "We're moving in. Stay in place and report any changes out here."

"Roger that, Marshal."

I glanced at the others, praying each of us walked out of this safe and sound.

"Ready?"

Everyone nodded. Looking at them, fear and determination filled me. Whatever it took, I'd make sure they, along with Dani, made it home. Hopefully, I'd be with them. Was this what Mom felt before her last assignment? Or Dad? Hadn't my family paid enough already?

Pushing aside the doubts, I took off at a jog. The sooner I reached the storefront, the sooner this ended. With each step, I eased my control over my fire aspect. By the time I reached our target, I wanted every advantage I could get.

"Well, well, well, look what the cat dragged in."

Two men stood in front of the glass door leading inside the storefront. Like the windows, the glass was coated over with a mixture of dust, bird droppings and a layer of either soap or paint. That alone made it stand out from the rest of the strip mall where small shops operated. Or they had the last time I was in this part of town. Now it looked like the entire strip had been abandoned.

Something else I needed to look into.

Better yet, something to let Griffin and his cops investigate.

"Hey, Sophie, do these mutts belong to you?" I jerked a thumb at the two men, grinning as they growled at my characterization.

Sophie, in her wolf form, padded across the lot to stand next to me. The men took one look at her and their scents changed. Wariness, followed by a touch of fear. But, being foolish males, they decided to posture instead of being smart enough to submit.

"That bitch doesn't scare us," one of them sneered, ignoring Griff's growl as he moved to his sister's side.

He might not have shifted, but he was all wolf just then.

"Alpha, I leave them to you."

Sophie looked up at me and gave a very human nod.

"Submit or shift and fight," Griff said. "Those are your only options."

Both men laughed. It sounded hollow, especially when Sophie growled. Magical energies built around her, energies I recognized signaled a shift. Curious, and not about to let her be attacked by these two while in the middle of shifting back to human, I waited. Then I chuckled almost evilly. It seemed I wasn't the only one who hid a secret or two.

Instead of shifting to human, Sophie's form blurred as bones broke and reformed. It didn't take long. Gone now was the wolf that sat next to me. In its place was a hybrid, something I'd only read about. She stood on her hind feet. More wolf than human, a reminder of how some of the old movies used to portray werewolves. She now stood as tall as me, with the additional inches I'd added during our run to the strip center.

"Submit." Her voice, deeper than when she was human, rumbled in her chest and the hair on the back of my neck stood on end.

Foolishly, one of the men pulled a gun. Sophie moved quicker than any of us expected. One moment, the man stood a few feet away from us. The next moment he hit the front wall of the storefront and slid down to the sidewalk with a sickening thud. Blood trailed down the wall where he hit. Sophie threw back her head and howled, challenging not only the man's companion but every wolf close enough to hear.

I bent, retrieved the man's gun and tucked it under my belt at the small of my back. As I did, Sophie stalked toward the second wolf, still in his human form. The front of his jeans turned dark as he pissed himself before dropping to his hands and knees, head hanging low. Not satisfied with his show of submission, Griff kicked him in the ribs, sending him sprawling.

"Make sure he won't bother us, but leave him alive. I need to have a conversation with him."

Griffin nodded. As he reached down to grab the man by his collar with one hand, he reached for his cuffs with the other. "We're going to have a little chat about showing the proper respect to the local alpha."

Another chill ran down my back as he did. Griff was pissed, not only because of the disrespect to his sister but to the fact the wolf and his companion dared act against the pack and against the town. I didn't doubt he wanted the wolf to stand trial under pack law and, for the moment at least, I was inclined to agree.

"You think these cuffs will hold me, cur?"

"No, but this will."

Before I could react, Griffin drove a silver knife into the man's right shoulder. A second knife appeared in his hand moments before he slammed it into the man's left thigh. The wolf howled in pain and frustration. While I normally didn't approve of gratuitous violence, I nodded in approval. One thing the movies got right was that silver was the bane of all weres. He wouldn't be able to shift to his wolf form as long as the knives remained where they were. I trusted Griffin to make sure they were removed before they did permanent damage. But that would wait until we finished our business here. All I cared about was finding Dani and I continued toward the storefront where I saw others through the glass.

"Boys, you really should have paid attention to the lesson we just taught your friends outside."

I shook my head, a smile on my lips. Just inside the door crouched two werewolves. Shifted, they were smaller than the one outside and certainly smaller than Griff or Sophie. That meant they were young. Hopefully, they wouldn't make me kill them. Especially if they were as young as I suspected.

One of them, easily differentiated from its companion by its lighter coat, growled and moved forward on stiff legs. The other remained silent as it tried moving to one side in an attempt to place us between the two. Behind me, I felt magic building as Sele and Elle prepared to counter anything they might try. Before they could, Sophie was there and the two instantly dropped to their bellies. It wouldn't have surprised me if they covered their eyes with their paws and tried to look very, very small. Instead, their muscles quivered and the stink of fear rose from them.

"Shift," Sophie growled. "Ripley, go. I will deal with them."

I nodded and glanced around. A single door split the back wall. Locked or not, it wouldn't keep me out. If I couldn't open it, Sele or Elle most certainly could. If they failed, Romy most certainly could.

The door opened under my touch. Either those beyond it never thought we'd find them or they believed they could beat us. Either way, I planned to teach them just how foolish they'd been.

A short corridor opened onto a larger area that had once been the storeroom. The scene inside sent a chill of fear through me. Drake, Yousef, two more wolves in their shifted form, ranged around the room. A witch, the one who'd presented herself to me as Ker, stood in the middle of a magical circle in the center of the room. But it was the sight of Dani laying motionless inside the circle, surrounded by sigils I didn't need Razor to explain. Black magic rose inside the circle, focusing on Dani.

I'd kill them, each and every one of them, if any harm came to Dani. "Sele."

"We've got her, Ripley."

Good, because I had something else to deal with first. Then I would deal with the witch.

"You and I have some business to deal with, Drake."

35

CHEATER, CHEATER, NO CHICKEN DINNER

"Walker."

I have to admit it. He made my name sound like a hiss Layla would be proud of. Instead of putting the fear of God into me as he expected, his anger and frustration amused me. Especially when he dropped his eyes to the badge clipped to my belt, a badge he hadn't given me. With another hiss of breath, he looked beyond me to where Layla and Razor stood before casting a quick glance to where Sele and Elle stood outside the magic circle, softly talking as they compared notes. Inside the circle, the witch seemed oblivious to them as she continued raising her dark magic and centering it on Dani.

He swallowed hard and a thin line of sweat ran down the left side of his face. I scented his fear on the air before anger and something else, something I couldn't identify, replaced it. Determination flashed in his eyes and I sighed slightly. He wasn't going to make this easy.

"Leave, Walker. This doesn't concern you."

He sounded more confident than he was. I knew it as did he. Now to see who blinked first.

I'd be damned if it was me.

"But it does." I shrugged out of my mother's jacket. There was no way this ended without a fight and I didn't want to risk the jacket. "You made it concern me when you lied about the Conclave appointing me as senior marshal."

Yousef started in surprise at that and glared at Drake before quickly composing himself. Interesting. How far and how deep did Drake's lies go?

Well, there was no time like the present to find out.

"You also made it my concern when you failed to supply me with the intel I needed to not only figure out what was going on here but to help protect the people of this zone. If that's not enough, you also made it my concern when you interfered with the pack, coercing and convincing its alpha and others to go against Conclave law. But your real mistake was in taking Dani. That mistake will cost your life unless you release her now." I handed my jacket to Razor who, in turn, handed it to the now human Cal.

"You forget one thing, Walker. I represent the Conclave. I have the force and authority of it behind my actions here."

I stared at me in surprise when I grinned before shaking my head.

"Wrong. I've had several very interesting conversations with Isabel Mankowitz in the last twenty-four hours. It seems she's had some concerns about you for a while now. She also corrected your *oversight*. I am now the official senior marshal for the Zone." Now it was my turn to show at least one of the tricks up my sleeve. "And, by her authority, I have warrants for your arrest as well as yours, Yousef."

"The fuck you say!" Yousef instantly shifted into a defensive stance, his hand going to the small of his back where I knew he carried either a knife or a gun, possibly even both.

"I wouldn't if I were you." I nodded to where Layla, more cobra than human, sidled in his direction. "But don't worry. I'll deal with you shortly."

Drake's lips peeled back in a snarl. Then he chopped a hand through the air, as if doing so would not only silence me but end the standoff between us. Fool. The only way it would end was with either him in custody or me dead.

And I didn't plan on being dead any time soon.

"Take care of her, Yousef." He never took his eyes off me as he gave the order. "After all, we wouldn't be in this position if you'd done as ordered months ago."

"And what was he supposed to do?"

"Take you out of the picture, preferably permanently but as long as you did nothing to upset my plan, I didn't care."

"Thank you for the confirmation. I'll make sure Isabel knows as soon as we're done here."

"You'll be telling her nothing, bitch," Yousef drawled. "Mr. Drake, it will be a pleasure to deal with her for you. No charge."

"Aww, surely I'm worth something for your trouble."

"Especially since she's going to wipe the floor with your sorry hide," Griff commented as he moved to stand to my right.

As he spoke, Sophie, still in her hybrid form, moved to my left, her attention on the two wolves standing protectively between us and Drake. "Submit or die, wolves." Her deep voice rumbled in the room, almost echoing off the walls.

"Stop!" Drake ordered as the two hesitated.

"Deal with them, alpha. We don't have time to waste with their foolishness." I turned my attention back to Drake and Yousef. "Now, you two can either surrender now or see how foolish it is to underestimate me."

"Always so cocky and yet too cowardly to follow in your parents' footsteps." Yousef motioned for Drake to step back. "Let's see which of us is truly best suited to be a marshal."

"Please." I gave a dismissive wave. "You proved that the moment you threw in with Drake and acted against the Conclave and its laws. By Conclave decree, you are both criminals and subject to a kill order if you fail to surrender. I told Isabel I would do my best to bring you in to face the charges against you. To be honest, however, I'm more than happy to play your game. How do you want to settle this?"

"So eager to meet your death, Walker?" He shook his head as if disappointed. But the gleam in his eyes betrayed his excitement.

"Yousef, you really haven't learned anything about me, have you?' I grinned, relaxed, watchful. "I rarely say anything I don't mean and I will always do my best to protect this town, the Zone, and the people in both. I don't need to be a marshal to do so. But being one does give me some liberties to act I wouldn't have otherwise."

"It's going to be a pleasure to deal with you, Walker." Yousef took a step to his left, watching to see if I matched his move. "Before we're done, you'll be on your knees before me, begging for mercy. Maybe Drake will let me keep you as a pet. You won't be of much use for anything else by the time I'm finished with you."

"Such big talk for such a little man." I held my right hand up and measured a small distance with my thumb and forefinger, the insult clear.

"I'll show you small." Anger suffused his face.

"Big words." I glanced at Griff who all but slouched insolently at my side. "If you're so good, why did you continually refuse to train with me. Every opportunity you had to spar with me, to get down and dirty, you refused. Makes me think you're afraid of being beaten by a woman."

"I'm not afraid of anyone, especially not you." This time, he took another step to his left and then another.

"I think he wants to dance, Griff. You and the others keep an eye on Drake. Help the sisters if you can. I won't be long dealing with this poor excuse for a human."

"I'm going to enjoy breaking you just like I enjoyed watching your mother being beaten and broken."

The world stopped. My blood ran cold. Every part of me demanded action, justice. Whether he spoke true or not, he punched my last button. That part of me from Surtr demanded release. The idea of frying him to a crisp called to me. But it was too quick and it wouldn't give me the chance to question him. If he spoke true, the circumstance of my mother's disappearance was worse than I thought.

The part of me from Morrigan wanted to shift. If I gave in, my hybrid form would put Sophie to shame. It would also teach everyone in the room with me how foolish it was to cross me. But that was a secret I didn't need to reveal. Not yet at any rate.

At least that's what I told myself as I struggled to maintain control.

"Tell me, Drake, why the hell did you choose a fool like him to be your errand boy?" I flicked a quick glance over Yousef's shoulder to where the man stood. "He can't keep his mouth shut. He says things I guess he thinks will intimidate me, maybe shake me, but instead only make me more determined to put the kill order the Conclave gave me to good use. Is he always this much of an idiot?"

I snapped my fingers, as if the answer suddenly dawned on me.

"Of course he is. He doesn't realize that his inability to settle in and become part of the community here became suspicious long again. Just like he doesn't realize I suspected something was up where he's concerned for the last several months. Of course, I could say the same about you, Drake. Tell me, how long have you been actively working against the Conclave?"

Drake's mouth thinned and one hand fisted at his side. Other than that, he showed no reaction. On the other hand, Yousef's face once again flushed with anger and his feet shuffled as he tried to decide whether to attack or not. Interesting. Neither tried denying what I said and neither showed any inclination to back off.

Good.

"Tell me something, Yousef. Do you think Drake's been completely honest with you about everything I can do?"

Yousef's shoulders jerked as he forced himself not to turn to where Drake stood.

Good. He did have doubts. I could work with that.

"Don't listen to her," Drake drawled.

"I suggest you not listen to him, Yousef. He's still keeping secrets from you. What you saw me do at the fire is only part of my abilities. Now ask yourself why your mentor, the traitor you chose to follow, has been keeping you in the dark about me. Perhaps he hopes you manage to kill me but that I will deal a fatal blow to you in the process. After all, we both know Drake hates loose ends and, if you do manage to kill me, you then become just that: a loose end."

"She's trying to throw you off your game, Yousef."

"Not at all. I look forward to a fair fight." I smiled and relaxed my body, letting them both see I didn't have any worries about dealing

351

with Yousef. "Tell me, *Marshal*, do you know how my parents trained me? How about Red or Gemma? And let's not forget about Razor and Layla." Without taking my eyes from his face, I motioned to where all but Gemma ranged around the room, looking as if they were bored by all this.

"Then there's the fact I've trained with Alpha Starke, Chief Starke and other members of the pack. Think about that before you decide to make a move against me. You know me well enough to know I'm not bluffing when I say you won't leave here alive if you force the issue. There's one more thing you should know. For every bruise, every cut, and every tear you've caused Dani to suffer, you'll pay tenfold."

"You don't scare me, Walker. You're nothing more than a bartender pretending to be something you're not."

"Don't say I didn't warn you."

Waiting, ready for whatever he might do, I centered myself. Yousef sneered and seemed to be waiting for me to make a move. Interesting. More interesting was how the fingers of his left hand began working, drawing sigils in the air next to his thigh. That explained so much I didn't understand before. His file, the one Drake sent me when he said Yousef was coming to "help" me, mentioned he was a low-level para with no real powers or talents. I hadn't believed it then and now I had confirmation my suspicions were right.

One corner of my mouth lifted as the energies around him grew and began to swirl like an eddy in the lake. I'd figured he was some form of magic user. But the way he manipulated the energies around him said he was a witch. Something he'd denied when I asked before about his talents and abilities. Fortunately, he had as little discipline as a witch as he did as a marshal. Still, it was good to know what I was dealing with.

I inhaled once and pulled on my abilities as one of Surtr's *children*. The familiar warmth filled me, and I wrapped myself with still metaphorical flames. I wouldn't do the final shift unless absolutely necessary. No need to singe my friends just to deal with the two fools standing in front of me.

As they say, the best laid plans of mice and men. Or, in this case, descendants of gods.

A gunshot sounded, echoing off the walls. A split-second later, I staggered back, almost dropping to my knees. Pain seared through my upper chest. Tears burned in my eyes and the room darkened around me before energy flowed through me. I dragged in a painful breath, looking around for the source of the shot.

Behind and to one side of Yousef, Drake stood with a gun in one hand. Before I could react, Sele. Her hands moved rapidly through the air and a blast of wind erupted from them. Drake's eyes widened in surprise and he flew back, his feet leaving the ground. He hit the far wall with a sickening thud, sliding down and laying motionless. As he did, Sele extended her hand and his gun flew through the air and into her grasp. Then she turned to me, her eyes flashing in an anger so deep it surprised me.

"Deal with him, Ripley." She motioned to Yousef before turning her attention back to the witch circle.

"Do try to deal with me now, Walker."

Without warning, he hit me with a blast of energy that forced me to fight to stay conscious.

"You're a coward, just as I suspected," I rasped.

Pain forgotten, the blood from my wound ignored, I released control. Soon he'd learn how foolish he'd been to resort to dirty tactics.

I grew—or the room grew smaller—as I faced down the bastard. His eyes widened in fear, and he staggered back a step. Amusement rumbled deep in my chest as I stepped forward. The floor beneath my feet turned to goo, melted by the flames now enveloping my body.

"N-no. You won't win."

Yousef retreated again. As he did, he forgot his own weapons. His hands drew more sigils in the air. Tears of frustration filled his eyes as Razor countered each one before they could activate. As he did, I continued stalking Yousef, wanting him as far from the others and from the witch circle as possible without actually leaving the room.

"You've already lost, Yousef. You just don't know it."

"Big talk when you're bleeding and hurt."

"Trust me, I'm not bleeding any more. Fire tends to stop blood by cauterizing the wound." I took another step in his direction, relishing the fear in his eyes and the stench of it in the air. "You betrayed your oaths to the Conclave, Yousef. You betrayed me and those I hold dear. Your own words tell me you betrayed my mother. All of that is enough to carry out the death warrant I have on you. But you can stop that with a few simple answers. Tell me what I want to know and you'll live." At least for a little while.

"Go to Hell!"

36

CONSEQUENCES CAN BE HELL

I laughed, the sound out of place in the basement. Then I waved the others back. If he wanted a fight, I'd give him one. But it would be one I choreographed and controlled. I needed to know what his agenda, not to mention Drake's, happened to be. Over the last few minutes, it became clear they'd been planning something for years, possibly decades. But what and how had they managed to keep it hidden from the Conclave for so long?

"Trust me, Yousef, Hell doesn't scare me." I lifted a hand, flames dancing almost a foot over my palm. "Perhaps you'd like me to give you a quick introduction into what to expect?"

He paled but refused to back down, much less surrender. Instead, he once more began drawing on the energies around him. This time, before Razor could respond, I waved him off. Yousef was mine. He'd pay for what he did and, if necessary, I would pull the information I wanted out of him. Then he'd learn what real pain really was.

"You don't scare me."

"I should." I dropped my hand and once again assumed a fighting stance. "You have one last chance, Yousef. I will kill you if you force me. Hell, I might kill you even if you don't. The only way to walk out of this room alive is to answer my questions, starting with telling me everything you know about Drake's plans, what actions he's taken in this Zone and others, and what you know about my mother's disappearance."

"I don't owe you an explanation about anything."

He flung another ball of magical energy my way. I sighed and countered with a fireball that enveloped it before impacting the wall behind Yousef.

"Too bad you aren't a water witch, much less a Water Elemental." I shook my head and lifted my left hand. A moment later, a ball of fire about the size of a baseball rested on my upturned palm. "I wonder what would happen if I threw this and you failed to stop it. How long do you think you'd survive?"

Faced with the possibility of being turned into a crispy critter, he panicked. He threw everything he magically could at me. One part of me laughed as both arms flung magical energy in my direction. He tried forming spells but couldn't remember the words to his incantations. Behind me, Razor muttered about fools who were going to wind up killing themselves with a backfiring spell. Then he countered the latest of Yousef's spells, telling me to quit playing around.

"Enough!" I slashed a hand through the air, flames trailing after it. "Answer my questions or die. The is your one and only chance."

I never said Yousef was the smartest person in the room. I didn't expect him to be the most foolish. Although, considering the last few days, perhaps I should have. Especially when he didn't stand down.

Instead, he reached behind him for what I assumed was his gun. Before he had a chance to wrap his fingers around it, Romy acted. Without doing much more than turning in his direction, she chanted something under her breath and reached out with her right hand. I could stop my laugh as Yousef suddenly reached to grab the pistol flying through the air from behind his back. At the same time, Layla, now a massive cobra from my worst nightmares, slithered between him and the witch sisters, assuming a protective position.

"Let me go and I'll tell you everything I know, including why he wants the girl." Yousef jerked his head to where a groggy Drake now sat with his back to the wall.

Sweat poured off his face, and not all of it was caused by the energy he expended with his ill-advised magical attacks or by rising temperature in the room as my flames grew. He was scared. Terrified really. As he should be.

"Tell me!" I hurled a ball of flame at him, no longer caring if he got more than singed around the edges.

He frantically worked to counter it, failing. The smell of scorched material filled the air. The skin of his face and hands blistered as the fireball came close enough to burn before I called it back. Gasping in pain, he dropped to his knees, his hands beating at his clothes to dampen any flames that survive.

"I've got him," Griff said softly, almost cheerfully, as he moved to cuff Yousef's hands behind him.

Then he extended a hand, catching a small leather bag Razor tossed him. I moved so I could watch as he forced Yousef's hands together, fingers entwined, into a small ball. Then he fitted the bag over his hands, holding them tightly together. I nodded in approval as understanding dawned. That simple bag and the way it tightly contained his hands, prevented Yousef from drawing any more sigils.

"Yousef Asghar, by order of the Conclave, I am taking you into custody. The warrants signed out against you allow for the search of your person, you local residence, your vehicles, as well as the search of any property you hold interest in, real or personal. Do you understand?"

"I-I need a doctor." He knelt there, unable to resist as Griffin secured his ankles before moving to stand behind him, a hand resting on Yousef's head as a reminder not to try anything foolish.

"That's up to you." I pulled back my flames until they were more wisps than anything. A quick check confirmed they obscured the parts of my body that could have gotten me arrested for public nudity otherwise. "Answer my questions and you'll get a healer. Otherwise, I will execute the kill order. It's up to you. Griff, take him out of here. Have your men secure him somewhere he can consider his options."

My stomach turned at the thought of denying him treatment, but what choice did I have? He wasn't badly injured. I might be many things but a sadist I'm not. But I could play the part when necessary, especially when people I cared for were at risk.

Besides, I had something else to deal with before spending any more time on Yousef.

Roderick Drake.

"Your turn, Drake. You get the same deal I offered Yousef. Answer my questions and live." At least long enough to stand trial before the Conclave. "Refuse, try to lie to me, fight me, and all bets are off."

He slowly climbed to his feet. Even though he gave every indication of still being dazed from his close encounter with the wall—thanks to Sele—his eyes burned with a hatred that sent a chill down my spine. Not that he scared me. He'd been on the Conclave for years and I doubted he spent much time sparring, much less being in real fights. But I had learned my lesson not to underestimate him. So I watched and waited, wondering how he'd react.

"You have no authority over me." He spoke softly, almost conversationally. "Unless you want to find yourself answering to the Conclave, leave. You have already caused too much of a delay."

"Drake, you're a fool. Call Isabel if you doubt me. I'll even let you borrow my phone."

The phone I'd fortunately left in my jacket pocket when I shrugged out of the jacket and handed it off. As if we'd rehearsed it, Razor produced the phone and crossed the room in Drake's direction. Six feet from him, Razor knelt and placed the phone on the concrete floor and slid it in Drake's direction.

"Call her or answer my questions. You don't have any other choices."

One corner of his mouth jerked slightly. That was my only warning. One moment, he stood there, ignoring the phone, his eyes locked on mine. The next, energies flowed around him, swirling, speeding up and slowing down. I inhaled quickly, surprised. Then I smiled, amusement filling me.

This was going to be fun.

No one moved as Drake shifted faster than any shapeshifter I'd ever seen. While that would have concerned me under most circumstances, today I counted myself lucky. Drake lived up to his name. Where once stood a man, a drake straight out of mythology stood. Normally, that might be a frightening prospect, but not now. Who could be scared of a wingless dragon that looked like its growth had been badly stunted, leaving it looking more like an overgrown iguana than a dragon?

"You fool." I smiled and shook my head in pity. "You don't have a clue, do you?"

He stretched his neck, the scales scraping against one another in a hiss. Then he raised up on his back legs, a rather sad attempt at intimidation. It would have been much more effective if he had wings. Hell, he would have been more intimidating with a knife or gun and still in his human form than he was right now.

"Do you really think you're going to intimidate me as a *drake*? Perhaps you should have done your homework into who and what Surtr was and what I, as one of his direct descendants, can do." I tsked once, before turning my head and grinning at Sophie.

He opened his mouth in what he might have wanted to be a roar, but a hiss sounded instead. The nails of his feet clicked against the concrete as he shifted positions. He wanted out. He wasn't a fool after all. Not that I'd allow it. He was about to find out how badly he'd stepped into it by targeting me and my friends, the people who were family to me.

"Fair warning, Drake. This little stunt is only delaying our conversation, not preventing it. Be ready to answer my questions very soon, starting with why you betrayed my mother. Then you're going to tell me exactly what happened to her."

He reacted as expected. Hissing again, he stepped forward. One step, two. Then he stopped, his head cocked to one side in question when I failed to move aside or react in any way. Instead, I stood my ground, all but daring him to try to gain the advantage.

"You don't scare me, Drake, but I should scare you. Now shift back. Your time's up." I waited a moment. "Shift back, now!"

He fought the order. His head swung back and forth, angry hisses filling the room. I waited, giving him a few moments to realize he no longer controlled the situation. His hisses mixed with the sounds of his claws scraping against the concrete floors, his scales rubbing against one another as he writhed in frustration.

"You have no choice, Drake. Your kind answers to me just as the wolves answer to those of Morrigan's line. Shift back. I won't ask again."

The energies swirled around him, dark and angry—and completely powerless against me. At least for the moment. I watched, trusting the others to make sure no other d surprises waited for us.

Unlike his initial shift, his return to human took time. Several long minutes later, he stood before us, naked as the day he was born. Unlike most shapeshifters, he did not look like he lived in a gym and posed for the covers of paranormal romance novels. Pale, paunchy, he more closely resembled an accountant who spent most of the behind a desk than anything else. Well, he was about to learn he should have stayed behind that desk instead of trying to betray the Conclave.

Not to mention betraying me, my mother, and everyone else in Denham Grove.

For a moment, no one said anything. Drake and the two were-wolves supposed to guard him and who were now cuffed, hobbled and on their knees behind him, eyed us warily. Sophie, now in her human form, and her brother returned to their positions on either side of me. Sele and her sisters continued to work to break the witch circle. Inside the circle, the witch paid them no attention. I hoped we wouldn't regret that later.

"On your knees, Drake." My voice might have been soft, but the command was clear.

Against his will, his will, he dropped to his knees. The moment he did, I nodded to Griffin. He understood and moved quickly. Once Drake, he bent and dragged his hands behind him. The sounds of handcuffs ratcheting close filled the air. Once done, Griff remained where he was, his hands resting on Drake's shoulders, a reminder not to try anything foolish.

"All right, Drake, we're going to have a quick conversation. I'm going to ask the questions and you're going to answer. I suggest you remember how easily I forced you to shift back. Now think about how easy it will be for me to force you to answer my questions. If I have to do that, you will not leave this basement. I will simply force the infor-mation from you and then execute you per the Conclave's kill order. Understand?"

Sweat pricked out on his forehead yet he remained silent. I sighed softly. Before I said anything else, Griff bent and whispered something in his ear. The color drained from Drake's face and he swallowed hard.

"I understand," he muttered.

"Louder. Everyone needs to hear."

Because I wanted witnesses if I had to appear before the Conclave to defend my actions.

"I understand."

"This won't take long." I hoped. "Did you order the attack on Red's warehouse?" "Yes."

Okay. I understood how this was going to go. He'd only give me what I asked for. He might think that a good strategy, but it wasn't. All it did was piss me off. For now, however, I needed to keep my temper in check.

"Why and was anyone else involved?"

"He knew too much and was starting to ask questions I couldn't afford to have answered. No one else was involved."

I didn't believe him about no one else being involved. I probably hadn't asked the right question, but that could wait. He'd admitted being behind the attack. Time to move on.

"What questions was he asking?"

"Go to hell."

"Do you really want me to drag the information out of you?" I gave him a few moments him to consider what I said and all it implied. Then an alternative dawned on me. "You know, I really don't have time to deal with you. The Conclave's orders give me wide discretion on how to proceed. I could kill you right now and the Conclave wouldn't bat an eye. I could take the time to force the information from you. But I don't have time for that. I need to deal with the last headache you've left for me." I jerked a thumb in the direction of the witch circle and then turned my attention to Sophie.

"Alpha, this man—and I use that term loosely—violated pack laws. He interfered with the pack and corrupted your predecessor and other members of the pack. He sent them against pack allies, with orders to kill and maim. Would the pack claim justice for him?"

Sophie looked at Drake and a slow, predatory smile lit her expression. "We not only claim it, Marshal, we demand it."

This time, Drake's gulp was audible. He began trembling and struggled against Griff's grip on his shoulders. I didn't doubt he'd try to run—or shift—given the chance. Well, I wasn't going to give him that chance.

"Drake?"

"All right." He almost spat it out. "He was asking about the girl, demanding I open my files on her to him. How he knew I had information on her is beyond me, but I couldn't risk him finding out the truth."

"And what is that truth?" This time, I didn't hesitate. I put enough power in my voice to force an answer.

"That she is an aether elemental." My brow wrinkled, not understanding what he meant. Then I heard all three sisters gasp and turned toward them.

"Sele?"

"I'll explain later, but it means we have to stop that bitch from finishing her ritual now!"

"Then get that circle down." I spun around to once again face Drake. "One more question. What did you have to do with my mother's disappearance?"

He struggled to keep from answering. His eyes closed, brows furrowing together. His jaw clenched in an attempt to stop the words from escaping. As he did, Griffin's fingers dug into his shoulders, knuckles turning white. One corner of my mouth lifted in approval as Drake gasped in pain. That was enough for the words to start pouring out.

"Stop!"

One hand fisted at my side. Anger, stronger than I'd ever felt before, filled me.

When Sophie rested a hand on my arm, I shook it off. I didn't need her concern or understanding. I needed this bastard's blood. He set my mother up. He ordered Yousef to follow her and make sure it was done in such a way no one suspected him. Conclave approval or not, he would die by my hand for his betrayal.

"Why?"

"Because she figured out what I was doing and was going to sell me out to the rest of the Conclave." He showed no remorse.

"Get him the fuck out of here." I watched as Griffin hauled him to his feet and all but dragged him out of the room.

"Ripley, are you all right?" Sophie asked.

I shook my head. I was anything but all right and I wouldn't be until I learned everything about what that bastard had done and why he did it, starting with my mother's disappearance. But that had to wait. Getting through the witch's circle and stopping her ritual took precedence.

And I had a feeling we didn't have any time to waste. It had to be now or never.

As if sensing what I had in mind, Elle hurried to stop me. Before she could reach out, and probably burn the hell out of herself since flames still danced over my skin, I shook my head. Then I tried to stop me. I stepped closer to the circle.

Magical energies washed over me as I neared. A million imaginary ants crawled over my skin. My heart pounded as I carefully reached out, a warning not to do anything stupid.

But this wasn't the time for caution. I had to get to Dani and I had to stop the witch. If doing so short-circuited my nervous system—or worse—I didn't care. Not as long as it saved Dani. Hell, I was already injured, probably badly. If this was the last thing I did, so be it as long as Dani and the others were safe.

"Ripley, don't!" Elle said.

Sophie called for her brother. Sele and her sisters increased their attempts to disrupt the circle. I heard them. But it was like background noise, an angry mosquito buzzing around my head. Ignoring them, I stepped over the edge of the circle and the world exploded around me.

Every nerve ending came alive, pain exploding, forcing me to my knees. The world around me darkened, as if all the light was sucked out of existence. The only sounds were my pulse thundering in my ears and my lungs struggling as I tried to draw a breath.

Then light replaced the darkness in an explosion of light and magical energy. Guess I did it. I proved that one descendant of Surer with more than a little of Morrigan in her as well would disrupt a witch's circle. Not that I ever wanted to do it again.

Damn, but it hurt.

At least I seemed to be in better condition than Ker, or whoever she really was. The moment the circle fractured and exploded, she collapsed. Good. That was good.

She couldn't hurt Dani if she was unconscious.

Or dead.

Please let her be dead. I so didn't want to ever have to do this again.

"B-bind her. C-can let h-her use m-m-magic again." I forced the words out, struggling to not only remain on my feet but conscious.

"No need," Sele said, her voice grim. "When the circle's energies rebounded on her, they burned her out. My guess is she suffered a cerebral hemorrhage. She's dead."

"G-good." I tried to lever up onto my feet and failed. Giving up, I dropped to my butt. The floor was good enough for now. "Razor, Dani." I couldn't finish my thought.

"I've got her, Ripley. Layla and I will take her home. Don't worry."

"And you're going with them," Sophie said as she quickly crossed the room in my direction.

I wanted to argue. I needed to go through everything onsite, see if there was any evidence the Conclave could use. Hell, evidence I could use. Sophie said something, but she sounded a mile away. I tried to say something, but my mouth and brain didn't want to cooperate. Fear clinched a tight fist around my heart. Then the floor rose up and met my face as everything went dark.

.#

37

DID ANYONE GET THE NUMBER
OF THE TRUCK THAT HIT ME?

I didn't want to wake up. Pain from my wounds, exhaustion and uncertainty were not comfortable, especially when I wasn't sure where I was. Then I recognized my mother's room. I lay on the large bed, a quilt I recognized covering me. From somewhere beyond the closed door, I heard muted voices. I wasn't alone. But the fact the house wards let them inside meant they were friends and people I'd specifically attuned the wards to.

Hissing as I sat up, I slowly made my way to the en suite. After cleaning up, I studied my almost healed wounds. Either I'd been unconscious longer than expected or Sele or one of her sisters had healed me. I might hurt, but not like I would have otherwise. Either way, I wasn't going to argue, not when I'd gone into that day unsure if I'd come out alive.

But that brought up several questions, starting with Dani. I needed to see her to be sure she was all right. Then I needed to hear what she could tell me about what happened. After that, I'd deal with Drake and Yousef. They owed me an explanation and then they owed me their lives.

The moment I stepped back into the bedroom, Dani almost bowled me over. She wrapped her arms around me and buried her head against my chest. Holding her close, I carefully made my way back to the bed where I sat and pulled her onto my lap. I'm not sure how long we sat here, saying nothing, just reassuring one another we were there and all right.

When Dani finally looked up, I gently wiped away her tears and stopped her before she could apologize. Then I told her we needed to talk, but I wanted everyone to hear what she had to say. If that was all right with her. She nodded once. Then she looked at me, her head tilted to one side. Tears burned my eyes as she reached up to kiss my cheek and hug me again. Then she climbed to her feet and moved to the closet, which was now filled with my clothes. A quick look around the room showed what I hadn't noticed before. Things from my apartment had been moved in. Someone, probably Layla and Sophie, had been busy.

How long had I been out?

I let her choose something for me to wear, grinning slightly as she brought me a pair of well-worn jeans, a tee shirt and then dug in one of the dresser drawers for underwear. For the moment, she was mother henning me much as I had her over the years. Thanking her, I grabbed the clothes and disappeared into the en suite once again to dress.

Downstairs, I found everyone but the sisters. In their place was Gemma. She explained they had opened the café, wanting the town to see things were getting back to normal. The last two days—TWO?!?!—had been busy for everyone. When they found out what had been going on, they showed up in force to help however they could. Some went out to Gemma's to clean up and make repairs. Others went to the storefront where Dani had been held to make sure nothing had been overlooked there and then to cleanse it of any residual magic. Others set up roaming patrols, not just of the town but of the area closer to the rift. Fortunately, there had been no real issues. Whatever had been going on with the rift seems to have calmed down.

And that left me with new questions.

Leaving the elephant in the room alone for the moment, I asked about the pack. Griff assured me things were in hand there. The previous alpha was dead as were those who had attacked Gemma's and who worked with Drake and Yousef. It meant the pack numbers would need to be increased but he and Sophie would be very careful about who they welcomed in the months and years to come. He also wanted to discuss my role with the pack once we had everything else in hand. I nodded, understanding. I wouldn't take control of the pack. It wasn't my place to. But after revealing my lineage and my power over pack members, I would have to be more involved than I have been up until now.

As for Drake and Yousef, they were being held in two special cells at the jail. The jails had been warded by Gemma and the sisters. The men could neither leave the cells without the wards being removed nor could they communicate with one another. They only saw Griff or Razor. And they wanted out, demanding their freedom, especially Drake who threatened all of us with the wrath of the Conclave if we didn't do as he said.

And that brought up the next question. What about the Conclave? To my surprise, it was Red who answered. He'd reported to the Conclave what happened and provided them enough proof to not only keep them off our backs but to get them to agree to leave the two men in my custody, at least until I had a chance to interrogate them and then report back to the Conclave. Red did say he fully expected the Conclave to demand I hand them over. This was the sort of thing at least some of the other members would want to sweep under the rug. Oh, Drake and Yousef would pay for what they did, mainly because it brought negative attention to the Conclave.

I nodded. I expected as much. I'd deal with that when the time came. But now I had other things to worry about. First, I wanted to hear what Dani could tell me. Then I needed to meet with our prisoners. Then and only then would I contact the Conclave.

Dani couldn't tell us much. When Yousef breached the wards here and let the others inside, Aras did everything he could to protect her while Red tried to slow the attackers down. At my look, Razor assured me Aras would be all right. He'd returned to the forest to finish healing. Layla was checking on him daily and reported that several of his kind had arrived the day before to help him. That relieved me because I knew it would help keep Dani from worrying too much about him.

When Aras fell and they grabbed her up, she was hit with something. Gemma's best guess is a sleep spell. She really didn't know anything else until she woke here after everything was said and done. At my look, Gemma assured me she was all right. They hadn't hurt her —we stopped that from happening. Nor did she have any attachments or compulsions or anything else attached to her. I nodded and smiled at the girl in reassurance, relieved nothing worse happened. Still, I'd be talking more with Gemma later. I wanted to make sure she hadn't held anything back because Dani was there.

Before we could discuss anything else, Dani wanted to know what happened with her now. To my surprise, Red spoke up. If I agreed, she'd stay here with me. Until the warehouse was rebuilt and he was satisfied no one could breach his defenses again, no one would be living there. He would take over my old apartment. I nodded in agreement when he glanced in my direction. Dani looked at me, her eyes wide with hope. I grinned and assured her this would be her home as long as she wanted.

After she went off with Layla to work on making up her lessons, I turned to the others. It was time to deal with our "guests" at the jail.

It wasn't easy and it wasn't pretty. Yousef tried pulling the "I was just following orders" excuse that failed to work for so many Nazis. When I informed him we would be going through his home and belongings, he tried to get through the wards to get to me. In the process, he said he'd kill me given the chance. I should have been drowned when I was a kid or dealt with at the same time my parents were. I simply activated the outer layer of wards, stopping all sound from entering or exiting his cell. Then I turned to Razor where he'd been standing out of sight of the cell. I wanted a truthsayer to question him. Griff would supervise. If the truthsayers sensed even the smallest lie or evasion, I wanted someone to strip the truth from him. I didn't care if it wound up damaging the man. He was already facing a death sentence, one I planned on carrying out. Razor said he'd have them here by end of day. Thanking him, I told Griff I was ready to see Drake.

The interview was almost anti-climactic. He wouldn't talk. Even though he knew I could force him because of who and what we were, he kept silent. The only thing he said as I prepared to step away from the cell was that I'd be answering to the Conclave. When I said they'd left him to me, he paled. Any remaining color in his face drained away when I said my next stop would be my office to report to the Conclave and then I'd be making a trip to his home and his office where I would be securing any and all records, paperwork, and other evidence that might point to his crimes against our people. With that, I stepped away, nodding for the wards to be brought back up.

Now it was time to get to work.

38

EPILOGUE

One week later, I stood in front of my closet, staring at its contents. I was sorely tempted to grab a pair of jeans and a shirt and go about my business. But I couldn't. Not today. Today, was anything but normal. Of course, I could say the same about the last couple of weeks had been. Unfortunately, I had a feeling it was going to be a very long time before life went back to anything resembling what I thought of as normal.

Today, I wasn't Ripley Walker, bartender and bouncer. I wasn't even the local marshal. Today, I represented the Conclave as its senior marshal for the Zone. As such, in less than two hours, I'd be there when the Conclave announced its final judgment on Drake and Yousef. No one doubted what it would be. Not only had more than enough evidence been gathered to convict them, but they made attempt to deny their actions. That made it simple for everyone except me.

For the first time as marshal, I'd be carrying out a Conclave death sentence. It would happen immediately after Isabel announced their sentences. No waiting around years for an appeal in the paranormal court. It wasn't necessary when we could, and did, use truthsayers for confirmation of guilt. Once Gemma did just that, the two would be taken outside of town and I'd deal with them.

And with their deaths, I'd be left with unanswered questions about my parents, especially my mother. But that wouldn't stop me. I would find out what happened to Mom. Then I'm make anyone else involved pay. She would be avenged.

For now, I needed to look the role of senior marshal and executioner. I cast a look at the bed and fought the urge to crawl between the sheets and hide from the world while I licked my wounds, physical and emotional.

My cellphone buzzed and danced across the top of the dresser. I reached for it, fully expecting it to be Sophie. When we spoke last night, she asked if I wanted her to pick me up. Who am I kidding? She didn't ask. She told me she'd pick me and what time to be ready. A quick glance at my watch confirmed I still had time. So if she was already here, she'd have to wait until I finished getting ready.

"Ripley Walker?" a man's voice I didn't recognize asked.

"Yes. Who's calling?"

"Marshal, the name's Karl Bruner. I'm the senior marshal for the Northeast Zone."

I thought for a moment. Then I did a mental finger snap. The Conclave appointed him to take a team to search not only Drake's office and residence but Yousef's as well. I'd read his reports about the problems in his own sector and wondered why he was calling on this of all mornings.

"What can I do for you, Bruner?"

"Karl, please."

"All right, Karl. I hate to be brusque, but I need to leave shortly."

"I know and that's why I'm calling."

My stomach did a slow flip and then a flop as possible explanations dawned on me.

"I'm listening."

"Ripley, we just finished the going through the last of Drake's holdings up here. We found some things you need to see before the Conclave convenes to hand down their sentences."

I swallowed hard, praying he wasn't about to tell me someone else on the Conclave had my sector in their sights.

"What did you find?"

"I'm sending you several digital files. The first includes financial records tying him and Yousef to one another for much longer than I think anyone suspects. Under the table payments for the bastard who never should have been one of us to turn a blind eye to some actions and others to make sure certain so-called troublemakers disappeared."

I hissed out a breath as my phone pinged, announcing the arrival of an email. I crossed the bedroom to the small table in front of one of the windows. My tablet rested on the table and the screen activated at my touch. I quickly pulled up my email client and scanned the first few pages of the file. It was worse than I imagined. But it also left no doubt Drake and Yousef worked against all our kind for their own financial benefit. If this didn't put the final nail in their coffins, I didn't know what would.

"Got it and I appreciate you sending it on. This should tip the scales if anyone on the Conclave still hesitates dealing with those two as they should be."

"There's more, Ripley."

I frowned at the hesitation I heard in his voice. "What?"

"You should be getting another file in a moment. It includes photos of a pocket diary we found in some of his files. The diary's more than ten years old. I had my team pull it when they sent me a picture of the outer cover because I recognized it as the sort of diary some of our fellow marshals used to carry."

For a moment, the world seemed to slide to a stop. He couldn't be saying what I thought he was. Could this have something to do with my mother?

Or maybe even my dad?

Before I could ask, the promised second email arrived. I opened it and my knees gave out. Blindly, I reached out for the chair next to the table and dropped onto it. I recognized the handwriting shown in the second photo, an image of one of the interior pages of the diary. The writing wasn't something most could decipher, but I could. It was a mix of code and various para languages and scripts my parents taught me when they began teaching me to read.

Mom.

The diary had to be hers. But how had Drake gotten it?

"I take it you recognize it," Bruner said.

"It belonged to my mother."

"Can you read what she wrote?"

"Yeah. It's something she and my father taught me."

"I'm going to send you a complete copy of the diary. I'd appreciate it if you let me know what it says after you've had a chance to go through it."

"All right." I took one last look at the image and then shook myself. I needed to focus and find out what else he had to say. "Did you find anything else?"

"Too much, really. If you didn't already have those two dead to rights, I'd suggest asking the Conclave to hold off passing judgment and sentence on them. But nothing here will change the outcome. All it would do is prove they deserve to die slowly and painfully as many times as possible."

"But?" I heard a very large *but* in there.

"There are others who will have to answer for their own crimes. It's going to take a long time for our people to go through everything we found."

"Tell me this, Karl. Have you found anything to implicate any of the rest of the Conclave in illegal activities?"

"Nothing on the sitting members."

I closed my eyes and counted to ten. "But you found information about former members, didn't you?"

"We did. Also, some of their staff members have been implicated. But no one currently associated with the Conclave seems to be involved."

"All right. Get me what you have as soon as possible. In return, I'll send you everything I've learned and everything I suspect. In the meantime, if you need me and I'm not available, contact the local pack alpha, Sophia Starke. Another contact to make is our police chief, Griffin Stark. He is the alpha's brother and her second in the pack. I'll send you their contact information as well as information for a few others who have proven their loyalty."

"Appreciate it." He paused and I waited, wondering what else he might be about to drop on me. "Ripley, thank you. I'm speaking for all the marshals. You managed to do what none of the rest of us have— you found the bastards betraying not only us but all paras. If you need anything, let me know. I promise, you will have all the help you need."

"Thanks, Karl." I considered whether I should say anything else. "There is one thing. During the fight before we took them into custody and then during their interrogations, both Drake and Yousef pretty much admitted they set up my mother. That bastard Yousef said he watched as she was attacked and then dragged away by redhats and harpies. Then he and Drake worked together to cover up what really happened. It's clear from what they've said this past week that there are others involved in what happened then and what's been happening now. Check your sector records and ask around. Find out if any marshals or anyone else who worked for the Conclave, especially for Drake, disappeared on assignments that should have been routine. We need to make sure no one else has fallen victim to them."

Not to mention needing to find out just how deep this cancer runs."

"Will do," he said. "I suggest we set up regular briefings between the two of us and some of our fellow senior marshals."

"Agreed. It's past time for us to start working together, beginning with sharing information. Can you take care of setting it up?"

"Of course. I'll send you the list of those I'm contacting and when we'll meet by end of day."

"Thanks." I felt the wards on the property warning someone approached. "I need to head out now. Send me everything you can and I'll brief the members of the Conclave. I'll touch base with you when we're done here."

"Thanks, Ripley. Watch your six."

"You do the same."

We'd no more ended the call when my cellphone pinged with another incoming message. I glanced at the display and smiled slightly even as I rolled my eyes. Sophie. Checking in for the third time since she woke me at six.

You about ready?

Almost. Are you riding in with Griff?

No. He got called out an hour ago. Thought I'd grab a ride with you if that's ok.

I chuckled softly. I doubted Griff had been called out. More than likely, he left early to make sure everything was ready for today. Since learning the Conclave was coming, he'd obsessed about safety measures in town. Not that I blamed him, especially after recent events.

The last thing we needed was for something to happen to a member of the Conclave.

You have ten minutes, I texted back.

No problem. I'm outside. I'd appreciate it if you'd tell the house to let me in.

I chuckled softly. The protections on the house and property were now probably the strongest in town. Unless the protections were keyed to someone, I had to lower them to allow the person in. The past week had been so busy, I hadn't had a chance to attune them to Sophie and a few select others. The only exceptions were Dani and Layla, who came every day to give Dani her lessons and who, unless I missed my guess, planned on discussing the possibility of homeschooling her with me as soon as the Conclave finished its business with Drake and Yousef.

You're clear, I texted a few moments later and hurried downstairs to greet her.

"I'm surprised. You're ready." Sophie gave me a cocky grin as I stepped outside, closing the front door behind me.

"Gee, I wonder why? Could it be because someone started calling hours ago to make sure I didn't oversleep?"

She chuckled, not at all intimidated by my glare. Instead, she made a show of looking at me from head to toe. Since two could play that game, I did the same to her. Not that I expected to find so much as a hair out of place. Dressed in dark slacks, white silk blouse and grey jacket and leather boots that matched the jacket, she looked professional and ready to get this over with. Not that I blamed her.

"Well, do you approve?" I waved a hand at my own black boots, slacks, shirt and jacket. The only thing missing was my Stetson, which currently hung on a peg in my room.

"You almost look professional," she teased as we walked across the yard to where my black SUV waited. "Seriously, Ripley, are you ready for today?"

I slid in behind the steering wheel and waited for her to fasten her seatbelt before answering.

"I'm not sure." I gave a slight shrug and then backed out of the driveway. She looked at me in concern, waiting for me to explain. "We both know what's going to happen. The Conclave will hand down a death sentence for those bastards. Don't get me wrong. They deserve it. People we care about were hurt, some even died, because of what those bastards did."

"But?"

"But we also know their machinations weren't limited to Glenham Grove. There's no way they are the only ones involved and they both refuse to name their accomplices. I'm afraid they're going to take information we need to the grave."

She nodded, understanding my concern. "Something else is bothering you."

I blew out a breath. She knew me too well.

"I got a call this morning from Karl Bruner."

"I don't know the name." Her brow furrowed in concern.

"He's the senior marshal for the Northeast Zone. The Conclave asked him to head the team that searched not only Drake's home and office but Yousef's as well." As well as a few other locations, but there wasn't time to go into that right now. "He wanted to give me a head's up about some of what they've found so far." I pulled up to the stop sign and checked for oncoming traffic before continuing down the street. "Among other things they found, they came across confirmation that both those bastards were involved in what happened to Mom."

"Ripley, are you okay?" Sophie reached out and lightly rested a hand on my arm.

"I honestly don't know." No, that wasn't right. I did know. I was pissed and wanted nothing more than to make those two suffer as much as I had because of what they did. "There's no question based on what they found that both Drake and Yousef have first-hand knowledge of what happened to Mom and that they were both involved with setting her up."

"What?" Her anger spiked enough I not only felt it but could scent it. When I dared take a quick look, her eyes glowed yellow, confirming her wolf was close to the surface.

"Sophie," I drawled.

I waited as she inhaled deeply and closed her eyes. Unlike her brother, her control was the strongest I'd ever seen. If what I learned came this close to forcing her into a shift, I needed to be careful how I told the others.

"Sorry." She scrubbed her hands over her face. "Just tell me. I've got my wolf under control now."

"Short version." Because that's all we had time for. "Yousef was there when Mom was ambushed, just like he said. He watched as she fought and was then overwhelmed. Worse, he didn't do a fucking thing but look on as Redcaps and what sounds like harpies fell on her before disappearing with her body. He stayed long enough to make sure she didn't get away, assuming she was still alive, before making his way back to report to Drake."

My hands gripped the steering wheel so tightly the leather wrapping it creaked in protest. As it did, I wanted more than anything for his neck to replace the wheel. No, that would be too quick, too easy. I wanted him to suffer as my mother suffered, as I'd suffered. Then I'd get serious about making him pay for his crimes against me and mine.

"There's more, isn't there?"

I nodded. "Bruner discovered something else in the papers and sent images for me to confirm if I could."

"What?"

"Mom kept a pocket diary. So did my dad. They explained once that they used the diaries to record their impressions and thoughts about their various assignments for the Conclave. The one Bruner's search turned up was the one Mom had on her that last mission. There was a note attached saying Red found it and turned it over to Drake."

And that was something he and I would be discussing as soon as I had a chance. At least Drake couldn't decipher Mom's script. That might be the only reason he hadn't destroyed it long ago.

"It's really your mother's?"

It reassured me some that Sophie found it as unbelievable as I had when Bruner first mentioned it.

I nodded. "Yeah. I recognized her handwriting."

"But why did Drake keep it?"

"My guess is he never thought anyone would look for it. Even if they did, he doubted they'd understand its importance. He certainly didn't." Something I'd be eternally grateful for.

"Soph, Mom had her own form of shorthand. Part cypher, part really bad handwriting, and part a combination of various para species' script. Think shorthand with cuneiform, hieroglyphics, Zapotec and a couple of others. She and Dad taught it to me, telling me it was our secret and that it was important to use it so I always remembered it."

"Ripley, that means you should be able to read what she wrote."

"Bruner sent me a couple of pages via email. I could read them." Or at least most of what was written on those pages. "He promised to send me the rest of it as soon as he could. I'm hoping it might answer at least some of our questions."

"Have you told the Conclave?"

I shook my head. "You're the first I've told."

"What about Bruner?"

"He's leaving it to me to tell them."

Which was enough to convince me he was as worried about recent events as was I.

"So, what are you going to do?"

Wasn't that the million-dollar question?

Before I could answer, my cellphone buzzed. I reached up and tapped my left earbud, answering the call.

"Ripley, it's Gemma."

My brow knitted. Why was she calling when we'd be seeing her in just a few minutes?

"Gemma, what's up? Has something happened?"

Hearing my concern, Sophie sat up straighter and turned to look at me.

"I'm at the courthouse. We need to talk before you go inside."

"Gemma, you're worrying me."

"I don't know if you need to worry or not, child. It's about your mother."

I sucked in a breath. "W-what about her?"

"Something's happened. Something's changed. I don't know what, but I can sense her. For the first time since she went missing, I can sense her."

I slammed on the brakes, reaching out with my right hand to brace Sophie and ignoring the honking of a car horn behind us. My heart pounded, threatening to burst through my chest like the creature in the same movie that was the source for my name. Somehow, I remembered to breathe. At least I think I did. I couldn't be sure of anything except the fact Gemma just said the last thing I expected.

"What do you mean?" My voice came out as a harsh croak, and I shook my head when Sophie looked like she might say something.

"I'm not sure, child. I sensed something and it felt like your mother."

I swallowed against the lump in my throat.

"I-is she alive?"

Sophie hissed in a breath.

"I don't know. I can't tell. It felt real. But that doesn't mean it happened in the moment I felt it. It could be that with everything that's happening, it finally broke through whatever shielded it from me."

Or it could be tied to Mom's pocket diary and my own emotions as I read the few pages Brunson sent.

I leaned forward, resting my head against the steering wheel. A moment later, I blew out a breath and sat up. I needed to get a grip and figure out what to do.

"Gemma, I learned last night Mom kept a pocket diary during that last assignment. Apparently Red found it and handed it over to Drake. This was before he started to suspect something was off about the bastard. One of the teams found it yesterday when they were searching Drake's home and office. They emailed images of some of it to me to see if I recognized it. Could that be what triggered what you felt?"

"It's possible. Your emotions as well as those your mother felt as she wrote in the diary could do it, especially if she made an entry near the time of the ambush."

"And?"

For a moment, she didn't answer. As I waited, I flipped on the turn indicator and pulled away from the curb. We were less than two blocks from the courthouse, and I had a feeling we needed to get there sooner rather than later.

"Do you know if she had it with her when she fell?" Gemma asked in return.

"I don't know for sure. My best guess is that she did and she somehow managed to hide it where Red found it later." Something I'd be talking to him about as soon as possible.

"If she did have it with her, it's possible her energies are still tied to it. Do you know if the location where it was found had been warded?"

I shook my head before realizing she couldn't see me. "I don't know."

"Find out. If it was, that could be why I didn't sense it before now."

"Can you tell me anything else?"

"I can't tell if she's alive, but she isn't dead."

I swallowed hard, focusing on not wrecking out. If I'd been standing, my knees would have given out. As it was, I really wanted to pull over again and let Sophie take over driving.

"All right. We're almost at the courthouse." I checked the time. "Meet us at the café. We need to talk before I see the Conclave and we finally deal with Drake and Yousef."

I once again tapped my earbud. As the call ended, I turned onto Main Street. Next to me, Sophie waited. I could feel her curiosity and concern. Fortunately, she was a good enough of a friend and she knew me well enough to understand she needed to give me time before saying anything.

"Are you all right?" she asked as I pulled into the parking lot across the street from the courthouse.

"I don't know." And that was the truth. "Gemma's going to meet us. I need to talk with her before everything gets started this morning. I'd like you to stay. I have a feeling I'm going to need a friend."

"Rip, you're worrying me."

Hell, I was worrying me. How could I expect her to understand what was going on when I didn't? Then, as she reached out and lightly rested a reassuring hand on my arm, I drew a deep, shaky breath. I could do this. I couldn't fall apart. Not until I told her what Gemma said, not until I'd talked with Gemma, and not before we dealt with Drake and Yousef once and for all.

"Soph, Gemma said she can suddenly sense my mother. She doesn't know why any more than she knows what had been blocking her all these year. Nor can she tell if Mom's alive. All she knows for sure is that Mom isn't dead."

Sophie's jaw dropped and she stared at me in disbelief. Then she shook herself, the movement very canine even if she was still buckled in. She said nothing for a moment. Instead, she reached for my hand and held it firmly between hers, letting me know she was there for me.

"What are you going to do?"

"Talk to Gemma, then the Conclave, and then deal with those bastards."

Then I'd figure out my next step.

One thing was certain. Their deaths wouldn't close the door on what happened. Questions about what happened to my parents and why needed to be answered. I also wanted to take another look into the accident that cost Dani's parents their lives. Then there was identifying who plotted with Drake and Yousef against the best interests of the Conclave and our people.

But it all started with my mother. If she still lived, I would bring her home. If not, I'd lay her to rest before hunting every last person, human and para, responsible for what happened.

And may all the heavens and the hells help anyone who got in my way.

REQUEST FROM THE AUTHOR

It has long been said that the best form of advertising is word of mouth. That is especially true when it comes to books. Friends and family members trust reviews and suggestions for books that come from people they know.

That word of mouth goes even further in this digital age. If you enjoyed this book, do me a favor. Spread the word. Tell people on your various social media accounts. Leave a review. If you're a blogger, write a post about it. All that does help. Besides, it is the one way we, as authors, know you really enjoyed our work.

Thanks!

ABOUT THE AUTHOR

I'm older than twenty and younger than death and that's all you'll get from me about my age. After all, it's not polite to ask a woman how old she is. I'm a mother, a daughter and was a wife. I've spent most of my life in the South and love to travel. The only problem with that is my dog always thinks I've abandoned him when I do and it takes weeks to reassure the poor thing and my cat resents the fact I came back before he could figure out a way to kill the dog and hide the body. My house is haunted - it is, really. I swear it. What else explains the table that plays music and the light that comes on by itself? - but it's mine and I love it. Okay, I'm a little strange. But that makes life interesting.

———

To keep up-to-date on new releases, specials, please sign up for my newsletter.

ALSO BY THE AUTHOR

Writing as Sam Schall

Honor & Duty Series

Taking Flight

Battle Bound

Battle Wounds

Battle Flight

Vengeance from Ashes

Duty from Ashes

Honor from Ashes

Fire from Ashes

Betrayal from Ashes

Risen from the Ashes

Victory from Ashes

Destiny from Ashes

Writing as Amanda S. Green

Nocturnal Lives Series:

Nocturnal Origins

Nocturnal Serenade

Nocturnal Interlude

Nocturnal Haunts

Nocturnal Challenge

Nocturnal Rebellion

Nocturnal Revelations

Cat's Paw

www.ingramcontent.com/pod-product-compliance
Lightning Source LLC
Chambersburg PA
CBHW021428240626
47153CB00001B/68